A Year Like No Other

ALSO BY PAULINE LAWLESS

Because We're Worth It

If the Shoes Fit

Published by Poolbeg.com

A Year Like No Other

Pauline Lawless

POOLBEG

Published 2011
by Poolbeg Press Ltd
123 Grange Hill, Baldoyle
Dublin 13, Ireland
E-mail: poolbeg@poolbeg.com
www.poolbeg.com

1

A catalogue record for this book is available from the British Library.

ISBN 978-1-84223-463-1

Typeset by Patricia Hope in Sabon 11/15
Printed by CPI, Mackays, UK

www.poolbeg.com

ABOUT THE AUTHOR

Pauline Lawless was born in Dublin but she has lived most of her life in the midlands. She was educated at Belgrove School, Clontarf, and St Louis Convent, Balla, Co Mayo.

She started writing after she retired from business and her first novel, *Because We're Worth It*, was a bestseller in 2009. Her second book, *If the Shoes Fit*, also a bestseller, followed a year later. She adores Paris and so it was a perfect setting for this, her third novel, *A Year Like No Other*.

Pauline has five children and seven grandchildren and now divides her time between Ireland, Belgium and Florida. When she's not writing she likes to escape to the golf course and also enjoys playing bridge.

Visit her website at **www.paulinelawless.com**.

ACKNOWLEDGEMENTS

I have enjoyed continuing my love affair with Paris while writing this book. I sometimes longed to leave everything and head straight there as I wrote. I hope my readers enjoy escaping there for a little while with me. *À Paris!*

Once again to all at Poolbeg: Kieran, Sarah, David, Lee, Lisa and Sarah a big thank you. To Paula Campbell, thanks for your continued faith in me and believing that I really can produce three more books! Thanks to Barbara Devlin, who lifted my spirits greatly when I heard how much she had enjoyed reading the manuscript.

To Gaye Shortland, the best editor any writer could have. Your advice and guidance is invaluable and makes my books so much better than I could manage alone.

To my lovely daughter Ciara who once again was called on to proofread even though she has a very busy new life in Galway. I promise we'll have another trip to Paris soon and have champagne at the Ritz once more!

To my wonderful family who are always there for me and especially my daughters-in-law Anil in Munich and An in Brussels who are both very supportive and whose comments I value highly.

A thousand thanks to all my friends in Ireland, Belgium and Florida. Your interest and encouragement is much appreciated and gives me a great deal of pleasure.

Grateful thanks to fellow Poolbeg writers Mairead O'Driscoll and Mary Malone. I have valued your unstinting help and advice since I first started writing.

Finally, to the most important people of all – you, the readers – I hope I haven't let you down and that you enjoy this story as much as the others I've written. Thanks to those of you who have visited my website **www.paulinelawless.com an**d left such kind comments. Hope to hear soon how much you've enjoyed this book too.

To JM
With all my love.

Aussi à Moe Moe – Grands Bisous xx

1

"Paris? You can't be serious!" Felicity cried, the shock registering on her face. "Please tell me you're joking, Maxwell?" Her voice wobbled as her eyes searched her husband's.

"I'm afraid not, dear," he replied gently, looking away uncomfortably. "It's Paris, I'm afraid – for a year." He shifted from foot to foot, not knowing what to say to make it more acceptable. He wondered if he were tall, dark and muscular instead of small, blond and rotund – cuddly, his daughters called him – might he be able to handle this situation better. He was easy-going and jovial and hated confrontations and rows.

"Oh God, not Paris," Felicity continued, her plummy well-modulated voice rising uncharacteristically. "You know I detest France. Nobody speaks English there and the French are so rude. Do we *have* to go?"

Max sighed, at a loss for words to calm her.

"Well, I suppose you could stay here in London and I could commute every weekend," he suggested hopefully, thinking of what bliss it would be to have a Felicity-free working week.

"Oh, no, that's out of the question," she replied, panic flitting across her face. "You couldn't possibly manage without me."

The reality was that he could manage perfectly well without her but he knew Felicity would never manage without him to take care of her.

Max sighed again as he watched her pacing up and down, her pencil-thin body taut with anxiety as she struggled to cope with the news. Felicity, always a lady, in her cashmere twinset and pearls with not a hair out of place, was doing her best to retain her composure but failing miserably.

In fairness, the fact that he was being sent to Paris had come as a complete surprise to him too. He'd been hotly tipped to be taking over in either Dubai or Hong Kong, so when the president of the bank informed him that he'd be joining the new finance group in Paris, it had come as quite a shock. It was a fantastic opportunity for him and a great step up in the banking hierarchy and he was already very excited at the prospect. He'd known, of course, that Felicity would be less than happy with the news and so her reaction to it came as no surprise.

"How can I possibly face my friends? They're all madly jealous at the prospect of my moving to Dubai or Hong Kong and now I have to tell them that I'm just popping across the Channel," she sniffed.

"Seriously, dear," Max tried another strike for his freedom, "I would of course find it very difficult to cope without you but I couldn't bear for you to be unhappy. Perhaps the best solution is for you to stay here in London and I'll come home at weekends. What do you think?"

"No, I wouldn't hear of it," she reiterated. "I've never shirked from doing my wifely duty, so if I have to come to Paris with you, I will. But I really don't know how I'll survive there," she shuddered, clasping her arms even tighter around her flat bosom.

Max sighed. "This is a big promotion for me, Felicity," he explained gently, putting his arms around her. "If I make a success of this – then who knows – the sky's the limit."

"I need a drink," she said, breaking away and going to the cocktail cabinet where she poured herself a gin and tonic. She sat down carefully in the leather armchair, back ramrod straight and legs crossed in a ladylike manner as she took a very unladylike gulp from her glass.

"What will I do for friends in Paris? At least I would have

known Gloria in Dubai and Diane and Myrtle in Hong Kong," she said, dangerously close to tears. "And of course, everyone speaks English there."

"Well, you'll have the other wives in Paris. There are four others on this project with me and no doubt they'll be bringing their wives too, so you'll surely make friends with them."

"Are any of them English?" she asked hopefully.

"I'm afraid not." He moved over to pour himself a large whisky, throwing his eyes up to heaven. He eased himself into his favourite armchair, willing this conversation to be over.

Felicity was English to her very backbone, he thought. She hated foreigners with a vengeance and truly believed that every other country was uncivilised. She wore her Englishness like a mantle and without it she was lost. Once out of England, she was out of her comfort zone. Would she survive in France? He sighed. One thing he knew, Felicity or not he was heading to Paris. This job was too good to pass up. If she insisted on coming with him, then she would just have to adapt.

He loved his wife dearly but she was a product of her very conservative, upper-class background. She'd barely had any contact with her parents as a child and had been packed off to boarding school at eight. Her mother, Georgina, was a veritable dragon, domineering and controlling and as a result Felicity was crippled with insecurity and low self-esteem and was generally a bundle of nerves. From time to time her genes showed through and she could be haughty and arrogant, like her mother, but only ever with Max and their two daughters, never with outsiders.

He'd been christened Maxwell, after his grandfather, but had been known as Max all his life. He liked the name Max – it suited him – but Felicity insisted on calling him Maxwell.

"Max is so common, darling," she'd said.

'Common' was the biggest sin in Felicity's book. So it was that, like so many other men, his wife was the only one to call him by his full name.

Their two daughters Alexandra and Philippa suffered the same fate. From a young age they had called each other Alex and Pippa as had he, but despite this Felicity still insisted on using their formal names, which made them squirm with embarrassment in front of their friends. Now aged sixteen and eighteen and quite the little rebels, they frequently protested. But still Felicity persisted, causing many an unholy row.

Alex was in her first year at Cambridge and wanted to be a journalist. Pippa was a boarder at Benenden School and one week wanted to be an artist, the next a model.

Felicity was a wonderful mother but, when the girls reached their teens, she couldn't understand how it had happened that her two charming little daughters had turned into these argumentative, rebellious teenagers. Max had tried to explain that they were simply growing up but poor Felicity just didn't get it. She was in a time warp and could be heard sighing regularly, at their hairstyles, clothes, music and just about everything else.

Both girls were thrilled when Max broke the news that they were only moving to Paris and not the Middle or Far East.

"Cool, Pops," Pippa had squealed, hugging him. "Now I'll be able to pop over with my friends at half term."

"That's great, Pops. Paris is much closer." Alex smiled. "Harry and I will be able to visit often." Harry was the latest squeeze.

Max tried to envisage Felicity's reaction to all these teenagers invading her space. She could barely cope with her own two, never mind all their high-spirited friends.

Felicity called her younger sister, Penelope (Penny to everyone else).

"Penelope, you won't believe where we're going. Not Dubai or Hong Kong – but Paris," she said, stifling a sob.

"Oh you lucky duck!" was her sister's reply, much to Felicity's surprise. "You always land on your feet. Imagine it! Afternoon tea in the Ritz every day and the fabulous designer shops of the Rue du Faubourg Saint-Honoré on your doorstep – not to mention all the chic parties that you're sure to be invited to." She sighed dramatically. "I'm green with envy."

This stopped Felicity somewhat in her tracks. "What about Dubai or Hong Kong? I was really looking forward to one of those."

"Can you imagine the toll the Dubai sun would take on your face, Felicity?" Penny took great care of her own face and body. "Seriously! Have you even considered that? And Hong Kong is very over now, you know, definitely old-hat. Consider yourself lucky, girl." She sighed again. "I wish Jeremy would whisk *me* off to Paris for a year. You wouldn't hear *me* complaining!"

Somewhat mollified, Felicity had to agree that she hadn't thought about the skin damage she'd incur in the hot desert sun. At thirty-nine, that was the last thing she needed. She had a typical English rose complexion and inspected her face regularly for signs of aging. So far, so good – she had great genes and had taken reasonable care of herself over the years – but she wasn't getting any younger and one could never be too careful.

"And just think, it means you'll be escaping from Georgina's clutches for a whole year, you lucky thing. God, I've just realised that means I'll have to cope with her on my own while you're away," Penny groaned.

"I know, I'm sorry, but you're much more able to deal with Mummy than I am. She still terrifies me. And we're just across the Channel, if you need me."

Felicity hadn't thought about the bonus of escaping from her mother's demands for a year. That put a new light on things.

Next she rang her cousin Gloria in Dubai, who burst into tears at the news that Felicity would not, after all, be joining her there.

"Oh, dear, how shall I ever stick this place without you, Felicity?" she'd cried. "It's so damn hot. I can't put my nose outside the door. As for our fellow-Brits – all nouveau-riche, my dear, not at all the class of people we're used to."

Well, Felicity thought, patting her mousy-blonde hair, so much for the fantastic life she raved about last time I spoke to her!

Next, she rang her old school-friend, Myrtle. Things were equally bad in Hong-Kong.

"I'm terribly disappointed that you're not coming out," she told Felicity, "but, honestly, you've had a lucky escape. Things have changed dreadfully here. Not the same at all. And Diane has turned out to be a prize bitch. We had a dreadful row and now we don't talk at all which, I needn't tell you, is very embarrassing when we meet at functions."

Phew! Felicity thought. I have had a lucky escape. Imagine being caught between those two! The more she heard, the more she was beginning to think that Paris wasn't so bad after all. It was at least within driving distance of London. She brightened up at the thought that they could quite easily pop back to London – every weekend if they wanted to.

2

It was six thirty and Ashling was in the kitchen, putting the finishing touches to the pasta dish for dinner. Her two little girls were spending the night with their grandmother, as they did every Friday.

When she heard Kieran's key in the door she wondered why he was home so early. He was rarely home before nine.

"Hi, honey, I'm in the kitchen," she called out. "How come you're home so early?"

He burst in, his big bulk filling the room as he waved a bottle of champagne. "Stop cooking! *We* are going out to dinner tonight, to celebrate!" he cried, putting the champagne on the table and swinging her around off her feet. "I got it, Ash, I got the job! *We* are going to Paris, *chérie*!" he laughed.

"Oh my God, are you serious?" She looked at him, her green eyes wide with disbelief.

"Yes, yes, yes!" he cried ecstatically, pumping the air.

She hugged him, jumping up and down, her auburn curls dancing. "Oh my God, I can't believe it! Paris!" she cried, clapping her hands, her face aglow. "How come? Tell me all!"

"Let me just chill this a little more," he said. He set about putting some iced water in the wine cooler for the champagne.

She pulled out a kitchen stool and sat at the breakfast counter watching him and drumming her fingernails as she waited with mounting excitement for him to finish. He's so damn handsome, she thought smugly, and he's mine.

Sitting opposite her at the counter, he finally regaled her with the details of his good news.

"The CEO, Mr O'Reilly, called me into his office just as we were closing and told me that I'd been chosen for the Paris project," he said, reaching for her hands. "I just couldn't believe it." He was grinning now from ear to ear.

"What about Bill and Conor? I thought you were sure it would go to one of them?"

"I was. They're both older and more experienced than me, so I really didn't think I stood a chance, but Mr O'Reilly explained that what they want on this project are new ideas and new ways of looking at things." He was still beaming like a Cheshire cat, his hazel eyes shining. "So all that extra overtime I've put in has finally paid off."

"I should hope so," she replied sharply, thinking of the rows they'd had over the long hours he spent at the office. Seeing his disconsolate face she relented. "I'm very proud of you." She got down from the stool and went around the counter and kissed him. She knew his career was very important to him and sometimes felt that she took second place to it. He was a consummate workaholic. She hoped that this move would mean that they could spend more time together as a family.

"Oh, Ash, I'm so excited. It's quite a feather in my cap," he said, holding her tight.

Ashling fetched two champagne glasses as he opened the champagne. *Pop!*

"My favourite sound," she sighed happily.

"Let's take these inside," he said, putting his arm around her waist.

When they were seated on the comfy leather sofa, he raised his glass to her.

"To Paris!"

"To Paris and to my wonderful husband for making it all happen!" She smiled as she touched her glass to his.

"Besides the promotion for me, Ash, I was thinking of how much you would love living there for a year." He smiled at her above the rim of his glass as he took a sip of champagne.

"It's a dream come true. You know I always wanted to live there but . . ."

"Don't remind me. I know how I scuppered that plan. Maybe this will make up for it." He reached over and kissed the tip of her nose.

"Oh, it will," she said, nodding her head vigorously.

It was true. She'd been in her last year of journalism at college and had started making plans to spend a year in Paris, to perfect her French, when she'd met Kieran at a U2 concert. It was love at first sight. He was ten years older than her and already making waves in the banking world where, aged only thirty-two, he had already been promoted to branch manager. He'd swept her off her feet with his rugged good looks and his easy-going sense of fun. He was tall with light-brown hair and laughing hazel eyes and the muscular body of the rugby player he was. A gorgeous hunk, her sister Fiona had called him the first time she'd met him. He was her perfect Prince Charming and she'd known instantly that she wanted to spend the rest of her life with him. By the time her exams came around, she realised that she couldn't bear to be away from him for a week, let alone a whole year, and so she had abandoned all thoughts of moving to Paris. Instead she'd got a job as a junior reporter with the *Sunday Independent*. Two years later they'd had a dream wedding and three years after that Orna was born, followed eighteen months later by Ciara. All thoughts of Paris had flown out the door by that stage.

And now this! Her dream of living in Paris was going to be realised, albeit a little late. The girls were now almost six and four-and-a-half years old, the perfect age for this move. She had no doubt that they would pick up the language in no time and she would make sure she nurtured it in them.

Luckily she had continued with her French and had even gained her diploma from the Alliance Française in Dublin. Now it would certainly pay off. Speaking French in Paris is a must, she'd been told – otherwise the locals would just ignore you.

"Lucky you kept up your French," Kieran remarked, accurately reading her thoughts.

"I know. I should be as fluent as any Frenchwoman by the time I come home," she grinned, taking a big gulp of champagne, spluttering as the bubbles went up her nose.

"You sure you won't have a problem taking a year's sabbatical from the job?" he asked, as he handed her his handkerchief.

"Not at all – people do it all the time. I will need to give one month's notice so that they can find my replacement, of course. When do we leave?"

"I start work at the end of August so we need to be there before that."

"That gives us just over two months. I'll hand in my notice tomorrow so I'll be free from the end of July to prepare for the move. What about a school for the girls?"

"That will be no problem. Mr O'Reilly tells me that there are very good international schools in Paris and we will have someone there to help us find one, and a house too." He patted her knee reassuringly.

"Oh, I'm so excited," she cried, her bright green eyes sparkling. "Paris! I can't wait!"

"I'm pretty excited too," he said, nuzzling her neck. "What do you say we take this champagne and excitement up to bed right now?"

"I thought you'd never ask," she grinned back at him, feeling the lovely familiar passion rising inside her. "*Je te désire passionément*," she whispered huskily, moving towards the door. "That means I want you very, very much," she laughed at him, seeing the bewilderment on his face.

"Let me just call Frères Jacques and book a table for later," he said, giving her a pat on the behind.

"*Quel derrière!*" he said, in a quite diabolical accent. "That does mean 'lovely bum', doesn't it?" he asked, grinning at her as he dialled. This was something he'd heard at the Moulin Rouge nightclub on one of his many rugby trips to Paris.

She wiggled her backside – just like Marilyn Monroe in *Some*

Like It Hot – all the way up the stairs as he followed her, trying to concentrate on his phone conversation.

After they'd made love, Ashling lay propped up in bed, sipping champagne, and feeling blissfully happy. She laughed as she heard Kieran singing loudly in the shower. It was a long time since he'd done that. Come to think of it, she couldn't remember when they'd last made love either. He was always too tired or stressed, because of work, and it was beginning to worry her. Their sex life had always been fantastic but lately it had become a non-event. She hoped that this move to Paris would be good for them both and bring them close together again. Lying back on the pillows she took another sip of champagne, smiling secretly to herself.

3

Meanwhile in New York, Taylor was lounging in the bath, taking care not to wet her newly coiffed blonde hair. She frowned in irritation when she heard the knock on the bathroom door.

"Maria, I told you I did not want to be disturbed," she snapped at her Mexican housekeeper, who wouldn't have dreamt of disturbing her at this time, not even if her life depended on it.

"It's not Maria, it's me." Her husband, Brandon, poked his blond head around the door.

"Oh for heaven's sake, Brandon, you know better than to disturb me in my bath," she said irritably, lifting up the cooling eye-mask she was wearing.

"I need to talk to you, Taylor," he replied.

"Yes, well, it will keep till I'm finished, I'm sure," she said, replacing the mask and sinking her size-zero body lower in the tub.

"I suppose," he sighed, closing the door.

He stood sipping a whisky, gazing out the living-room window of their Fifth Avenue penthouse apartment, feeling very alone. Looking out over Central Park he watched a young couple stop and kiss, their arms wrapped around each other and he thought how lucky they were. Next, he saw an elderly couple walking hand in hand, the old man gently guiding his wife, and he envied them too.

Sinking onto the large comfortable sofa, he kicked off his shoes and stretched his long legs as he thought about his marriage. Sadly, he'd accepted a long time ago that theirs was a loveless relationship. He longed for some TLC and affection but he didn't even get that. As for sex – that had become obsolete years ago! He knew it was no way to live. He was going to give this Paris job a chance in the hope that the change would do them both good – City of Love and all that! Secretly, he had his doubts that anything could save their marriage. If things didn't improve between them in Paris, he would definitely have to do something about it.

Sighing, he hit the remote and began to flick through the channels.

An hour later, his wife breezed in and headed straight for the drinks cabinet.

He turned down the TV volume. "Taylor, you must be the only woman in New York who can bathe three times a day and still not have enough," he remarked, his eyes taking in her new hairdo. He reckoned it was a shade blonder than before, achieved no doubt at enormous expense. Everything about Taylor was achieved at enormous expense. She had to be the most high-maintenance woman in the city, he thought.

"What is it you wanted to talk about, Brandon?" she asked coldly, as she mixed herself a martini.

"I'm being sent to Paris to head up a new project." He watched her face closely for her reaction.

"So?" she queried, raising one perfectly threaded eyebrow.

"So – it's for a year and I'm afraid you'll have to accompany me as there will be a lot of entertaining to be done."

"Accompany you? To Paris?" she asked, her composure deserting her as she digested this news.

"Yes, dear, that's what executive wives do – unless they have a career of their own, that is."

"But what about the children?"

"Oh come off it, Taylor," he said irritably, getting up and going to pour another whisky for himself. "Mike and Mia are not exactly children. They're in their twenties, for God's sake, and they have their own lives in California now. They don't need you here."

He smiled grimly, thinking that she had never seen much of the twins anyhow, not even when they'd been little. Taylor was not exactly the maternal type. Once she'd presented him with the required son and daughter, she'd declared that that was that. They'd had separate bedrooms ever since. The whole process of pregnancy and birth had disgusted her. The children had been raised mostly by nannies and it was his one regret that he'd been so busy climbing the corporate ladder that he'd missed a lot of their childhood. Lately he'd been trying to make up for that. They'd both graduated from college in Los Angeles where Mike was now working with one of the major television companies. Mia, who had qualified in oenology, was working with a winemaker in Sonoma. Brandon made a point of travelling there every two months or so to visit them but Taylor steadfastly refused to travel with him to "that trashy movie place" as she called it. As a result she'd seen hardly anything of the twins during the past four years.

"And what about all my charity work?" she demanded, breaking into his thoughts.

"I'm sure they'll survive without you for a year," he replied with some satisfaction.

Taylor's whole life was a whirlwind of charity lunches, dinners and meetings. Not that the charities themselves were ever foremost in Taylor's mind. It was what New York socialites did with their time. Besides the endless preparation for these events, mainly at Elizabeth Arden's Red Door Spa – there were the endless shopping trips to Bergdorf's and Saks and occasionally to Europe, looking for that perfect dress.

"Think of the designer shopping, my dear," he added, watching the flicker of greed in her eyes. "You'll be right on their doorstep."

"And I can fly back for the Sweet Charity Ball in November?"

"Of course, if you wish."

"Business class?"

"But of course," he sighed, knowing damn well she wouldn't consider travelling any other way.

"First class?" She was really pushing it now. Luckily Concorde was gone or she'd be insisting on that!

"No, Taylor," he replied, looking at her with distaste. "Business class is quite comfortable enough. We don't want to bankrupt the project before we even start."

"Huh!" she snorted. She'd see about that!

Brandon could see that she was taking care not to frown and perhaps cause a wrinkle. Not that she could, he thought wickedly, with all that botox in her forehead!

"Well, I suppose I don't have a choice but to go, do I?" she pouted.

"No, actually, you don't."

Taylor knew when she was beaten. "Let me warn you, it will cost you," she shot back at him, her cold grey eyes glittering.

"I don't doubt it," he replied dryly. He could almost feel his credit card heating up as he spoke. God, but he was married to a bitch!

4

"Jazz, we have to talk," Hans said, pouring two beers.

Jazz knew that they were heading for a showdown. She guessed what was coming and felt a knot forming in her stomach.

She'd met him thirteen years before when she'd joined the bank where he worked. She'd just returned from Paris at the time, on the rebound from her first big love and Hans had made her feel good about herself again. Somehow they'd drifted into a relationship. They'd moved in together and it had worked out perfectly well but over the years they'd become more like good friends than lovers. There was no magic in their relationship and Jazz wondered if she could have done something to make it happen. Maybe, but in any case it was now much too late. It wasn't anything major that had gone wrong – they'd just grown further and further apart over the years.

Jazz was absorbed in her career, quickly making her way to the top of the banking ladder, leaving Hans on the bottom rung. Perhaps things might have been different if she'd made the commitment to start a family but she hadn't wanted that. She hadn't been prepared to give up her exciting job to settle into motherhood. If she couldn't have given it one hundred per cent then she wasn't prepared to do it at all. She'd seen too many colleagues trying to juggle motherhood and a career and was convinced it didn't work.

Like Jazz, Hans had been happy enough to plod along as they were but now something had changed. She couldn't figure out why he'd chosen today to confront her about their relationship. He'd had a few drinks after work which had perhaps given him Dutch courage, or maybe it was something else. She'd been offered a fantastic job in Paris which she desperately wanted to take but he wanted her to turn it down. This was causing tension between them. She'd been mulling it over for a week now and still hadn't made a decision.

Carrying two glasses of beer out to the terrace of their Frankfurt apartment, he sat down opposite her as the late evening sun shone down.

"I think you'll agree with me that we're at a crossroads," he started, stumbling over the words.

She nodded her agreement, her glossy dark hair catching the sun as she moved her head.

"Sweetheart, we can't go on like this. It is decision time," he continued, staring into his glass.

"What do you want us to do?" she asked, wondering for a moment if he'd met someone else. She could hardly blame him. She'd been very preoccupied with work lately, working overtime and at weekends too. Still, the thought of being on her own filled her with fear. She was comfortable with him. She looked at him, her anxiety showing in her smoky brown eyes.

"I think it's time we got married and had a baby," he said, shocking her into silence. "Neither of us is getting any younger, you know."

Jazz didn't need to be told that. Every time she went back to her home in Munich, her mother, her aunts and even some of the neighbours who'd known her from the time she'd been a baby, reminded her that her biological clock was ticking.

"When are you going to make me a grandmother, Jasmin?" Mami constantly asked. Jasmin was her real name. It was Hans who had started calling her Jazz. The name suited her, he'd said, as jazz music was all about improvisation and she was constantly improvising in life. She'd been secretly pleased by this.

"Your mother keeps hoping you'll have some good news for her soon, Jasmin," her aunts and neighbours were fond of saying.

Her mother had long ago given up any hope of being the mother-of-the-bride and would happily settle now for being a grandmother.

"You're not getting any younger, you know," was her refrain and now here was Hans reminding her of that same fact.

If she was honest, it had been preying on her mind lately. She would be thirty-six next birthday – pushing the big four oh, which she dreaded. Then her biological clock would wind down, for sure. The last thing she wanted was to be like those celebrities 'thinking' about having a baby, although well into their forties. She felt they should be thinking about being a grandmother – not an old mother. But did *she* want a baby right now? She wasn't sure. In her heart she knew that what she didn't want was a baby with Hans. He was not really father material and she knew that deep down she didn't truly love him. Maybe if she'd met the right man . . . well, it was a bit too late to be thinking of that now. She sighed.

"I'm sorry, Hans," she replied sadly, "but I think marriage would be a dreadful mistake right now."

He looked crestfallen. "Well, I guess that's that then," he said, gulping his beer and licking his upper lip with his tongue. "I think it best then if I move out as soon as possible."

"No, there's no need for you to do that," she told him, reaching over for his hand and making a quick decision of her own. "I've decided to take the Paris job, so you can stay on here. I think a temporary break from each other might be a good idea. They say absence makes the heart grow fonder," she smiled, wondering if that was really true.

"I suppose, but I can't wait forever," he said, looking soulfully into her eyes, relieved that she wasn't giving up on them completely.

"No, no, of course not. Please let's take this year out to see how we feel," she said, running her perfectly manicured finger around the rim of her glass.

"Okay, whatever you say. I'll go along with that," he agreed, not wanting to lose her completely. "Paris it is."

Filled with guilt at the excitement she was feeling, now that she'd decided to go to Paris, she got up and wrapped her arms around him, cuddling him like a child.

5

Sophie Durbuis lay in bed, snug in the crook of her husband's arm, her head on his shoulder as they discussed the exciting project that they were about to embark on.

Yves had been surprised and delighted to be asked by Bank National de Paris to lead the international group that would be based in Paris for the coming year. Because of his previous international banking experience they'd felt he was the right man for the job. It would be a very big and important project and he was incredibly excited by it. He would need someone to help the families of the bankers involved to relocate, and who better to do this than his wife, Sophie, a born and bred Parisienne, who knew the city like the back of her hand. She had worked in real estate and like him, had perfect English, thanks to the four years they'd lived in Washington. She was the obvious choice for the job. She hadn't worked for five years since the birth of their son, Pierre, but now that the little fellow was well settled in school, Sophie was ready to get back into the workforce. This would be a good way to start.

Yves sniffed his wife's short dark hair, loving the scent of coconut that always clung to it.

Sophie's mind was racing with ideas.

"I'll email all the wives today," she told him, reaching for her Blackberry to take notes. "I have to get started right away and find out what they require for accommodation and which area they would like to live in," she said, tapping away on the keys.

Yves laughed aloud at her enthusiasm. "So much for any hope I had of a romantic morning," he cried, kissing her upturned nose. She grinned back at him.

"You brought me into this," she replied, kissing him back. "Unfortunately, all of Paris decamps to the south of France for the month of August so I have to work fast."

"That's my girl," he said, taking the Blackberry from her and pulling her into his arms. "But I think it can wait for half an hour," he added, his voice husky.

"Only half an hour?" she asked coquettishly, feeling herself getting aroused.

"That depends," he replied, starting to caress her.

She sighed happily.

What a lovely message, Ashling thought as she read the email. Sophie said how much she was looking forward to meeting them and helping to make their stay in Paris a happy one. She had enclosed a questionnaire asking for information about them and their families and what their needs might be in relation to accommodation. She also enclosed a map of Paris explaining the different areas which were known as *arrondissements* and, seeing it, it hit home to Ashling that her dream really was about to become a reality.

Looking at the map, Ashling felt a frisson of excitement. She knew exactly where she'd like to live – St-Germain-des-Prés, on the left bank. Although she'd only been to Paris once before, to celebrate their second wedding anniversary, she felt she knew it intimately from all she'd read about it. In fact, she had conceived Orna on that trip and when Kieran had suggested that maybe they should call her Paris, she'd quickly vetoed it. Thanks be to God she had. Can you imagine it? To name your child after that awful tacky Hilton woman – unthinkable!

This area where she wanted to live was where writers like James Joyce, Sartre and Hemingway had hung out in the Les Deux Magots and Café de Flore. The thought that these same cafés might soon be her locals filled her with anticipation. It would all depend, of course, on where the girls would be going to school and she hoped that she could find one within walking distance of this area. The wonderful Paris Metro would take Kieran to his office every day and take her to explore this magical city. Without hesitation, she requested Sophie to try and find a good school and apartment in this 6th arrondissement or as close as possible to it.

Felicity read the email with interest. Thank goodness there was someone there to help her. She had dreaded the thought that she might have to drag around Paris looking for accommodation. She could never have coped with that. She had no idea where she wanted to live and was in a tizzy about it. Finally, it was her sister, Penelope, who showed her the way. '*As close as possible to the Ritz and Rue Saint-Honoré,*' she wrote on the questionnaire, taking her sister's advice. She didn't worry too much about how Maxwell would get to and from work. That would be his problem. After all, he was the one dragging her to Paris.

Taylor read the email wondering who the hell this woman thought she was, to be organising her life for her. On second thoughts, she realised that, as she didn't speak French, it would probably be necessary to have someone do this kind of thing for her. She could look on her as a kind of personal assistant. Yes, her friends would be very impressed when she dropped that into the conversation. She rang around some of the girls who had been to Paris and told them that her personal assistant there wished to know where she wanted to live. She finally spoke to the wife of an ex-ambassador who said that the Avenue de la Grande Armée was the only possible address but it was frightfully difficult to get a place there. That wouldn't stop Taylor.

She sent off a reply to Sophie, with a long, long list of her requirements in an apartment on the Grande Armée. Looking at the map she saw that it was actually a continuation of the Champs-Élysées. How great was that! She hoped Brandon appreciated all that she was doing for him.

All of this had brought on a headache so she popped a Vicodin and washed it down with a vodka and soda and waited for the lovely feeling that she knew would follow.

Jazz read the email with mixed emotions. She'd spent a year in Paris when she'd been twenty-one and just out of university. There, she'd fallen in love for the very first time. She'd lost her virginity in the Hôtel de Lutèce on the Île Saint-Louis – that little island in the centre of the Seine. She'd been certain, at the time, that the charming sophisticated Frenchman was her Mr Right and had dreamt of living happily ever after with him, in Paris. The shock when she discovered, after nine months, that he had a wife and two kids out in the suburbs, had broken her heart and she'd never returned to the city. Since then, Paris had held bitter-sweet memories for her. Now, her heartbreak buried, she thought that the Île Saint-Louis would be the perfect place to live – just across from Notre Dame and surrounded by terrific restaurants and bars.

Sophie read the replies she received with interest. It was funny, she mused, but she could tell from just a simple email what these women would be like. Ashling – what a lovely name – was sweet and obviously cultured and intelligent.

Felicity, well, she was something else! A bundle of nerves – Sophie guessed, from the numerous emails she received from her – and a snob too, from the sound of it. Wanting to live close to the Ritz, indeed! Did she expect to be having tea there every afternoon? She obviously had no notion of the cost of it. 45 the last time Sophie was there. And as for shopping on Rue du Faubourg Saint-Honoré and the Rue de Rivoli! Only pop stars could afford it nowadays. She seemed to be very English and Sophie, reading between the lines, could sense that she was extremely apprehensive about coming to live in Paris.

As for Taylor, Sophie knew instinctively that she would not like this woman. She was the one that irked her the most. Such a long list of demands! She wanted a four-bedroom apartment on the Avenue de la Grande Armée, with three reception rooms and five bathrooms. What was it about Americans and bathrooms? Had Taylor any idea how much property in that area cost? Well, Sophie sighed, I'll see what I can do for her but I don't hold out much hope. Taylor had also requested a housekeeper and cook. Her husband, Brandon, was obviously very wealthy and Sophie had a premonition that she would have a lot of trouble with this obnoxious woman.

As for Jazz – well, she was a dark horse. A complete mystery. Jazz hadn't given much information about herself or her husband in her email. She'd requested a bijou flat on the Île Saint-Louis, so she obviously knew Paris well. Sophie knew what to expect from the other three women but not from Jazz. What a strange name, she thought.

She spent every moment of the next few weeks looking at properties which might suit each woman. As she'd expected, she'd had no joy on the Grande Armée but had found a nice place close by on Avenue Kléber which she hoped would meet with Taylor's approval.

The closest she could get to the Ritz for Felicity was actually closer to the Opéra but when she pointed out that it was in the most sought-after area of Paris, Felicity nervously emailed back that she supposed it would have to do. Later, however, having studied photos of the apartment, she said she was more than happy and that it was almost as nice as their Holland Park house in London.

Ashling from Ireland had thanked Sophie for her help and was obviously very excited about coming to live in Paris. She sounded lovely and was very concerned about finding a good bilingual school for her daughters. Sophie knew just the school for them. Her own son, Pierre, was a pupil there and she could highly recommend it. She'd found a darling town house for them, not far from her own, and although it wasn't in the 6th arrondissement it was bordering on it and within walking distance of the school and the Luxembourg Gardens. She guessed that Ashling would be delighted with it.

She'd had no response from Jazz except a curt 'thank you'.

Sipping a kir before dinner, she recounted all this for Yves.

"What do you know of Jazz's husband?" she asked him.

"Don't even know if she has one," he replied, busy reading the financial pages of the *New York Post*.

"What do you mean? Surely, he's coming to work for you?" She looked perplexed.

He looked up from his paper. "No, darling, *Jazz* is coming to work on the project," he explained, smiling. "She's a banker with Deutsche Bank in Frankfurt."

"Oh my God!" Sophie cried. "I thought she was an accompanying spouse. She must think I'm an idiot talking of things to do when the men are working." She looked crestfallen. "I feel such a fool."

"You're never that, *chérie*," he replied, patting her knee. "It's my fault entirely. I should have told you." He got up and brought her a file with information on the people involved.

Reading it, she felt even more foolish when she read of Jazz's achievements. She would have to apologise for her mistake. Reading the files of the others involved, she saw that they were all very high-powered achievers in the banking world. This was obviously a very important project and she was proud to be a part of it.

Felicity and Max were sitting having breakfast in their beautiful London home when she broached the subject.

"We'll take the car to Paris," she announced calmly, sipping her green tea.

"Of course we won't," he said emphatically, looking up from his paper to see if she was serious. She was. "Nobody in their right mind drives in Paris."

"We absolutely have to have a car in France," she insisted.

"In the name of God, why?" he demanded. "Where would we park it? You want to live right in the city centre. There is no garage with the apartment." He was trying to keep cool, but it was difficult.

"I'm sure Sophie will find a garage to rent close by," she said petulantly.

"Why on earth do we need a car in Paris?"

She looked at him nervously, wringing her hands. "Maxwell,

you know I'm terrified of flying and I'll need to come back here frequently to see the girls and check up on things." Her voice was wobbling and her eyes starting to fill with tears.

As always, they softened him and he felt like a cad. He relented. He realised that he was asking a lot of her – to leave her family and all of her friends. She would be right out of her comfort zone, on her own all week, in a strange city, with nothing to do and no friends. The fact that she had hardly any French would be a huge drawback. He knew she'd never have the confidence to use the schoolgirl French that she had now mostly forgotten. Of course she would need to know that she could travel back to London frequently and flying truly did terrify her.

He remembered the time they'd been on holiday in Cuba. The airline that was due to take them home collapsed the day before they were due to fly. They were stranded in Havana for three days, which was no hardship for Max, but poor Felicity had suffered panic attacks and palpitations. She thought she'd never get home, and when they finally landed at Heathrow she'd declared, "That's it. I'm never flying anywhere again." That pretty much put paid to exotic holidays! The idea of travelling from India or South Africa by car was a little daunting, even for Max.

So, now, against his better judgement, he kind-heartedly agreed. "Okay," he told her, wanting to assuage her fears, "we'll take the car to Paris."

She smiled at him, relief flooding her face.

6

On the 28th of August they were all en route to Paris.

Taylor sipped the champagne that had been offered to her as soon as she'd taken her seat on board the flight from JFK. Brandon was immersed in the *Wall Street Journal*, as usual. She'd already taken two Vicodin before leaving the house and now she washed down a Valium with the second glass of champagne, wishing that they would hurry and serve dinner so that she could settle down for a good night's sleep. Thank goodness for first class!

Taylor wasn't happy with the seat they'd been allotted on the flight.

"How come people are allowed to take children in first class?" she hissed at Brandon, scowling at the little boy seated near them.

"They can take them to the moon if they're willing to pay for them," he replied disinterestedly.

In fact, the little boy was extremely well-behaved and the stewardess informed Taylor, when she complained, "Actually, his father is chairman of the company."

Brandon smiled to himself. He hoped that might shut her up for a while. Miffed, she put on her eye mask, reclined her seat into a bed and slept for the remainder of the flight.

There was a chauffeur waiting for them at the airport in Paris, holding a placard with their name on it. He whisked them to their apartment on Avenue Kléber where Sophie was waiting for them in the lobby.

Brandon saw her first and let out a long low whistle.

"That can't be Yves's wife, surely," he remarked. "She's much too young." He didn't add 'and beautiful and sexy', which is what he was secretly thinking. My God, she had the face of an angel! He had met Yves in New York at business meetings a couple of times and had taken him to be in his late forties. This lovely girl wasn't a day over thirty.

Taylor frowned at him. "Probably some insignificant little secretary," she snorted, looking jealously at the lovely young woman approaching them.

"Welcome to Paris. I'm Sophie, Yves's wife," she smiled and kissed Brandon on both cheeks.

Taylor shrank back as Sophie turned to kiss her but seeing her husband frowning, she succumbed to the kiss.

"Yves will be here in a . . . Oh, here he comes," Sophie said, smiling at the handsome man coming towards them.

Taylor understood what Brandon had meant. Yves was certainly older than Sophie but his tall figure exuded an energy and youthfulness that made him appear younger. His jet-black curly hair was quite long with a just-got-out-of-bed look that matched his sleepy, smouldering dark-brown eyes. He oozed sex appeal. Taylor caught her breath. He was *the* most divine man she'd ever seen. She, who had not been attracted to any man for as long as she could remember, found herself blushing. A true Latin lover, she thought, as he took her hand and brought it to his lips. Paris was looking more attractive by the moment – if all the men were like this!

He and Sophie showed them up to their apartment which was on the third floor of the beautiful old building, and even Taylor had to admit that it was impressive. Yves explained that it had been built in the mid 19th century, during the famous Baron Haussmann's renovation of Paris, which had given them the beautiful city of today. It was an exquisitely elegant house with high ceilings and beautiful antique French furniture. As she went from room to room Taylor could just imagine herself entertaining here. She had invited all her friends from New York to visit and she had no doubt that they would come. They would be green with envy, she thought smugly. She naturally nabbed the largest bedroom for herself leaving Brandon with a smaller one.

There were fresh flowers everywhere and bowls of fruit. The fridge – an American one, thank God – was chock full of food, all the staples that Sophie had thought they would need. She hadn't known that Taylor didn't *do* cooking. There was champagne in the fridge and the bar was also well stocked.

Taylor immediately excused herself, without so much as a thank-you, and headed for the shower, throwing what she thought was a seductive glance at Yves on the way. All in all, Paris was looking promising, she thought, as she enjoyed the hot streams of water which flowed over her body from the many jets of the Jacuzzi

Meanwhile, Sophie made coffee while Brandon and Yves discussed business.

"Thank you so much for arranging all this," Brandon said to Sophie, waving his arm around the apartment. "It was very kind of you."

She blushed at the compliment. He was utterly charming. All her Paris friends would just adore him. She sensed that he genuinely liked women and wasn't just interested in getting them into bed – which was what most Frenchmen wanted. He was also very attractive and exuded an inner strength. The kind of man one could always depend on. She flashed a brilliant smile at him.

Shortly afterwards Yves excused them. "I'm sorry, but we must go. I spend Saturdays with my son Pierre and I can't be late. Today I am taking him to see an American football match!" He shook hands with Brandon. "We'd like you and your wife to come to lunch tomorrow so that everyone can get to meet each other. We will send a car for you at noon. Is that all right with you?"

"Wonderful, I look forward to it," said Brandon.

"*À demain* – until tomorrow," Sophie said, kissing him on both cheeks.

As he kissed her he recognised the wonderful scent of Hermès Vetiver Tonka. God, she was a beauty!

Although he was only five years old, Yves had already taken Pierre to the Stade de France to see France play rugby, to Roland Garros for the French Open Tennis and to Le Mans for the Formula One racing. Yves worshipped his little son and treasured his Saturdays with him.

Pierre was ready and waiting and in a state of high excitement when his parents arrived home.

"He was worried that you'd be late, Monsieur," his nanny, Cosette, told them, putting on the little boy's jacket.

"Of course I wouldn't be late," Yves said, sweeping him up in his arms.

"Say goodbye to Maman and Cosette and then off we go."

Pierre kissed both women and Sophie gave him an extra squeeze. She adored this solemn dark-haired child more than anything in the world. He was such a good little boy and very affectionate.

"Have a good time, my little angel," she said, waving them off. Then she turned to the nanny, whose day off it was. "Off you go, Cosette, and have a nice day."

Looking at her watch, Sophie saw that, if she hurried, she could have an hour in the gym before it was time to go and meet the English couple.

Max and Felicity were hopelessly lost on the Paris ring road. They were going round and round in circles, unable to find the correct exit. Max's temper was getting more frayed by the minute as Felicity kept issuing directions, which was why they were in such a muddle. In fact, if she hadn't forgotten the bag with the GPS in it, they'd not have been lost in the first place. Eventually they found the exit for the Champs-Élysées and pulled into the Marriott Hotel there, which was where they'd arranged to meet Sophie.

They paged her at reception and were unprepared for the charming girl who arrived, smiling.

She's very young and oh so pretty, Felicity thought enviously.

She's bloody gorgeous, was Max's first thought. She reminded him of a young Audrey Hepburn. She had beautiful big brown eyes set in a gamine face and short black hair. She also had the same chic and elegance for which Hepburn had been renowned.

"I'm Sophie. Welcome to Paris," she said in perfect English, with just a hint of an accent. They shook hands.

"I'm Felicity and this is Maxwell," Felicity said, feeling quite old and plain beside her.

"Call me Max, please," he said, ignoring the dirty look his wife threw him.

Sophie nodded. "You had a good trip?" she enquired.

"I wouldn't quite say that," Max said, smiling.

She laughed a lovely tinkling laugh. "Paris is not easy for driving, *non*?" She winked at him.

"I'm famished," Felicity said, wanting to break up this cosy little chat and steer the conversation away from driving in Paris. "Can we get something to eat here?"

"But of course, forgive me," Sophie apologised. "We will go on the terrace and have lunch. You have had a long journey." She led them out to the terrace where they were seated at a table under a billowing white parasol.

Over a delicious lunch, Sophie explained that the couple from America had arrived earlier that morning and were now sleeping and that the others would arrive later in the afternoon.

"My husband Yves and I have arranged a lunch tomorrow so that everyone can meet. We will send a car for you, around noon. If you agree."

"Splendid," said Max. He couldn't wait to meet his future colleagues and hear more of the project.

Felicity was apprehensive and hoping that they wouldn't be seeing too much of Sophie during their stay. Maxwell was obviously very taken by her and it was Felicity's greatest fear that one day he would leave her for a younger, more attractive woman. She knew she'd never survive without him.

After they had finished eating, Sophie took them to their apartment.

"She's lovely, isn't she?" Max remarked as they pulled out after her car.

"If you like that type," she sniffed.

They followed Sophie to the apartment which was even nicer than the photos had suggested. Max then drove with her to the garage and deposited the car there.

Ashling's youngest sister, Fiona, who was still at university, drove them to Dublin airport.

"Are you sure you don't want to take me with you?" she asked, fluttering her eyes at Kieran.

"Quite sure," he replied, laughing. "One Murphy woman is as much as I can handle!"

"Well, don't forget, if you need a baby-sitter, I'm always available. Paris! So romantic," she sighed dramatically.

"Well, it's business actually but I'm sure we'll find time for a little romance too," he said, winking at his wife.

"I certainly hope so, or else I might have to take a French lover while you're busy working," Ashling said coquettishly. "They're famous for that, you know."

"Don't you dare," he said, smacking her on the backside.

In a flurry of kisses they said their goodbyes.

It was all so exciting! Ashling had never flown business class before. She loved the private lounge where there were free drinks and snacks and a lovely hushed, calm atmosphere – a far cry from the chaotic noise and bustle of the terminal below. The girls were very well behaved, loving the new pink Barbie pull-along cases that they were hauling around and not really understanding what was happening except that they would be going to a new school.

"Champagne?" Kieran asked.

"It's a bit early, isn't it?"

"It's five o'clock somewhere," he grinned, pouring one for her and one for himself. "To Paris and an exciting year ahead!" he toasted her.

"To Paris and a year like no other!" she replied, smiling up at him.

Ashling drank her champagne and waved hello to some people that she knew from work. This was the life and it was only just beginning. She felt that she was on the brink of an exciting adventure.

She felt quite special as she entered the aircraft and turned left into business class. The steward greeted her with another glass of champagne and she sank into the large comfortable leather seat. Once they were airborne she could recline it and snooze but she had no intention of missing a second of this fantastic experience. The meal served by the Air France steward was as good as in any top-class restaurant. And the wines . . . oh my God, they were divine! The girls were happily colouring in the books the steward had given them. They'd decided they wanted to sit together and were quite at home in this new environment. Ashling sighed happily as Kieran squeezed her hand.

"Have I told you lately that I love you?" he asked, quoting her favourite song.

"Not since this morning," she said, smiling into his eyes.

"Well, I do. Very much."

"Do you think it's allowed to kiss in business class?" she asked him, looking around.

"Why not? It's Air France, after all," Kieran said, reaching over and kissing her deeply.

Over his shoulder, Ashling saw the steward pass by and pulled away, blushing furiously, but he grinned at her cheekily and sighed, "*Ah, l'amour – c'est magnifique!*" as he went on up the aisle.

Ashling took Kieran's hand and lay back in her seat. "Paris, here we come!" she said quietly, smiling to herself.

Jazz had decided to take the TGV speed train to Paris. She preferred travelling by train as, since 9/11, flying had become a nightmare. She reckoned by the time she got to Frankfurt airport and checked in, she could be halfway to the Gare du Nord in the centre of Paris. That's presuming the flight wouldn't be delayed, which was happening more and more lately. They could keep their flights – train it was. It took just under four hours from the centre of

Frankfurt to the centre of Paris. How cool was that! She travelled premier class, of course, and Sophie had organised a limousine to meet her.

Things had been very strained with Hans since they'd decided to take this break. At times she felt panic-stricken and at other times she recognised that they were together from force of habit and she could not envisage being married to him for the rest of her life. How would she cope with being a singleton again – at the age of almost thirty-six? It scared the hell out of her, but was it better to stay in a dead relationship? God, I sound like Carrie Bradshaw on *Sex and the City,* she chuckled to herself.

She knew that those she worked with considered her a confident, extremely capable woman. And she was – at work – but in her private life it was another story. She had no confidence in herself whatsoever but she would never let anyone come close enough to discover that fact. Except Hans of course, and now he was probably gone.

She sighed as the limousine drove up along the Seine and then caught her breath, feeling a flutter in her stomach as she spotted the Île de la Cité – with the imposing Notre Dame Cathedral – and the smaller Île Saint-Louis in the distance.

Crossing on to the smaller island, the car pulled up at one of the tall narrow buildings that backed on to the Seine.

"You must be Jazz?" said the very chic attractive girl who approached her, smiling. "Welcome to Paris. I'm Sophie." She kissed her on both cheeks.

Jazz had forgotten about this charming Gallic custom.

"Hello, Sophie. Nice to meet you at last!" she said and turned to take her luggage from the trunk of the car.

"*Non, madame. Permettez-moi!*" the chauffeur said, lifting the luggage out.

"*Merci, Claude,*" Sophie smiled at him. "Claude will take it up for you," she told Jazz, as she opened the front door of the house.

"Careful, it's very heavy," Jazz warned Claude, in excellent French.

"Oh, you speak French," Sophie exclaimed, as they entered the cute old-fashioned lift. "Would you prefer to speak in French or English? I'm sorry I don't speak German."

"No problem, and I prefer English – my French is a little rusty," Jazz smiled as the lift ascended.

Sophie was amazed at how flawless her English seemed to be.

They took the lift up to the very top floor where Sophie opened the door to the sweetest little apartment Jazz had ever seen. There were casement windows in the bedroom and large French windows in the living room, which opened on to a balcony. Sophie waited for Jazz's reaction as she stepped out into the sun.

"Oh my God, Sophie, it's fantastic!" she exclaimed as she saw the terrace with its little table and chairs and a sun-lounger. Best of all was the magnificent view. Across the rooftops of Paris she could see the Sacré-Coeur Basilica shimmering in the sunlight. Down below, the tourist boats chugged up and down the Seine. It was truly breathtaking.

"This view is the pièce-de-resistance, isn't it?" Sophie said, pleased that Jazz was as impressed as she had been with the bijou apartment.

"It's perfect, just perfect," Jazz murmured as she looked out her bedroom window and saw the Eiffel Tower in the distance.

"Shall I make us coffee?" Sophie asked her.

"Coffee? Is there some here?"

Sophie smilingly opened the cupboard which was full of jars and food.

"Oh my God!" Jazz exclaimed again. "Where did they come from?"

"I stocked up for you," Sophie replied, opening the fridge to show Jazz that it was also full, with even a bottle of champagne chilling.

"You're so kind," Jazz told her, mortified to feel tears coming to her eyes. "Thank you so much."

"Perhaps you would prefer a glass of champagne to celebrate your first day in Paris?"

"Why the hell not?" Jazz replied, wiping her eyes. "As long as you'll join me."

They sat on the balcony, feeling the heat of the sun and sipping champagne. Looking down at the tourist boats, Jazz murmured, awe in her voice, "I can't believe I'm living here again."

"Please excuse me but I did not realise you were a banker. I thought you were a wife," Sophie apologised.

"Don't give it another thought – and I'm definitely not a wife!" Jazz laughed, but it sounded hollow, even to her ears.

Sipping the champagne she was surprised to find herself telling Sophie about Hans and how she suspected that it was over for them.

"Maybe that's good," Sophie said. "You must be madly in love with the man you marry, otherwise what's the point? I am sure that you will find true love in Paris. Everyone does," she assured this beautiful girl.

Jazz didn't tell her that she already had – many, many years ago.

Driving home, Sophie thought that Jazz would certainly have no shortage of suitors in Paris. Although she had been dressed in simple blue jeans and a white shirt, her long dark hair in a ponytail and wearing practically no make-up, Sophie could see that Jazz was a very attractive, sexy woman. Her eyes were amazing – a deep smoky brown and fringed with long curly dark lashes. Her legs were as long as any supermodel's although she was not the skinny size zero of many of them. No, Jazz was all woman and Sophie suspected that Yves would fancy her – big-time.

Ashling and Kieran enjoyed the drive in the limousine that had met them at the airport, craning their necks to take in all the famous sights they passed and pointing them out to the girls. When they passed the Café Les Deux Magots, Ashling let out a squeal of joy. Not far from there, the car pulled up outside a very grand townhouse. Sophie was inside, waiting to greet them. Ashling felt big and ungainly beside the petite Frenchwoman but found her extremely charming and liked her instantly.

"What's your name?" Sophie asked Orna, squatting down to her level.

Shyly Orna told her. "And this is Ciara, my little sister," she added, trying to pry her away from Ashling's legs.

"Ciara's a little shy at first," Ashling explained, "but once she gets to know you she'll never stop talking!"

"They're so sweet, and what lovely names you all have," Sophie remarked.

"Yes, they're Gaelic. Ashling means 'dream vision' in Gaelic. It's usually spelt A-i-s-l-i-n-g in Ireland, but foreigners never know how to pronounce that!"

"Yes, I would pronounce that Ace-ling," Sophie agreed with her.

Ashling loved the house. It was on three floors, very spacious and beautifully decorated, but most of all she loved the location. Opening the kitchen cupboards, she was surprised to see they were well stocked.

"This is fantastic," she cried. "Thank you so much, Sophie."

"Mummy, look!" Orna called out. "The fridge is full too and there's chocolate yogurt in it!"

"I've left some champagne there too, to celebrate your first day in Paris," Sophie said.

"You're so kind," Ashling said, moved by this gesture.

"We'd like you to join us for lunch tomorrow where you'll meet all the others involved in the project. It's very informal so please bring the girls with you and they can meet my son Pierre." She smiled at Orna, who was taking all this in, fascinated by the lovely lady with the funny accent.

"I'll send a car for you, at eleven thirty. This is okay?"

"Perfect," Kieran and Ashling said simultaneously.

When Sophie had left, Ashling threw her arms around Kieran's neck. "Please pinch me to tell me I'm not dreaming," she asked him. "*Ouch!*" she squealed, as he did what she'd asked.

Kieran took the girls up to their pretty bedroom where they put away their dolls and toys. Meanwhile, Ashling explored the contents of the fridge and rustled up a delicious supper for them.

They were all tired, more with excitement than anything else, and after the girls were tucked up in bed, Kieran took her in his arms.

"I'm so happy and excited," she sighed.

"Me too. Come to bed and I'll show you how much," he grinned, grabbing the bottle of champagne from the fridge and opening cupboards looking for glasses.

"I'm getting fond of this," she said, smirking at him. "Bed early in the evening, with champagne."

"You better get used to it, woman," he said huskily. "You're in Paris now."

"And my husband has turned into a Latin lover. Yippee!" she cried, clambering up the stairs ahead of him.

7

Sophie had intended wearing a midnight-blue Balenciaga two-piece to the lunch but as the weather was so glorious she scrapped that plan and chose her simple dove grey Roland Mouret dress. It suited her to perfection, showing off her very tiny waist and petite figure. Her legs were deeply tanned so she decided to dispense with tights and completed the look with pearl-grey Manolo Blahnik shoes which made her look at least four inches taller. A silver cuff and silver earrings completed the ensemble. It was perfect for an informal lunch, she figured.

Leaning on the doorframe, watching his wife twirl in front of the mirror, Yves remarked, "Simple but devastating, my darling. You'll be the most beautiful woman there."

"You haven't seen Jazz yet. She's a knockout. I could never compete with her," she said, making a little grimace.

"You can compete with anyone," he said, coming and putting his arms around her waist from behind. "Mmmm . . ." he buried his face in her neck, "if we had time I'd make you take it all off and come to bed with me."

"Stop it!" she cried. "We don't have time. Our guests will be here in ten minutes," but she was smiling as she said it.

Secretly she would have loved nothing better. She adored sex with her handsome husband. She knew people thought he was too old for her but in bed he satisfied her totally. In fact she had a job keeping up with him. A far better lover than many men half his age! They still sometimes made love twice a day and she loved it. "Later," she whispered to him as she brushed past him.

Pierre was sitting with his nanny who was reading to him, when they came downstairs.

"You look very pretty, Maman," he said, reaching up for a kiss.

"Thank you, my darling," she replied. She was sure he would break some hearts when he was older. He had his father's looks and charm. "Okay, men. We're ready. Let them come!"

Taking their hands, she led them into the courtyard garden.

Ashling gave the girls' hair a last brush before leaving. They looked beautiful. Their long hair, a red-gold colour just like their mother's, hung like silk curtains down their backs and was held back with white rosette hairbands. They wore ballet-length, white smocked dresses and white leather Mary Jane shoes. They were a picture in prettiness and had been warned to be on their best behaviour.

They were the first to arrive at the lunch and the door was opened by a beautiful young man who turned out to be the butler-cum-waiter. He showed them through the house – which Ashling noted was like something out of *Homes & Gardens* – into a beautiful courtyard where Sophie and Yves waited with the most adorable little boy Ashling had ever seen. He had a mop of black curls, big brown eyes and dark olive skin. He was like a mini-version of his father. She noted that he was wearing what was obviously a very expensive blue-and-white suit – probably Baby Dior, she thought.

"*Bienvenue*, lovely to see you again," Sophie said, as she welcomed them with a kiss. "And how pretty the girls look! I wanted you to be here first so that the children could meet before the other adults arrive."

"Pierre, come and meet Orna and Ciara," she called, beckoning him over.

He came shyly forward and Sophie introduced the girls.

"*Enchanté*," he said to each of them, bowing slightly from the waist.

His manners were impeccable and the girls were mesmerised by him. Ciara was clinging on to Ashling's leg but when she saw Orna smile and take his hand, she followed suit. Pierre spoke a little English as he was in a bilingual school and was proudly showing it off. Sophie gave them some juice and settled them at a table together, while the waiter, who was called Jacques, handed the adults a flute of champagne.

"What a beautiful home you have," Kieran said, as they raised their glasses.

"Thank you, we love it," Yves replied.

"We're really pleased it's such a glorious day and that we can have lunch out here in the courtyard," Sophie told them.

"It's quite exquisite," Ashling exclaimed, looking around.

The paved courtyard was lined with bay trees in wooden containers and a myriad of colourful flowers adorned numerous pots, both standing and hanging and also lining the windowsills. There were four small fountains with water gently cascading and four Grecian statues, one at each corner. But the pièce-de-resistance was the interconnecting gazebos, beautifully draped with white voile curtains. Under the larger one was a large round table, stunningly set with a centrepiece of white roses and green-and-white china and linen. The smaller one housed a bar. Dotted around the courtyard were many white wrought-iron tables and chairs under white parasols. The children were seated at one of these. It was all so beautiful that Ashling felt like she was in a scene from a movie.

"How clever that you are dressed to suit our colour scheme," Sophie remarked, admiring Ashling's long green-and-white floaty dress and matching sandals. She was also wearing a sweet straw sunhat.

"Very wise to be wearing a hat under this hot sun," Yves remarked.

"With this Irish skin, I have no choice," Ashling grimaced.

"You look very pretty, my dear," Yves replied, noting her creamy fair skin with its smattering of freckles and her long red-gold curls. "Red hair and green eyes, that is very Irish I think." He smiled at her appreciatively.

"A typical Irish colleen, that is what you say, *non?*" Sophie asked.

"I'm afraid so," Ashling replied, shrugging her freckled shoulders and laughing.

Twenty minutes later Jacques came through to the courtyard with Taylor and Brandon. Taylor was dressed all in black and dripping in gold chains, while diamonds and emeralds sparkled on her fingers and ears. Sophie noted that her suit was Chanel and she wore a large black hat, presumably to shield her face from the hot August sun. She looked completely out of place in the lovely summer garden and her ensemble was more suited to a funeral than a garden party. She looked formidable indeed and reaffirmed Sophie's first impression that she would never, ever like this woman.

Brandon was even more gorgeous than she remembered. He was incredibly handsome, very tall and slim with blond hair going slightly grey at the temples. He had a kind face and a gentleness about him that she knew all women would find very attractive. His deep, very blue eyes held her in their gaze, as he reached forward to kiss her. He made it feel like an intimate kiss although she knew it wasn't. She caught her breath, feeling the persuasive power of his charm. Only one other man she'd ever met had possessed the same quality and that was Bill Clinton – whom she'd met at a reception in Paris. Both men focused intensely on you when they were talking to you and both had that same aura and charisma that was totally irresistible. Blushing slightly, she introduced Ashling and Kieran while the waiter offered them champagne.

I can tell she's going to be a bellyful of laughs, Ashling thought bitchily as she shook Taylor's limp hand. The other woman looked Ashling and Kieran over in her supercilious way and instantly dismissed them. Brandon, however, was charm personified and both of them warmed to him immediately. Ashling couldn't understand what he was doing with this dragon of a wife.

"Goodness me, is that children I see?" Taylor exclaimed, catching sight of the kids quietly sipping their juice. She made it sound as if she'd spotted some exotic animals. Unwelcome ones, at that!

"Yes, the two girls are mine," Ashling said, immediately on the defensive, "and the little boy is Sophie's."

"How quaint," Taylor remarked, ignoring the dirty look Brandon was throwing her.

"They're very sweet," he said, trying to undo the damage.

"Sorry, I didn't catch your name properly?" Ashling said to him.

"My husband is Brandon Cartwright Hartford Junior – a very prestigious East Coast family," Taylor informed them haughtily.

Ashling caught Brandon's look of annoyance. No love lost there, she thought.

As they sipped their champagne Brandon told them that his great-grandfather had hailed from Ireland, from Co Kerry. "Hence the 'Brandon'," he explained. "I believe there's a mountain called Brandon there."

"Indeed there is. Mount Brandon, near Tralee," Kieran informed him. "Kerry is a beautiful county with fabulous scenery and very friendly people."

"So I've heard. I'm definitely going over for a visit while I'm here in Europe. I've always wanted to visit Ireland. Maybe I'll even get to climb Mount Brandon." He smiled, showing a set of perfect white teeth.

Ashling gathered, from the look of distaste on her face, that Taylor wouldn't be accompanying him.

Another couple arrived just then, whom Yves introduced as Felicity and Max Parker-Scott, from London.

"Maxwell," Felicity corrected him.

"Max," her husband insisted, ignoring her glare.

"Well, which is it to be?" Brandon asked, smiling.

"Please call me Max," Max reiterated, shaking hands with everyone.

Taylor looked at Felicity in sympathy.

Ashling felt an urge to giggle. Taylor and Felicity were both bristling with self-righteousness. Both of them were very slim – no, make that skinny – and not more than a size two dress size, she figured. They were the epitome of the social x-rays that Tom Wolfe wrote about in *Bonfire of the Vanities* who believed they could never be too rich or too thin.

From what Ashling could see of Taylor's hair under the hat, it was very expensively cut and coloured. Her face was completely unlined, eyes pulled tight and lips puffed up and the only time she showed any expression was when she narrowed her glittering eyes in disapproval. This she was doing now as she regarded the others with an air of superiority.

Felicity, on the other hand was very English, wearing pearls – real ones, Ashling guessed – over her beige cashmere twinset which must have had her sweltering in this heat. Her mousy-blonde hair was up in a chignon – like Princess Anne – and between that and the frumpy black heels she wore, she looked older than she probably was. She spoke with a plummy English accent and sounded exactly like the Queen and all the other royals. Ashling half-expected a clatter of corgis to be following her around. Felicity smiled a tight little smile as she shook hands with them and kept glancing nervously at her husband. Ashling got the feeling that she was extremely nervous and uncomfortable.

Sophie caught Ashling's eye and smiled conspiratorially at her. For her part, she was hoping that she wouldn't have too many dealings with Taylor in the future, although she had her doubts. This type of woman was always trouble. Beckoning with a nod to Ashling, she turned to the company and said, "If you'll excuse us, we'll just go check on the children before lunch."

They moved away together towards where the children were sitting.

"What harridans!" Sophie remarked, throwing her eyes up to heaven.

Ashling agreed. "We'd better not let that Taylor near the children. She looks like she'd eat them up," she said, giggling.

"Not a chance," Sophie replied. "They'd be much too fattening."

The two of them pealed with laughter.

"Look, Maman," Orna cried, "Pierre has brought Ciara and me a present!"

Ashling was shocked to hear her little daughter calling her 'Maman'. Then she saw the book that Orna held up. It was *Easy French for Children*.

"He's been teaching us to speak French," Orna said, smiling adoringly at Pierre.

"How lovely!" Ashling exclaimed. "Did you say thank you to Pierre?"

"*Merci, Pierre*," Orna said shyly.

"*Merci, Pierre*," Ciara parroted her sister.

"My God, I can't believe it!" Ashling cried. "They're speaking French already."

"Pierre is a regular little teacher," Sophie laughed. "You'll be amazed how quickly they'll pick it up." Clapping her hands lightly, she called, "Come along, children, and Papa will take you in to Cosette for lunch. Yves, do you mind?"

Yves smilingly came forward. "Come along, children."

"It's too hot for them to eat out here," Sophie explained to Ashling, as Yves ushered them inside.

Minutes later, Jacques came through into the courtyard with a stunning girl. All conversation stopped as everyone regarded the leggy beauty who had joined them – alone – it appeared.

"Jazz, welcome!" Sophie went to greet the new arrival, kissing her on both cheeks.

"Thank you, Sophie," the girl replied, a perfect smile lighting up her face.

"Come, let me introduce you," she said, taking Jazz's hand. The girl was wearing a short, off-the-shoulder, red silk dress which showed off her smooth tanned shoulders and curvaceous body to perfection. She was tall and dark-complexioned with huge smoky brown eyes and a heart-shaped face. Her long black glossy hair cascaded around her shoulders, reminding Ashling of Catherine Zeta Jones in the film *Zorro*. She was wearing black-patent Louboutin heels, their red soles matching her dress. Her perfectly shaped, smooth, tanned legs seemed to go on forever. Her only jewellery was a pair of big gold hoop earrings and a small gold watch. Ashling watched as Sophie came towards them with the new arrival. Gosh, she was even more gorgeous close up and her only make-up appeared to be lip gloss and kohl. Ashling felt downright frumpy beside her.

"I'd like you all to meet Jazz, from Frankfurt," smiled Sophie, as they reached the little group. "Jazz, let me introduce the others. This is Ashling, from Dublin."

Jazz kissed Ashling on both cheeks. "Oh, Dublin, how wonderful," she said, her voice warm. "I've been there often. A great place – great *craic*," she added, pleased that she'd remembered the Irish word for fun.

Ashling warmed to her straight away.

The same couldn't be said for Taylor, who held out her hand limply. She looked Jazz up and down in a supercilious, rude manner.

Felicity appeared crestfallen as she looked at the girl before her. How on earth could she compete with all these beautiful women, she wondered? Like Taylor before her she greeted Jazz coolly. She was already in awe of Taylor and admired her enormously.

Jazz got a much warmer welcome from both Brandon and Max – too warm, from the frosty expressions on their wives' faces. They both kissed her and even Kieran seemed bowled over by her. Jazz was incredibly sexy-looking but Ashling had a feeling that she was not aware of the effect she was having on the men.

Jazz accepted the flute of champagne from an obviously admiring Jacques.

"Is your husband not with you?" Felicity enquired, in a polite but curious voice.

"I don't have a husband," Jazz replied.

"How come?" Taylor quizzed her. "Isn't your husband a banker on this project?"

"No, actually, *I'm* a banker on this project," Jazz informed her coldly, enjoying the shock on Taylor's face.

Hurrah! Good girl, Ashling cheered her silently. That put the snooty bitch in her place.

"Fantastic!" Brandon exclaimed enthusiastically, making matters worse. He was thinking that Jazz would certainly brighten up the workplace.

Felicity looked at Maxwell anxiously to see how he was reacting to the newcomer. She was apprehensive to think that he would be working every day with this girl. Not only was she gorgeous but clever too, she thought jealously.

Taylor pointedly turned her back on Jazz, seething at this girl who had upstaged her. All the men were hanging on her every word. Fools! She felt a headache coming on and went into the bathroom where she downed her second Vicodin of the day. Thank God for these little pills. They were her lifesavers.

"I think I'll sit down, if you don't mind," Jazz excused herself, some time later. "These heels are not for standing in!"

"I don't know how you walk in them at all," Ashling remarked, shaking her head. "I couldn't."

"Walking isn't a problem, it's standing around that kills me." Jazz plonked herself down on one of the wrought-iron chairs, crossing her fabulous legs. Ashling sat down with her as Sophie went to check on the lunch.

"It's so beautiful here, isn't it?" Jazz remarked. "You'd never think that we were in the centre of Paris." She flashed a smile at Jacques as he replenished their glasses. "And Sophie found me the cutest apartment. You'll have to come and visit."

"I'd love to."

Jazz already felt that she had made a friend. There was something warm, humorous and open about the Irishwoman. Sophie, too, was just lovely and obviously someone to be relied on in any crisis. She had done the right thing in coming to Paris. Everything was going to work out beautifully. She glanced around the charming courtyard and breathed a sigh of relief and contentment. At that moment her eyes widened in shock. Suddenly she was frozen in time and felt that her blood had stopped flowing through her body. For a moment she feared she might faint.

Coming into the courtyard with his arm around Sophie, was Yves, her lover from all those years ago. It can't be, this can't be happening, she thought, her heart hammering violently in her chest. In a panic, she looked around for a way out but there was no escape. They came towards her.

Sophie was smiling. "Jazz, I'd like you to meet my husband, Yves."

"*Enchanté, madamoiselle,*" he smiled, taking her hand to his lips, staring deeply into her eyes.

Her heart had now moved up into her throat and her mouth was so dry that she couldn't utter a word.

"I look forward to working with you," he said, showing no flicker of recognition.

Jazz took her cue from him. She let her breath out slowly, hoping that nobody had noticed her reaction.

"Thank you," she managed to reply and took a large slug of champagne. It went down the wrong way and, spluttering and coughing, she excused herself to make her way to the bathroom.

Once inside, she locked the door, sat on the loo and tried to stop shaking. She couldn't believe it. She felt she was living in a nightmare. Seeing Yves again had given her such a shock and brought back all the old memories. He was as gorgeous as she remembered and, if anything, the years had made him even more handsome. His body was more muscular now and his jet-black curly hair, still long, had begun greying at the temples. His dark-brown eyes had not lost their magnetic attraction and she'd felt herself drawn to him once again as she had been, all those years ago. Closing her eyes she recalled their lovemaking. She'd been such an innocent but he had gently taught her how to reach the heights of pleasure. She'd been drunk with lust and she'd fallen deeply in love with him. It had been crazy and wild and now here he was, disturbing her equilibrium once again.

She wondered what he thought of her. She had changed a lot in fifteen years. Her hair had been dyed blonde and short back then, now it was long and its natural dark colour. Her body was certainly in better shape now – toned and more voluptuous – and the scruffy student denims replaced by sophisticated designer gear. Was it possible that he hadn't recognised her? No, of course not! They'd been so close. He probably hadn't wanted to upset Sophie. She certainly couldn't be the wife he'd been married to back then. She was much too young.

How could she possibly work with him every day? Would she ever be able to resist him? Here, I go – ruminating like Carrie Bradshaw on *Sex and the City* again – she chuckled to herself. Somehow that helped her get back her cool and she splashed some water on her face. Then she brushed her hair and reapplied some lip gloss to her lips and kohl to her eyes. Finally she felt calm enough to go out and face him once again.

Just as she finished, she heard a knock on the door.

"Jazz, are you okay?" It was Ashling.

"I'm fine," Jazz replied, opening the door, a bright smile on her face.

"Oh, good," Ashling mumbled. "I was worried that something was wrong." Her voice held a note of concern.

"Absolutely not," Jazz assured her, her voice light.

Ashling wasn't totally convinced as they linked arms and went back to join the party.

8

Lunch was just about to start as they rejoined the group. They moved across to the large gazebo, grateful for the shade it provided from the hot sun. There were place names on the table and Ashling found that she was seated between Max and Brandon. Thank God I'm not beside Taylor or Felicity, she noted with relief.

"We have tried to separate husbands and wives, to make it more sociable," Yves smiled, "but please feel free to circulate any time you wish."

To Jazz's horror, she was seated beside Yves. She would very much have liked to circulate right then and there but of course that was out of the question.

To Felicity's delight, she was seated beside Taylor who had her in thrall. She was so looking forward to hearing more about Taylor's wonderful life in New York which, she gathered, was tremendously exciting. Watching the two of them nattering away, Ashling reckoned that it would be a case of them and us.

She and Jazz were getting on terrifically well together.

They started with tiny morsels of various canapés or *amuses-bouche*, as Sophie called them.

"It actually translates as 'amuse the mouth'," she explained to them.

"I never knew that," Jazz remarked. "How cute!"

The first course of foie-gras with an onion confit was delicious.

Taylor declined to have any. Felicity was enjoying hers when Taylor launched into how it was made.

"Do you know they force-feed the poor geese to make their livers as large as possible?" Taylor remarked maliciously.

Brandon glared at her, furious with her for such abominable rudeness.

Felicity dropped her knife and fork with a clatter and pushed her plate away. There was no way she could eat the foie gras now after hearing that. Max shifted uncomfortably in his seat, embarrassed by the whole thing.

"Actually, it depends on the producer," Yves explained gently. "The good ones do not do that and this is from the very best producer in the Auvergne."

The others ate on in silence, enjoying the wonderful flavour and ignoring Taylor and Felicity.

The next course was a wonderful dish of seared scallops with baby asparagus which was truly divine. Taylor again declined, saying that she didn't trust seafood. Felicity didn't finish hers – probably in support of her new friend, Ashling guessed.

After a sorbet, the main course of lobster thermidor was served but there was filet mignon for those who did not like lobster. Taylor was again being awkward, although this time she was alone and even Felicity tucked into the wonderful lobster with gusto. Ashling noted that for all Taylor ate of her steak, they might as well not have bothered putting it on the pan. She played around with it and ate about two morsels before pushing it aside. I'll certainly never invite her to dinner with us, Ashling vowed.

Finally, the dessert trolley arrived. It was divine. Ashling couldn't help herself. She just had to try everything. Sitting in front of her loaded plate she noticed that Taylor and Felicity had practically nothing on theirs. That figures, she thought disgustedly. How do they resist it? No wonder they stay so slim.

To Ashling's relief, she saw that Jazz had also helped herself generously which made her feel a bit better!

Jazz obviously enjoyed her food although she had a fantastically toned body.

"I don't know how you do it," Ashling wailed. "How will I survive the next year here with all this delicious French food?"

"Well, if I didn't work out a lot, I'd certainly be overweight," Jazz confided.

"Me too," Sophie nodded in agreement.

"Well, if you two need to work out then I definitely need it too," Ashling said, ruefully. "I never lost the weight I gained when I was pregnant with the girls." She patted her stomach with a grimace.

"Sophie is introducing me to her gym on Tuesday night," Jazz remarked. "Why don't you come with us?"

"May I?" Ashling asked, hopefully.

"Of course you may. It's a date," Sophie smiled.

"I like a woman who enjoys her food," Brandon, his deep blue eyes twinkling, smiled at Ashling as she tucked into her heaped plate.

"Me too," Max agreed.

If looks could kill Ashling would have been stone dead by the venomous glares that flew her way from Taylor and Felicity.

As the lunch progressed Ashling began to think that she had never met such a mismatched couple as Max and Felicity. He was the life and soul of the party and kept them entertained with his jokes and funny stories. Felicity on the other hand was ever so prim and proper and didn't relax at all. He was small and rotund – she was tall and skinny. They were like chalk and cheese yet he seemed devoted to her. That didn't, however, stop him flirting with the other women, despite Felicity's uptight face. Ashling had a feeling, however, that he was only doing it out of chivalry and wasn't altogether serious. She guessed Max was really a man's man. When he heard that Kieran had played rugby for Leinster they got into a deep discussion about the game, across the table. He was also a keen golfer and he and Kieran discussed the pros and cons of various drivers and clubs, and courses they'd played.

As the wine flowed, so did the conversation. Yves was so attentive to Jazz that she found it embarrassing. He monopolised her all through the meal, practically ignoring Taylor who was on his other side and desperately trying to gain his attention. It was obvious to everyone that he found Jazz very attractive. Nothing subtle there, Ashling thought. God, if Kieran behaved like that with another woman, I'd kill him! Sophie, however, seemed to be taking it all in her stride. Maybe it was because Brandon was keeping her entertained which was certainly no hardship for her. Despite the glares that his wife was throwing him all through lunch, he continued to chat with her, laughing and joking with her. She seemed to be enjoying it.

Can't say I blame her, Ashling thought ruefully.

He was, without doubt, the most charming man she'd ever met. He was devilishly attractive, six-foot-four at least, with dark-blond hair and those wonderful blue eyes which lit up when he spoke. He had a deep sexy voice and a very hearty laugh which he used often. She wouldn't blame Sophie if she fancied him. Even Ashling wasn't immune to him and for a brief moment wondered what it would be like to be in bed with him. Shocked at herself for thinking such a thing, she excused herself and went to the bathroom.

Jazz followed her in.

"Are you okay?" Ashling asked, seeing a strange look of panic on Jazz's face.

"Yes . . . no . . ." Jazz stammered. "I mean –"

"Yves is being a bit much, is that it?"

"Yes," Jazz blushed. "Ashling, would you mind changing places with me?" she whispered.

"Not at all. I'll go and grab my glass and sit beside him. Then when you come out, you can sit in my place."

"Gee, thanks," Jazz said, relief in her voice. "Are you sure you don't mind?"

"Course not. After all, he did say we should feel free to circulate," Ashling reminded her as she left the bathroom.

Jazz had found that the chemistry between Yves and herself was as strong as it had been the first time they'd met. Every time his hand brushed her skin – which it did often – it was like an electric current scorching through her body. She wanted him so badly that it hurt and she knew that he wanted her too. It shocked her that she still felt this way about him.

Leaning over the washbasin, she cried, "Oh, God, what am I going to do?"

She would have to work with this man for the next year. How could she do it, feeling as she did? And, to top it all, his wife was so lovely. "Oh God," she cried again, her head in her hands. Splashing some water on her face she composed herself and went back to the party.

Ashling had done as she'd promised and was seated beside Yves. They were deep in conversation. He looked up soulfully at Jazz as she sat down beside Brandon and she could see the disappointment in his eyes. She immediately regretted what she'd done and longed to be back sitting close to him. Even though they were now separated, she was acutely aware of his presence.

After dinner the children joined the party again and Jazz was enchanted with them. They all took to her too and she played with them, swinging them around and around for ages, until she finally cried out, "Mercy, mercy!"

"Come along, children!" Sophie clapped her hands. "Leave Jazz alone now, she's had enough." Taking the girls by the hand she took them indoors to get them some juice as Jazz put her shoes back on.

"You're very good with them," Ashling remarked, as Jazz flopped into a chair.

"I love kids," Jazz replied, but Ashling heard the wistfulness in her voice.

"You've never had any?"

"No. I guess I never met the right man."

"Have you ever been married?"

"No. I've lived with someone for close on thirteen years but we're splitting up, so I guess you could say I'm single again and highly unlikely to have children at this stage," she said, a pang in her voice.

"Never say never," Ashling said gently, patting her hand.

The party broke up shortly afterwards as the cars arrived to take them home.

Before they left, Sophie handed each of the women an envelope containing information on things to see and places to go in Paris and its environs.

Taylor was silent in the car on the way home but Brandon recognised, from the set of her lips, that it wasn't because she had nothing to say. Taylor would never discuss anything private in front of the hired staff so she stayed mum until they had left the car and were inside the house.

"How could you embarrass me like that with that French slut?" she hissed at him, as she made for the drinks cabinet.

"I take it you mean Sophie, our generous hostess?" he enquired, raising an eyebrow.

"She's generous all right, with her flirting and I daresay her favours," she said through gritted teeth, as she mixed herself a large martini.

Brandon looked at her through hooded eyes. "She's a lovely lady, a great hostess, charming, friendly and kind. What exactly is your problem there?"

"You were laughing with her all through lunch," she hissed. "I noticed you eyeing up the German tart too."

"Oh, now you're talking about Jazz," he said lazily, "the very bright, intelligent young woman who is a director of a very prestigious bank in Germany. Let me also mention that she's extremely good company and funny too – as opposed to you, my dear, who was a right pain in the arse all day."

"Stop being so vulgar," she spat at him. "It doesn't suit you." Her body was rigid as she sat back in the very comfortable sofa.

"Unlike you," he drawled, as he poured himself a whisky, "who underneath that veneer of gentility, is as vulgar as they come."

"Don't throw my background at me!" she screamed at him. "You're a shithead." She leapt up and made to fling her glass at him but he grabbed her wrist, stopping her in her tracks.

"Don't even think about it, my dear," he said. "I know what's wrong with you. Jazz and Sophie are young, pretty and attractive, not to mention extremely sexy, and you're downright jealous." With that he turned on his heel and went into his study.

Knocking back what was left of the martini in the glass, she poured another large one and took a Vicodin with it. Curling up on the large sofa, she cursed Paris, France and French and German women in particular. How she missed New York!

All the way home in the car Felicity enthused about Taylor. Max couldn't understand how she admired that cold obnoxious woman so much. Max had disliked her intensely. Her hubby, Brandon, was a jolly good chap and Max was looking forward to working with him.

"Did you see the disgraceful way Yves was behaving with that German woman?" she remarked, her voice censorious.

"Not particularly," he replied. "He's French. They fancy themselves as lovers so probably he was just acting the part. With a wife like Sophie, I couldn't imagine him straying."

God, Maxwell is so naïve at times, she thought, as they arrived at their apartment.

"Anyway, I really liked that Irish chap and his wife," he continued, getting out of the car. "We must invite them over for supper sometime."

Felicity shuddered. Not if I can help it, she thought. To her delight, Taylor had invited her to go shopping the following Tuesday. She couldn't wait.

That evening, as Ashling looked through Sophie's information, she marvelled at all the opportunities that were available in this wonderful city. She spent the evening curled up on the sofa looking at all her options.

There was a French Literature course being held in the Sorbonne which would be great for her French; an art appreciation course being run at the Louvre; a wine course and a cordon bleu cookery course. "Eat your heart out, Julia Child!" she laughed, thinking of the famous American cook who had done a cordon bleu course right here in Paris and then introduced French cuisine to America. She was played by Meryl Streep in the film *Julie and Julia*, about a girl who for a year had worked her way through every one of the

524 recipes in Julia Child's cookbook. In fact, having seen the film, Ashling had gone straight out and bought the book herself and now here she was with a chance to follow in Julia Child's footsteps.

Reading about the music lessons at the Conservatoire she thought briefly that she might take up the piano again or even start learning the cello. It was so exciting. She was spoilt for choice! She planned to use this year to improve herself in as many ways as possible.

One thing she'd definitely decided on, having been surrounded by slim women all day, was that she would start back on her Weight-Watchers plan tomorrow morning and hopefully, between that and her gym sessions, she would be a new woman when she returned to Ireland next year.

9

The following morning Jazz and the three men were collected by car and driven to the Finance Ministry at Bercy, where their office would be located.

None of them were prepared for the fortress-like building where they would be spending the next year. Brandon and Jazz would be sharing an office and working together and Kieran and Max were another team, in another office. Brandon thought that Jazz looked extremely elegant in her cream trouser suit, her hair coiled up on her head. She looked totally different to how she had looked at the lunch on Sunday. Now, she was every inch the businesswoman, though a very sexy one.

He considered himself something of a connoisseur where women were concerned. Ever since Taylor had decided, after the twins were born, that she no longer wished to have sex with him, he had done what any full-blooded male would do – he found his pleasures elsewhere. He was always discreet and always honest with the women in question. It was an arrangement which suited both parties. Occasionally things began to escalate to more than just a sexual relationship and, when that happened, Brandon immediately finished it. He himself had come from a broken home and it was something he would not inflict on his twins, despite the loveless marriage in which he was mired.

He had found out, from sad experience, that women in banking were mostly cold, ruthless and career-driven. He supposed that Jazz, for all her attractions, was the same. She hadn't got where she was today by being sweet and feminine, which was the kind of woman that attracted him. No, beautiful as she was, Jazz was definitely not his type but he would have no problem working side by side with her.

Yves welcomed them and told them that after coffee they would be meeting with the French Finance Minister. They were all agog to know what exactly they would be working on. Yves's secretary, a cute young blonde called Chantal, brought in the coffee as they ruminated on what it might be.

Twenty minutes later, in the Minister's office, they found out. They would be working on a project, which if it turned out to be viable, would have repercussions for financial institutions worldwide. He explained to them that they would be working under the utmost secrecy and must swear not to discuss any aspect of the project with anyone other than themselves and, even then, only in the office. They would report to him every Friday and he in turn would report back to the finance ministers in their home countries. There was another group in Beijing – their counterparts – who were working on the same project and the results from both groups would be pooled together. He then outlined the nature of the project and what part each one of them would play. As he finished, he stressed the importance of what they were doing and wished them well.

They trooped back silently to their offices, thinking of what he had said. The importance of the project was starting to manifest itself and each of them felt honoured and proud to be the ones chosen to carry this out.

Meanwhile, Sophie was taking Ashling to the school on Quai d'Orsay, to view it and meet with the headmistress. The children were giggling in the back of the car, Pierre proud and delighted to be showing off his school to the girls. It was a bilingual Montessori school and, having checked it out online, Ashling felt it would be perfect for the girls. The fact that Sophie had chosen it for Pierre was commendation enough but, still, she wanted to see it for herself before making a decision.

She needn't have worried – it was perfect. The headmistress showed them around and Ashling loved the atmosphere of the place. The girls thought it was cool. Having spoken to the headmistress, it didn't take Ashling long to make up her mind. Ms Coleman assured her that they would be speaking French in no time at all, which thrilled her. There was a bus which would collect them and drop them home, if she so wished, but as it was only a ten-minute walk away, she said she'd probably walk them there and back in fine weather. They would start school the following Monday and both Orna and Ciara were wildly excited about it, as was Pierre.

Leaving the school, they took the kids to McDonald's for a treat.

"Not my idea of a treat," Sophie admitted, "but Pierre loves it. Can you believe it? French children preferring McDonald's to a good restaurant! What's our country coming to?" She laughed, throwing her eyes to heaven.

"Kids everywhere seem to love it but they grow out of it," Ashling assured her while ordering two black coffees and three kids' meals.

There was a big play centre there so when the children had polished off their chicken nuggets, they disappeared to work off their high spirits.

Sophie's phone rang. She spoke so fast that Ashling could only catch part of the conversation but she gathered that Sophie was very excited about something or other.

"That was Yves," Sophie told her, her eyes shining. "We have all been invited to a reception at the Hôtel de Ville, on the 18th of this month. This is a great honour – to be invited by the Mayor of Paris!" She was barely able to contain herself.

"I don't think I can go," Ashling replied, a worried frown on her face. "I don't have a baby-sitter."

"Don't worry," said Sophie, making a face as she sipped the awful coffee. "I have a girl who baby-sits for me when Cosette is away. She loves children and also speaks English. Let me call her to see if she's free."

Again the rapid French and then she rang off, beaming. "No problem, Nicole will be delighted to do it."

"Great! What would I do without you? You're a gem!" Ashling said, giving her a hug.

"I know," Sophie replied, her eyes twinkling. "I tell myself that every day."

Laughing, they gathered up the kids and set off for home, Ashling happy that she'd found the perfect school for her little daughters and now, it seemed, the perfect baby-sitter also. She would never have managed without Sophie, she thought, meaning it sincerely.

10

On Tuesday morning as Brandon and Max were busy settling into their exciting new project, Taylor and Felicity were hitting the shops. They had met at nine thirty and set off down the Rue du Faubourg Saint-Honoré. As Taylor dragged her into one designer shop after another – salons, Taylor called them, but they were just fancy shops as far as *she* could see – Felicity marvelled at her friend's composure. She swept in as though she was their most important client and as a result they treated her as such. Felicity was very intimidated by all these chic Parisian saleswomen. It was one thing shopping in John Lewis and Selfridge's in London – and she was even intimidated there – but Paris was something else! She envied the other woman's confidence and bravura and wished she had even a fraction of it herself.

It was breathtaking to see the speed at which Taylor could spend. No procrastination for her! She ordered 2000 worth of clothes in the first fifteen minutes they were out and within two hours she had racked up over 12,000 worth of goods. Paris Hilton had nothing on this girl!

Felicity found herself admiring a narrow snakeskin leather belt in Gucci and Taylor insisted that she buy it.

"Go on, Felicity, you've bought nothing at all! You'll make me feel bad if I have all this stuff and you have nothing," she'd insisted.

Embarrassed, Felicity had given in and bought it but had been shocked at the price tag of 350. Seeing this, she'd been tempted to back down and change her mind but she couldn't. What would Taylor think of her if she did?

"What do the men think we'll be doing all day in Paris? It's like taking a child to a candy store and then saying they can't have anything," Taylor said in her New York drawl. "They owe us – big-time."

Felicity was inclined to agree with her and felt better after that.

"I'm exhausted," Taylor declared, unsurprisingly, shortly after eleven thirty. "Let's go and have coffee. The Ritz is just around the corner."

Felicity had wanted to visit the Ritz ever since she'd seen those very sad, last pictures of Princess Diana leaving there on the night she died. It was with a feeling of awe that she entered the elegant hotel. She had been to Claridge's and some other top hotels in London with Maxwell but nothing prepared her for the opulence and grandeur of the Ritz in Paris. She had to stop herself gaping as she walked down the plush carpeted hallway with its glass cases showing the frighteningly expensive merchandise on sale in the boutiques opposite. Taylor was totally unfazed and, spotting a divine jewelled Judith Leiber evening bag, was its proud owner three minutes later. Another 2000!

In the restaurant, Felicity couldn't help but notice the expensive jewels on the other women seated there. There was an air of calm, the staff were very friendly and attentive and thankfully they all spoke English. When the coffee and tiny sandwiches and pastries arrived, Felicity sighed in pure bliss. This was the life! Why was I so concerned about coming to Paris? It's really frightfully civilised. Of course, I didn't know that I would meet such a wonderful friend as Taylor. And an American at that! It just goes to show – one should never prejudge.

Discussing Princess Diana, Felicity was very impressed to hear that Taylor had actually met the princess, two years before her death.

"Yes, she attended a charity luncheon I was at. Beautiful woman," Taylor said nonchalantly. Felicity sighed with envy. "And of course,"

Taylor continued, "the Duchess of York and I are good friends. We meet often at charity events. She's quite a celebrity in the States, you know."

Felicity didn't like to point out that, contrary to popular belief, she was no longer the Duchess of York, just plain Sarah Ferguson, and no longer in favour with the Royal Family and their supporters. She suspected that Taylor would be most displeased if she mentioned this so she kept her mouth shut and kept it to herself.

Before they parted she screwed up the courage to invite Taylor and Brandon to lunch the following Sunday. To her joy, Taylor said they'd come. It was great to have found such a good friend so soon, Felicity thought happily as she made her way home.

That evening, Ashling found her way, as directed, to the gym where Jazz and Sophie were waiting for her.

"Gosh, this is great," she said, as she kissed them both on the cheeks. "I'm only five minutes' walk away from here. How fantastic is that? This is one terrific city."

"You can say that again," Jazz remarked as they went inside. "I had to pinch myself as I was walking across the Seine. It's so beautiful."

Sophie checked them in as guests and they left their bags and jackets in her locker. They changed into workout clothes and Ashling felt very self-conscious in her leggings and long T-shirt when she saw the smart gear of her two friends. Of course, they had fabulous figures and had no need to cover up like she did. The ladies' locker room was state of the art and so was the gym they entered shortly afterwards.

A tall blond Adonis came bounding over to Sophie.

"*Bonsoir*." Sophie kissed him on both cheeks. "I've brought you two new victims," she laughed. "This is Ashling, from Ireland."

"Hi, welcome," he said, in a very pronounced Australian accent.

"And Jazz, from Germany."

"Wow! What a great body," he whistled, looking Jazz up and down in appreciation. "Hi, you're *very* welcome," he said, enthusiastically.

Jazz was dressed in tight black shorts and a fuchsia mini-vest-top which showed off her perfectly hard tanned stomach and long, slim legs.

"You don't look like you need my help," he grinned cheekily, admiration showing in his eyes.

"Believe me, I need it to keep in shape," she grinned back, finding this friendly guy very much to her liking. He looked like a surfer, all blond and tanned and muscular with startlingly blue eyes. Well, working out won't be so difficult with this hunk in sight, she thought.

As Jazz was an experienced gym-goer, he let her choose what machines she wanted to work on. Sophie headed for the treadmill while Hugh took Ashling in hand. He couldn't believe that she'd never visited a gym before. There were sweating bodies, male and female, on almost all of the machines.

"It's the busiest period," he told her, seeing her look of anxiety.

"I'll be coming in the mornings once my little girls start school next week."

"That will be much quieter," he assured her. "Not many men then. Mostly young mothers like yourself."

"Whew, that's a relief!"

He was very patient and gentle with her as he explained the various machines and then set her up on the treadmill next to Jazz.

Ashling felt like a hulk as she walked on the treadmill while all around her others were running on them. Jazz actually had hers inclined as she raced along beside her. She was barely breaking a sweat while Ashling was perspiring like mad and out of breath. It brought home to her just how out of condition she was. She then went on the bike and after only five minutes gave up, almost in a state of collapse. Seeing how fresh her two friends were made her more determined than ever to get in shape. This is it, she told herself. It starts tonight! She went out to the reception desk with Jazz and they both signed up for the year.

They went into the café afterwards and over Perrier water they discussed the reception in the Hôtel de Ville.

"What should I wear?" Ashling wanted to know.

"A classy cocktail dress, I think," Sophie advised.

"I don't really have anything suitable, I'm afraid," Ashling replied, thinking of her wardrobe of hippy-style dresses.

"It will be a very chic affair," Sophie informed them, her eyes glowing with anticipation. "Everyone who is anyone will be there. It should be fabulous."

"Why not treat yourself to something new?" Jazz suggested. "I'll come shopping with you on Saturday, if you like."

"Would you?" Ashling asked her. "I'm useless on my own. I never know what suits me."

"Sure. No problem, I love shopping. It'll be fun."

Ashling recounted this conversation to Kieran when she got home.

"Yes, of course you must buy something nice," he replied. "It looks like we'll be invited to lots of receptions here although Yves says that this one can only be topped by being invited to the Élysée Palace."

He was in terrific form, loving his job and pleased that Ashling and the girls were settling in. All he needed now was to get in a good round of golf but he couldn't see that happening any time soon.

11

The following Saturday morning, Ashling went to meet Jazz for their shopping expedition. Kieran and the girls accompanied her as he was taking them on to the Tuileries Gardens for the morning. They were very excited about visiting the carnival there.

"They're so cute," Jazz remarked as they left.

Again, Ashling heard that sad note in her voice.

"We're going to Galeries Lafayette," Jazz told her as they made their way to the metro. They had to look at the map to check their route as neither of them was as yet familiar with the underground system.

"Oh God, I'm aching all over after the gym this week," Ashling complained as they got on the train.

"You know what they say – no pain, no gain," Jazz laughed, showing her no compassion at all.

"You're cruel," Ashling cried, mock-punching her.

Hurtling along under the Seine and streets of Paris, Ashling thought how badly an underground system was needed in Dublin. It was far easier to get around this huge metropolis of Paris than her home town of Dublin. Thinking of how the Celtic Tiger had deserted Ireland made her sad but happy to be where she was right now. Things were still dire back there, by all accounts, and set to get worse.

They entered the massive department store with its huge domed ceiling and circular foyer and Ashling felt relieved. She had been afraid that Jazz would want to take her to one of the snooty designer boutiques and she didn't have the confidence for that. This store was beautiful and not at all intimidating.

"When I was a student and didn't have a cent to my name, I used to come in here and look up at that dome and all the levels of beautiful clothes going round and swear that one day I would come back and shop here," Jazz said, smiling wistfully. "And now, here I am."

"I didn't know you lived here before." Ashling was surprised.

"Oh yes. It's a long story. I'll tell you about it sometime. But now let's find a dress for you."

Ashling stood by as Jazz whizzed around pulling dresses off rails. With her arms full, she ushered her friend into the fitting room where Ashling proceeded to try on the clothes Jazz had picked out. She came out wearing them, one by one, and at each Jazz shook her head.

"No, not right," she remarked tersely after each one. They were either too tight – too loose – too long – too short – too frumpy.

Back in the shop, Ashling was beginning to despair until Jazz pounced on a gorgeous green dress. Ashling looked at the label. Issa, she read. "That's the brand so many well-dressed celebrities are wearing nowadays," she said excitedly.

Jazz hustled her into the fitting room again and when she came out wearing the dress, she got the thumbs-up from a beaming Jazz.

"Perfect!"

"Do you not think –"

"It's perfect! The colour is exactly the green of your eyes and it really suits you. It makes you look slim too."

"Maybe not slim exactly," Ashling grimaced, "but slimmer, that's for sure."

Looking at herself in the mirror she could see that Jazz was right. The dress was very flattering.

"I don't know how you knew to pick this one out," she said as she twirled around. "I'm useless. I'd never have known what to choose."

Next Jazz ushered her down to the shoe department where she insisted that Ashling try on a pair of green-and-navy Sergio Rossi shoes. They were much higher than she normally wore but amazingly they were very comfortable.

It was incredible how much slimmer her legs looked in these heels. Jazz certainly knew what she was doing where fashion was concerned.

"I'm so grateful," Ashling told her. "I would never have chosen these or the dress, by myself. Now I'll feel much more confident on Thursday night."

Jazz looked at her and thought that if only she could lose about ten kilos, she'd look sensational. With her red-gold hair and green eyes, she was so pretty, but the weight was holding her back. She debated whether she should say this to Ashling or not. Better not, she decided. She didn't know her quite well enough yet.

Jazz then dragged her along to look at a Herve Leger dress that she was thinking of buying. She tried it on and, when she came out of the fitting room, Ashling thought that she had never seen anyone look more beautiful.

The dress was a silver metallic sheath and it followed the curves of Jazz's wonderful body like a second skin. It had a V neckline front and back and came to about five inches above the knee.

"Wow!" Ashling let out a low whistle. "That is sensational on you. It fits you like a glove!"

"That's the point of these bandage dresses," Jazz informed her, as she turned this way and that in front of the mirror. "They're really very flattering."

"You don't need much flattering," Ashling said enviously.

After Jazz had paid for her dress, Ashling invited her for a glass of wine to say thanks for her help.

They went to a nearby café where Ashling ordered a glass of chardonnay and a coffee.

"Aren't you having a glass of wine?" Jazz asked.

"No. I've started a diet. I seriously want to lose about a stone and a half."

"How much is that in kilos?" Jazz wanted to know.

"About ten kilos."

Jazz smiled. "If you can lose that ten kilos by Christmas, we'll be back in here buying you a Herve Leger dress too!"

"I wish," Ashling said, not very convinced.

"Trust me. Let that be your motivation. I'll drink to that," Jazz toasted her, relieved that she hadn't been the one to suggest that Ashling lose weight.

Jazz went to the gym after the shopping trip and was flattered by the obviously smitten Hugh's attentions. He practically ignored the other clients' efforts while he concentrated on her workout. He asked her out for a drink afterwards but she laughingly declined. She had enough man trouble at the moment, thank you very much. She thought about Yves constantly and all the old feelings she'd had for him had resurfaced. She was trying to figure out what to do about him – not to mention Hans who had been calling her constantly. It was obvious that he missed her. Rediscovering her feelings for Yves made her realise that there could never be a future for Hans and herself now. She knew that she would have to go back to Frankfurt soon and tell him face to face that it was over. Not for her the Daniel-Day-Lewis-style fax to Isabelle Adjani, finishing their long relationship! She was not looking forward to that meeting with Hans.

Hugh came up to her as she was leaving.

"Hey, Jazz. A group of my friends and I are taking a boat down the Seine tomorrow for a picnic – Aussie-style. Why don't you join us?" he asked, his blue eyes twinkling. Seeing her hesitation, he added, "It'll be good *craic*."

"Where did you hear that word?" she asked him, surprised.

"My dad is Irish – and I have a lot of Irish friends here in Paris." Seeing that he'd caught her interest, he cajoled her. "They'll be there tomorrow. How about it?"

She looked at his boyish, handsome face. She could well imagine that he would be great fun. He had such zest for life.

"Why not?" she smiled at him.

"Bloody great!" he whooped. "I promise you, you'll have a great day."

They arranged to meet up the following morning and he bounded off, a huge grin on his face. She couldn't help but smile.

That night, Ashling rang her.

"I just want to say thanks for today. I really enjoyed it and I love my new gear. Kieran is very impressed."

"That's great. I can't wait to see you in it, all dressed up."

"We were wondering if you'd like to come to lunch tomorrow."

"Sorry, I can't. I've arranged to go with Hugh from the gym on a picnic down the Seine."

"Wow, that's great," Ashling laughed. "My God, Kieran is right. You *are* a femme fatale."

"No, no, it's not like that," Jazz protested. "He's much too young for me but it sounds like it will be fun. His dad's Irish, you know, and so are a lot of his friends here. In fact," she giggled, "what persuaded me to go was when he said it would be great *craic*."

"I'm sure it will be. Have a great day. I'll be dying to hear all about it."

12

Max was not at all pleased when Felicity told him that she had invited Taylor and Brandon for lunch on Sunday. He could sense how manipulative Taylor was and feared that his wife would be completely dominated by her. However, when he saw how occupied and happy Felicity was, preparing for the lunch, he thought that it was better than having her moping around the house all day, waiting for him to come home and entertain her. To his delight she had even encouraged him to go and play golf on the Saturday. Much as he despised Taylor, he was grateful for small mercies!

When Taylor told Brandon on Saturday that she wanted to pull out of Felicity's lunch the following day, he adamantly refused to do so.

"The poor woman has done all her shopping by now and maybe even cooked some things. Absolutely not! We're going and that's that," he told her, brooking no argument.

So Taylor reluctantly set out for Felicity's lunch on Sunday, dreading the boring ordeal ahead. She'd taken two Vicodin that morning and also taken a few slugs of vodka, from the bottle she kept stashed in her bedroom, before setting out.

Felicity had produced a meal fit for a king. Cooking was her big passion and she was incredibly good at it. Even so, she was in a tizzy as she put the finishing touches to the starters in the kitchen – but she was very pleased with the result.

"Lovely place you have here," Brandon remarked, as they sat down at the table, "and very central."

"Yes, we're very happy with it," Max replied.

"A bit on the small side," Taylor remarked archly. "Ours is a lot bigger. But then you have no staff, do you?"

"Goodness, no," Felicity laughed nervously. "What would I need staff for?"

"Well, I for one couldn't live without a housekeeper and cook," Taylor replied snootily, then shut up when she saw the glowering looks Brandon was throwing her way.

Felicity dished up the lunch and even Taylor couldn't resist eating all the delectable food on her plate.

"What a wonderful meal!" Brandon lauded Felicity when they'd finished, as Max beamed with pride at his wife.

"You absolutely must share your secret with me," said Taylor. "Even though I have a cook, she doesn't turn out food this good. How on earth did you find such a good caterer, in such a short space of time?" She leaned in to Felicity conspiratorially. "I insist you give me his name," she demanded.

"Well, actually, I cooked everything myself." Felicity blushed.

"Good heavens!" Taylor cried, dropping her spoon with a clang. "You can't be serious."

"She's deadly serious," Max said, beaming broadly. "The old girl is quite a dab hand in the kitchen." He reached across and patted Felicity's hand.

"You can say that again," Brandon smiled at her, patting his stomach. "Where on earth did you learn to cook like that?"

"Well, when I was little, I was always hanging around the cooks in my grandmother's kitchen –"

"Cooks, you say? Just how many did she have?" Taylor was agog.

"My wife is very modest," Max commented. "Her grandmother was actually a friend of the late Queen Mother. Felicity is the daughter of Lord and Lady Delmere."

For once Taylor was speechless and Brandon took great delight in the shock on his wife's face. As he guessed she would, when she came to, she did a total about-face and smiled at Felicity, who was now elevated to 'best-friend-forever' status – or BFF as Mia called it.

"How wonderful, my dear," she purred. "To think that my best friend is the daughter of a lord and lady!" Reaching out for Felicity's hand, she grabbed it. "My friends back home will be green with envy. I will insist you meet them all when they come to visit." She smiled around the table, suddenly a much perkier, happier person than she'd been earlier.

"Oh, it's not that important any more," Felicity blushed. "I'm afraid the estate is not what it used to be . . . death duties and all that," she finished off lamely.

"Nonsense! An estate – how wonderful!" Taylor gushed. "You must take me down to visit. I insist."

Embarrassed, Felicity got up to clear the table and Brandon almost laughed out loud at Taylor's transparency. Catching Max's eye he could see that he wasn't fooled either. They smiled at each other.

"True blue blood," Taylor was saying to no-one in particular, while the subject of her musing was stacking dishes in the dishwasher.

After that, the afternoon went with a swing and the two men enjoyed each other's company while Taylor pumped Felicity for information about the English aristocracy. She even got a bit tiddley and left insisting that Felicity join her for a day's shopping again the following week.

When she arrived home, flushed with wine and her discovery, she rang everyone she knew to tell them about her new aristocratic friend. Brandon couldn't bear to listen and went into his study to escape. Eventually, much to his relief, she went up to her bedroom. She took a Valium and was quickly asleep, dreaming of stately homes in England.

Meanwhile Jazz was, in fact, having great *craic*. It was a wonderful day. There were about twenty people in the group – Australians,

Irish, and a couple of Americans and they were all very friendly and made her feel welcome. They sailed down the Seine for about an hour and then pulled in at a bar owned by a friend of Hugh's where they had a wonderful barbeque with lots of wine and beer. They finished up with a sing-song which, Jazz remembered, was how the Irish finish every party.

All day Hugh had been very attentive to her, refilling her glass frequently and making sure she was okay. She could see that many of the other girls fancied him and were trying to attract his attention but he didn't seem too interested. She knew they were wondering what the story was between them. She was really glad that she'd accepted the invitation and many of his friends said that she would have to join them again the following weekend.

As she was saying goodbye to him, he leaned over and kissed her cheek lightly. He was very sweet and she hoped they'd be good friends. They could be, if he accepted that there could be no question of romance.

13

The girls came into Ashling's bedroom at six in the morning, madly excited at the prospect of starting in their new school. Ashling groaned. She realised that she might as well get up. In this hyper state, they'd never let her sleep anyway. She groaned anew as she got out of bed. She was still stiff from the sessions she'd had with Hugh in the gym last week but planned to hit it at least three times a week, now that she would be free in the mornings.

She dropped them off at school, happy that they were in good hands, and headed straight for the gym where Hugh greeted her enthusiastically.

"G'day," he flashed his neon smile at her. "You'll enjoy your workout today. It's mostly young mums like yourself here."

Looking around she saw that this was true and a few of the other women even waved at her.

God, he was gorgeous, she thought, as she stepped on the treadmill. He came over shortly afterwards to offer his encouragement and help while all the time pumping her about Jazz. Seeing his eyes light up as he spoke of her, Ashling realised that he was really keen on her friend.

"We had a wonderful day yesterday," he told her in his very attractive Australian drawl. "All the guys were crazy about her."

"You included, I guess," Ashling laughed.

"Definitely! She's amazing," he said, awe in his voice. "She's not just beautiful and sexy but also highly intelligent and very genuine." He made a face. "It's not easy to find all that combination in one girl, trust me." Looking wistful, he added, "I only wish she felt the same about me."

"Give her time. I think she's just coming out of a relationship," Ashling advised him gently.

"Yeah, well, maybe you'll put in a good word for me," he said, his very blue eyes looking hopeful.

"Of course," she said, patting his arm. He really was a darling.

"How was the hot date?" Kieran teased Jazz at work, his eyes twinkling.

"It wasn't a date," she blushed, playfully punching him on the arm. "We're just friends."

Yves, who was standing nearby, overheard their conversation.

"What is this you say?" he asked Kieran.

"Our Jazz has an admirer. A very gorgeous handsome Australian hunk, from what I hear," he grinned.

Jazz started to protest once more but could feel the colour rising even more in her cheeks. Yves looked directly at her, his intense brown eyes piercing hers. Then pressing his lips tight together, he turned and walked away, but not before Jazz had seen the disappointment in his eyes. She sighed. Life was so difficult.

Brandon didn't feel like going home on Monday night. He couldn't bear to face Taylor. He had no doubt he would once again have to listen to her calling those she hadn't already, regaling them with the news that her new best friend was the daughter of Lord and Lady Delmere. She'd had no time for Felicity before she'd discovered who she was but now she was the bee's knees. This just emphasised how unbearably shallow Taylor was. She disgusted him. He could hardly bear to be in the same room as her at the moment. Now reluctant to go home, he asked his colleagues if they would fancy going for a drink after work.

"Sorry, but I want to get home to hear how the girls got on today. It was their first day at school," Kieran excused himself apologetically.

"Sorry, mate," Max said. "I'm afraid Felicity will have dinner waiting for me."

Seeing his look of despondency, Jazz succumbed. "I'll join you, but only for an hour as I have to hit the gym later."

When Yves heard that she was going, he changed his mind and said he'd love to join them too, ignoring the fact that Sophie would be expecting him home.

They retired to a bar around the corner from the office and as they entered Jazz was aware of the envious looks she was getting from the other women there. Not surprising, given her two gorgeous escorts!

As Yves was ordering the drinks Jazz turned to Brandon.

"You okay?" she asked, noticing the strain around his eyes.

"So, so," he replied. "Personal problems."

He didn't elaborate and Jazz didn't press him although she could well imagine that, with a wife like Taylor, his life couldn't be easy.

Yves returned with their drinks.

Looking across the table at her two handsome colleagues, Jazz reflected that though they were both hugely attractive, it was Yves who set her pulses racing and she felt sure that he must have that effect on every female he came in contact with. His young blonde secretary, Chantal, was there with a group of other young girls and came over to say hello. Jazz was sure, from their body language, that they'd been intimate.

When Chantal left and Brandon went for a second drink, Yves leaned across to Jazz, his eyes boring into hers.

"I have to see you alone," he murmured, his voice low.

This was what she had been waiting for since she'd met him again. Her heart started hammering in her chest. She couldn't drag her eyes away from his.

"Why?" she whispered huskily, her heart soaring with happiness. She still meant something to him after all.

"Because you're the most exciting woman I've ever met." His eyes smouldered as he spoke.

Her heart plummeted. She had thought he was going to mention their previous liaison. She was bitterly disappointed when he said nothing. "I c-can't," she stammered. "It – it wouldn't be right."

He was so close to her that she could hardly breathe. She closed her eyes and then felt his lips brush hers. Trembling, she longed to give in to him but pulled away.

"Please, *chérie*," he whispered.

Before she could reply Brandon had returned. She knew from his manner that he was unaware of what had taken place.

She could barely concentrate on the conversation after that and made her escape as soon as she could. She was beginning to worry that Yves didn't remember her after all. Was that possible? She knew she'd have to find out.

Brandon arrived home to find Taylor curled up on the sofa, her hand wrapped around a martini and on the phone yet again. He quickly surmised, from the saccharine tone of her voice, that she was speaking to Felicity. It irritated him beyond all reason.

When she had finished, he couldn't restrain himself.

"You are the most two faced, insincere woman alive," he fumed. "You had no time for Felicity until you heard that she was aristocratic. Now, you're fawning all over her. You make me sick." He turned his back on her and moved to the bar where he poured a large whisky for himself.

She sipped her martini, smiling smugly.

"You should be pleased that I'm mingling with the true aristocracy. This can only help your career," she purred.

"I don't need your help, thank you," he replied, clenching his fist with irritation.

"Touchy, touchy," she mocked him. "I do believe Paris does not agree with you."

He walked out of the room, unwilling to start a slagging match with her. He knew from experience that that was a waste of time. He went into the kitchen to find something to eat. She had nothing to do all day, but still there was no sign of a table set for dinner. Mimi, the cook, had prepared a coq-au-vin which he reheated in the microwave.

As he ate it he wondered how on earth he had thought that Paris would improve his marriage in any way. It was time that he accepted it was past saving.

14

On Tuesday morning Ashling walked the girls to school and then walked along the Boulevard St Germain, enjoying the warm sunny day. She oohed and aahed at the beautiful baby and children's shops along the way. One in particular, Tartine et Chocolat, had the most divine dresses and shoes for the girls. Although they were horribly expensive, she vowed that she would indulge in them at some future date.

She continued on down to the famous café, Les Deux Magots, and almost had to pinch herself to make sure she was really there. The tables on the terrace were all occupied and the fumes of Gauloise cigarettes assailed her as she passed by. The French were ardent smokers and the smoking ban simply meant that the outside terraces were all packed whilst the insides of cafés and bars were practically empty. It was the inside of this one she wanted to see and, as she'd suspected, it was practically empty. She ordered an espresso from the friendly waiter who was dressed in black tails and white shirt with a long white apron tied around his waist. She tried to avoid looking at the delicious pastries in the glass case as she reverently took in her surroundings. The thought that this was where James Joyce, Ernest Hemingway, Simone de Beauvoir, Sartre and many other famous writers had sat penning their masterpieces, filled her with awe.

As a journalist, she had toyed with the idea of trying her hand at writing a novel and she harboured a secret hope that Paris, and this café in particular, might give her inspiration.

Looking around, she saw that there were still writers at work here. There was an elderly woman in the corner scribbling away in a notebook, biting the end of her pencil from time to time. To her left was a young hippy type, his glasses halfway down his nose, banging away on his laptop. Against another wall was a very handsome man who, with his silver beard and silver hair, reminded her of a younger Kenny Rogers. He also had a laptop in front of him. He wasn't typing but was staring into the distance, as if in another world. Oh God, Ashling thought, I hope he doesn't have writer's block, a phenomenon she'd heard a lot of.

She noticed that there were sockets all around the wall so obviously it was quite okay to work on a computer in here. She'd brought a notebook with her and thought that she might just begin a diary, for starters. If nothing else, it would be a memoir of her wonderful time in this city. She had so much to recount already that the time flew by as she scribbled away, and before she knew it, it was midday. The café started to fill up and she decided that she'd better order lunch. She ordered a salad. The old lady and young hippy had left but the silver-haired man was still there and he was busy tapping away now, thank goodness. He looked up and caught her eye and nodded at her, smiling. She noticed that he had a lovely smile, his teeth a brilliant white against his deep tan. His smile lit up his dark hazel eyes, which made him very attractive. She nodded shyly back and then turned her attention to her salad, which looked divine and tasted divine too.

Leaving the café, she walked slowly along the Seine, soaking in the wonderful sights. How lucky I am, she thought as she made her way to the school where the girls were even more exuberant than they'd been the previous day. After giving them a snack, the three of them walked to the Luxembourg Gardens where the girls made a dash for the playground. Ashling marvelled at all the activities going on. She was particularly amused by all the people sitting at tables in the shade, playing bridge. There must have been fifty of them. "Well, I never!" she exclaimed. "They should do this in Stephen's Green. How wonderful!"

As she waited for Kieran to come home that evening, she was very tempted to open a bottle of wine but was afraid it would wreck her diet if she did. Luckily, she hadn't because Kieran didn't put in an appearance until nine thirty. She was pissed off waiting for him and his dinner was ruined. She'd eaten with the girls at six o'clock, thank goodness.

"What on earth kept you?" she asked him as he came in.

"Sorry, love. There's so much to do. I just couldn't get out any earlier." He bent to kiss her but she turned her head away.

"Your dinner is ruined," she told him coolly. "I hope it's not going to be this late every night, Kieran, because I really couldn't handle it."

"Sorry, sweetheart. I'll try and get out earlier in future."

She plonked the spoilt dinner in front of him and, leaving him on his own, went in to watch television. She was furious with him. She'd hoped that things would change here but he was working just as much as ever. After his dinner he went straight up to bed, saying that he was shattered. Ashling had to really resist the temptation to have a drink. She was furious with him. It wasn't as if she had all her family and friends here in Paris to keep her company. She must remember to check with Jazz to see if she and the others were putting in the hours that Kieran was. Somehow she doubted it. Sometimes ambition could be a bad thing, she thought bitterly.

By Wednesday Jazz was in a state of indecision. She tried her best to avoid Yves but it wasn't easy. She swung wildly between telling herself that she did not want to get involved with him again and fighting the longing that she felt for him. She could think of nothing else. More than anything she needed to know if he remembered her. Jazz tried not to let her thoughts of him interfere with her work although it wasn't easy. She caught Brandon, with whom she shared an office, looking at her speculatively from time to time. He even asked her once or twice if she was okay.

"Fine, just fine," she replied, busying herself with her computer.

He wasn't convinced. Something was bothering her but he didn't want to pry. He hoped she'd tell him in her own good time. They'd become good friends and he found her extremely intelligent and efficient in business. Not surprising that she'd risen so high in the banking world. He wondered why it was that she wasn't married. Surely she must have men chasing after her constantly. She had everything any man could want. She was beautiful and sexy, highly intelligent with a lovely personality. He was beginning to discover that she was not as hard-bitten and ruthless as other banking women he'd known. In fact, he suspected that underneath the professional exterior, she was soft and vulnerable. He really hoped that she'd meet a nice guy in Paris. If you couldn't find love in the city of romance, where could you find it?

Felicity and Taylor went shopping on Wednesday morning and it was a re-run of the previous shopping trip they'd had together, except that this time Taylor was fawning over her like there was no tomorrow. Every shop they visited was regaled with the fact that Felicity was the daughter of Lord Delmere. Felicity found this highly embarrassing but Taylor could not be stopped.

As before, Taylor spent a fortune and Felicity wondered how she could possibly afford it. She figured Brandon must have bottomless pockets because, as far as she could gather, Taylor had not worked since her marriage, which was over twenty years ago. By midday, Felicity was exhausted and relieved when Taylor led the way to the Crillon Hotel for lunch.

"This is my treat," Taylor insisted, grabbing the bill. "After all, I was the one who invited you to come shopping with me."

"It's too kind of you. Please let me share it at least."

"No, no, no! You can return the compliment when you invite me to visit your estate in England," Taylor gushed.

Felicity flushed a bright red and didn't know what to say. She hadn't the nerve to tell Taylor that there was no estate any more. It had all disappeared in death duties and taxes. She really didn't know how she could get out of this.

She was relieved when they said goodbye. She admired Taylor enormously and was delighted to be her friend but honestly, she was exhausting. Felicity by now felt she hated shopping and didn't think that she could survive another shopping trip with her. Still, she guessed that was the price she would have to pay if she wanted to be Taylor's friend.

Ashling took her computer to Les Deux Magots on Wednesday. The silver-haired man was already there and smiled at her as she sat down. He had a devilish grin and somehow he reminded her of a song by Kris Kristofferson that she'd loved years ago, "The Silver-tongued Devil". This would be her nickname for him. She copied what she'd written the day before on to her computer and continued recalling all that had happened since she'd arrived. The time flew by and she lost count of the coffees she consumed. It was the lunchtime crowd coming in that made her realise the time. She ordered a Greek salad today and when she'd finished, packed up her computer and smiled at the Silver-tongued Devil and her waiter Remy, who was delighted with the very generous tips that Ashling was leaving him. He guessed she was a foreigner. The French were measly with their tips!

On Friday, Remy greeted Ashling like an old friend and had her coffee before her before she even asked for it. The Silver-tongued Devil was there and so busy tapping away on his computer that he didn't notice her come in. She guessed he was a writer. If so, then she was glad that it seemed to be going well for him today. She enjoyed writing her diary and was thinking that maybe she should try her hand at writing a novel. She left as the lunchtime crowd came in, waving goodbye to the Silver-tongued Devil as she left.

15

Sophie rang Ashling the week of the Hôtel de Ville party.

"I was thinking that you might like to bring the girls over to play with Pierre on Saturday morning and they can meet Nicole, who'll be baby-sitting them that night."

"That would be lovely."

"Then *we* can head off to the hairdresser and beauty salon in peace," Sophie added.

"Well, I hadn't actually thought about going to a beauty salon. I usually wash my own hair too," Ashling admitted.

"You do?"

Hearing the surprise in Sophie's voice, Ashling quickly said, "Well, maybe I *should* go."

"Absolutely," Sophie replied, in a relieved voice. "This will be a very chic reception," she explained gently, not wanting to intimidate Ashling but anxious for her to look as good as possible. "I've made an appointment with my coiffeuse, Odette. Would you like me to make an appointment for you too and maybe with the nail salon also?"

Looking at her short unmanicured nails, Ashling agreed quickly. In for a penny, in for a pound! Obviously French women pampered themselves as much as Americans, with their weekly manicures and pedicures. Well, when in Paris . . . do as the Parisiennes do, she told herself.

Arriving at Sophie's on the Saturday morning, she met Nicole, who was a lovely young girl of eighteen. The girls took to her instantly and it was with a light heart that Ashling set off with Sophie for the salon. Cosette, Pierre's nanny, would also be with the children so the two ladies had the day to themselves.

Ashling was glad that Sophie was with her as the salon was a very swish place with gorgeous young stylists who sported kooky hairstyles and trendy black-and-white uniforms. Alone, she would have felt intimidated but as Sophie was obviously a cherished client they made a fuss of Ashling too.

Odette, who had dark hair with purple streaks and a band of bright pink in front, took Ashling in hand. She suggested taking all the weight away from her long curly hair and layering it, while still leaving the length. Ashling was relieved that she hadn't suggested a space-age haircut like the one she sported herself and relaxed even more when Odette admired the lovely auburn hues in her hair. No purple or pink streaks then either, thank God! Sipping a camomile tea, she was amazed at the finished result. It was really lovely and much smarter than her old style.

"How lovely, *chérie*," Sophie remarked, smiling. "You look much younger like this."

Ashling had to agree with her.

They then went for a facial and make-up session. Ashling didn't dare admit that she'd never had a facial before. That would have made her out to be a total peasant to these sophisticated women. She loved the feel of her skin afterwards and the make-up artist even managed to cover all her freckles. She was thrilled with the result. She knew she had never looked as good as this before.

Finally, when she went for a manicure the girl suggested that she put on gel nails. Ashling had never been able to grow her nails so, with Sophie's encouragement, she succumbed. An hour later, with beautiful red toenails and long French-polished fingernails Ashling felt chic and groomed for the first time in her life. It surprised her how much she'd enjoyed all the pampering.

"You look wonderful, *chérie*," Sophie smiled at her.

"I feel wonderful," Ashling grinned back at her. "I must do this more often."

"But of course. Every woman deserves to be pampered," Sophie stated with conviction.

When they arrived back at Sophie's, the reaction Ashling got from Nicole and the children made it all worthwhile.

"Mummy, you look beautiful," Ciara cried, rushing up to her and hugging her knees.

"You look very pretty, madame," Nicole said admiringly.

"*Très jolie*," Pierre said shyly.

"*Très jolie, Maman*," Orna repeated, determined to speak the French she was learning from Pierre. She parroted his every word.

"Thank you, my darlings," Ashling said, pleased as punch with this reception.

Jazz was seated at her dressing table, feeling very apprehensive about the evening ahead. Although Yves had acted professionally towards her in the office all week, the chemistry between them was undeniable. Although they had found themselves alone once or twice he had never alluded to their previous relationship. She wondered if he was purposely ignoring it, and if so, why? Hard as she tried she couldn't get him out of her mind. She knew it was crazy but she couldn't help it. He had somehow relit the fire that she'd thought had been quenched all those years ago. She sighed as she put the finishing touches to her make-up, a mixture of dread and excitement filling her heart.

Ashling was dressed and ready when Kieran rushed in, running late as usual.

"Sorry, darling." Pulling off his tie, he stopped dead in his tracks. "Wow! What have you done? You look sensational," he cried, whistling like any building-site worker.

"You like it?" she asked him, twirling around to give him the full view.

"Like it? I love it," he exclaimed, taking her in his arms.

"Careful, don't mess my hair," she cried, pushing him away. "And hurry up or we'll be late. The car will be here for us in ten minutes."

"Spoilsport," he grinned, as he took the stairs two at a time.

Ashling chatted to Nicole as she waited for him.

"What are you studying?" she asked her.

"English and Anthropology. I did a TFFL course during the summer so I'm qualified to teach French to foreigners. If you have any friends who want to learn French, I would be happy to teach them," the young girl replied. "And of course I will teach Orna and Ciara while I baby-sit," she added, smiling. Ashling was delighted to hear this. She gave Nicole last-minute instructions and then it was time to go. She felt relaxed knowing that the girls were happy and in good hands.

They collected Jazz who was looking more stunning than ever in her silver metallic dress, her dark curls tumbling around her shoulders.

"I'll be the envy of every man there tonight," Kieran remarked, "with the two best-looking women in the room on my arms."

"Don't bet on it," Ashling said with a laugh. "We're in Paris now. You'll be inundated with beautiful, chic women."

"Well, I wouldn't swap you for all of them," he said, giving her a playful squeeze.

Jazz smiled at them, wishing she could have a relationship like theirs.

Felicity had been in a nervous state all day. She hadn't slept a wink last night, so worried was she about the reception. She'd expressed her fears to Maxwell that morning but he just brushed them aside.

"Don't worry about it. You'll be fine," he said, kissing her goodbye as he left for work.

Honestly! Men are useless, she'd sighed as she stood surveying her wardrobe for the fifth time. She was in a flurry of indecision about what to wear. Taylor had been no help either. Felicity had thought that she'd show some interest – but when she'd rung her to ask her advice, she'd cut her off with a curt, "Darling, surely you can decide that for yourself. Sorry, have to go, just rushing out to the beauty parlour." Felicity had felt like crying. She felt so alone. Eventually after much dithering, she opted for a black suit and her pearls. Black was always safe.

Now as she looked around the glittering crowd in the Hôtel de Ville, Felicity realised that she'd got it wrong yet again. She felt dowdy and plain beside all these chic, elegant women. Even Ashling was looking glamorous in an emerald green dress. And as for Jazz – well, she always looked fantastic but was even more fantastic tonight. Felicity sighed enviously, looking around for Taylor who appeared not to have arrived yet.

Jazz and the men were whisked away by Yves to meet some other bankers and Sophie was off somewhere meeting with old friends.

"You look wonderful," Felicity said shyly, as she greeted Ashling. "What have you done to your hair? It's lovely."

"Do you really think so?" Ashling blushed and patted her hair, surprised and pleased with the compliment. Maybe she's not so bad when she's away from that dreadful Taylor, Ashling thought, feeling sorry for Felicity who was obviously nervous and uncomfortable.

"How are you settling in?" she asked her. "Have you been out to see the sights yet?"

"Oh, no," Felicity replied. "The only sights I've seen are the boutiques on the Rue du Faubourg Saint-Honoré. I went shopping there twice with Taylor. What an experience!" She laughed nervously and Ashling joined in.

"Aren't they dreadfully pricey?"

"Unimaginable!" Felicity exclaimed. "I needn't tell you, I didn't buy very much but Taylor almost cleaned them out!"

She's quite pretty when she smiles, Ashling thought. She also realised that Felicity's very upper-class English accent was genuine and not put-on, as she'd suspected when she'd first met her.

"Unfortunately, I haven't a word of French so I wouldn't have the confidence to go out and about on my own," Felicity admitted, as she accepted a glass of champagne from a passing waiter.

"Yes, I imagine that would be a huge drawback," Ashling sympathised, as she also took a glass from the handsome young man.

"To tell you the truth, I'm pretty homesick for England. I don't know how I'll survive the next year here." She couldn't stop the wobble in her voice and was terrified she might start to cry.

Ashling heard it and her soft heart melted as she wondered how she'd cope if she was in Felicity's situation.

"Have you considered learning French?" she asked.

"Goodness no! I did study it at boarding-school but was hopeless at it. I'm sure I'd be useless at it now too."

"Nonsense! You're older now and besides you now have the benefit of living in France. You should give it another go. You'll never know till you try. Look, my baby-sitter teaches French and she's a lovely sweet girl. Why don't I give her your phone number? You can always pack it in if it doesn't work."

"Does she speak English?" Felicity asked nervously.

"Perfectly. Trust me, you'll get on fine and even a smattering of French will help you enormously here." She smiled confidently at the other woman.

"I'm very grateful," said Felicity, as she wrote her number for Ashling.

Ashling felt very sorry for her. She had absolutely no self-confidence whatsoever. Without thinking, she continued, "Look, I'm planning on taking the open-top tourist bus around the city next Tuesday while the girls are at school. Why don't you come with me?"

Felicity's eyes lit up. "Oh, that would be lovely. Are you sure you wouldn't mind?"

"Of course not, it'll be nice to have company," Ashling assured her. "I'll give you a call to arrange a time to meet."

At that moment Taylor arrived beside them. She was a vision in purple silk, diamonds sparkling on her ears, neck, wrist and at least six fingers. She dazzled.

"What are you planning?" she queried, air-kissing Felicity and giving Ashling a brief nod.

"Ashling has kindly invited me to join her on one of those open-topped buses next Tuesday, to see all the famous Paris sights," Felicity told her excitedly.

"Oh my God," Taylor drawled, "how dreadfully touristy and naff!"

Felicity's face fell. Of course, Taylor was right. It was a very naff thing to do.

"I was going to ask you to come shopping with me next Tuesday," Taylor informed her as she hailed a waiter imperiously.

"S-s-sorry, Taylor, but I've pr-pr-promised Ashling," Felicity stammered. "Maybe some other day?"

Ashling saw the patronising look Taylor gave Felicity and felt like slapping her face. Supercilious bitch, she thought.

In fact, Taylor had had no intention of going shopping again with Felicity. She had found her a drag the previous week when they'd gone shopping together. Felicity hadn't bought a single thing. I ask you — a woman who doesn't like shopping! Taylor hadn't thought the species existed. And although Felicity was an aristocrat she was incredibly boring. However, she could overlook that because of who Felicity was. Lord Delmere's daughter!

"Oh my goodness, there's the American ambassador and his wife!" Taylor cried out. "I must go and say hello." She strutted off, practically knocking people to the floor in her haste.

Felicity looked after her dolefully. "Oh, dear, I think I've upset her."

"She'll get over it," Ashling snorted. God, what an obnoxious woman the American was!

Jazz was completely unaware of the interest she was arousing in the men she met. They were gallant and charming but none of them held a candle to Yves.

She was aware of his presence every moment and, when they were separated occasionally, she could catch him glancing at her from across the room. It was as if an electric current connected them. His touch on her back or arm set her pulse racing and her desire for him overwhelmed her. She had not felt this alive since the last time she'd been with him, sixteen years before. She knew now with a certainty that she had no future with Hans. He had never aroused these feelings in her. She was nervously apprehensive yet wildly excited at the same time. She knew that it could come to nothing. After all, he was happily married to Sophie. Of course, she thought ruefully, he had been happily married to someone else the first time she'd met him and it hadn't stopped him then!

She rejoined Ashling and Felicity who were deep in conversation with a very handsome couple. Ashling introduced them as the Irish ambassador and his wife. As they continued speaking Jazz watched Yves surreptitiously as he spoke to Sophie. They appeared to be easy with each other but she couldn't discern any particular chemistry between them. Even as he spoke to his wife, his eyes were searching for *her*.

"Do you agree with me?" the Irish Ambassador was asking them, as Jazz realised that she hadn't heard a word he had said.

"Absolutely," Ashling replied, looking askance at her.

"Oh, yes, definitely," Jazz said lamely, blushing with embarrassment.

"Are you okay?" Ashling asked her, after the couple had moved away.

"Sorry. My mind was somewhere else," Jazz apologised sheepishly.

"Look if you want to talk anytime, my ears are available," Ashling told her as a murmur went around the room.

They looked towards the door where there seemed to be something happening.

"Oh, my God! It's the President and his wife," Jazz, who because of her height could see above the crowd, exclaimed excitedly.

Ashling and Felicity strained to see them but they could only get a glimpse of the head of the First Lady, who was very tall, having once been a supermodel.

A short time later Yves came towards them, his eyes glowing.

"Come along, ladies," he said, smiling. "The President wishes to meet all of you."

Excitedly, they followed him across the room to where the rest of their group were waiting.

"Can you believe it?" Ashling whispered to Kieran. "We're going to meet the President of France."

"I'm more interested in seeing his wife," Kieran said, grinning.

"You would!" said Jazz. "I believe she's had quite an interesting past."

"And present, from what I hear and read," Ashling grinned. "There's supposedly a lover on the scene," she added wickedly.

"*He's* no slouch either," Kieran informed them. "The rumour is that he has a mistress tucked away too. Lucky man," he teased, as Ashling punched him jocosely.

"You can't believe everything you read in the tabloids," Sophie said. "And so what if he has? What's so wrong with that?" She shrugged her shoulders in the Gallic manner. "In France it's perfectly acceptable to have a lover. Both for men and women," she added nonchalantly.

The others looked at her, quite shocked. Jazz couldn't believe her ears. Did this mean that it would be okay with Sophie if she were to take up again with Yves? She honestly didn't believe that. But maybe the French truly *were* different.

Felicity couldn't believe her ears. She was relieved to have caught up with Maxwell again. She hated how he left her alone at these functions but she supposed it was his job to circulate. Thank God for Ashling, she thought, annoyed with Taylor who was now pointedly ignoring her.

On the way home in the car Jazz and Ashling discussed the evening.

"What a great night," Ashling enthused. "I can hardly believe it. Wait till I tell my sister that I met the President of France and his wife!"

"I was surprised at how short he was," Jazz remarked. "His wife towered over him."

"I was surprised she was so plain," Kieran commented.

Both girls agreed with him absolutely.

"I thought he'd never let your hand go," Ashling grinned at Jazz. "He was certainly taken with you."

Jazz laughed. "It was embarrassing. I practically had to yank it away from him."

"Our femme fatale," Kieran commented. "I thought the First Lady was going to clock you one."

"I thought Taylor was going to clock *you* one," Ashling laughed. "The look on her face when the President spent so long talking to you was nothing short of murderous."

"That's because he barely glanced at *her*," said Kieran, who disliked Taylor as much as the women did.

They had arrived at Jazz's apartment. She invited them up for a nightcap.

"No thanks, I'm bushed and I've got to work in the morning," Kieran said.

Jazz was relieved. She wanted to be alone to sort out her thoughts and feelings. And if she was honest, she wanted to be alone to relive the night and the precious moments she'd spent in Yves's company.

Max was pleased to see that Felicity and Ashling had hit it off and happy when she told him that they would be doing the tour of Paris together the following week. He disliked Taylor more and more each time he met her. He couldn't understand what Felicity saw in her. He hoped that her friendship with Ashling would draw her away from that awful woman.

16

Taylor peered in the mirror the following morning and noticed with horror that she had a frown-line on her forehead and a few tiny lines had reappeared around her eyes. Oh my God, I absolutely must have some botox injections immediately, she thought in a panic. She was a favoured client of the best plastic surgeon in New York and she wouldn't let any French quack within a mile of her face. There was nothing for it. She would absolutely have to return to New York immediately.

Brandon was loath to agree to it but she eventually wore him down. She left on Monday morning, looking forward to the break.

Felicity was in good form as she went to meet Ashling on Tuesday morning. She had been a bit worried that she'd upset Taylor but thank goodness everything was okay. Taylor had called her on Sunday to say that she was heading to New York for a few days and had been very friendly indeed. Maxwell still thought that she was obnoxious but Felicity was sure that he had got it wrong. Now she was looking forward to her day with Ashling, whom Maxwell thought was a lovely warm, genuine lady.

They met up in the Place de l'Opéra and, as it was a glorious day, they went up to the front seat of the open-topped bus. From there they had a wonderful view of the stunning city. Ashling turned out to be as good a guide as the official one and Felicity found herself falling in love with Paris. Ashling slowly warmed to the other woman and discovered, as she'd suspected, that Felicity had absolutely no self-confidence. As they travelled around Paris, they learnt a lot about each other.

Felicity was amazed when she found herself divulging things that she'd never told another soul. Somehow, Ashling had that effect on people. She was warm and kind and invited confidences and you knew you could trust her. Felicity totally relaxed in her company and was having a wonderful time. They stopped off at the Trocadero and had a coffee before walking down to the Eiffel Tower, which was even more amazing in reality than all the photos they'd seen. Hopping back on another bus they continued the tour, Felicity gasping at the sheer size of the Louvre.

"I'm planning to visit one museum every week, till I've covered them all," Ashling informed her. "I'm starting next week with the Louvre." Smiling at Felicity, she suggested, "Why don't you join me? I'd be delighted if you could."

"Are you sure? I'd love that," Felicity replied, her eyes glowing.

You know, she's actually quite attractive, Ashling thought, looking at the other woman. She saw that Felicity had beautiful skin and perfect teeth. She was the quintessential English rose. If only she'd do something with that mousy hair and maybe wear a little make-up, she'd be quite lovely, she decided. And her wardrobe could certainly do with a big shake-up. Mostly, of course, it was Felicity's diffident way and lack of confidence that detracted from her. What a shame, Ashling thought, and she wondered why it was that she had so little self-esteem. She was delighted to hear that Nicole had been in touch with her and that Felicity was starting French lessons the next day.

"She sounded lovely on the phone and will even come to my home," Felicity told Ashling. "I really hope I'm not too stupid to learn."

"Don't be daft! I'm sure you'll do fine."

When they arrived at Notre Dame they got off and, after exploring the cathedral, they went for lunch in a small bistro overlooking the Seine. It was perfect. When Ashling heard about Felicity's love of cooking she had an idea.

"Have you considered doing a cookery course while you're here?" she asked.

"Oh no, I couldn't. I'd have to conquer the French language first."

"There are lots of courses in English. They're in the info booklet Sophie gave us. You should really consider it," Ashling suggested, as she speared another piece of her delicious chicken salad.

"You think so? I'd really love that."

"You could maybe be the next Julia Child."

"Don't be silly." Felicity blushed at the very idea.

"I'm going to the Cordon Bleu school this week to enquire about a wine course. I'll make enquires about English-speaking cookery courses for you, if you like," Ashling offered.

"Would you? I'd really appreciate that." Felicity was almost pathetically grateful.

After finishing their coffee, they took the bus for the last leg of the tour. Ashling hopped off at the Quai d'Orsay to pick up the two girls from school while Felicity went on to the Opéra which was close to her home.

"I haven't had such a good time in years," she told Ashling as they said goodbye, blushing shyly as she did so.

"It's only the start," Ashling replied, giving her new friend a big hug.

On Thursday, Ashling was in Les Deux Magots again but the Silver-tongued Devil wasn't there. The old lady she'd seen on her first day was there again, still biting the end of her pencil in between her scribbling. There was also another old man on a computer in the corner. Ashling wondered what they were all writing. It was so exciting to be a part of it.

Before she collected the girls, she visited the Cordon Bleu school where she enrolled in the wine course. She loved wine but knew nothing about it, so where better to change that than in France? She was very excited about it and looking forward to the course. It would be strange to be a student again.

Max would never understand women. He'd really expected that Felicity would give him a hard time but here she was, settling in far better than he could have hoped. She'd had her first French lesson and, amazingly, she'd taken to it with gusto. She played the language tapes Nicole had recommended continuously and he could hear her repeating the phrases aloud as she prepared dinner in the kitchen. She had even begun talking about doing a cookery course and, when Kieran rang to invite him to play golf on the Saturday, she told him to go ahead. Wonders would never cease!

He was beginning to see that being away from her insufferable mother was probably the best thing that could have happened to Felicity. Her mother was a control freak who bullied her and constantly undermined her confidence. It was no wonder that she was such a nervous wreck.

Her ancestors had been members of the aristocracy and had owned a large estate in Wiltshire, but her grandfather's gambling as well as the taxes, death duties and the escalating cost of maintenance, had brought her father's generation to the brink of poverty. Still, there was no denying that Felicity had blue blood running in her veins. He had been rather in awe of her family when he first met them. It surprised everyone, not least him, when the shy, diffident Felicity stood up to her mother and despite much opposition, insisted on marrying him – a bright, brash East-Londoner, with less than perfect manners but oozing with ambition. That she had done this made Max realise just how deeply she loved him.

They made a good couple. Her genteel manner had rubbed off on him and her connections had been a great help on his climb up the corporate banking ladder. She, meanwhile, was happy to be living the good life with none of the money worries that had blighted her parents' lives.

She was happy to be a stay-at-home wife, looked after comfortably by her husband. She'd never worked outside the home and had no interests other than cooking and gardening. She was like a throwback to the forties or fifties. Modern womanhood had bypassed her. He'd spent their entire married life taking care of her and as a result she'd become totally dependent on him. Many of his friends envied him – at least, those married to demanding, ambitious career women did. But in the last few years, he'd begun to find Felicity's dependence on him a bit wearing and at times he longed for a strong independent woman, like the wives of so many of his colleagues.

Now he found his hopes raised that away from her mother's bullying, his wife might actually become more independent. It was certainly looking good.

After the gym on Friday, Ashling did a little window shopping before heading to Les Deux Magots. The hippy student and the Silver-tongued Devil were both there and the older man waved as she came in, giving her a bright smile. She brought her diary up to date and at lunchtime ordered a shrimp salad. As she was waiting for Remy to bring it, she caught the eye of the Silver-tongued Devil, who, she realised, must have been watching her. He flashed her a dazzling smile which was so infectious that she found herself smiling back. As if in slow motion she watched as he got up and came over to her table, smiling all the while.

"Hi, I'm Corey Danz," he introduced himself. "I've noticed you here for the past few weeks. Could I entice you to join this old gentleman for a glass of wine? As we both appear to be writers, I thought we should get acquainted." He had a very pronounced American accent.

"Well, it's a bit early in the day for me to be drinking," she replied.

"Nonsense! It's a special occasion meeting a fellow writer." He gave her a smile that would have lit up Paris, and proffered his hand.

She couldn't help smiling back. "I'm Ashling," she said shyly, shaking the hand.

"Ah, an Irish colleen," he smiled again. "What a pleasure to meet you."

Remy arrived just then with her salad.

"The *plat du jour* for me, please, Remy," said the American. "And could you bring a bottle of the Fèvre Chablis Grand Cru Vaudésir, please?"

The dish of the day turned out to be a Coquilles St Jacques – delicious scallops – and the chilled wine was the loveliest Ashling had ever tasted.

"This wine is wonderful," she said as she sipped it. "I've just enrolled in a wine course and am very excited about it."

"You look different this week." He cocked his head to the side and scrutinised her intently which made her blush. "I know. It's your hair – you've changed it. I like it. Very attractive!"

Now she really blushed, embarrassed yet pleased with the compliment.

Corey turned out to be a fascinating companion and he seemed to know a lot about wine.

"I'm not really a writer," Ashling confessed. "I'm a journalist. At the moment I am just keeping a diary of my experiences in Paris but I would love to be able to write a novel."

"Have you tried?" he asked.

"No, I'm a little afraid I wouldn't be any good."

"You'll never know if you don't try. If all the writers in the world felt like that, we'd have no books at all. And believe me – we're always afraid that the book we're working on is no good. It's part of the territory." He smiled encouragingly at her.

"What do you write?" she asked him.

"Thrillers, mostly, but I'm always hoping that I'll write *the* great literary novel one day."

She laughed at this, surprised that an established writer should feel insecure.

"You must follow your dream," he told her. "If you don't find inspiration here, you'll never find it."

She learned that he was from Florida and was divorced with two grown-up children. She found herself telling him about her family and the reason she was in Paris. They talked as though they'd known each other for years and it was with a shock that she saw it was time to collect the girls. In a flurry, she said goodbye and almost ran all the way to the school. He was such a fascinating man and she hoped she'd get to talk to him again.

Later that evening she went online to check if there was a writer called Corey Danz. Nothing came up. She wondered if he was just having her on, but she didn't think so.

17

Sophie and Yves had invited Orna and Ciara to visit Disney Paris with them on Saturday and as Kieran had a date to play golf with Max, Ashling arranged to meet up with Jazz. She thought Jazz looked strained and wondered if everything was going okay at work. They went shopping and she was surprised by the amount of stuff Jazz bought.

"Retail therapy. Nothing to beat it!" Jazz smiled but Ashling heard a tremor in her voice.

"Is everything okay?" she asked.

"Let's break for lunch and I'll tell you all about it over a glass of wine."

They found a cute little bistro in Les Halles and they both ordered the turbot which was recommended by the maitre d'. Jazz also ordered a bottle of Sancerre which she lashed into.

"Jazz, can I ask you a question? What time do you finish work every evening?"

"I generally leave at six so that I can go to the gym on the way home. Why?"

"Well, Kieran rarely arrives home before nine and I just wondered if all of you work so late."

"Max usually leaves with me but I know Brandon generally stays on working late. Mind you, I don't blame him when he has that dragon waiting for him at home." Seeing the stricken look on Ashling's face, she quickly added, "I'm not for a minute suggesting that's the reason Kieran stays late." She could have killed herself for putting her foot in her mouth like that. "Kieran and Brandon both have more responsibility than Max or I do, and I know the French Minister is very pleased with Kieran's performance. He's a bit of a workaholic, I suspect. Am I right?"

"Are you ever!" Ashling retorted. "I thought that I'd see more of him here than I did in Dublin but it's no different."

Jazz was surprised by how bitter she sounded. As the waiter refilled her glass, she let out a long sigh. "God, men are the root of all our problems, aren't they?"

"Don't tell me you're having man problems," Ashling exclaimed, surprised that anyone as gorgeous as Jazz could have any problem whatsoever.

"Major *men* problems . . . plural," she sighed. She then told Ashling all about Hans.

"I'm really sorry, Jazz. You never know, maybe it will work out between you."

"That's the problem. I don't want it to work out any more. I realise that I don't love him. He rings me once a week but I need to go to Frankfurt to tell him it's over. I don't want to finish with him on the phone. I don't think that's fair, do you?" She looked to Ashling for confirmation that she was doing the right thing.

"I agree, but the sooner you tell him, the better."

Jazz sipped her wine slowly and, moved by the concern in Ashling's eyes, blurted out, "You see, I love someone else."

"Who?" Ashling was mystified. Could her friend have fallen in love with Hugh already?

"Yves."

Ashling almost fell off her chair. Choking on her wine, she repeated, "Yves?"

"Yeah. Crazy, isn't it?"

The waiter brought their meal but Jazz hardly touched hers. He refilled their glasses and Jazz ordered another bottle.

"Don't you think it's a bit early to get sozzled?" Ashling asked gently, visions of her having to carry a drunken Jazz out of the bistro flooding her mind.

"Not at all! It's five o'clock somewhere, as I've often heard you say."

She then told a shocked Ashling about the romance she'd had with Yves when she was twenty-one. Ashling couldn't believe her ears. Now *she* stopped eating and listened in disbelief.

"So that's why you acted so strangely that first day we met at his house," she exclaimed.

"Yes. You can imagine the shock I got when I saw him again." Jazz looked stricken.

"Oh my God, I can't begin to imagine! Has he said anything to you?"

"He said that he wants to talk to me . . . alone. The thing is, I don't think that he remembers me," she said miserably.

"Surely he does," Ashling reached for her friend's hand. "You can't just forget someone like that – not after you've been nine months together."

"I don't know. I don't know what to do, Ash. I'm so confused."

She had taken to calling her Ash, like Kieran did. Somehow, it sounded right.

"Are you going to meet him? It's a bit difficult, isn't it, what with working with him and of course there's Sophie to think about." Ashling bit the side of her thumb as she thought about this.

"Well, you heard her say that it's perfectly acceptable for French men to take a lover, didn't you?" Jazz asked, hopefully.

"True, but I'm not sure how serious she was – and, in any case, I'm not sure she'd be too happy if it was you."

"I don't know what to do." Jazz poured another glass of wine for herself. Ashling refused any more.

"I suppose it won't hurt to meet him and talk. Maybe then you'll be clearer about your feelings," Ashling advised. Her heart went out to Jazz. What a predicament to be in.

"That's the problem. I'm afraid of what my feelings will be. I just find him irresistible."

"He *is* pretty dishy, I must say. What about Hugh?"

"Oh, Hugh's just a pal. Nothing more," she smiled. "Besides, he's much too young for me but I do enjoy his company a lot and that of his friends." She sighed.

"Well, that was a pretty enlightening lunch," Ashling laughed, trying to lighten the mood, as the waiter brought the bill.

"My treat," Jazz insisted. "After bending your ear like that, it's the least I can do." Her voice was beginning to slur ever so slightly.

"That's what friends are for." Ashling patted her hand. "No doubt, I'll be bending your ear at some future date. I'm sure things will work themselves out, but please go carefully." She tried to sound convincing but deep down she wasn't so sure. What a mess!

"I will. Thanks for listening. There's no one else I could confide in here. I'll let you know what happens."

"Do that," Ashling said as she helped Jazz out of the restaurant and into a taxi.

18

Taylor had had a great five days in New York and had driven the maid, Maria, mad with all her demands. She hadn't realised how much she'd missed the Big Apple. She'd lunched and dined every day with various friends and greatly embellished her life in Paris. They'd been, as she'd hoped, all green with envy when she casually mentioned that she'd met the President of France. She'd regaled them with the fact that her best friend was the daughter of Lord and Lady Delmere of England and gloated when she saw their envious glances. Only her old friend, Marilyn, seemed to be delighted for her good fortune.

"I'm so happy for you, honey," she'd drawled in her south Texan drawl. "How I would love to be in your shoes, living in the city of lovvve." She sighed dramatically. "How great is that!"

"Why don't you come over for a visit? I'd love to have you there," Taylor had said, excitedly.

"I'd sure love to, honey," Marilyn drawled, "but I'm in the middle of a verrrrry hot affair at the moment. Mum's the word, you know how it is," she'd winked.

Taylor had guessed that the guy in question was married.

It was with some reluctance that Taylor had left New York. She was very disgruntled when she arrived back in Paris. She would have liked to have stayed away longer but Brandon had booked a tour of the Champagne region for the weekend and so she'd had no choice.

They travelled down on a luxury coach to Ay and the guide explained all about how champagne was made and what Champagne Houses they would be visiting. Brandon found it fascinating but Taylor was bored and quickly went to sleep. She slept all through the drive through the vineyards and when they arrived in the tiny village of Hautvillers, Brandon had to wake her up.

"Where are we?" she asked, yawning.

"We're at the abbey where the monk Dom Perignon discovered how to make champagne," he explained.

"Will there be champagne to drink here?"

"Don't be ridiculous, Taylor. It's a church."

"I'm going back to sleep," she replied, closing her eyes.

Furious with her, he had no choice but to let her be and he left the coach with the other passengers, mostly Americans, who had witnessed the scene. How embarrassing!

Their next stop was the Champagne House of Moët & Chandon and Taylor accompanied him reluctantly for this one.

While the tour guide was explaining the method of making champagne, she called out in a loud voice, "When the hell are we going to get to drink it?" Brandon was mortified as all the other people on the tour looked at her strangely. The tour guide, who was French, stared her down.

"French people are abominably rude," she exclaimed in a loud voice.

"Not half as rude as you," commented another American in the group. "It's people like you who give Americans a bad name in Europe," he added, his voice angry.

Brandon was so embarrassed that he felt like walking off and leaving her. The guy was right, of course. She was being unacceptably rude. He couldn't understand it. She drank a lot but never normally got drunk yet here she was going hell for leather at it. She drank 'shampoo' – as she called champagne – for breakfast, lunch, dinner and every hour in between.

As he put her to bed that night, she ranted on about bloody France and French people. She then started crying and saying how much she missed New York. He felt pretty bad about that but unfortunately he couldn't change anything. He couldn't transport the New York social scene to Paris. Thank God!

Later, sitting alone on the terrace of a restaurant in Epernay, he wondered where they were heading. He was honest enough to admit that he didn't love his wife any more – well, not the woman she'd become – but yet, he had loved her once. She'd been different then of course.

She'd grown up on the wrong side of the tracks of a small country town in South Dakota. Her family were dirt-poor and Taylor longed to escape from the poverty and hopelessness she saw all around her. She was a wild child and very beautiful and impatient to get away from the small town where everyone knew everyone's business. At sixteen, she'd made her escape and headed for the Big Apple. New York mesmerised her and she loved its fast pace and air of excitement. This was living! She took a variety of jobs from waitressing to bar girl and finally, having worked hard to shake off her country gaucheness, landed a job in Saks 5th Avenue, first as a packer and then as a salesgirl in the perfume department. The women she saw every day filled her with envy. Spoilt, pampered and oh-so-chic, she longed to be like them.

Her opportunity came one Christmas when Brandon came in to buy perfume for his mother. She saw instantly that he was upper-crust and it didn't hurt that he was also extremely handsome. With every ounce of charm that she possessed she set about ensnaring him. He obviously fell for it as three days later he was back to buy perfume – for his grandmother this time, or so he said. By the end of the sale he had asked her out to dinner and six months later she was Mrs Brandon Cartwright Hartford the Third, with the dream wedding that she'd always wanted, minus her family of course.

His parents and family were horrified at his choice of bride but could not dissuade him. Brandon had to admit that for the first couple of years they'd been happy as Taylor settled into the lifestyle she'd only ever dreamed about. Then along came the twins and her lack of interest in them shocked him. That, and the fact that she thereafter refused to have sex with him, started the rot. He tried to ignore the problem as he immersed himself in his work but it didn't go away.

That was when she started her frantic climb up the social ladder of New York, but no matter how hard she tried, she was never accepted by the old-moneyed East Coast matrons. Her only friends – if you could call them that – were the nouveau riche, all desperately trying to climb the ladder with her.

And so it had festered on until it had come to this. Sitting alone in a restaurant in Champagne, seeing other happy couples all around him, made him realise just what he was missing. Life was too short to spend it without love and he'd done it for long enough. He felt desperately sad that somehow he'd failed Taylor but he knew for certain that he did not want to spend the rest of his life with her.

19

On Saturday night Kieran arrived home just as Yves and Sophie dropped the girls off, after their trip to Disney Paris. Ashling tried to usher them out as quickly as possible, not wanting them to see the state Kieran was in. Clearly, he'd had quite a few drinks after his golf game and was much the worse for wear. Normally it never bothered her but tonight it did. Ignoring him, she got the girls ready for bed. They were hyper after their very exciting day and, although they were desperately tired, it took her ages to settle them down. When she got back to the living room, Kieran was snoring away on the sofa. Angrily, she went to bed and left him there. Hours later she heard him coming into bed but she pretended to be sleeping. Jazz was right. Men were the root of all women's problems!

Kieran, realising that he was in the doghouse, suggested that they all go out for breakfast on Sunday morning. Ashling loved how all of Paris thronged the cafés on a Sunday morning, where the smell of freshly brewed coffee and freshly baked baguettes and croissants was like an aphrodisiac. She couldn't resist having just one croissant but without the butter and jam that Kieran and the girls were piling on theirs.

"Mmmm . . . this is the life," she murmured, much to Kieran's delight.

"How about we take a trip on a boat down the Seine?" he suggested, which elicited squeals of delight from the girls. "And then," he whispered, "we'll go into the Tuileries Gardens and you can go on the carousel and the big slide."

Orna and Ciara jumped up and down, clapping their hands at the thought of such treats. Ashling couldn't help smiling at their excitement.

"*Merci, Papa, merci, Papa*!" they chorused, making her laugh out loud.

Diners at other tables smiled at the two pretty golden-haired girls and their handsome parents. Such a happy family, they thought.

As they walked to catch the Bateau Mouche for the boat journey, Kieran stopped at a flower-seller's stall and bought a bunch of freesia for Ashling.

"I'm sorry," he said, sounding like a little boy. "I promise, I'll try to be home earlier from now on."

She couldn't stay angry with him any longer. Reaching up, she kissed him and they walked on happy again, hand in hand, towards the Seine.

At the same time, Max and Felicity were strolling in the gardens of Versailles. As a treat, Max had booked the tickets earlier in the week, knowing how much Felicity wanted to see the château and the musical fountains. She was overcome with emotion as the fountains started up. What a ninny she was to have been afraid to come to Paris, she thought. Penelope was right. Thank goodness they hadn't gone to Dubai or Hong Kong. Best of all, they were travelling back to London the weekend after next, to collect the girls – Penelope was on half-term break and Alexandra was taking time off university. Although she found them very difficult since they'd become teenagers, she missed them dreadfully.

She had to admit, life in Paris was much better than she'd expected it to be. She was actually quite enjoying it! Of course, not having Mummy around constantly berating her and telling her she was useless, was a bonus. She was putting off ringing her mother but she knew she'd have to face it soon. In the meantime, she'd forget all about her and just enjoy herself.

Jazz spent Sunday with Hugh and 'the gang', as they referred to themselves.

She was glad that she'd confided in Ashling the day before. It had lifted a weight off her shoulders although her friend had no solution for her problem. Well, she'd just let things take their course, she decided, accepting another glass of wine from Hugh. Although her mind was constantly on Yves she cheered up as the day wore on. The gang were so ebullient and effervescent that it was hard to be down for long in their company. They went to a steak house in St Denis where Jazz ate possibly the best steak she'd ever had.

"Argentine beef – you can't beat it," Hugh grinned. The owner of the restaurant, a friend of his, was from Argentina.

"Do you have contacts all over this city?" Jazz asked laughingly, as she cut into the deliciously tender rib-eye.

"Pretty much," he grinned, chewing as he spoke.

Later that evening as they strolled home, Jazz said, "I hear that you're planning to go to America. How long do you think you'll stay in Paris?"

"Oh, probably another six months or so. I want to visit Ireland and from there I'll head to the US. That's my final destination."

"What do you plan to do there?" Jazz was curious.

"I hope to open my own gym in California. That's my goal. They say America is the land of opportunity!"

"What about girlfriends and romance?"

"I had my fill of that in Australia," he replied, making a face. "I just haven't met the right girl yet." He flashed his gorgeous smile at her and she pitied all the poor young girls that he'd probably left in his wake. "Although, after meeting you, maybe I have?" He cocked an eyebrow at her hopefully.

Though she wasn't sure how serious he was, she decided to make a statement to make things absolutely clear. "Oh no, Hugh, I'm sorry, but thank you for the compliment. Apart from the fact you're nine years younger than I, my love life has enough complications at the moment. I definitely couldn't handle any more."

"Tell me about this complicated love life of yours. You seem like such a strong woman that I reckon you could cope with anything."

"I wish," she laughed, ruefully. Then, whether it was the wine or the moment or his gentle enquiring face, she found herself telling him all about Yves and her past relationship with him. Then she mentioned Hans and how he wanted to marry her.

"Whew! See what you mean by complicated." He let out a long whistle. "What are you going to do about it?"

"No idea," she replied honestly.

"You'll sort it out," he told her confidently. "If I was ready to settle down, you would be the first woman I'd want to be with," he said gallantly.

"You're very kind," she said, touched by his words, "but honestly, I'm much too old for you. You'll find a nice young girl eventually, when the time is right."

"I'm not being kind. I'm being honest," he replied, reaching over to kiss her cheek.

Somehow, she felt better after that and lying in bed that night she thought how lovely he was and how, in the future, some young girl would be very lucky indeed to find love with him. Talking to him decided her on one thing – she couldn't go on prevaricating like this. She would agree to meet with Yves and take it from there.

20

Brandon was relieved that the dreadful weekend was over as he walked into the office on Monday morning. He noticed that Jazz was much perkier than she had been the previous week.

"Had a good weekend?" he asked.

"Yes, thank you, very good – and you?"

"Don't ask!"

She guessed that meant a no and didn't pursue it. She was waiting nervously for Yves to come into their office, as he did every morning, but instead of Yves it was his secretary, Chantal, who came instead. She really was a very pretty girl, with very long blonde hair, a great body and fantastic legs. She perched on the edge of Brandon's desk, her already short skirt riding up another few inches. Jazz had to hand it to her – she knew how to highlight her assets. She was wearing exquisite, nude-patent Jimmy Choo shoes, the heels of which must have been five inches at least.

"I am sorry," she said in her attractive broken English, "but Yves can not come today because 'e go in the 'ospital . . . 'ow you say . . . appendix . . . *non*?" She threw Brandon a dazzling smile. "Okay now. No problem, but 'e can not come work this week."

"I'm sorry to hear that," Brandon smiled back at her. She really was a beauty!

Jazz's heart plummeted. Typical, Murphy's Law! Just when she'd decided to talk to Yves, he's out sick for a week. She hoped he was okay and that it was, as Chantal said, not serious.

"We'd better ring Sophie and check out that he's all right," she suggested to Brandon, hoping that he'd do it. She would have felt bad talking to Sophie right now when she was planning to meet up with her husband.

"Yes, I'll do that right away," he said to a relieved Jazz. "Thank you, Chantal." He smiled charmingly at the young girl once more.

Chantal made no move to go but sat swinging one perfectly tanned leg backwards and forwards.

"You like coffee?" she asked him.

Catching the amused glint in Jazz's eye, he turned to her and asked, "Jazz, coffee?"

"Yes, please." She grinned back at him.

"Make that two coffees, please, Chantal," he said, as she hopped down from his desk.

"What an operator," Jazz remarked when she'd gone. "You better watch yourself there. She has the hots for you!"

Brandon threw his head back and laughed. "You have to admit that very few men would be able to resist that!"

"And I take it you're not one of them!"

He could see she was enjoying this.

"I didn't say that," he shot back, "but she is bloody gorgeous."

With that, the lady in question arrived back with the coffee. There were three cups on the tray. She was obviously joining them. She sat down beside Brandon and it was obvious that she was making a play for him as she flirted and fluttered her eyelashes and crossed and uncrossed her legs. She must have a diploma in 'How to Attract Men' Jazz thought. Having watched Chantal in action for ten minutes, she decided that it was more than a diploma she had – it was a degree – and a master's one at that! So this was how Frenchwomen did it!

Brandon finally told Chantal he had some work to do and she reluctantly took her leave. Jazz said nothing but sat grinning at him.

"What could I do?" he said, shrugging his shoulders helplessly but it was obvious to Jazz that he'd enjoyed every moment of it.

Ashling was in very good humour. Putting on her beige trousers that morning she was amazed to find that they were loose around the waist. "It's not possible, is it?" she said aloud, barely daring to hope. Taking them off again, she hopped up on the scales. To her delight she had lost seven pounds since she'd started dieting. Holding her breath in hope, she then tried on her favourite 'Not Your Daughter's Jeans'. Exhilarated that they fitted her – it had been over a year since she'd been able to wear them – she was buoyant as she dropped the girls to school and set off to meet Felicity for coffee. She had booked two tickets for a walking tour of the Louvre which was due to start at nine thirty. Felicity was very excited about it. Over coffee she told Ashling all about the visit to Versailles.

"It was wonderful, truly wonderful," she said, her eyes glowing.

"I'm dying to go but I think the girls are too little. It would be too much for them."

"Oh no, they'd love it," she assured Ashling. "The musical fountains are enchanting and the gardens, not to mention the château, are simply stunning. I'm sure they'd love it. There are lots of restaurants so, as long as you pace yourselves, it should be no problem."

"Great, we'll take them so," Ashling replied, smiling at Felicity's obvious excitement. She seemed like a different person to the nervous, uptight woman she'd first met.

"Here, I brought you some brochures from the Cordon Bleu school. I've enrolled in a wine course and I gather the cookery school is first class." She took the brochures out of her bag and handed them to Felicity.

"Thank you so much. I'll check them out later." She smiled her gratitude at Ashling. Really, she was so silly to have thought Irish people were all boors. No one had ever been as nice or as kind to her as Ashling.

They had a marvellous time in the Louvre and were mesmerised by the graceful Venus de Milo and also the sculpture by Canova of Psyche and Cupid. Both were breathtakingly beautiful. They were surprised that the Mona Lisa was so small. They had expected a much larger painting. And yes, they both agreed, her smile was very enigmatic. Ashling was fascinated by the painting of Napoleon's Coronation. Pointing out his sisters to Felicity, she whispered, "That's Pauline Bonaparte there. Canova also did a very famous sculpture of her which is in the Villa Borghese in Rome. She's almost naked and reclining on a chaise longue."

"Oh, I have a copy of that at home," Felicity said excitedly. "My sister brought it back to me from Rome. It's very pretty."

"Yes, she was the great beauty of her day. I'm fascinated by everything to do with the Bonapartes. They were a fascinating family."

"Gosh, you're so well informed," Felicity said, feeling embarrassed at her own lack of knowledge.

"Well, I read a lot and I'm a real Francophile." Ashling smiled. "I'm fascinated with Louis XIV and his court also."

After the tour they went for lunch and Ashling shared the good news of her weight loss.

"Congratulations! But don't lose too much. *I* wish I could *gain* weight," Felicity grimaced. "I think it's because of my nervous energy that I stay slim." She then shyly told Ashling about her life. Ashling felt sorry for her, thinking how differently they'd been raised. Her mother sounded like a right dragon. Poor Felicity! No wonder she was a nervous wreck. Looking on the bright side, she suspected that this year in Paris would be a godsend for her. Look how much she'd changed since they'd first met three weeks ago. She seemed a much calmer, happier woman. After their lunch, they hugged goodbye and, as Felicity made her way home, she marvelled again at how cultured and educated the Irish girl was. It just shows how stupid it is to have pre-conceived ideas of people, she thought, acknowledging that she herself was often most guilty of it.

21

The following morning Ashling went to the gym with a spring in her step.

Hugh greeted her warmly. "Hey, girl, you're sure toning up," he remarked, flashing his lovely smile. "You're looking good."

"Yeah, well, I lost seven pounds since I started here," she said proudly.

"Bully for you. It sure shows," he said, admiration in his voice.

It was true, she *was* more toned. She had even started running on the treadmill – on the flat, it's true – but she was getting there. She didn't collapse in a heap when getting off the cross-trainer any more. It would take time, she knew, but it would be worth it.

After the gym she made her way to Les Deux Magots. Corey was there, sitting staring into space. As she sat down, he came over to her.

"I'm so glad to see you," he said. "When you didn't come in yesterday, I was worried that I might have frightened you away."

"Don't be silly," she laughed, "of course not! I like to visit a different museum or place of interest once a week and yesterday I went to the Louvre with a friend. It was wonderful," she told him.

She saw the relief that flooded his face.

"And," she continued, "thanks to you, I've decided to try writing a novel. I'm going to start today, as soon as I catch up on my diary."

"What kind of novel? What genre?"

"Well, as I'm in France and I love historical novels I thought I'd set it in the time of Louis XIV. I always found him a fascinating character and I've read a lot about him and his lovers. What do you think?" She looked at Corey hopefully.

"Very wise. They say you should write the type of book you like reading and also of course you should write about what you know. Looks like you've got it in one." He smiled encouragingly at her and she felt relieved. "Will you join me later for lunch and let me know how it goes?"

"I'd love to."

"See you in a couple of hours then."

The time flew by and she couldn't believe the time when Corey came to her table. "Well, how's my fledgling novelist? How did it go?" he asked.

"It's amazing. I started on it and the words and ideas just seemed to come. I'm really enjoying it."

"To a future bestseller!" he toasted her. "I have every confidence in you."

He really was very sweet and so encouraging, she thought, as she walked to collect the girls from school. For some reason she hadn't mentioned him to Kieran. She didn't know why. It was nice having a secret friend.

Felicity was more than proud of herself. The day after their visit to the Louvre, she'd taken her courage in her hands – which she admitted was unheard of for her – and braved the cookery school that Ashling had recommended. To her delight, they were starting a cordon bleu course in two weeks' time and it was in English. She'd been so impressed with them and they'd been so nice to her, that she'd signed up on the spot. She knew that Maxwell wouldn't mind the exorbitant price that they were charging. He would be happy that she'd found something that she really wanted to do and of course it would mean that he'd feel less guilty about leaving her alone in a strange city every day. She couldn't wait to tell Taylor and Ashling what she'd done, not to mention Maxwell. Wouldn't he be surprised!

Surprised was an understatement. Max was gobsmacked. He didn't recognise this confident woman (well, not confident exactly, but certainly not the nervous, diffident woman of old) and he was truly proud of her.

"Splendid!" he said. "This will be marvellous for you." Heaving a sigh of relief, he mentally thanked Ashling. What a great girl! He knew it was she who had boosted Felicity's confidence.

Jazz was amused by the antics of Chantal. It was obvious that she wanted to get something going with Brandon. Every morning, first thing, she arrived bearing three cups of coffee and croissants or pretty little pastries. She obviously knew the way to a man's heart was through his stomach as she watched Brandon devour the delicacies with gusto. Mind you, she was obviously appealing to his eyes too and each day she wore an ever shorter skirt with a different pair of glorious heels and sat swinging her gorgeous legs under Brandon's nose. She had taken to wearing her long hair down and it would fall forward, silkily brushing his face, as she placed his coffee before him. The scent of Chanel No. 5 would assail him and Jazz knew that it was only a question of time before he succumbed to her charms. She had to admire the girl. She was a pro when it came to seducing men.

"I could sure use some of her techniques," Jazz remarked to Brandon ruefully, after Chantal had left the office.

"You don't need them," he declared gallantly. "She's very attractive but you're a true beauty – and you also have a terrific brain, while I'm not too sure about Chantal's!"

This did not make Jazz feel any better and she wondered why Yves had chosen Chantal over all the other secretaries. Obviously, he was more into looks than brains. Suddenly, she felt very jealous of the young blonde girl.

Despite what he'd said to Jazz, Brandon was not immune to Chantal's charms. It had been quite a while since he'd had a woman and this girl was certainly easy on the eye. One afternoon, when Jazz was out of the office, she came in and blatantly asked him to meet her one evening.

"Chantal, I'm a married man."

She laughed a tinkling laugh. "I am married too. I don't want you for to marry. No, I like for you to make love with me." She laughed again and then reached forward and kissed him on the lips, her little tongue probing his mouth. God, she was offering it to him on a plate. She would arouse a saint, he thought to himself, and I'm no saint!

He watched her, hips swaying and hair swinging as she left his office. At the door, she turned and winked at him. He knew it was only a matter of time before he gave in and the thought excited him.

Ashling knew that Kieran was making a conscious effort to be home earlier each evening but he was still arriving home just as the girls were going to bed so he got to see very little of them. His birthday was the following Saturday and she had arranged a surprise dinner party for him. Sophie had assured her that Yves would be well enough to come and Jazz had asked Hugh to accompany her so she wouldn't feel like an oddity amongst all the couples. Ashling would have preferred not to have had Taylor there but unfortunately she had no choice but to invite her. She warned everyone not to say a word to Kieran. Max had promised her that he would take Kieran to golf on Saturday so that he wouldn't twig about his surprise party. It should be a great night.

Thursday had been a long tough day at work.

"I could murder a beer," Brandon said to Kieran. "You coming?"

"I promised Ash I'd get home early – but maybe one quick one," he said, seeing the disappointed look on Brandon's face.

The bar was crowded and as Brandon came in he spotted Chantal across the other side of the bar with two girlfriends. She waved and raised her glass to him in a salute.

"I'd like to buy a drink for those three girls over there," he said to the barman, pointing to Chantal.

"Isn't that Yves's secretary?" Kieran asked.

"Yes. She's been very kind bringing us coffee every morning," Brandon replied, fiddling with his key ring.

"Ah-ha!" Kieran grinned. "Something's up here. She doesn't bring Max and *me* coffee every morning."

"Maybe you don't have my charm," Brandon laughed as the barman brought their drinks.

Kieran finished his beer before Brandon was even halfway through his.

"Sorry about this but you know how it is. I'll be in the doghouse if I don't get home pronto." He looked sheepish as he left.

Brandon understood. Unfortunately, he had no incentive to go home. There would be no wife waiting for him with a nice meal and a loving word. No, no need to rush home. He was ordering a second beer when Chantal came over and stood before him.

"Thank you for the drink. You are alone, *oui*?" she asked. "The Irishman – 'e is gone?"

Brandon nodded yes. "Can I get you another drink? How about your friends?"

"They leave also," she smiled sexily at him.

She sat down close to him and the scent of her excited him. Her skirt had rolled up over her thighs and he caught a glimpse of a lace stocking-top. As she leaned close to him, her top fell open, revealing the top of her soft rounded breasts.

"I want very much to make love wiz you," she whispered, her voice husky with desire. "You come with me now?"

Brandon didn't stand a chance. He wanted her just as badly. She was much younger than he but it didn't seem to bother her. He realised it had been far too long since he'd had a woman. Silently, he followed her out of the bar, drinks forgotten.

She took him to her small apartment which was nearby.

"What about your husband?" he asked, terrified that he might walk in on them. She pealed with laughter. "My 'usband is at our 'ouse in Normandy – 'e work to make cheese with 'is family but I stay 'ere, in the week, because of my work."

Looking around, Brandon saw that it was just a one-room studio. He wondered if she'd taken other men there before him. He didn't care. All that mattered was that he was here now. He wouldn't think of Taylor. She wasn't interested in him anyway. He wasn't used to this straightforward approach by a woman but he wasn't complaining. When in Paris . . . he told himself. In New York, the women he'd bedded had wanted to be wined and dined first and then seduced. Obviously, Frenchwomen had no need for such pretence.

Chantal slowly undressed him and then herself. She was wearing a delicious white lace basque, stockings and a tiny thong. He could see her beautiful body through the lace and suddenly he couldn't wait to take her. She made him wait as she peeled it off, piece by piece. He could barely restrain himself. Her body was magnificent as she slowly climbed on top of him and brought him to ecstasy. He had never experienced sex like it. Her expertise was incredible.

She then lay back and showed him what she wanted and her obvious enjoyment aroused him once more. This time they climaxed together and it was pure pleasure. Sated, they lay panting and she smiled at him.

"I guess you *beaucoup* sexy man. Always, I can tell. You make Chantal very happy. We do this again, *oui?*"

"Yes, please," he said, barely able to believe what was happening. It was as if all his birthdays had come together.

Jazz knew, the moment Chantal entered the office on Friday morning that something had happened between her and Brandon. There was an intimacy and sexual vibe in the air that hadn't been there before. When Chantal left, she looked over at Brandon and he winked back at her. So, the male has pounced, Jazz thought, smiling to herself. Well, perhaps not. More like the female has devoured. Poor Brandon, she wasn't sure he'd be able to cope with Chantal's wiles. It would be interesting to watch.

22

Kieran was a little put out that Ashling had forgotten his birthday. He'd thought they might do something special together, as a family, but when Max rang to ask him to play golf, she told him to go ahead as she was meeting Jazz for lunch.

"Well, I like that," he muttered, feeling neglected. She hadn't even remembered it was his birthday.

In fact, Ashling had been in a tizzy for two days trying to keep the party a secret.

When he arrived back from golf on Saturday evening, Max surprised him by asking if he could come in for a drink.

"Yeah, sure," Kieran said, looking at him strangely. This was out of character. Max normally wanted to get back to Felicity as soon as possible. In fact, now that he thought about it, Max had delayed more than usual after the golf.

Entering his house, he was surprised at the silence. Normally he would hear the TV or Ashling talking on the phone or the girls playing. Not tonight. With Max in tow he opened the living-room door and couldn't believe his eyes. All his colleagues were there and they all erupted into a mixed version of "Happy Birthday" and "*Bon Anniversaire*". He was bowled over.

"So you didn't forget, after all," he said to Ashling as she kissed him.

"Of course not, you ninny!" she laughed.

Then they were all upon him, clapping him on the back and offering gifts.

"I need a drink," he said, to much laughter, and Brandon handed him a glass of champagne. "What a surprise – but a lovely one."

The night went with a bang. Hugh was introduced all round and everyone loved him, with the exception of Yves – he was very quiet all night but everyone assumed that it was because it was his first day out of hospital.

Brandon sat with him for a while. "That's a pretty little secretary you have," he remarked casually.

"Chantal? Yes, she's hot – and very talented – if you know what I mean." He winked at Brandon. "What a body!"

As Brandon had suspected, Chantal had shared her favours with Yves. Maybe she still was doing so, for all he knew.

"She's a nice kid," he said nonchalantly, changing the subject.

Jazz tried to avoid Yves all night but she was aware of his eyes on her every moment. He tried to take her to one side but she felt it wasn't the time to talk, not with Hugh and Sophie both there, so she excused herself.

"So that's the lucky man," Hugh whispered to her after he'd been introduced to Yves. It was obvious to him that Yves was crazy about Jazz. He never took his eyes off her all night. Mind you, Sophie was pretty gorgeous too. Lucky sod, Hugh thought.

Taylor was as high as a kite. She had taken two Vicodin and an Oxycontin before leaving the house, anticipating a boring evening. Topped up with the champagne she consumed at the party it was no surprise that she was spaced out. Ashling thought that she must have had quite a skinful before arriving at the party to get so drunk so quickly. Even Felicity was having trouble understanding her. Taylor kept going on about Felicity and Lord somebody or other. It was obviously embarrassing Felicity who kept moving away. Ashling had prepared a cold buffet and so, luckily, people weren't stuck beside Taylor at the dinner table all night. Brandon took her away quite early, furious with her as he'd been having a great time. He couldn't understand how she was so drunk. In New York she had never let herself get into this state. Here in Paris she didn't seem to care. He wondered if it was more than just alcohol she was taking. Despite Taylor's behaviour he felt very relaxed, thanks to his session with Chantal. He hoped they'd get together again soon. He'd forgotten just how great sex could be.

Felicity was really enjoying herself and had even found the courage to chat with Jazz, who she'd discovered was lovely and not a bit stuck-up.

Why was I so silly? Felicity asked herself. Just because she's beautiful, I was intimidated by her. So stupid! Jazz was interested in the cookery course and asked her all about it. She also wanted to hear about her trip to Versailles and Felicity happily regaled her with all the details. Jazz really was a charming girl, she decided.

As she thanked her hostess for a lovely evening, Ashling asked her if she'd like to visit the Musée d'Orsay the following Tuesday.

"I'd love to," Felicity beamed.

Max was thrilled with this new woman his wife was becoming. He privately thanked Ashling for her help.

Everyone left the party saying what a great night they'd had. Ashling was pleased and when Kieran took her to bed and made love to her it seemed like her world was perfect.

23

Yves was in and out of Jazz's office all day on Monday on some pretext or other.

"He's like a hen on a hot griddle," Brandon remarked after Yves's sixth visit. Jazz guessed that he was trying to get her alone. His chance finally came late in the afternoon when Brandon was out of the office.

"Please, Jazz, I really need to talk to –" he started.

She pre-empted him. "Okay, Yves. I'll meet you."

His face lit up and he took her hand to his lips. "You're so beautiful," he whispered. "I cannot stop thinking about you."

She found herself melting under his intense gaze and she was trembling with excitement. They arranged to meet on Wednesday evening after work. For the rest of the day she was floating on air. This was what she'd hoped for and she longed for the time to fly by until she could be with him.

Brandon was also waiting for Chantal to say something about another meeting. He was really looking forward to being with her again but he didn't want to push it. His patience was rewarded when she emailed him on Tuesday and asked him to meet her on Thursday evening, at her place. He, like Jazz, was full of anticipation. Their office fairly buzzed with excitement.

Taylor was bored. She had hoped that some of the Americans she'd met in the Hôtel de Ville might have invited her to drinks or dinner but the only invitation that had come her way was to a book-club meeting. It was the most boring two hours she'd ever spent in her life. The only good thing about it was that she'd secured the names of two American doctors who, she was told, were very generous with their prescriptions. Thank God for that! The Vicodin she'd brought with her from the States wouldn't last forever. Luckily she'd had some in her bag that day, which helped her get through the boring afternoon. The women were just like the snooty, old-money matrons of New York. All a clique – no newcomers welcome! Well, she didn't need them. They were boring old farts anyway. What she needed was fun and she knew just the person to provide it.

That evening she phoned her friend, Marilyn, in New York.

"You absolutely *must* come over to Paris," she cried. "I'm dying of boredom here."

"Hey, I'd love to, honey," Marilyn drawled, her Texan accent even more pronounced over the phone, "but I'm flat broke. That bastard Frank is late with the alimony again." Frank was her latest ex-husband who had fallen on hard times and was working his butt off just to meet his alimony payments. He knew that Marilyn could spend in a day what it took him a week to earn.

"Don't worry about money, sweetie. I'll book your flight. How soon can you come?"

"Oh, honey, you're soooo generous. I'd love to come. To tell you the truth, I need to lie low for a while here. You know that politician I was goin' out with? Well, blow me down if the press darn well didn't' get hold of the story. All friggin' hell broke loose. Like all men, he chickened out an' so I'm here with the paps parked outside my door, afraid to show my purty little face outside. It's worse than bein' Tiger Woods' mistress, I'm a tellin' ya!" She roared with laughter.

Taylor laughed with her. "God you're a tonic, Marilyn! I *need* you here. Please say you'll come."

"Well, if you really need me, honey, what can I say? Sure I'll come. I miss you too and anyway I'm sick of American men. Have some nice guys lined up for me." She was laughing her husky laugh again as she rang off.

Taylor was over the moon. This was just what she needed to brighten up her life. Marilyn was such fun. She was outrageous. The matrons of Paris better watch out and lock up their menfolk! With Marilyn around anything was likely to happen.

They'd become friends as teenagers, both thrilled to have landed a job in Saks and both on the lookout for a rich husband. Marilyn had found four. Her boredom threshold was low and no husband had lasted more than five years. They'd kept in touch throughout and Taylor was now looking forward to having her visit. Giggling, she mixed herself another martini before going online to check for flights.

Ashling didn't make it to Les Deux Magots on Monday as she had a lot of cleaning up to do after the party and then on Tuesday she went with Felicity to the Musée d'Orsay. They loved all the Impressionist paintings and had settled into an easy friendship.

As they walked along the Seine to the bistro they'd spotted earlier, Felicity confided, "I have to call my mother tonight and I'm dreading it."

"Is she really so bad?" Ashling asked.

"She's worse." Felicity made a face. "It sounds crazy, I know, but she intimidates me so much that I end up a nervous wreck in her presence and that drives her ballistic. I just can't seem to say or do anything right when she's around," she sighed.

Ashling couldn't even imagine how that could be possible. She had such a warm, loving relationship with her mother and couldn't wait for her to come and visit. She rang her at least twice a week and loved talking to her. She felt sorry for poor Felicity. Her mother sounded like a dragon.

"Maybe you should just stand up to her. You know, she'll probably admire that. She probably hates you being so submissive."

"Yes, probably," Felicity said, without much conviction, as they arrived at the bistro.

They ordered and settled down to their lunch.

"You look wonderful, Ashling," Felicity remarked admiringly. "I can see you've lost more weight and your new hairstyle really suits you."

"Thanks. I'm delighted with what I've lost and also with my new hairdo. It has given me a boost."

"I know what you mean. I wish I could look smarter," Felicity confided, patting her mousy hair.

"A new hairstyle would do wonders for you, you know," Ashling suggested gently, conscious that she was now stepping into the role Sophie had played in her own case. "Why don't you let me make an appointment for you with Odette, the girl who did my hair?"

"Oh, would you? That would be wonderful," Felicity's eyes were shining. "I'm always overwhelmed by these smart salons."

"No need to be, she's really sweet and I'll come with you," Ashling reassured her, delighted that Felicity had agreed to go. Once she got her inside the salon she'd make sure that her friend got the whole works. She was determined to make the appointment for as soon as possible.

Felicity finally screwed up the courage to ring her mother after she'd had two gin and tonics.

"Hello, Mummy," she started.

"This must be you, Felicity," her mother barked. "You know I don't want to be called 'Mummy'. For God's sake, my name is Georgina. Can't you manage that?"

Instantly, Felicity found herself like a terrified child again. "Sorry, Mum . . . eh . . . Georgina," she mumbled. She would never get used to calling her mother by that name. "How are you and how's Father?" She could never call her father Nigel either and she knew he wouldn't want her to.

"Nigel's fine," her mother dismissed him with a sniff. "And how are you getting on with those dreadful French people? Have you seen sense and decided to come back to civilisation?"

Listening to her mother, Felicity began to realise why she herself was so bigoted against other nationalities. She'd been raised with these blinkered ideas. God, her mother would have a fit if she knew that her best friend was Irish! This thought almost made her giggle. Somehow that gave her the courage to reply; "Actually, Georgina, I'm quite enjoying it here. The French are surprisingly civilised."

She heard her mother's sharp intake of breath and sensed her disbelief. She continued quickly before her mother could start a tirade.

"Actually, the reason I'm ringing is because we're coming back to the UK next weekend to collect the girls and I thought we might visit you and Father on Saturday."

"Felicity, you know Saturdays are very busy for me. I can fit you in on Sunday morning."

The familiar haughty tone boomed across the line. Years of her mother's dominance and her own acquiescence almost made Felicity agree. Then she remembered Ashling's advice.

"Sorry, Georgina, but that doesn't suit *me*. We're taking the girls out on Sunday to Lulworth Castle and heading straight back to Paris from there. Well, don't worry. Maybe we'll catch up next time I'm home. Love to Dad. Byeee!"

She hung up before her mother could say another word and perhaps reduce her to a quivering jelly, as she so often did. Felicity's hands were shaking and clammy as she replaced the phone on its stand. She couldn't believe what she'd just done. She'd stood up to her mother, on her own, for the first time in her life. She let out a whoop of joy and punched the air, whirling around just as Maxwell came through the door.

"What the hell?" he exclaimed, totally taken aback to see Felicity behaving in this way.

"I did it, I did it!" she cried exultantly. "I stood up to my mother – excuse me, *Georgina* – and it feels great!" She punched the air once more.

He laughed, delighted and happy. "Well, it's about bloody time, is all I can say," he said, hugging her.

"It feels great," she admitted, a little more subdued. "I feel a great release all of a sudden, like I'm free."

"You always have been, sweetheart," he said. "You just never had the courage to see that." He kissed her then and she felt safe and secure and most of all, loved just for herself.

Meanwhile, Georgina stood looking at the phone unable to believe what had just happened.

"I don't believe it," she said aloud.

"Don't believe what, dear?" her husband Nigel, who had entered the room, enquired.

"Felicity hung up on me."

"Surely not. Felicity would never do that."

"That's what I thought too but she just did." Her aristocratic, plummy voice was full of dismay and disbelief.

"Did you upset her?" her husband asked uneasily.

"Of course not," she snapped back at him. "I told her I wasn't free for her to visit on Saturday and that I would see her on Sunday morning instead, but she said *she* wasn't free then. And then she hung up, just like that. Can you believe it?" Her voice was filled with awe, then fury. "How dare she!"

Nigel hid a smile, wary of being caught up in this battle his wife had waged on his gentle daughter since forever. Felicity had been such a sweet child, always anxious to please, but of course nothing she could ever have done would have pleased Georgina. He wished he could have protected her from her mother's wrath but he had been equally intimidated by his domineering wife. He often felt that he'd failed his daughter. She'd always been timid and nervous and became more so with each year that passed. This had infuriated Georgina even further.

He had been happy when, for the first time in her life, Felicity had defied her mother and insisted on marrying Max. It was a good marriage but Felicity's confidence had not improved very much. She'd been too browbeaten by her mother who still had her at her beck and call.

He had hoped that a year in Paris, away from her mother's influence, would help his daughter to gain in confidence and stand on her own two feet. And now it looked as though that may very well have happened. As Georgina banged and stalked around the kitchen, he prayed that Felicity had found the strength, as *he* never had, to finally stand up to her mother.

Jazz spent the days counting down the hours, and finally the minutes, until she would meet with Yves. Time had never seemed to go so slowly but eventually the hour had come and it was with a mixture of apprehension and excitement that she entered the bar where he had suggested they meet. It was just around the corner from her apartment.

He was waiting for her and her heart soared when he took her in his arms and kissed her. She knew then that whatever he might say to her, she would not be able to resist him for long. It was as if it was completely outside her control. He had a bottle of champagne on ice and as she sipped it his hand was in contact with her body all the time, caressing first her back and then her thigh. She was waiting for him to mention their previous affair but he didn't. In fact she couldn't remember afterwards what he'd said to her, she'd been in such a state of excitement and arousal, and more than a little nervous. It was obvious that he was very nervous too.

They finished the champagne and, taking her by the hand, he whispered, "Come!"

They left the bar and walked until they reached – "Oh God, I don't believe it," Jazz murmured. He does remember, she thought. It was the Hôtel de Lutèce where he had first brought her as a twenty-one-year old. She was touched. Entering the lobby, she had a sense of déjà-vu. It looked shabbier than she remembered but then in those days she'd thought it was paradise. God, she'd loved him so much. She was surprised that he had a key and didn't have to check in. She felt like a wanton woman as she followed him up the stairs and couldn't wait for what she knew would be a magical reunion.

It was the same room and pretty much as she remembered, but it seemed much smaller. As soon as he closed the door she was in his arms and then they were kissing, panting and pulling off each other's clothes. Falling on the bed, they clung to each other.

"Jazz, you are the most beautiful woman I've ever met," he

whispered in her ear, in between kisses. "I've never seen a more voluptuous body. You drive me crazy with desire."

Caressing her gently and kissing her all over, he finally entered her and it was every bit as good as before. He was as accomplished a lover as she remembered.

"I think I'm falling in love with you," he whispered in her ear, his tongue nuzzling it, giving her a delicious sensation. "I've never been with a woman like you before."

Her heart plummeted. Had she misheard him? No, she had not – and such a statement could only mean one thing . . .

As she lay there she tried to come to terms with the fact that he didn't remember her at all. How was that possible? She couldn't believe it. He had been her life for nine months and it had taken her years to get over him. In fact, she suspected now that she never had. I know I should get up and leave, she thought, as a tear slid out of the corner of her eye, but somehow she couldn't. She was ashamed of her weakness and when he started to make love to her again, all her scruples were forgotten.

Many hours later they said goodbye, clinging on to each other.

"I'll be counting the hours till we meet again," he said.

"Me too," she whispered.

24

Taylor laughed out loud when she saw Marilyn come through the doors of the arrivals hall of the airport. A porter was pushing her luggage which consisted of five Louis Vuitton cases. It looked like she was here to stay for quite some time. She was wearing a Burberry trench coat, Brian Atwood killer heels and over her arm a large Hermes bag. Her face was almost obscured by a massive pair of Gucci sunglasses. The paparazzi waiting outside had no idea who she was but were busy snapping away, sure that she must be a celebrity of some kind. She was waving her hand at them crying, "No comment, no comment!" although nobody had asked her anything. She squealed with joy when she caught sight of Taylor and they fell into each other's arms, laughing hysterically.

"You're such a howl," Taylor cried. "I am *so* glad to see you."

"Oh, Pareee, City of Lovvve, I am *so* happy to be here."

Marilyn threw her arms in the air, then turned and posed for the cameras once more.

"A limo!" she cried when she saw the car Taylor had waiting for her. "You always had such class, honey."

It's just as well I did order a limo, Taylor thought. All that luggage!

They chatted nineteen to the dozen all the way home and Taylor was gratified to see how impressed Marilyn was with the beautiful apartment.

"Oh hon, I'm sure gonna love it here!" She pirouetted daintily. "How about a little bubbly to celebrate?"

"Sweeetie, it's only 10 a.m.!" Taylor exclaimed in surprise. "Do you not want to go for a sleep?"

"Heck, no! I have to celebrate my first day in the beautiful Pareee and what better way than with a bottle of French champagne!" She pealed with laughter.

Her joie-de-vivre was contagious and Taylor found herself laughing too as she opened a bottle of champagne before sitting down to catch up on all the gossip. Two bottles later, they both decided that a nap might be a good idea.

How fantastic to have Marilyn here, Taylor thought, as she drifted off to sleep. Paris will certainly be more fun now.

Wow! How great it is to be in Pareee, Marilyn thought, as she wrapped the luxurious duvet around her. I just know this trip is gonna change my life forever. I'm *sooo* excited!

Mimi, the cook, a scowl on her face, cleaned away the debris they'd left behind. The housekeeper, Cecile, had left after less than two weeks of suffering Taylor's abuse. Mimi was left doing it all, cooking and cleaning, not that her mistress ate very much. Still, she felt sorry for the master, married to such a horrible woman. She hated Taylor but needed the job badly so she put up with her insults and demands, biding her time till she found something better.

Brandon arrived home from work to find both Taylor and Marilyn sipping wine and the unmistakeable smell of cigarette smoke in the living room.

"Brandon, dahhhling, how lovely to see you again!" Marilyn cried, throwing her arms around him.

"Marilyn, how are you?" he replied tautly, extricating himself from her embrace and going to open the windows to get rid of the stench.

He disliked Taylor's friend, with very good reason. He had always felt that her wild living and casual morals were a bad influence on his wife. She flirted with him constantly and she'd often let him know, in no uncertain terms, that she was available to him, despite him being married to her best friend. Needless to say he didn't take her up on the offer. He wasn't that stupid!

Taylor, however, admired Marilyn enormously. Being very low in the sexuality department herself, he guessed she envied her friend's lustfulness and sexual appetite.

And Brandon had to admit that Marilyn was certainly very sexually attractive. She always had that 'just got out of bed' look and her china-blue eyes and blonde hair made her seem almost childlike. Her small figure added to this, except for the large silicone breasts that were forever on show. They were completely out of proportion to her waif-like figure.

"I paid enough for these boobs," she was fond of saying, "so why not show them off? I must get value for my money." Then she would laugh riotously.

Taylor had toyed with the idea of having her breasts done too but luckily he had talked her out of it. Now here was Marilyn, larger than life, back in their lives and set to stay, if the amount of her luggage was anything to go by. She was still flirting outrageously with him and he was still ignoring her.

He'd been shocked to see the number of empty bottles and numerous cigarette butts in the bin when he'd gone into the kitchen for a beer. He hoped to God Taylor had not started smoking again. He'd had a hell of a job getting her off them years ago.

Ashling was delighted with the way her novel was going. She'd been to the English bookshop, Shakespeare & Co, and bought a copy of *The Sun King* by Nancy Mitford. This was a marvellous book about Louis XIV and his court which she'd read and loved years before and she knew it would be a great help with her research. She also spent hours Googling all the information that she needed and checking up on her facts. She had settled into a routine. Girls to school in the morning; Monday, Wednesday and Friday, gym for an hour; then to Les Deux Magots for coffee and two solid hours of writing before lunch, which she usually had with Corey, then a lovely walk by the Seine, revelling in this beautiful city and on to collect the girls from school.

On Tuesday mornings she visited a museum or art gallery with Felicity and from next week on she'd have her wine course on Thursday mornings. Life was pretty full and she loved it.

It was amazing how quickly Orna and Ciara had settled in. They were always full of news and excitement and she was delighted to hear how much their French was improving. It never ceased to amaze her how easily children could pick up a language.

Most afternoons she took the girls to the playground in the Luxembourg Gardens where they'd already made friends. Ashling would sit with the other mothers chatting as they watched their offspring enjoy themselves. Then home to cook dinner and, when the girls were tucked up in bed, she would write for another two hours. She had come to accept that Kieran would rarely be home before nine o'clock. Thank God she had her writing. It had come as a big surprise to find that she loved it so much and ideas were tumbling around in her head all the time. She could barely wait to get to the computer to get it all down. It was much easier than she'd imagined. Corey had insisted on reading the first few chapters and she'd been overjoyed when he'd commented that they were very good. He suggested that she perhaps give more detailed descriptions of the characters' appearance from the word go and she realised that he was of course right. She was grateful for his advice and did as he suggested. He was very encouraging.

Taylor, meanwhile, hadn't had so much fun in years. Marilyn was a tonic – absolutely outrageous! She had such zest for life that she left Taylor exhausted. They'd gone shopping and Taylor had enjoyed taking her to the gorgeous designer boutiques where all the assistants knew her by name.

"Gee, you have been busy, honey," Marilyn drawled.

For someone who had said she was skint, Marilyn managed to buy an awful lot, flashing a myriad of credit cards everywhere they shopped. In Prada, she fell in love with a jacket that was truly adorable.

"I absolutely *must* have this," she cried, turning this way and that before the mirror.

"It's beautiful," Taylor agreed, fingering the butter-soft suede. It fitted Marilyn's body like a glove.

"But I just can't afford it," her friend added, her china-blue eyes clouding over. "I'm up to my max on all my credit cards. Damn that Frank and his alimony!" She was like a little girl being denied a beautiful doll.

Taylor checked out the price tag. She blanched. Oh my God! Then she thought – Marilyn has come all this way to visit me, it's the least I can do for her. Taylor knew that Brandon would be furious if he knew. Well, he'd never know. She could always say it was something she'd bought for herself.

"We'll take it," she said to the salesgirl. "It's my present to you," she beamed at Marilyn. "I'm so grateful you came over to visit me."

"Oh, honey, I love you so much!" Marilyn hugged her and twirled her round. "Thank you so much. It's beautiful." She smiled at her reflection in the mirror.

"I haven't had such a good time since . . . I don't know when," Taylor told Marilyn over a bottle of champagne in the bar of the George V. "I guess I've become so tied up in the social charity scene in New York that I've forgotten how to really enjoy myself."

"Oh, don't depress me, honey. Them old fuddy-duddies are so up their own butts that the only time they enjoy themselves is when they're in the restroom.

She pealed with laughter and Taylor joined in. God, it felt so good to be able to let her hair down like this. Marilyn's sense of humour was infectious.

"I'm so sick of all them stuck-up cows back home," said Marilyn. "I've given up on all that social crap in New York. Who needs it? I'm aimin' to have a good time from now on." To prove her point she raised her glass to a good-looking guy at the next table, giving him a sultry look. "European men! Give them to me every time!"

Taylor laughed at her, watching as she flirted outrageously with the man. He obviously enjoyed it because ten minutes later he sent another bottle of champagne to their table.

"Cheers!" Marilyn smiled sexily as she raised her glass to him.

"Gosh, I don't know how you do it," Taylor said, admiringly.

Marilyn pealed with laughter. "Men are pussy-cats," she purred, knocking back the champagne.

As Ashling sat waiting for Felicity, she thought about Corey and wondered why she still hadn't told Kieran about him. What's there to tell, she reasoned, as she sipped her coffee. She hadn't told him that she'd started on her novel either. He was so tired every evening that he barely said more than a few words to her before going to bed. In the morning, he was up and gone as she was getting the girls ready for school. He never asked her what she got up to all day, so why should she volunteer the information?

She'd lost more weight and was feeling a lot fitter than she had in years. Not that Kieran noticed! Huh, some marriage, she thought, but that's not my fault. If he wants to put his career first, well, that's his decision and there's no point in my causing rows about it. It won't change anything. And to think I thought things might be different here! Thank God I've got a life of my own now – and my writing – it's turning out to be a lifesaver.

Felicity's arrival broke into her thoughts.

"I'm so nervous about going to this beauty salon," Felicity cried, sitting down and ordering two espressos.

"There's no need to be. I felt like that too but Odette is so sweet – all the girls are," Ashling reassured her.

And so it turned out to be. Odette took Felicity in hand and assured her that she would not do anything too drastic.

"No purple highlights or dreadlocks then," Felicity laughed, winking at Ashling.

A sleek smart bob and blonde and honey highlights later, Felicity beamed as she turned her head this way and that, admiring her new hairstyle in the mirror.

"This is fantastic!" she cried to Ashling, who had been busy writing away on her laptop while all this was going on.

"Now, you have to have a facial, and manicure and pedicure to go with the new hairstyle," Ashling ordered. If she'd asked her to walk on water, at this stage, Felicity would have happily done so. Ashling sensing this, decided to go for broke. "You'll need new clothes to go with this new you. What do you say we go shopping this afternoon and smarten you up?"

"Oh, Ashling, what can I say?" Felicity had tears in her eyes. "Can you spare the time?"

"No problem. The girls are going to a birthday party from school, so I'm free till six."

"I'm so grateful," Felicity said as the beautician came for her.

Ashling grinned with satisfaction.

On the off-chance, she rang Jazz and asked if there was any chance she could take a half-day to come shopping with them. She had a great eye and would know what to choose for Felicity.

"I'd love to," Jazz replied. "I need to get out of the office big-time. I'll explain later."

They agreed to meet for lunch before the shopping expedition.

The request couldn't have come at a better time for Jazz. In the cold light of day, she was ashamed at how stupidly she'd behaved. She should have left Yves straight away once she'd realised that he didn't remember her. She considered calling in ill to work on Thursday, not wanting to face him. He kept coming into the office hoping to find her alone, she suspected, and she knew Brandon was wondering what the hell was going on. Now Ashling had given her an escape route.

She had taken the next day off anyway as she was travelling back to Frankfurt to finish with Hans and collect her things. Then she planned on driving to Munich to visit her mother and leave her car and her stuff there. She hoped the break would give her a better perspective on things.

Now, as Jazz saw the two women arriving at the bistro, she let out a long whistle.

"My God, Felicity, I hardly recognise you. You look fabulous."

And it was true. Felicity looked beautiful. Her skin was glowing and the hairstyle was very becoming. It made her look ten years younger.

"I know," Felicity replied, unabashed. "I love it, I really do." She tossed her head, flicking her short, shiny hair from side to side. Her plummy upper-class accent always took Jazz by surprise each time they met. Ashling was used to it now and barely noticed it.

"God, Ash, this is some makeover!" Jazz grinned at Ashling, who gave a little bow.

After lunch they hit Galeries Lafayette and it was like a re-run of Ashling's search for a dress there. Jazz whizzed around, pulling garments off rails as Felicity tried on one garment after another. If Jazz and Ashling liked it on her, she bought it. 3000 the poorer, a happy Felicity insisted on treating them to champagne in the restaurant on the top floor. The two girls laughed at her enthusiasm.

"Maxwell will probably have a fit when he sees how much I've spent but really it's been years since I bought anything new for myself," she remarked, as the waiter popped the cork.

"I'm sure he'll be thrilled when he sees how great you look," Jazz told her.

"Exactly, you've got a whole new wardrobe there," Ashling assured her.

"True. If I tell him that Taylor spent more than that on one dress, he's sure to be happy," Felicity said mischievously.

They all roared laughing as they clinked their glasses together.

"To the new Felicity!" Jazz and Ashling chorused, delighted to see the change in her.

Felicity left after one glass as she wanted to be home before Maxwell, leaving the other two to finish off the champagne. Jazz went to pour some more for Ashling who put her hand over the top of her glass.

"Not for me thanks. That's my limit for today. I've lost twelve pounds already and I want to make it a stone by next weekend," Ashling said proudly.

"Well done, you look great."

Jazz gazed at her, seeming to hesitate, and Ashling waited to see what it was she wanted to add.

"I was out with Yves last night," Jazz went on quietly, refilling her own glass.

"I was wondering what you'd done about him. Did he remember you?"

"No, not at all. But I still love him, Ash – I can't explain it – I feel so alive when I'm with him," she whispered.

"Oh, Jazz!" Ashling groaned. "I just hope you don't get hurt. I wish I could do something to help," she offered, gently taking Jazz's hand.

"Thanks, but no one can. I know it's not right but I can't give him up."

Ashling saw the anguish in her friend's eyes. She didn't think this was the time to mention Sophie. God, what a mess!

"What about Hans?"

"I'm going to Frankfurt tomorrow and I'm going to tell him it's over between us. I'm dreading it."

"Well, I suppose it's only fair to him."

"Yes. I can't bear it when he calls me. I hate having to pretend."

Later, Ashling hugged a very disconsolate Jazz goodbye, wondering where it would all end. She was glad that her own life was simple and uncomplicated.

Felicity was sizzling with excitement as she waited for Maxwell to come home. She kept looking in the mirror, not believing that it was her own reflection she was seeing. She looked so totally different and she hoped that Maxwell would like her new look as much as she did. She was wearing a new Donna Karan soft jersey royal-blue dress and matching heels and she felt elegant and smart, and even a little sexy. Jazz had insisted that she buy an uplifting Wonderbra and it had done wonders for her shape. She quivered with apprehension as she heard Maxwell's key in the door.

"Hello, love," he called out, coming into the living room.

She was standing by the window and Maxwell stopped dead in his tracks when he saw her. He stared at her, saying nothing, and with a sinking heart she thought that he didn't like her makeover.

"Felicity?" he said, as if he didn't really believe it was her.

"Yes," she croaked.

"What has happened to you?" He didn't move.

She started to cry. "You don't like it," she said, disappointment in her voice.

"Don't like it?" he repeated as he moved towards her. "I love it. You look fantastic." He took her in his arms as she smiled through her tears.

"I'm so glad," she mumbled, "because I love my new look too."

"You ninny," he laughed, drying her eyes. "How could I not love it? You look wonderful. This calls for a celebration!"

He gave her a long kiss, then went and took a bottle of champagne from the fridge. Pouring two glasses, he handed her one and raised his glass to hers. "To my beautiful wife," he smiled, and they clinked glasses.

Felicity couldn't stop beaming at him as she sipped the champagne.

"How did this happen?" he asked her.

She explained that Ashling had inveigled her into the hair and beauty salon and then Jazz had joined them for the shopping spree.

Thank you, Ashling and Jazz, he said silently.

"You may not be so happy when you see how much I spent," she told him, tremulously.

"I don't care how much it cost. It's been worth every penny," he assured her, stroking her cheek.

He was still gobsmacked. To think that she'd had the courage to go along with it! He was extremely proud of her.

Felicity sighed with happiness. Tomorrow she would be travelling back to London feeling like a new woman and seeing her girls once again. She wondered what *they* would think of her new look.

Brandon felt his world was tilting slightly out of kilter and he could do nothing about it. He hoped Taylor wasn't smoking again. That first night with Marilyn, they went out to a local brasserie to eat. Any time Marilyn wanted a smoke, Taylor went outside with her, so he had his doubts.

Since then the two women had been on the tear, arriving home late every night, completely out of it and high as kites. He'd never seen Taylor so drunk. It worried him. Although he didn't love her any more, he *was* her husband and felt a responsibility for her. He'd thought that having Marilyn here would help her settle in Paris, now he felt it might not have been such a good idea after all.

As if all that was not enough to worry him, something strange was going on with Jazz. He suspected it was something to do with Yves who was obviously very smitten with her.

She'd arrived into the office that morning looking more businesslike than ever in her navy pinstripe suit and white shirt. Her hair was held tightly back in a comb, no curls escaping on her neck and forehead as had been the case for the past few days. The only thing that hadn't changed was the four-inch killer heels. Something had happened! Brandon didn't know what but he was as curious as hell. Jazz was an enigma. A fascinating woman, actually, and he would love to know what was going on in that head of hers. He guessed he never would as she was the ultimate professional again now. She was acting like the hard-nosed female banker he'd expected in the first place. Women! You never knew where the hell you stood with them!

"Is everything okay?" he'd asked her for the umpteenth time.

"Fine, fine," she'd replied, but it was patently obvious that everything was not fine.

Then at lunchtime she'd upped and left, saying she needed to take the rest of the day off. She was heading to Germany the following day so he wouldn't see her again till Monday. Yves's face, when he told him she was gone, was the picture of misery. Seeing his dejection at this news, Brandon was convinced that there was something going on between them. Was Jazz out of her mind? Surely she could see that Yves was a serial womaniser? Brandon shook his head. He could never understand how otherwise intelligent, bright women stopped using their brains where men were concerned.

The only bright spot in his life at the moment was Chantal. He couldn't wait to see her again. She had texted him to say that she was very excited about seeing him tonight. Not half as excited as he was, he bet.

145

And the wait was worth it. She was as lovely as he remembered and they made love three times, each time better than the last. She was so adventurous that even he was surprised at some of the things she suggested. She was totally without inhibition or guile. She loved her body and she loved sex and it all seemed so natural.

They didn't talk very much – there was too much action going on – and he felt a bit of a cad. This wasn't how he usually treated women. He was a gentleman and he thought that he should show her some appreciation.

"Would you like to come out for a romantic dinner with me some evening?" he asked, as they lay perspiring after the last session of lovemaking.

"*Non, merci*," she replied, stroking his face. "You are kind, but I like better to make love with you than go eat. I eat wiz my friends."

She was unbelievable. He'd never met a woman yet who turned down the offer of a romantic dinner. This was a first. Well then, he decided, he'd buy her something nice to show his appreciation. She clung to him as they parted.

"I can't wait till next time. I text you," she said, kissing him lightly. He shook his head. She was amazing and very beautiful. She was just what he needed in his life at this moment. He left, wondering what would face him when he got home. Two drunken women and the stench of cigarettes, probably!

Yves was devastated. He couldn't understand why Jazz had left for the weekend without talking to him. He was crazy about her. What a body! He got aroused just thinking of her. She was passionate and sensual – everything he wanted in a woman. He thought of her silky olive skin, her strong toned thighs and her soft heavy breasts and felt himself go crazy with desire for her. And underneath it all there was a smouldering intensity that he couldn't quite fathom. She was the most exciting woman that he'd ever been with and he'd been with hundreds – so many hundreds he'd lost count decades ago.

He'd been thrilled when she'd agreed to meet him and more than surprised when she'd gone meekly with him to the hotel. Her unbridled passion had taken him by surprise and the sex had been awesome. She had enjoyed it as much as he had.

He had hoped to catch her alone this morning but Brandon was always there. Finally, after lunch, he went into their office determined to get her on her own, only to find that she'd left.

"Where's Jazz?" he asked Brandon, looking around as if she might step out from behind a cupboard at any moment.

"She had to go home," Brandon explained. "Women problems, I suppose."

"Well, I'll see her tomorrow then," said Yves, disappointment in his voice.

"No, she won't be in tomorrow. She's going back to Germany for the weekend."

Yves couldn't understand it. Was she avoiding him? He was furious with himself for not getting her mobile number from her. He wondered why she hadn't contacted him. She'd gone very quiet at one point the night before. Was it something he'd said? He was trying to remember but for the life of him he couldn't. Still, there was something niggling in his brain. There was something disturbing him that he couldn't quite put his finger on.

25

Ashling stopped by Corey's table in Les Deux Magots, to say hello.

"I missed you yesterday," he said, his face lighting up at the sight of her. "Why don't you join me for a quick coffee and tell me what exciting things you were doing."

She sat down, laughing, as Remy placed her coffee before her. He was delighted to see her too. She told Corey all about Felicity and the make-over and the shopping spree.

"She was like a different woman completely by yesterday evening."

"You're the Irish Mother Teresa," he teased her.

"Go way with you!" she smacked him playfully.

"Is this the friend you go to museums with every week?"

"Yes. Felicity is from London. Sadly, she won't be able to come with me any more as she's starting a cordon bleu course." Ashling made a face. "It won't be as much fun alone, I'm afraid."

"Hey, why don't you let me come in her place?" he suggested, his eyes lighting up at the idea. "I spend far too much time in here and I haven't seen anything of Paris. It will do me good. What do you say?"

She hesitated, but then seeing his dazzling smile and his delight at the idea, she succumbed.

"Why not? That would be great," she replied. After all, what harm was there in it? They would only be going to museums. "Well, better get back to some work," she said, leaving him to start into her novel again.

"See you for lunch?" he asked.

"Sure."

Over lunch – yet another salad! – Corey suddenly asked, "Is your marriage happy, Ashling?"

"Oh, yes," she replied. "Kieran is great but he's a workaholic. I don't see all that much of him."

Corey heard the catch in her voice. "What does he think about you writing a novel?"

"Well . . . em . . . I haven't actually told him yet," she admitted.

Corey said nothing but raised his eyebrows in surprise.

"But, I will, I will . . . soon," she added.

Corey wondered why she hadn't shared such an important part of her life with her husband. It didn't sound like her marriage was as happy as she was making out. He was growing fonder of Ashling every day. She was so warm and open, without guile, and she had a bright intelligent mind. She was a beautiful woman in every way – inside and out. He loved her company. She brightened up his life and the days he didn't see her seemed dull by comparison.

Marilyn and Taylor were drinking in the Crillon bar when they spotted the guy who had sent them over the champagne in the George V, sitting at another table with a friend. He nodded and smiled at Marilyn and within minutes a bottle of Bollinger appeared with a note from him, asking if he and his friend could join them. Marilyn smiled sexily at him and told the waiter to tell him it would be her pleasure. He came to their table and introduced himself as Louis and his friend as Christophe. They were obviously very wealthy and wearing very expensive clothes and jewellery. One didn't hang out in these hotels drinking Bollinger unless one had pots of money.

This was the start of a riotous evening as they went on to dinner with the two men. Halfway through the evening Marilyn noticed that Taylor was flagging and beckoned her to follow her into the ladies'. Once inside she took a mirror and small packet of white powder out of her bag and poured the powder on the mirror. Taylor watched fascinated as her friend made two little lines and, through a small straw, expertly sniffed the powder up her nose.

Marilyn then made two more lines and handing a straw to Taylor, instructed her to do the same.

"I've never done this," she said, shocked yet fascinated at the same time. "What is it?"

"It's only cocaine, the party drug, honey, and we're sure havin' a party. Go ahead – you'll feel a million dollars after it. Where do you think I get my energy from? Nourishing foods?" She pealed with laughter.

Taylor did as she was told and couldn't believe the effect it had on her. She felt her head clear, her tiredness fall away and a rush of energy engulf her.

"This is wonderful," she exclaimed to an amused Marilyn.

"It sure is, honey. Everyone who's anyone takes it nowadays."

Rejoining the party, Taylor felt like she was walking on air. She felt witty and funny and for the first time in over twenty years, really sexy. Why hadn't she done this before? She hadn't been living at all. Well, all that was about to change!

Much later they fell into a taxi, waving at Christophe and Louis who had Marilyn's promise that she would call him.

Taylor didn't know how her friend managed it. Men flocked to her like bees around a honey-pot. It was her looks that attracted them at first but then her zest for life and the knack she had of making them feel special had them falling in love with her within ten minutes of meeting her. No man was safe when she was around. If the Pope was present, Marilyn would have tried to seduce him – well, maybe not the present one, he was a bit long in the tooth – but all men were fair game to her.

Taylor knew that many people thought Marilyn was a nymphomaniac, or at best a sex-addict, but it wasn't the sex her friend craved, it was the love and attention of men. She needed them to want her and it made her feel complete when they succumbed to her charms. Marilyn equated sex with love and affection and so she sought it constantly.

Her mother had been an alcoholic and her very handsome father had abused her from the age of eleven. Even so, she had adored him and had confused his abuse with love. He'd been obsessed with his idol, Marilyn Monroe, and eventually left his wife and the fourteen-year-old Marilyn for another blonde Monroe lookalike. Ever since then Marilyn had modelled herself on the tragic star – same platinum hair, smile and flirtatious ways. She even had that same vulnerability that Monroe had had and this quality drew men to her just as they'd been drawn to the star. She lived in hope that her father would return and love her again.

It was quite sad, Taylor thought, but at least it hadn't stopped Marilyn enjoying life.

26

When Jazz arrived at the apartment in Frankfurt, Hans was so pleased to see her that she almost lost her nerve but gathering sher courage she did what she knew she had to do. He made coffee for them both and when they sat down she broke the news as gently as she could.

"Hans, I'm really sorry but being away has given me the time to think and I think we should call it quits."

"Have you met someone else?"

"Yes," she said, miserably, not wanting to lie to him. She reached out for his hand.

"Well, that's it then," he shrugged, pulling away from her and wrapping his hands around his coffee mug.

"We'll always be friends, I hope," she said gently. "You can stay on here until I return from Paris. That'll be no problem."

"Are you absolutely sure, Jazz? What if it doesn't work out with this guy?"

"Whether it does or not I'm afraid it's over for us."

"I'll miss you," he said glumly. "I honestly hope you know what you're doing."

She collected her things and, giving him a final hug, left for Munich. Driving along the autobahn, listening to Michael Bublé on the CD player, she knew she'd done the right thing finishing with Hans. It was time to move on.

Felicity was ever so excited about seeing her two girls again. She and Max had travelled across on the ferry from Calais to Dover so that they could pick Pippa up from her school in Kent, on their way up to London. They were outside the school, ready and waiting along with a lot of other parents, when all hell broke loose and 500 teenage girls erupted from its halls, whooping at the thought of the long half-term break. Pippa was one of the first out, long blonde hair flying, socks falling down her ankles, tie askew. In former times Felicity would have tut-tutted disapprovingly about her young daughter's state of dress but today she ignored all of this as she waited with growing excitement to hug her little girl.

As Pippa hurtled towards her, Felicity held her arms out but the young girl stopped dead in her tracks. Staring at her mother, her mouth open and eyes startled, she said, "Mummy, is that really you?"

"Yes, darling. Don't you like it?" Felicity became very apprehensive.

"Like it? I lovvve it. You look fantastic. Really cool!" She threw herself at Felicity who hugged her tightly.

God, she'd really missed her girls. She felt tears come to her eyes but was determined not to cry. Pippa would be mortified!

Max stood by beaming at them and then Pippa was hugging him too.

"Gosh, I couldn't wait for this weekend. I've really missed you both," the young girl said as she slung her bag in the trunk of the car. "And I'm dying to see Alex too. Tell me all about Paris. Mummy, you look fabulous, truly . . ." And so it went, all the way to London, Max and Felicity laughing at their youngest daughter's exuberance.

Alex was waiting for them at the house having come down from Cambridge the night before. They were touched to see that she had put flowers in the rooms and had stocked the fridge with food. She even had a bottle of champagne chilling.

She was equally amazed at the change in Felicity.

"Mummy, you look ten years younger," she said admiringly. "You look really chic."

Felicity smiled in delight at her daughter's words. "Thank you, Alex," she said. "I've really missed you and Pippa so much."

Max and her daughters stared at her in wonderment.

"Mummy, you just called us Alex and Pippa," Pippa said, stunned. All of their lives their mother had insisted on calling them Alexandra and Philippa, which they hated.

"Yes, well, it's time I called you what you like to be called," Felicity replied sheepishly.

"You'll be calling me Max next," her husband said laughing.

"And why not? If that's what you want."

"This calls for champagne," Max beamed, getting out the glasses.

Pippa was thrilled to be allowed one glass – her first ever.

"A toast," Max said. "To my lovely, chic wife!"

"*Merci,* Max," she replied, as they all laughed. This made the bubbles go up Pippa's nose and they laughed even harder.

Felicity smiled at the three people she loved most in the world and thought how lucky she was.

Her sister, Penny (no longer Penelope) came around that evening with her husband and another bottle of champagne was opened. There was a real party atmosphere as she told them all about Paris and the people she'd met there. They were amazed at the change in Felicity. When she told them that she was learning French and was starting a cordon bleu course in a week's time, they all congratulated her.

"I'm green with envy," Penny said, sighing.

"My God, Felicity, you went away a mouse and came back a lion," Penny's husband, Jeremy, who was nothing if not blunt, remarked.

"Jeremy!" Penny exclaimed, glaring at him, afraid that he might have hurt her sister's feelings.

"It's okay, Penny. He's right," Felicity smiled at him.

"Probably because you've got out from Mother's clutches," Penny remarked grimly. "She's very put out that you're not going to see her while you're home."

"That's too bad," Felicity said coolly. "I offered to go down tomorrow, but that doesn't suit her."

Alex and Pippa exchanged relieved looks. They dreaded visiting their grandmother as much as Felicity did. She tried to put them down at every turn too and they hated how she demoralised their mother.

"At last, she's standing up to the old bag," Alex whispered to her sister.

Taylor was exhausted. She just couldn't keep up with Marilyn. Where did the woman get her stamina? All the drinking and late nights were killing her and if it wasn't for the little white powder that Marilyn shared with her, she would never have stuck the pace.

They'd gone out to dinner at the Moulin Rouge with Louis and Christophe on Saturday night and she didn't know whether it was the sight of all that naked flesh or what, but the two men became very amorous as the evening wore on. Initially, they were both obviously rivals for Marilyn's attention but somewhere along the line, she had decided that Louis was the one for her. After copious bottles of champagne and wine, Louis invited them back to his apartment for some more.

Taylor wasn't too keen to go. She was tired.

"Come on girl," Marilyn beckoned her into the ladies' cloakroom.

Lining up some lines of coke, she snorted them and then laid out two lines for Taylor who'd become expert at it now.

"Honey, this is the last of my angel dust and Louis has promised me some more if we go back with them. Please, hon?"

Taylor, as the drug began to take effect, felt a rush of energy. She panicked at the thought that there might be no more cocaine left. It was what was keeping her going. She needed it desperately so she agreed to go along with them.

"Have you any cash?" Marilyn asked.

Taylor opened her purse and took out a wad of notes. There was 150 in it.

"Great, that'll do," Marilyn drawled, taking it from her.

"Where does he get it from?" Taylor wondered.

"Montmartre, I think. There's where all the drug dealers hang out."

Back at his place, Louis opened a bottle of champagne and then laid out some more lines of coke which they all snorted. Taylor felt wonderful – clearheaded and as light as air. This was great stuff! Marilyn and Louis were getting it off already and he had started to undress her. They moved to the bedroom.

"Come on, babe, let's join them?" Christophe said, as he slipped his hand inside her blouse.

Taylor panicked. This wasn't what she wanted. She didn't want to have sex with anybody. She hated sex. Grabbing her bag, she said, "I have to go."

"Don't be a spoilsport, honey," Marilyn called out. "Come on, join in!"

Running faster than a cyclist on the Tour de France, Taylor bolted from the apartment and hailed a taxi. Trembling with relief she arrived home. It was four o'clock in the morning.

She was still sleeping at noon the following day when Brandon opened the door to a very dishevelled Marilyn dressed in a low-cut cocktail dress that clung to her every curve. For a brief moment he could have sworn it was Marilyn Monroe at the door. Brushing against him as she passed she gave him a sexy look, then blew him a kiss and smiled as she wiggled her way into her bedroom. He sighed. The sooner *she* goes back the better.

He's so gorgeous, Marilyn thought as she showered before going to bed. She hadn't had much sleep the night before. Whew, these French guys were some studs! Still, she'd rather be in Brandon's bed any night of the week. Marilyn could hardly believe her luck when she received the phone call from her friend asking her to come to Paris. Taylor claimed she was bored. Can you imagine? I wouldn't be bloody bored if I was married to a gorgeous hunk like Brandon. Taylor was so spoiled. She had Brandon and oodles of money, was living in the most beautiful city in the world, but she still wasn't happy. She was bored! She was always whining on about her awful childhood. Huh! I could teach her a thing or two about awful childhoods! But what was the point dwelling on it? I wasn't going to let my parents ruin my life and I haven't.

Marilyn had been shocked when Taylor had admitted to her, early on in her marriage, that she hated having sex and intended to stop once her babies were born. Marilyn had thought that her friend was off her head. How could she not like sex? Taylor had stuck resolutely to her decision and Marilyn supposed that Brandon must have sought sex and solace elsewhere. Who could have blamed him? He was a young virile man and with his handsome good looks and irresistible sex-appeal, he would have had no trouble finding women willing to hop into bed with him. She'd hoped that maybe she'd stand a chance with him but despite letting Brandon know that she was available, he had shown no interest in her.

She hadn't seen much of him in the intervening years as he'd been busy carving out his illustrious career and she'd been busy marrying and divorcing her various husbands. She and Taylor had met often however, mostly at charity functions and from what she could gather, their marriage was a sham. Taylor was a fool. Seeing their relationship first-hand, Marilyn knew it was only a matter of time before they divorced and then she'd be there, ready and waiting to console him and offer him her shoulder to cry on. She was nothing if not opportunist. After all, Paris wasn't called the City of Love for nothing!

27

Meanwhile Ashling was enjoying a wonderful weekend. With Max gone, Kieran had no golf on Saturday and feeling guilty about the long hours he'd been working, suggested that they go to Versailles for the weekend. Ashling was delighted. Having heard how great it was from Felicity, she was very excited about the trip. They needed to spend some quality time together as a family. Besides, she wanted to see the very place that she was writing about every day in her novel. It would surely inspire her to walk in the selfsame salons and corridors of her characters. It was so exciting!

Kieran had booked them into the Trianon Palace Hotel, the most luxurious hotel in the region, and it was pure bliss. The girls were fascinated with their interconnecting room and their own phone on which they could ring their parents. The bathrooms were sheer decadence and all in all it was a great success.

There was so much to see that the kids were exhausted that evening. Ashling put them to bed at seven and, leaving them in the capable hands of the hotel baby-sitter, she and Kieran went for a meal in the beautiful dining room. It was a Gordon Ramsay restaurant and the food and wine were superb. She could see Kieran relaxing more and more by the minute.

"You're finding this job stressful, aren't you?" she asked him, as they waited for the dessert to be served.

"Very. You see, Ash, it's not like Dublin. Here I'm working with the crème-de-la-crème of the international banking world and I really feel I have to prove myself," he admitted. "Brandon is a genius and Max is pretty bright too. As for Jazz, she's the most exceptionally brilliant woman I've ever worked with, so you can understand how competitive it is."

Ashling patted his hand. She'd never heard him talk like this. He'd always been top dog in Ireland.

"So you see," he continued, "as I'm not in the genius category, I have to work even harder to come up to scratch. So please understand it if I'm not always home as early as you'd like."

Her heart went out to him and she cursed herself for being so selfish. The dessert trolley arrived just then and she had to restrain herself from choosing a bit of everything. She'd lost four more pounds and didn't want to ruin her diet.

She'd been delighted to see the Muscat de Beaumes de Venise dessert wine on the menu as she'd had it before and loved it. They'd ordered a glass each.

"Mmmm . . . delicious," Kieran remarked as he sipped it.

"I'm really looking forward to my wine course," she smiled at him over the rim of her glass.

"Soon you'll be an expert and leaving me way behind," Kieran teased.

"Yeah, I'm really looking forward to that," she laughed.

"Are you happy here, Ash?"

"Absolutely. I love Paris. It's all I expected it to be."

She still didn't tell him about her novel or about Corey. Somehow, it wasn't the right time. She didn't want to spoil the mood. They went to bed and made gentle love and she swore that she wouldn't complain any more about him overworking. He had enough to contend with.

Brandon was checking his bank accounts on Sunday afternoon and was shocked by how much Taylor had been spending. Not just on credit cards, but taking out of the wall too. 500 since last Tuesday! It was incredible. He would have to tackle her about it but their hours never seemed to match up any more. He was out at work all day and she was out gallivanting with Marilyn every night. She'd spent all day Saturday in bed and hadn't come in till four again this morning. She was now sleeping off the hangover that she more than likely had.

At two o'clock she surfaced looking like the Wrath of God. She came into the kitchen for a coffee and when he mentioned that he wanted a talk with her, she swore at him. "Not now, for God's sake. Do I look in a condition to talk?" she snarled.

"Self-inflicted," he couldn't resist saying.

She stormed out and, after taking two Vicodin, soaked in a warm bath for an hour. Then she snorted two lines of coke which made her feel much better and went down to face the music. God, how did I ever exist without cocaine? she asked herself. Marilyn was still sleeping.

"How can you be spending so much?" Brandon asked her after she'd mixed a martini for herself.

"Well, Marilyn is broke. That skinflint of a husband hasn't paid her any alimony recently, so as her friend, I have to help her out," she explained irritably.

"May I remind you that it is my hard-earned cash you're spending? I have no objection to supporting you in the grand style to which you're accustomed but I'll be damned if I'll support your friends as well," he said coldly.

She stuck her tongue out behind his back as he went to pour himself a coffee.

"And what's with all this drinking? My drinks bill must be in the hundreds this month with all the alcohol you two are consuming."

"Spoilsport," she said. "You're just jealous that we're having a good time."

He shook his head, perplexed. He was shocked as he saw her go to pour another martini for herself. It had only taken her five minutes to drink the first one.

Just then Marilyn surfaced, looking as bright as a new penny. How did she do it, he wondered? She had to be on something. She blew him a kiss as Taylor handed her a martini. This was their breakfast. It was going to be another long night of boozing, he guessed.

28

Ashling was thrilled when she stepped up on the scales on Monday morning. "Yyeeesss!" she cried. "One stone gone!" All her hard work dieting and in the gym had paid off. It felt so good to be able to fit comfortably into her jeans and skirts.

With a light heart and lighter body she skipped into the gym on Monday morning.

"Hi there, Ash!" Hugh greeted her. "You look hot, girl!"

Ashling laughed happily. "I've lost a stone to date," she told him.

"It shows, trust me," he eyed her appraisingly. "Okay, so we need to step up the workout now."

"Slavedriver!" she complained, but in fact she found it was getting easier every week. She was now running on the treadmill – and it was tilted!

She was glowing as she entered Les Deux Magots. She stopped by Corey's table and had a quick coffee with him. She felt energised and couldn't wait to get stuck into her novel once more. She actually missed her writing at the weekends and was always anxious to get back to it again. The characters in her novel had become her friends and she missed being away from them.

As she settled down to write she wondered how Jazz had got on in Frankfurt.

Corey meanwhile was admiring her as she tapped away. He'd

even found his writing had improved since he'd met her. She was his inspiration, his muse! He hoped her husband appreciated her.

Jazz looked strained after the weekend.

"How was Germany?" Brandon asked her.

"Fine," she replied, not very convincingly.

"You okay?" He looked at her sympathetically, sensing something was wrong.

"Just about," she replied with a grimace. "I finished with my boyfriend of thirteen years at the weekend, so I'm feeling a little sad."

"Why did you finish with him?" He guessed he knew the answer to that.

"I realised that I didn't love him enough to spend the rest of my life with him."

"There's someone else, isn't there?" he asked gently.

She nodded her head.

"Be careful, my dear. I don't want to see you get your heart broken."

The look in her eyes worried him. He wanted to protect her from Yves. She didn't deserve to be messed around and he had no doubt that she would end up hurt.

Yves came into the office just then. He looked rumpled and as if he hadn't slept all weekend. Jazz thought that he'd never looked more desirable.

This time he'd come prepared and he slipped her a note which said, 'Please meet me in l'Excelsior at lunchtime'. This was the bar around the corner.

She debated for about thirty seconds whether she should go or not but she knew that she would. She wanted to see him more than anything. She tried not to look at Brandon, not wanting to see the sympathy she knew would be in his eyes.

Yves was waiting for her when she came into the café. The look of relief on his face lifted her heart. She slid onto the banquette seat beside him.

"I was afraid you wouldn't come," he said, raking his hair with his hand. "Why didn't you contact me last Thursday? I was worried sick all weekend. I haven't been able to sleep. Did I do something to upset you?" He looked wretched.

Her heart melted.

Pulling her close he whispered, "I missed you so much."

She was lost. Looking into his smouldering eyes she was transported back in time. Her feelings for him were still the same. She should never have left Paris all those years ago. They might have been married by now with children if she hadn't run scared. They were meant to be, she was sure of that. The chemistry between them was electric. She knew he felt it too. She tried not to think of Sophie.

"Please meet me tonight?" he begged, after she'd ordered a sandwich and a coffee.

"Okay," she agreed, without hesitation. She wanted it as much as he did.

Felicity was hugely excited at having the girls in Paris. She found that she was enjoying their company enormously. They were thrilled with the apartment and ran from room to room exclaiming loudly at everything they saw. 'Cool' was the utmost compliment and she heard them say it frequently.

"I've been looking things up on the internet and I have a whole pile of things I want to do," Alex informed her on their first evening. Secretly, Felicity was happy that she'd dumped her boyfriend, Harry, so it would be just the four of them for the week. She'd had a major job persuading Pippa not to invite the whole of her class at school.

"You can bring two friends for the New Year," she'd promised her younger daughter.

Now, as they sat around the table on their first night, Felicity shared her plans for the week with them.

"I thought we'd have a girls' night on Thursday night," she told them excitedly, "so I've invited some of my friends for supper. Dad is going to disappear for the night." She smiled at Max.

"I *have* offered to play barman," he said, "but unfortunately, it's strictly girls only."

They could see from the way he was beaming at Felicity that he was okay with it.

Brandon sighed with relief to find that Marilyn was out for the night. "I presume she's met some poor sucker who's been taken in by her charms," he remarked sarcastically to Taylor, who was sitting nursing a martini when he came in.

"Don't be so mean," she glared at him.

There was no sign of any dinner in sight so he went into the kitchen where Mimi had left a beef stroganoff ready for reheating. She'd also set the table with three places.

"Are you eating with me?" he asked Taylor.

"No, I'm not hungry, you go ahead," she replied, as she poured herself another martini.

"Taylor, you have to eat," he said with concern.

"I'm not hungry."

Come to think of it, he thought, as he ate his dinner, I haven't seen her eat anything much lately. He wondered if it was because she was burning the candle at both ends. She seemed to be surviving on alcohol. He'd have to keep an eye on her and make sure she was eating. Bloody Marilyn! She wasn't helping matters. He would have to do something about her. She couldn't stay indefinitely with them. She'd have to find a place of her own.

Coming back into the living room, he poured himself a whisky and sat down opposite his wife. She seemed listless.

"Taylor, do you know how long Marilyn is planning on staying?" he asked.

"Dunno."

"She can't stay here indefinitely. I think two weeks is quite long enough to put somebody up. If she wants to stay in Paris longer she'll have to find a place of her own," he said, trying not to sound too hostile.

"You're cruel," Taylor cried, spilling her drink as she rushed from the room, stifling her sobs.

Lord, I can't even have a conversation with her any more, he thought, a worried frown on his face. Sighing, he sipped his drink and turned on the television.

Taylor came in thirty minutes later, in her dressing gown, and she seemed like a different person. She mixed herself another martini and sitting down opposite him said, "Okay, I'll talk to Marilyn about moving out."

He was mystified. She appeared to have had a personality change. She was bright-eyed and lively. He couldn't understand it. Not for the first time he wondered if she was taking something. He would have to keep a closer eye on her from now on.

Jazz arrived at the hotel where Yves was waiting in the room for her. She fell into his arms. The world fell away and all she cared about was being with him. He was like a drug, a drug she couldn't give up. She was transported with love and pleasure. When they made love it was very intense and even better than the last time. They didn't talk very much but kept whispering sweet nothings to each other. It was sheer bliss and she could barely bring herself to say goodbye when it came time for them to leave. She hoped he felt the same way but she couldn't say.

Yves was fascinated by her. There was something mysterious beneath her surface that he couldn't fathom. She spoke little which came as a surprise. Most women he bedded never stopped talking. She was different to any woman he'd ever known. She gave herself so freely, holding nothing back and he revelled in her body which was so soft and voluptuous. He would have liked nothing better than to have stayed with her till morning, making love to her again and again, but there was no way he could stay out all night.

As it was, he knew Sophie guessed that he had a new mistress. She must not suspect that it was Jazz. They had an open marriage but there were limits. They'd both agreed that they could have other partners but somehow he knew that that didn't include friends or people they both knew. Sophie would not be happy if she thought that Jazz was his latest conquest.

"Wednesday, same time?" he asked, showering tiny kisses on her face and neck.

She nodded silently, her eyes closed in pleasure. She didn't know how she could wait over forty hours to be in his arms again. But she had no choice.

29

On Tuesday night, as Taylor and Marilyn were polishing off another couple of bottles of wine and a few lines of cocaine, Brandon was savouring the delectable Chantal. She was the perfect mistress. Her face lit up when he handed her the bottle of Chanel No. 5 perfume he'd bought for her.

"You don't 'ave to bring me present," she smiled at him. "Is enough you come."

He loved her quirky English and her cute accent. She came into his arms and he nuzzled her neck. She smelled so clean and fresh. Her blonde hair felt like silk and her skin like velvet. She was too good to be true. Simple and uncomplicated, she wanted him for sex and nothing more. He was more than happy to oblige. There would be no messy emotional demands from her. "I love my 'usband. I very 'appy with 'im," she'd said, laying her cards on the table the very first night they'd made love. He had no problem with that. They agreed they would meet in future on every Monday and Thursday night. It was a perfect arrangement for both of them.

The following night Marilyn was getting dolled up to meet Louis. Taylor was sitting on her bed watching as she primped and preened herself. She envied Marilyn's lush curvy body and sexiness. No wonder men were so crazy for her.

"Can you ask Louis for some more cocaine?" she asked her friend, handing her 200.

"Honey, you ain't used up all the last stuff he gave you, have you?" Marilyn asked her in a shocked voice.

"Yeah, well, I was feeling down at the weekend," Taylor admitted.

"Well, I'd go easy on it honey, if I were you. It's pretty addictive. But I'll get some more from Louis for you, if you want," she added, seeing Taylor's desperate look. Pocketing the 200, she decided that she'd have to keep an eye on Taylor's consumption of cocaine. She wouldn't want that on her conscience!

Marilyn didn't come home that night and when she hadn't come back by two o'clock the following day, Taylor was in a panic. She had finished all the coke and she desperately needed more. She couldn't think straight without it. She'd gone to the two American doctors and they'd both given her a prescription for Vicodin and Valium so she was okay on that score. Of course Marilyn had no idea that she was consuming them as well as the coke.

She left umpteen voicemails on Marilyn's phone but still her friend didn't contact her.

At around four o'clock Marilyn sailed in, as cool as a cucumber. Taylor was furious with her.

"Why didn't you answer my calls?" she demanded.

"Hey, honey," Marilyn drawled, "don't get your knickers in a knot. I was havin' *the* most fantastic sex of my life with Louis. You didn't expect me to stop mid-orgasm, did you?" She laughed uproariously.

The image of her doing that made Taylor laugh too. "Did you get the coke?" she asked then, nervously.

"Sure did, hon, but you better make this last longer than the last lot. This stuff's damn expensive." She rolled her eyes to heaven.

Taylor grabbed the sachet from her and swiftly lined up the powder. Inhaling deeply, she felt the rush of blood to her head. She relaxed visibly then and poured them both a glass of wine.

"Brandon was wondering how long you're thinking of staying in Paris, sweetie." She looked at Marilyn.

"Well, hon, that depends," Marilyn winked. "The way things are goin' I reckon I'll be movin' in with Louis before long."

Taylor felt a little put out. After all, it was she who had invited Marilyn to Paris in the first place.

"Don' worry, chicken. Even if I move in with him, we'll still see each other all the time."

Somewhat mollified, Taylor thought that maybe it was for the best. At least it would get Brandon off her back.

"That would be great. When do you think it'll happen?"

"I guess if I play my cards right it could be any day now." Marilyn winked again.

Poor Louis, Taylor thought. He'll be a wreck by the time she's finished with him.

30

Ashling started her wine course on Thursday morning and from the beginning loved every moment of it. For the hundredth time she thanked her lucky stars that she'd studied French for all those years. There were ten students on the course and they ranged in age from seventeen to seventy. What a mix! It was fascinating.

It was a ten-week course and each week would have two hours of theory and then an hour of tasting. The first week they learnt all about the grape varieties grown in France and she was amazed at the sheer number of them. To think that they used thirteen different varieties in Châteauneuf-du-Pâpe – a wine she loved and one that was hugely popular in Ireland – was incredible.

The lecturer, François, a young man about her own age, was wildly enthusiastic and she found herself being caught up in his enthusiasm. Her brain was practically scrambled after the theory session as she tried to remember all that he'd said. She'd taken lots of notes so she'd be able to study them afterwards.

The tasting session was an eye-opener and she agreed with François that she'd never be able to take a sip of wine again without analysing it. It was hugely enjoyable and they all laughed when he told them that their homework would be to open a different bottle of wine every evening for the coming week.

"No problem there!" Ashling said, to the amusement of the other students.

There was another Irish girl, Nessa, on the course and she and Ashling naturally gravitated to each other. After the class, they went for a coffee together.

"My head is swimming," Nessa laughed. "I need to sober up before I collect Cian from crèche." Cian was her three-year-old son.

"I have a couple of hours yet before I collect my girls, thank goodness," Ashling laughed with her.

"We *are* supposed to spit the wines out," Nessa remarked.

"No way! And waste all that delicious wine?" Ashling cried.

"I didn't notice anyone else using the spittoons either."

"No, they've got more sense." They both roared laughing.

All in all it was a very successful morning.

Pippa and Alex were having a wonderful time and adored Paris as much as Felicity did now. She was bonding with the girls more than she ever had and the three of them had some great giggles. She felt proud showing them around and secretly delighted at their amazement that she could even speak a little French.

"Mum, you're a revelation!" Alex cried.

"Yeah, you've morphed into a really cool mum," Pippa added.

God, was I such an ogress before, she wondered.

She took the girls shopping and even liked the clothes they were choosing. This was a first. She normally hated anything they liked. They grinned at each other, hardly able to believe it but not complaining. However, Felicity drew the line when Pippa wanted to have a tattoo.

"No, young lady, not until you're eighteen! Then you can decide for yourself."

"Cool," Pippa said, winking at Alex. She couldn't wait for her eighteenth birthday!

They were wearing their new gear on Thursday as they waited for the party to begin. Felicity had invited all the girls and of course that included Taylor. She was secretly relieved when Taylor called that afternoon to cancel. She'd become very strange lately. To tell the truth Felicity was beginning to dread her phone calls. She ranted on at times and Felicity often found it difficult to understand her. No, it was much better that she wouldn't be there.

Jazz was the first to arrive and the girls thought she was ultra-cool. Ashling was next and then Sophie, looking as chic as usual. The girls were very impressed with her and thought Ashling was a sweetheart. Jazz was a little uneasy to be in Sophie's company. She hadn't met her in ages and had purposely changed her gym times so as to avoid her but Sophie was as friendly as ever, which made Jazz feel dreadfully guilty.

They all thought Felicity's two girls were adorable and found them to be exuberant and full of fun.

"We can't believe how much Mum has changed since coming to Paris," Alex confided to Ashling.

"She's super cool now and she looks brill," Pippa chimed in enthusiastically.

"We can't believe that she's learning French."

"And that she loves it," Pippa said, with wonder.

Ashling was very proud of her friend and beamed with pleasure on hearing that her daughters approved.

Felicity had also invited Nicole – her French teacher and Ashling's baby-sitter – so that Alex and Pippa could meet her. The three young girls were getting on like a house on fire.

Despite what she'd said, Felicity had asked Max to prepare margaritas for everyone before he got out of their way and they went down a treat. Even Pippa was allowed have a diluted version, wrinkling her nose up as she tasted the salt on the rim of the glass.

"Yuck! Disgusting!" she exclaimed, but still she sipped it and was a little tiddley after it.

Alex and Nicole laughed at her, feeling very superior at the grand old age of eighteen!

As usual, Felicity had prepared a fantastic spread.

"My diet will be ruined," Ashling wailed.

"Nonsense, you can get back down to it tomorrow," Felicity said, matter of factly, handing her a laden plate.

They had a really fun night and when Max came in to say

goodnight he found them all a little giggly and having a great time. He was very proud of his wife.

Nicole was taking the girls out to meet her friends on Friday night. They couldn't wait.

"I think it was a big success," Felicity murmured to Max as she lay cuddled in his arms later.

"It certainly was, if all the laughter and giggling was anything to go by," he replied.

But she didn't hear him. She was fast asleep.

Pippa and Alex had a wonderful night out with Nicole and her friends. They were a big hit with the French boys who loved their English accents. They left, promising to join them on Facebook and to keep in touch.

They took the Eurostar back to London on Sunday where Felicity's sister, Penny, was meeting them. They were desperately sad leaving Paris and hugged Felicity and Max tight as they said goodbye. Felicity couldn't keep the tears in check as she waved goodbye to her babies. Thank God she was starting her cordon bleu course the following day or she'd have been totally miserable without them.

"I've never enjoyed a week so much," she said to Max, as they drove back home.

He smiled. Neither had he and it was all because of her change of attitude. Gone was the nervy woman, always harping at the girls and in its place was this much more relaxed person who was fun to be with. The girls certainly had enjoyed themselves too and couldn't get over the change in their mother. Felicity barely slept a wink all night, so excited and apprehensive was she about starting her cordon bleu course the next morning.

She arrived at the school at eight and was very impressed and not a little intimidated by it all. There were about twenty-five other students in the class and most of them were in their twenties, she guessed. There were two other women about her age there, and two men who looked to be in their forties. She was so glad that she'd had that makeover the week before last. She'd have felt a frump with her old hairstyle and her old mumsy clothes. She was surprised to see that there were more males than females there, but then all the best chefs in the world were men, weren't they? The students appeared to be a very diverse bunch from all corners of the globe but she was pleased to note that everyone was speaking English. Thank God for that!

They were welcomed by the director who explained the syllabus to them. It appeared very daunting but Felicity was determined to make a go of it. It had cost a lot of money and she wanted to prove to Max that it was money well spent. Everything about the school was ultra-professional and she was delighted when she was given her chef's hat and apron which she would have to wear at all times.

She and the two older women gravitated to each other and sat together for the first class. Sue was American and Becky was English, from London too. She was delighted to make their acquaintance. They had lunch together and she discovered that Becky was a widow and planned to open her own catering company back in London while Sue's husband was a diplomat and she was doing the course as she had a lot of social entertaining to do.

The day flew by and Felicity was exhausted by four but she knew she was going to love it. Thank God she'd had the courage to go for it.

31

Taylor had been very anxious for Marilyn to meet Felicity.

"Her father is Lord Delmere and they have a magnificent estate in England," she boasted. "She really is awfully posh. Wait till you hear her talk. She sounds just like the Queen."

Marilyn didn't like the sound of her one bit!

Taylor had rung Felicity two weeks ago to invite her and Max to lunch on the Sunday and had been very put out to hear that Felicity was going back to the UK collect her daughters. Then when she'd called and asked her to come last Sunday, she couldn't, because her daughters were leaving for London. Bloody children! They were nothing but a nuisance, Taylor thought angrily.

"Back to visit the estate?" she'd asked Felicity, hoping to impress Marilyn.

"Not exactly," Felicity had mumbled.

"Well, I have my best friend here from New York and I'm simply dying for you to meet her. How about coming shopping with us on Friday and we'll do lunch," Taylor said, enticingly.

"I'm dreadfully sorry, Taylor, but I've started my cordon bleu course and it's from eight till four every day, so shopping is out of the question."

"Can't you take a day off?"

"Definitely not." Felicity almost laughed at the suggestion.

"Well, maybe some evening then?"

"To be honest, I'm so bushed every evening that I'm only fit for bed."

"Oh, I see." Taylor was getting the feeling Felicity didn't want to meet her at all. "She's doing a cordon bleu course," she explained in an aside to Marilyn.

Marilyn rolled her eyes to heaven. The only cordon bleu cooking she knew about was what she ate in the fancy restaurants she frequented. She, like Taylor, didn't *do* cooking and knew that Felicity would most definitely *not* be her type.

"Well, how about lunch the following Sunday then?" Taylor wouldn't be deterred. "And Max is invited too, naturally," she added.

"That would be lovely, Taylor," Felicity gave in.

Her friend was acting very weirdly. She thought she detected a slight slurring of her words. She'd been that way at Kieran's party too. She wondered if Taylor had a drink problem. God love her, she thought charitably, I do hope not.

Felicity wasn't telling a lie when she'd said she was bushed every evening. Nothing had prepared her for the intensity of the course and all the information that she had to take in. Of course, as Sue and Becky agreed, it had been a long time since they had all been students so naturally it was more difficult for them than the youngsters. Felicity was relieved to hear that the other two women found it difficult also. It wasn't just her. And she loved it – loved every minute of it! She fell into bed after dinner and slept like a baby till the alarm went off at six thirty the next morning. Max assured her that she'd get used to it and that it would get easier with time. She hoped so. She was also having her French classes with Nicole two evenings a week. She didn't want to give them up as she felt she was improving rapidly.

Ashling and Jazz had both rung her to see how she'd got on at the course. It was so nice of them. She'd also received a Good Luck card from the two girls where they wrote that they were very proud of her. This touched her and she shed a few tears over it. She was so looking forward to their next trip in November.

Now she was sorry she'd accepted Taylor's invitation. She'd

really much rather put her feet up on Sunday afternoon and watch a film. Still, she had to keep a social life going or she'd have no friends left. She hoped Ashling and Jazz would be there.

When Taylor had mooted the lunch party to Brandon, he'd been surprised.

"We'll invite Felicity and Max. Actually I've already invited them. Yves and Sophie, Jazz and that Australian friend of hers . . ."

Brandon blanched. "You haven't invited them already?" he demanded.

"No," she replied, surprised at his vehemence.

"Thank God. Who else were you thinking of?"

"Well, I suppose we have to have the Irish here . . ."

"You mean Ashling and Kieran?" he glared at her.

"Well, they did have us to his birthday party," she said reluctantly, "and Marilyn and Louis."

He didn't ask who Louis was but could guess. It didn't matter. But at all costs he had to avoid having Jazz, Yves and Sophie at the same table. The thought of it made him break out in a cold sweat.

"That's too many," he told her. "Let's keep it to eight. We can invite 'the Irish', as you call them, another time – and as far as I know Jazz is going to Germany at the weekend." This was an outright lie. "We can have her with Ashling and Kieran another time."

Taylor was relieved. Jazz was too glamorous by half and for sure Marilyn would make a play for the Australian hunk. No, best to do as Brandon suggested.

"Okay, that's decided then," she smiled.

He wiped his brow. Phew, that was close!

Jazz rang Ashling on Saturday. "Are you going to Taylor's lunch tomorrow?" she asked her.

"Didn't even know she was having one. Are you going?"

"No. Brandon mentioned it and I think he was a little embarrassed about it but maybe it's for the best as Yves and Sophie are going."

Ashling couldn't have agreed with her more. "Why don't you

come around to us for lunch tomorrow? Kieran is taking the girls to the circus in the afternoon. I hate circuses so we can have the afternoon to ourselves."

"Thanks, I'd like that," Jazz replied. She'd declined to go out with Hugh and the gang. She just didn't feel up to all that jollity.

"Come around twelve," Ashling told her.

32

Ashling was shocked to see that Jazz had lost weight and had dark circles under her eyes.

"Are you okay?" she asked after greeting her. "You look stressed."

"Yeah, well, I'm not sleeping and I'm not eating. Love is great for dieting!" she laughed hollowly.

God, love is not very good if does this to you, Ashling wanted to say, but of course she didn't.

Jazz wanted to talk about Yves all day. She really has it bad, Ashling thought, her heart aching for her friend. She was surprised to hear that they were meeting almost every night.

"I don't see Sophie at the school any more," she told Jazz. "She's back working full-time. Do you think she knows about you and Yves?"

"I've no idea." Jazz didn't want to talk about Sophie or even think about her. The guilt and shame would be too much.

To change the subject, Ashling told her about the novel she was writing.

"Gosh, that's great, Ash. You'll be famous!"

"I don't think so," Ashling laughed. "It's not easy getting published but I do love it."

"I wondered what you did with your days, you dark horse!"

Ashling was tempted to tell her about Corey but she didn't. He was still *her* secret.

"Please don't mention it to anyone. I haven't even told Kieran yet," she admitted.

Meanwhile, Brandon was welcoming his guests. Taylor, as always, fawned over Felicity. "My God, you look fantastic," she gushed, stunned by the change in her. "I can't wait for my friend Marilyn to meet you."

"You look lovely, my dear," Brandon said, kissing her. He too was taken aback by the change in her. She looked downright chic!

Felicity was surprised to see that neither Jazz nor Ashling had been invited. She was disappointed and wondered why they hadn't been.

Yves and Sophie were the next to arrive followed closely by Marilyn and Louis.

"Hello, everyone," Taylor clapped her hands. "I'd like you to meet my friend, Marilyn."

There was a stunned silence in the room as everyone stared at the vision before them. For a brief moment they all thought that it was the ghost of Marilyn Monroe. She was wearing an identical white halter dress to the one Monroe wore in that famous picture of hers with her skirt blowing up. Brandon half expected her skirt to blow up around her hips any moment. Now *that* would have caused a sensation. Thank God it didn't!

"Hi, everyone," Marilyn drawled, her glossy red lips arranged in a Monroesque pout.

Introductions were made all around and Brandon took an instant dislike to Louis. His tan was too orange, his suit too shiny and his long black hair too oiled. He was obviously wealthy, judging from the diamonds and gold he wore, but then Marilyn wouldn't have been with him if he wasn't. He couldn't keep his hands off her. The poor fool was obviously besotted with her. This didn't stop her zooming in on Yves whose dark Latin looks clearly attracted her. She flirted outrageously with him and he, recognising a fellow sex-lover when he saw one, played along with her. Brandon hoped that they'd get it together and that he'd leave Jazz alone.

As she'd expected, Marilyn found Felicity boring. Ditto Max and Sophie. Yves was something else and she knew that she'd be seeing him again. He slipped her his phone number on the quiet. "Call me, please," he'd whispered in her ear. She sure would!

Sophie was very quiet today, Brandon noticed, and things seemed a little strained between herself and Yves. He wondered if she knew about Jazz. What a mess, he thought, not for the first time.

The lunch went with a bang. Mimi had worked all day yesterday and again this morning, cooking a delicious meal. Taylor hadn't lifted a finger to help. She even got Mimi to serve it up, afraid that she'd make a mess of it. Brandon was surprised that she seemed in such high spirits. She'd been moping around the house all week, probably because Marilyn was spending so much time with Louis. Thank God for that!

Over coffee, Marilyn announced that she would be moving in with Louis, the following day. The poor fool looked delighted but not half as delighted as Brandon was.

He noticed that Taylor had disappeared after that and when she hadn't come back after twenty minutes, he asked Marilyn if she'd seen her.

"I'll go find her," she offered.

Going into Taylor's bedroom she caught her friend in the act of popping a Vicodin into her mouth.

"What are you doing?" she asked, grabbing Taylor by the wrist. She took the bottle of Vicodin from her.

"Are you crazy?" Marilyn cried. "Do you know how addictive these are? They can kill you if you're takin' 'em with cocaine. It's a lethal mix. Oh, Taylor! If I'd known you were on these I'd never have given you coke!"

"I can handle them," Taylor replied haughtily. "I'm just taking them for my headaches."

Marilyn now understood how her friend got so high so quickly. She'd been taking a cocktail of drugs, on top of all the alcohol they'd been drinking.

"Taylor, you gotta stop! What you're doin' is dangerous." Just then, to her horror, she spotted a bottle of Oxycontin on Taylor's bedside table. "My Gawd, are you taking them too?"

Taylor wrenched her hand away from Marilyn's. "Leave me alone. I know what I'm doing. Go back to the party." She went into the bathroom and banged the door after her.

Marilyn didn't know what to do. Taylor needed help. Should she say something to Brandon? Taylor would never forgive her if she did. But if anything happened to her friend, Marilyn would never forgive herself. One thing was sure, there'd be no more cocaine going her way.

Brandon saw Marilyn returning. "Is she okay?"

"She's fine," she lied, looking at him bleakly. "She'll be back shortly."

Brandon didn't know what had transpired in Taylor's room but when Taylor returned he noticed the tension between the pair of them. Marilyn left shortly afterwards with Louis, and Taylor seemed in good spirits again.

33

Felicity was enjoying herself enormously. She hadn't actually learnt to cook anything yet but was learning all about the basics of French cuisine. On Monday morning they had to be in at half past six as they were being taken to the market where the chefs from all the top restaurants in Paris were jostling together for the wonderful fresh produce on offer. As usual, she had teamed up with Sue and Becky and with the two older men on the course – Giles who was Moroccan and Jean who was French. They formed a merry group as their instructor pointed out what they should look for when shopping. It was an eye-opener and by the time they'd finished at nine, they went into a market café where the smell of croissants and freshly brewed coffee was tantalising. Felicity ate twice as much as she usually did. All this studying was giving her an appetite and she was gaining weight, much to Max's delight. He'd always thought she was too skinny.

"Gosh, what will I be like when we start cooking food and tasting it?" she remarked to the others.

"You'll be lovely," Jean said gallantly, which made her blush.

"It's all right for you," Sue moaned. "You could do with a few extra pounds. I'm already overweight."

"Me too," Becky chimed in. "You're so slim, Felicity."

Felicity blushed again. She'd never received so many compliments.

She was having a simply wonderful time. She felt like a new person. Cooking was her passion and she was now with others who understood and shared that passion. Nothing could burst her bubble.

Jazz met Yves at lunchtime again. She couldn't stay away.

"I missed you so much, *chérie*," he said, holding her close. They'd decided to meet in a café further away just in case they ran into anyone from the office in l'Excelsior.

He stood up to greet her and kissed her deeply, pressing her body close to his. "I missed you," she whispered huskily, desire bubbling up inside her. If he'd asked her to go to their hotel with him right there and then, she would have. It was outside her control. She needed him so badly. They arranged to meet there after work and it took her all of her willpower to concentrate on her work that afternoon. No matter how much she wanted to be with him, her work was of paramount importance. She knuckled down to it.

She'd asked Brandon that morning how the lunch party had gone.

"Okay," he'd said without much enthusiasm, so she hadn't enquired further. "Felicity looked fantastic," he added. "I think she was disappointed that you and Ashling weren't there."

She was dying to ask how Yves had been but didn't dare.

"Sophie looked very strained," he volunteered, watching her for a reaction.

He got it. Her head shot up like a whip.

"How do you mean?" she asked, her heart in her mouth.

"Well, there seemed to be a lot of tension between herself and Yves."

Oh, God, she thought, putting her head in her hands. This is not what I want. I don't want her to be hurt.

Brandon pretended not to notice and lifted his phone to ring someone while she turned back to her computer, quaking inside.

Sophie was Yves's problem and if he didn't mention her then Jazz wouldn't either but she wondered where Sophie thought he was spending all his evenings. She must suspect that he had a new mistress. Please God she won't find out it's me, Jazz thought guiltily.

Marilyn called for her things and when she had packed everything up she sat down for a last drink with Taylor.

"Honey, please listen to me," she said, her Texan drawl much more obvious when she was upset, as she was now. "You are dicing with death here. Coke is fine but not when taken with Vicodin or Oxycontin. You'll shatter your liver, honey, if . . . if you don't kill yourself. I won't get you any more cocaine, Taylor. You have to stop." She took Taylor's hands in hers. "Promise me you'll ease up, honey, please?"

"Okay," Taylor nodded. Anything to stop this sermonising!

"Honey, I have to go. My taxi is waiting outside. You know where I am if you ever need me. Anyway, I'll call you tomorrow." She kissed Taylor and hugged her tight before going downstairs to summon the taxi driver to come and collect all six of her Louis Vuitton cases. (She'd arrived with five but with all the purchases in Paris, it was now six!)

When she'd left, Taylor poured another glass of wine and, curling up in the armchair, wrapped her arms around her ever-more-skinny frame. She was losing weight fast but she just couldn't face food any more. Tears rolled down her face. She knew Marilyn was right but she just couldn't face life without her pills. She'd cut back, honestly she would, she decided as she brought the half bottle of wine closer to her.

Ashling and Corey had decided to make their weekly excursions on a Tuesday as many museums were closed on Mondays. So, on Tuesday morning she met up with him in Les Deux Magots for their first museum outing. Even Remy smiled and wished them good luck as they left. She felt like a naughty schoolgirl playing truant from school. Ashling had decided that Napoleon's tomb at Les Invalides was to be their first port of call. It was fascinating and stunning and she discovered that Corey was as big a fan of Napoleon as she was.

"May I invite you to a special lunch, in honour of our first exploratory trip?" he asked when they'd finished, his dazzling smile lighting up his face.

"Why thank you," she replied shyly. "I'd be delighted to accept."

They walked across the Seine chatting companionably. He was a very imposing figure and she saw many women turn to look at him. She wondered how old he was. With his silver hair and beard it was very hard to judge but his skin was fresh and unlined.

"I feel honoured to be escorting such a beautiful young woman to lunch," he remarked. "Everyone is wondering how an old geezer like me could possibly have managed it." He laughed heartily, throwing back his head as he did so.

"How old are you, Corey?" she felt brave enough to ask, now that he had brought up the subject.

"Too old," he replied. "I'll be fifty-four next July."

"That's not so old," she replied honestly.

"Thank you, sweet lady," he smiled at her.

"I'm almost thirty-three," she grinned. "Same age as Jesus when he died."

He roared laughing at that, loving the way she volunteered her age so freely. Most women absolutely refused to tell their age until they got into their mid-eighties, when they started boasting about it.

They walked through the beautiful Place de la Concorde into the Place Vendôme and, with a shock, Ashling realised that he was taking her to the Ritz. She'd always wanted to visit it and when Felicity had described how fantastic it was, she'd promised herself that she'd go there one day, if only for a coffee. I mean, how much could they charge for a cup of coffee! She had been a huge fan of Princess Diana and she recalled the last photos of her going through the revolving doors, not knowing she was going to her death, and she felt sad.

The hotel was so opulent that it took her breath away.

The doorman saluted them. "Welcome back, Mr Corey."

Ashling was puzzled. Why hadn't he said Mr Danz?

They walked down the luxurious corridor and into the grandiose restaurant. It was magnificent.

Just then a very attractive blonde, another diner, came up to him. She spoke with an American accent.

"Mr Corey, I can't tell you how much I enjoy your books," she simpered. "I wonder could I possibly have your autograph?"

"Of course," he replied graciously, signing the menu she held out to him.

Ashling was puzzled. "Mr Corey?" she said, enquiringly.

"Yes. I write under the pseudonym Dan Corey."

"Oh, my God. You're not Dan Corey?" she cried in horror, bringing her hands to her mouth.

"No, I'm Corey Danz but my readers know me as Dan Corey," he said, laughing at her confusion.

"Why didn't you tell me? I've read all of your books. You're very famous!"

She felt foolish. All this time and she hadn't realised that he was the best-selling author Dan Corey. She blushed with embarrassment.

"I'm sorry if I didn't say anything, Ashling, but I prefer to be just Corey Danz to you. Now what are we going to eat?" he asked her, handing her the menu. "Champagne to drink, I think, to celebrate our first outing." He called the waiter.

She took her time reading the menu, trying to get back her equilibrium. She was having lunch with Dan Corey, one of the most successful authors in the world. Just imagine it. But no, she told herself, he wants to be himself and to me he'll be plain Corey Danz, my friend. She gave him a dazzling smile as she told him she'd like the scallops, followed by roast duck.

"Thank God, no salad today," he exclaimed, breaking into a hearty laugh. "I was beginning to fear you were a rabbit disguised as a beautiful woman, come to lure me away."

She pealed with laughter at the idea.

The sommelier arrived just then with their champagne. When he'd poured it Corey raised his glass and said, "To my beautiful Irish colleen and to many more lovely outings like today. Thank you. I haven't enjoyed myself so much in years."

"Neither have I," she replied and she meant it, truly.

Sophie knew that Yves was having an affair. When she asked him about it, he admitted it. She knew Yves needed to have other women besides her. They had an open marriage and it had worked perfectly well up until now. But something was different about this one. Before, he would meet his mistresses for an hour or two, once or twice a week, but this time he was staying out later and almost every night. When she asked him who it was he was seeing, he wouldn't say and this worried her even more.

He seemed distracted all the time and hadn't wanted to make love to her in over a week. That in itself was very unusual. There was nothing she could do about it except sit and wait it out until he grew tired of the lady in question, as he always did. Still, she had an uneasy feeling inside and it scared her.

After her wonderful day out with Corey, Ashling decided that she would have to tell Kieran about her new friend. She planned to tell him that night. She felt apprehensive about it which was silly as he was very much just a friend and she had nothing to be ashamed of. Still, she wasn't sure Kieran would understand that. Men were funny about their wives having male friends, unless they were gay of course, which Corey patently wasn't. She prepared a nice meal for Kieran and wrote another five hundred words of her novel when the phone rang.

"Hello, darling, it's me."

"Kieran, where are you? It's almost nine thirty."

"Well, we had a bit of a crisis here this afternoon and Max and I have had to stay on here working to sort it out. Sorry, babe, but I'll hardly make it by midnight. You go on to bed."

She sighed. "Well, I'll leave your dinner on the stove and you can heat it up when you come in."

"Don't worry. We've ordered in a pizza. See you in the morning. Love you."

Before she could respond, he had hung up.

"Some marriage this is," she said aloud, as she went to turn off the Irish stew he loved so much.

She wrote another five hundred words, pleased with the way it was going and at eleven o'clock closed her computer and with a yawn went up to bed. So much for telling Kieran about Corey! She'd also planned to tell him about her novel.

Well, it would have to wait for another day.

34

Marilyn was making love to Louis on Thursday evening when Taylor rang.

"Marilyn, can you get some more coke from Louis for me?" she asked. Her voice sounded desperate.

"Honey, I told you, as long as you're takin' all that other stuff, I can't give you more coke. It would be on my conscience, darlin'."

Taylor hung up on her.

"Who was that?" Louis wanted to know.

"It was Taylor, lookin' for more coke," she sighed.

"She surely hasn't finished the last lot I gave her? And what other stuff is she taking?"

When Marilyn told him he did a backflip.

"You're kidding me? She's crazy. She'll kill herself."

"I know," Marilyn said, bending over and putting her head in her hands. "I've told her she has to cut back or at least not take a cocktail of drugs. I dunno if she'll listen. What can I do?"

"What about Brandon? Does he know?"

"No, an' she'll kill me if I tell him."

Now he was really worried. After all he'd been the one to supply her with the cocaine. "This is too dangerous, *chérie*. We cannot be involved any more. You have to tell her that."

"Okay. I'll do it tomorrow," Marilyn assured him, as she pulled him to her to renew their lovemaking.

Taylor was desperate. She needed a fix. The Vicodin and Oxycontin were not enough any more. She needed coke to clear her head. Some friend Marilyn was turning out to be!

Where is she when I need her? Taylor asked herself bitterly. Well, I don't need her. I'll score my own coke!

Getting dressed, she took 300 from the safe and stuffed it in her bag. Out of habit she put her credit-card holder in her pants pocket. Brandon had drummed it into her never to keep her credit cards and cash together.

Slipping out, she headed to Montmartre, where Marilyn had said Louis got his stuff. It was after ten but with any luck she'd be there and back within the hour and before Brandon got home. He was out every Monday and Thursday night, usually until midnight, so she had plenty of time.

She hailed a cab. When she asked to go to Montmartre, the cab driver raised his eyebrows. He spoke English and tried to engage her in conversation but she didn't oblige.

"Better be careful here, madame," the cab driver advised, as he let her out at the Place Pigalle. "It is no place at night for a lady on her own."

"Oh, mind your own fucking business!" she said, getting out of the cab.

She stood on the pavement, looking around. The place was heaving. Within seconds a guy had approached her. This is easy, she thought. I should have asked the cab to wait for me.

"You want a little action, lady?" the stranger asked. "I got all the equipment and can go all night long, if you want," he said, pushing his crotch forward towards her.

"Go away," she cried, pushing past him.

"Huh ho, you prefer some girly action, is that it?" he leered at her and waved at a girl close by.

The very attractive black girl came forward and, standing in front of Taylor, opened her coat. She was wearing only a thong and

190

stockings. Taylor was shocked. "I please you better than any man," the girl purred.

"No, no," Taylor cried, breaking into a run. This place was so awful. It had looked glamorous the night she'd been at the Moulin Rouge with Marilyn and Louis but tonight it was plain seedy. Left and right she could see sex shops with flashing neon lights and she was constantly heckled by men inviting her to come into their club. She didn't notice the two men following her. They'd seen her getting out of the taxi and knew she wasn't looking for sex. One of them caught up with her.

"Can I help you?" he asked politely. "Are you looking for something?"

She was gasping for breath. He was well spoken and looked quite well dressed. How come they all knew she spoke English, she wondered. She didn't realise that she stood out like a sore thumb in her Versace leather coat, her gold and diamonds and her Hermès Birkin bag.

"Maybe some heroin?" he asked, again very politely.

"No, not heroin," she replied. "Coke. I need cocaine."

"No problem, madame. You got cash?"

"Sure," she said, letting out a sigh of relief.

" 100. Okay?"

"That's fine," she said, taking the money out of her bag and giving it to him.

He handed her a packet and she clasped it tightly in her hand.

"Thanks," she smiled at him. She'd got it, she'd got it! "Where can I get a taxi here?"

"If you take the next turn left, you will have no problem."

She smiled her thanks at him but, before following his directions, she slipped into the nearest café where she ordered a cognac. As the waiter was getting it she went into the ladies' where she snorted two lines of coke. The relief!

She sat looking around the café as she sipped her drink. The cocaine had hit the right spot and she felt exhilarated. Who would have thought that she would be able to go out in Paris and score some coke by herself? Take that, Marilyn! I don't need you any more, or Louis. I can manage it on my own. She laughed triumphantly, patting the little packet that she'd slipped into her pants pocket.

Throwing back the remains of the cognac she paid the waiter, telling him to keep the change. He smiled in delight.

She left the café and went in the direction the drug dealer had given her to find a taxi. She didn't notice him standing in a nearby doorway, nor the signal that he gave to his friend to follow her. Turning into the quiet street, she didn't hear the man coming up behind her. Next thing she knew she was knocked to the ground. He tried to grab her bag off her but she clung on to it. He started punching her then and the pain almost rendered her unconscious. She could taste blood as he took her bag and then he pulled her coat off her, roughly twisting her arms. Lastly he pulled her jewellery off her neck and wrists, leaving her bruised and bleeding. Mercifully, she then passed out.

While his wife was experiencing this trauma Brandon was safe in Chantal's arms, all thoughts of his wife far away. Chantal was so easy to be with and she was very sweet indeed. She'd promised to bring him back some local cheese from Normandy the following Monday and he offered to bring the wine and bread. They'd settled into a relaxed routine and the sex was still fantastic. He was becoming very fond of her. For now, she filled a need in his life.

Coming in quietly that night, he was relieved to see that Taylor had gone to bed. Going quietly into his own room, within five minutes he was sleeping. He was awakened by the shrill ringing of the telephone. Sleepily he fumbled for the handset, thinking that at this hour it must be a call from the States. They constantly forgot about the six-hour time difference.

"Good evening, is this Monsieur Brandon Hartford?"

"Yes," he replied, fully awake now. This was a French accent on the phone.

"This is Capitaine Moreau of the Paris Gendarmerie. I am calling from the Lariboisière hospital. I'm afraid I have some bad news. Your wife was admitted here tonight. Can you come, please?"

"No, there must be some mistake. My wife is here sleeping," Brandon said as he jumped out of bed and ran to Taylor's room.

He stood stock-still as he saw that the room was empty and that her bed had not been slept in.

"Sorry," he mumbled into the phone. "She's not here. Is she okay?"

"She's alive but unconscious. Can you come quickly?"

Brandon could barely speak. "Yes, of course, I'll come right away," he replied his voice and hands shaking. "What hospital did you say?"

"Lariboisière. It's quite near the Gare du Nord – the North Station. I'll be waiting for you. Good evening."

Brandon thought he was in the middle of a nightmare. Could this be happening? He jumped into his clothes and rushed out where he luckily found a taxi quite quickly. He couldn't think straight on the short journey there but still felt it must be all some horrible mistake. Taylor was probably out somewhere with Marilyn. Oh God, he cried, as he realised that probably they'd been in a car crash.

Running into the hospital he gave the night receptionist Taylor's name.

"Ah, yes, just hold on a moment," he replied, making a phone call. "The *capitaine* will be with you shortly."

"Where's my wife. I want to see my wife!" Brandon cried in exasperation.

"Monsieur Hartford?" said the dapper young man who came towards him. "I am Capitaine Moreau. Please come with me." He led him into a small room off the foyer. "Please, sit." The policeman motioned him to a chair.

"Please, I'd like to see my wife as soon as possible. What happened? Was it a car crash?" he asked, distraught. Visions of Princess Diana went through his head.

"No, not a car accident. She was attacked, in Montmartre, at about ten thirty this evening."

"Attacked?" Brandon repeated, not able to take it in. "What about her friend, Marilyn? Was she attacked too?"

"Your wife was quite alone. Luckily, a passer-by found her and called 15 for an ambulance."

"That's not possible! She'd never have been there alone. Not Montmartre, at night." He was sure now they'd got the wrong woman. "May I see her, please?"

"Yes, follow me, but let me warn you, she is not a pretty sight."

Moreau wasn't joking. Brandon barely recognised the figure lying in the intensive care room. Her face was bruised and battered and she had an oxygen mask on. She had cuts and bruises on her hands and arms and a deep cut at the base of her neck. She was attached to a heart monitor and the beep, beep of it was the only reassuring thing there. She had just regained consciousness, the nurse told him, but would need monitoring for some time.

"Oh God, Taylor, what happened to you?" he cried, taking her hand.

She opened her eyes and looked at him bleakly before closing them again.

"It's better if we let her sleep," the nurse said gently, leading Brandon from the room. "The doctor would like to have a word with you, if you would please take a seat."

He sat down heavily, his head in his hands. What was Taylor doing in Montmartre alone at that hour of the night? It didn't make sense.

"Mr Hartford? I'm Doctor Winters. I'd like to talk to you about your wife."

To his surprise, the young woman was American.

"Will she be okay? She's not in any danger, is she?"

"Not from her injuries, no. They're pretty superficial although I know it must look frightening. No, they'll heal quickly. I'm more concerned about her substance abuse."

"Substance abuse?" He looked at her as though she were talking Chinese. "What do you mean 'substance abuse'?"

"Well, your wife has a large amount of hydrocodone and oxycodone in her system, coupled with a substantial amount of cocaine."

This woman was nuts. What was she trying to get at? Taylor would never have taken things like that. He laughed nervously.

"Oh no, Doctor, I'm sure you're mistaken. My wife has never taken drugs except for the odd few painkillers and maybe Valium and she certainly has never taken cocaine." He laughed again.

"Mr Hartford, these substances I mentioned are not only painkillers but also opiates and your wife has been ingesting them in large quantities," she said gently.

"Oh my God," he stared at her bleakly. "And the cocaine?"

Doctor Winters looked towards Capitaine Moreau.

"She was carrying a substantial amount of cocaine on her person when she was admitted and had ingested some recently," the policeman said. "We suspect that that is the reason she was in that area alone, at that hour of the night. It's the centre of the drugs trade here in Paris." He looked sympathetically at Brandon. "I'm sorry."

Brandon was ashen-faced.

"Had you no idea that your wife was addicted to these drugs?" the doctor asked.

Brandon didn't know what to say. How was it possible that she'd been doing all this under his nose and that he'd been unaware of it? He didn't blame them for not believing him. He could hardly believe it himself.

"No," he said quietly, "I honestly didn't know, but then we lead very separate lives. We haven't shared a bedroom for over twenty years so she could be doing anything in private and I wouldn't have known." He thought for a while.

"She's been having a lot of mood swings lately but I assumed it was because she's been drinking very heavily. Oh, God, I can't believe it," he cried, burying his head in his hands. "What can I do?"

"Well, she'll certainly have to go into rehab. We have some very good facilities here in Paris," Doctor Winters informed him.

"She'd never agree to that. I'll have to take her back to New York."

"Wherever, but the sooner she gets treatment the better. If she goes on like this she'll kill herself," she stated firmly, trying to stress the urgency of it to him.

"When do you think she'll be able to come out and when will she be ready to travel?" he asked her.

"Just a day or two, I should think."

"Okay, I'll organise that," he sighed.

"In the meantime, we'll do our best to apprehend the person responsible for attacking her," the policeman assured him, "but I'm afraid that will prove very difficult. By the way, she had no bag on her when she was admitted so I presume it was stolen in the attack. She did however have these credit cards in her pocket which was how we traced you." He held out Taylor's wallet.

"Thank you, Capitaine," Brandon said, taking the wallet and sliding it into his jacket pocket. "I'm sorry about all this." He held out his hands helplessly.

The policeman smiled sympathetically at him as he bade him *au revoir*.

Brandon went in with the doctor to see Taylor once more. She was sleeping peacefully.

"You may as well go home and get some sleep," Doctor Winters said gently. "We gave her a sedative so she'll sleep till morning. We'll call you if there's any change." She felt sorry for the poor man. He was obviously cultured and a thorough gentleman. She'd believed him when he'd said that he'd had no idea what his wife was up to. It never ceased to surprise her the way some people lived. "If you need to talk to me again, I'll be happy to help in any way I can," she told him, shaking his hand.

She left him to his thoughts. They weren't good ones.

Wearily he left the hospital but he knew he wouldn't get much sleep. He poured himself a large whisky when he got home and sat mulling over the events of the night. He felt guilty and ashamed that he hadn't noticed what his wife had been doing. It said a lot for their marriage. Going into Taylor's room he checked her drawers and bathroom and found the Vicodin, Oxycontin and Valium as well as several other drugs and two empty bottles of vodka. How had it come to this? Well, he thought as he got wearily into bed, it's time I did something to rectify the matter.

35

Brandon rang Jazz the following morning to say that he would be late in to work.

"Can you continue on with what we were doing yesterday, till I get there?" he asked.

"Of course. Is everything okay?" She sensed he was not his usual self.

"No, I'm afraid not, but I'd prefer if you wouldn't mention this to the others," he said, lowering his voice.

"What's wrong?" she asked with concern.

"Taylor's in hospital. I'll explain all when I see you."

"Okay," she replied, a little flummoxed.

He also rang Yves to say he'd be late but didn't elaborate further. He then took the metro to the hospital. He knew there was no way he would find a taxi during the Paris morning rush-hour.

He arrived at the hospital to find Taylor awake and looking slightly better than the night before. They'd taken off the oxygen mask and had cleaned her up.

"How are you feeling?" he asked her as he sat on the edge of her bed.

"How do you think I'm feeling?" she retorted.

He sighed. She hadn't lost her sharp tongue along with everything else.

"I know about the drugs, Taylor," he said quietly.

She turned her head away from him.

"The doctor says you're very lucky to be alive but you have to stop. They recommend that you enter rehab."

"Not here in Paris!" she cried, attempting to sit up in the bed.

"No, I told them I'd take you back to New York."

"Thank God for that." She lay back down, grimacing. "What do they know here anyway?"

"Are you sore?" he asked sympathetically.

"What do you think? Of course I'm sore," she said sulkily.

"Have they said when you'll be able to come home?"

"No. They're talking of moving me to a ward but I absolutely refuse to go. If I can't have a private room, then I want to go home."

The nurse came in then and Taylor told her, in a haughty voice, that she would be going home if there was no private room available.

"I'm afraid you will have to speak to the doctor about that."

"Where can I find her?" Brandon asked the nurse.

"If you go out to the desk, the sister-in-charge will contact her for you."

Brandon did as she directed and ten minutes later a young male doctor arrived to talk to him.

"Monsieur Hartford, Doctor Winters is off duty at the moment but I am in charge of your wife's case. I must stress that it would not be wise to take your wife home at this point. I would not trust her to be on her own where she would have access to further prescription drugs. She needs to go directly from here to rehab. Is it possible that you can arrange that?" He looked at him enquiringly. "In the meantime, I think it will be possible to find her a private room, if that is what you want. It will be very expensive, of course."

"That won't be a problem, doctor, and I will try and organise a flight as soon as possible. I have a friend in New York who is a psychotherapist and he'll organise rehab for Taylor there."

"That's good. Please let me know when you're ready and I'll release her but in the meantime she's better off here under our supervision." He smiled sympathetically at Brandon. He'd been at the receiving end of Taylor's anger and felt extremely sorry for her husband.

"The doctor says you must stay here for a couple of days," Brandon told Taylor, "but the good news is that they've found you a private room."

"Thank God for that," she said ungraciously. "Can you go home and get me some clean clothes and my make-up? I need some towels and toiletries as well. I couldn't possibly use the awful stuff they have here. I'll call Mimi and tell her exactly what I want."

He threw his eyes to heaven. "I do need to go into work this morning, Taylor."

"It will take you less than an hour. I can't possibly go on looking like this." She looked disgustedly at the hospital robe they had given her.

Resignedly, he agreed to do as she asked. He arrived back at the hospital an hour later lugging a heavy case and a large bag. The sooner he got her back to the States the better.

Jazz waited impatiently for Brandon to come into the office and enlighten her as to the problem. She had noticed that Taylor had been acting very strangely lately. She had seemed out of it at Kieran's birthday party and Felicity had told her that she had acted awfully strangely at her lunch party the previous Sunday. Felicity had expressed concern that Taylor was drinking too much. Jazz was inclined to agree with her. It was no wonder Brandon had succumbed to Chantal's charms if he had to cope with a wife who was not only the most obnoxious woman Jazz had ever met but also an alcoholic.

Jazz had met Chantal during lunchtime in the Excelsior the previous Wednesday, and couldn't resist pumping her for information. She gathered that Chantal was happily married and that she left her husband in Normandy on Monday morning, returning there every Friday evening, which meant that Brandon wouldn't even have the pleasure of *her* company over the weekend. Jazz knew that being involved with a married person meant you were destined to spend every weekend alone. She wouldn't see Yves until Monday and it was killing her.

Nothing prepared Jazz for the bombshell Brandon dropped when he finally arrived at the office. He looked haggard as he slumped into his chair.

"Are you all right?" Jazz asked him, a worried frown on her face. "You look wrecked."

"I'm more than wrecked," he admitted, looking up at her.

"How's Taylor? What happened?"

"It's a long story. Any chance of a coffee?"

"Of course," she replied, going into the kitchen and coming back with two big mugs of coffee and a plate of macaroons. She placed them in front of him and pulled up a chair beside his desk.

"Shoot!" she said, as she sipped her coffee and bit into a macaroon.

"Can I ask you not to breathe a word to anyone? Promise?"

"Of course, I promise. What is it?" She was mystified.

"Well, Taylor was mugged last night . . ."

"What?" Jazz exclaimed, looking at him in shock.

"That's not the worst part," he continued. "It happened in Montmartre, when she was buying cocaine."

Nothing he could have said would have shocked Jazz more.

"Cocaine?" she repeated after him, spilling her coffee on the desk. "You can't be serious!"

"I'm afraid I am. And it's not only cocaine, they tell me she's addicted to prescription drugs and must go into rehab immediately."

"Oh my God, Brandon, I'm so sorry. I never would have guessed. I did think that maybe she had a drink problem . . ."

"She has that as well," he said putting his head in his hands. "I can't believe that she was taking all this stuff without my knowledge although I did notice a change in her personality."

"You poor thing," she said sympathetically as she came around the desk and gave him a hug. "What are you going to do?"

"She won't go into rehab here so I'm taking her back to New York as soon as possible and signing her into a clinic there."

"Can I help? Shall I go online and find a flight for you?"

"Thanks, Jazz, that would be great. If you can get a flight for Tuesday that will give me time to make arrangements in New York."

"I'll do it straight away. First class or business?" Going to her desk, she logged on to her computer.

"Better make it first. The more privacy we have the better. Will you be able to manage here while I'm gone? I should be back by Thursday morning."

"Of course I will. You take as long as you need to get everything sorted out."

"Thanks, Jazz. You're a jewel. And please remember, not a word to anyone. I'll just say Taylor was mugged and not go into details."

"You have my word," she assured him. "My lips are sealed. And Brandon . . ." she added shyly, "I appreciate your confiding in me."

Brandon waited until twelve thirty to call his friend, Bob, in New York, as it would be just six thirty in the morning there.

"Hi, Brandon, old buddy! How are things in gay Paree?"

"Not too good, Bob, I'm afraid. I have a problem."

He then explained to Bob what Taylor had been up to.

"Gawd, I'm real sorry, buddy, how awful for you. They're right when they say she has to stop immediately. I can arrange to see her on Tuesday when you get here and take her straight in. That okay?"

"Thanks, Bob. I appreciate that."

"See you Tuesday then. Give me a call when you get in."

"Will do. Till Tuesday."

Ashling had been looking forward to the weekend. They had planned to take the girls to the theme park, Parc Astérix, on Saturday and then Felicity had invited all four of them to lunch on Sunday. Jazz was also invited but unfortunately she'd already committed herself to lunch with Hugh.

However, these plans were scuppered by the phone call from Ireland at six that morning. Kieran's mother had suffered a stroke and he had to catch the first flight home. Luckily they hadn't told the girls they were going to Parc Astérix so she didn't have to disappoint them. She rang Felicity to explain that Kieran would not be able to come to lunch on Sunday.

"That's a shame but I hope you and the girls will come anyway," Felicity said.

"Of course, we'd love to," Ashling assured her.

"Did you hear that Taylor was mugged on Thursday night and is in hospital?"

"God no, how dreadful! What happened? How is she?"

"Well, Brandon didn't elaborate but said she's fine. She should be out in a day or two. He'll be at our lunch tomorrow."

"That's good." Ashling wasn't too keen on Taylor but didn't wish her any ill. "See you tomorrow then, Felicity. I look forward to it."

She took the girls to the Luxembourg Gardens and was surprised to run into Corey as she entered the park.

"What a nice surprise," he said, his face lighting up when he saw her. "And this must be Orna and Ciara." She was amazed and pleased that he had remembered the girls' names. He shook their hands solemnly and Ciara, as always shy with strangers, clung to Ashling's leg.

"Is your husband with you?" he asked, looking around.

"No," she grimaced. "He had to go to Ireland urgently this morning as his mother had a stroke last night."

"Oh, I am sorry," he said sympathetically. "May I stroll with you?"

"Of course," she smiled at him. "I'm just taking the girls to the playground."

The two little girls skipped ahead of them and when they reached the playground, Corey remarked, "You know the only thing I miss about home is doing simple things like this with my grandchildren." She heard the wistful note in his voice.

"Please feel free to borrow my two for an hour, if you like," she laughed.

To her surprise he did and was wonderful with the two girls, pushing them on the swings and the seesaw. They took to him very quickly and were enjoying playing with this man who reminded them of Santa Claus and was paying them such attention. Ashling could see that both Corey and the girls were having a whale of a time. After forty minutes he collapsed down on the bench beside her.

"My age is catching up on me," he laughed, panting and trying to catch his breath.

"You're great with them," she said.

"They look very like you," he replied. "I can see just what you were like as a little girl now. Orna is a real little extrovert. I imagine she'll be an actress or a dancer whereas Ciara is much shyer. I guess she'll be more a thinker and maybe a writer, like her mother."

Ashling was amazed that he had identified the girl's personalities so quickly.

"You're very astute," she told him. "Do you judge everybody so well?"

"Oh, yes, I sussed you out from the first moment I met you," he replied, a mischievous glint in his eye.

"Don't tell me," she laughed.

"I won't. It would only embarrass you," he said, his eyes solemn now.

Blushing, she got up to call the girls over.

"How about I take you all to Berthillon for the best ice cream in Paris?" he asked.

"Yes, yes, please!" the girls chorused, jumping up and down.

"I don't know," Ashling hesitated.

"Please, Mummy, please!" they begged her.

"Please, I'd love you to come," he said, looking into her eyes.

"Okay, then. I guess I'm outnumbered." She smiled at the three pleading faces. "Actually, I have been looking forward to tasting this famous ice cream since I came here and seeing as how I reached my goal weight this morning, well . . . I guess I owe myself," she laughed.

"You look fantastic," he said, appreciatively. "You definitely deserve a special ice cream."

He took the girls' hands as they walked down the Boulevard St Michel to the Île Saint-Louis where she was amazed to see an enormous queue outside the famous Berthillon ice-cream salon.

"This is the best ice cream in the world. There are queues here even after midnight," he told them as they took their place in the line.

Two American couples recognised him and, telling him they were big fans of his, asked for his autograph. He was very gracious and chatted away to them as he signed. They were thrilled to bits. Ashling guessed it would be the highlight of their holiday.

"Does this happen all the time?" she asked, as they moved forward in the queue.

"Yes, especially in New York. But I don't mind. They're my readers after all. It'll happen to you someday too."

"I wish," she sighed, as they reached the counter and tried to decide what flavour ice cream to choose.

Licking the coconut and violet ice-cream cone that she'd chosen, Ashling had to agree with him that it was the best she'd ever tasted. "Worth the wait," she smiled, getting ice cream on her nose.

He had gone for strawberry and chocolate, as had the girls.

"Yummy! This is del-ic-ious," Ciara said, in between licks, making them laugh.

"*Merci, Corey,*" Orna said. "*C'est très bon.*"

"*Merci, Corey,*" Ciara parroted her.

"They're adorable," he said to Ashling, "just like their mother." She blushed again.

They said goodbye then and Ashling felt that somehow the dynamics of their relationship had changed. Now she would have to tell Kieran about him because, sure as hell, her two daughters wouldn't be able to keep quiet about him.

36

Ashling was in good form when she arrived at Felicity's for lunch on Sunday. After greeting Felicity and Max she went into the living room where Brandon was sipping a whisky.

"Brandon, I'm delighted to see you and I was so sorry to hear about Taylor. How is she?" she asked, kissing him on both cheeks.

"I was in with her this morning and she's recovering well. She should be out tomorrow and then I'm taking her to New York on Tuesday to recuperate."

Both Felicity and Ashling thought that this was strange.

"I *am* sorry. Felicity told me she was mugged. How dreadful for her. Would you like us to visit her?"

"No, really, thanks all the same. She needs rest," he assured them.

"If there's anything we can do, please just ask," Felicity said.

"Thank you, I will. She was lucky really. It could have been much worse," he told them, grateful for their concern. "Where's Kieran?"

"He's had to go to Ireland urgently. His mother took ill on Friday night."

"Well then, you can be my date for lunch," he smiled at her, hoping to lighten the mood.

"I'll be honoured," she smiled back at him.

Felicity had excelled herself and Ashling was amazed at the wonderful food she dished up.

"You've definitely found your calling," she said, when they'd finished. "I haven't had such a wonderful meal in years."

"I agree," Brandon complimented her too. "You really are the most amazing cook."

Felicity blushed as Max beamed proudly at her.

"Have you considered cooking professionally?" Brandon asked her. "I would imagine you'd be hugely in demand as a caterer."

"What a brilliant idea," Ashling said enthusiastically. "You should do it, Felicity. It's so difficult to get really good caterers in Ireland, and I imagine that in London it's even worse."

"I might think about it," she told them, delighted with their compliments. "I have a friend on the course, Becky, who plans to start a catering company in London and she's asked me to go in with her, but I don't know yet. Anyway, I have almost nine months to decide."

They had a lovely day and Ashling thought uncharitably that it was all the better because Taylor was missing. Brandon was very good with the girls and played endless games with them. Taylor would have hated having them there.

"You're very good with children," she remarked, as he finished reading them a story. Orna and Ciara adored him and were sitting on his knees with their arms around his neck. "You must have been great with your own children."

"Sadly not," he grimaced. "I was too busy working when the twins were growing up so I saw very little of them. I regret it now."

Ashling disentangled her daughters from his neck and took them into the television room where Felicity put on the Disney Channel for them. She returned to Brandon.

"Brandon, about what you were saying," she said, as she accepted a glass of wine from Max, "I wish you'd mention that to Kieran. He hardly sees the girls and I'm afraid he'll regret it too, when they're older."

"I will try but it's not easy convincing a workaholic like Kieran that work is not the be-all and end-all. His work is very important to him."

"I know," she sighed, "but there has to be a balance between work and family-life surely, especially where children are involved."

"I agree, but it took me a long time to realise that and, by the time I did, it was too late, the children were grown. I missed out big-time," he added sadly.

He could see from the strained look on Ashling's face that this was becoming a problem for her. He hoped Kieran would see that quicker than he himself had. Ashling was no Taylor, willing to settle for a comfortable lifestyle. She wanted more from her marriage than a breadwinner and Kieran should realise that.

"I will bring it up with Kieran, if you like," he assured her. He was rewarded with a glorious smile which lit up her sparkling emerald eyes. *Her husband is a lucky devil. I hope I can talk some sense into him,* Brandon thought.

Meanwhile, Jazz was having lunch with Hugh and a group of his friends when her phone rang. It was Yves.

"Can you meet me this afternoon, *chérie?*" he asked.

"What time?"

"Four o'clock. I can get out for about two hours and I'd really like to see you."

"Of course I'll meet you. I want to see you too," she whispered, aware that Hugh could hear her. "Why not come to my apartment?" she added, much to his surprise.

"That would be wonderful," he said huskily, his voice full of desire. "*À bientôt!*"

"Yes, see you soon," she whispered back, her heart singing with joy at the prospect of this unexpected meeting.

She'd never invited him to her apartment before but now it was time. Today she desperately wanted him in her own bed where there would be no thoughts of other women he'd shared it with. She quivered with excitement at the thought of the evening ahead.

"I'm sorry, Hugh, I'll have to leave soon," she said.

"It's Yves, isn't it? Jazz, I hope you know what you're doing and that you don't get hurt." Hugh looked at her, concern in his face.

"Gosh, all my friends seem to think I'll get my heart broken," she said ruefully, trying to make it sound like a joke.

"I sure hope not," Hugh replied but without much conviction.

Sophie knew that Yves was lying to her. He'd said that he needed to go into the office for a few hours on Sunday afternoon. He had never done this once in all the years she'd known him. Now she knew for sure that it was serious with this other woman. She was frightened and pondered how she should react. She wished she knew who the woman was but it could be anyone. It could be someone he'd met in a restaurant, in a café, on the street, while buying the newspaper. Yves would never have a problem charming a woman into bed, wherever he met her.

He'd first met Sophie herself when she'd been getting on the metro. He was getting off and, on seeing her, he had turned around and hopped back on. By the time she'd got to her stop he had managed to get her phone number from her. He was irresistible when he wanted to be and she didn't underestimate her husband's ability where women were concerned. It could even be someone from work, she realised. She knew he'd had a brief fling with his secretary, Chantal, but that appeared to be over. She'd have to keep a close watch on this latest affair if it was as serious as she feared.

Jazz showered quickly and changed into some sexy underwear for Yves. She had just finished lacing up the corset when the bell rang. Spraying herself liberally with Angel perfume and slipping on her new, very expensive Carine Gilson silk negligée, she pressed the button to let him in.

He took her in his arms the moment he walked in and inhaled her scent deeply.

"You smell so divine, *chérie*," he murmured as he kissed her neck and slipped the silk negligée from her shoulders. "Oh, my God, you are so sexy," he exclaimed, his eyes roving over her body. The sight of her luscious breasts barely contained in the sexy cream-lace basque drove him crazy but, though he throbbed with desire for her, he took his time, caressing her body as he slowly undid the laces of the basque. Throwing it away, he started kissing her breasts and worked his way down her body, driving her crazy with desire too. She was panting with excitement as he undid the ribbons on each side of her tiny cream lace thong and let it drop to the floor.

Unable to wait a moment longer, she started pulling his clothes off him. When he was naked too, he lifted her up and she wrapped her legs around him as he carried her into the bedroom. For a brief second the thought entered his head that he had no condom – he always had a supply in the hotel – but it was too late to stop now and with a shudder he entered her. It was the best sex they'd ever had and it went on for what seemed like hours.

"I love you," she murmured, as she climaxed for the umpteenth time.

Afterwards, curled like spoons together, they fell into a warm relaxed sleep and she smiled, knowing that this was the happiest she'd ever felt in her life.

When Brandon arrived home that evening there were three voicemails on the machine from Marilyn. He rang the number she'd left.

"Brandon, daaahling," she cooed. "I've been tryin' to get in touch with Taylor but her phone has been turned off for three days now. Is she there with you?"

"Sadly not, Marilyn," he replied curtly. He held Marilyn responsible, in a way, for Taylor's predicament. His wife had been fine till Marilyn had hit town.

She heard the hostility in his voice. "Is everythin' awllrighty?" she asked, a little nervously.

"No, it's not damn alrighty!" he barked back. "Taylor's in the Lariboisière hospital. She was mugged in Montmartre last Thursday night, while buying cocaine."

"Oh my Gawd!" Marilyn gasped. "Is she okay?"

"Well, she's alive, if that's what you mean. But she's most certainly not okay. I'm taking her to New York on Tuesday where she's going into rehab."

"Oh my Gawd, I'm so saawry," she drawled. Her voice was

beginning to irritate Brandon. "Brandon, honey, I told her she was crazy to be takin' all them pills along with the coke. She knew that."

"You knew that she was taking all that stuff?" he asked, infuriated. "Why didn't you tell me?"

"Oh, sweetie, I'm her friend. I couldn't have' gone squealin' on her. You understan' that," she replied, her voice sugary sweet.

Some friend you are, he thought.

"I'll go visit her tomorrow. Poor thing!"

"Marilyn, don't you dare give her any drugs. I'm warning you."

"Course not," she replied, sounding affronted. "And Brandon, sweetie, you know I'm here, if you ever need me," she said, her voice now husky and intimate. "Anythin', anytime."

Disgusted, he hung up on her.

When Kieran arrived home that night, he was pretty shattered. His mother was holding her own but couldn't speak or move so it was very worrying.

"It was awful to see her lying there, Ash," he told her, tears coming to his eyes. "I felt so helpless. I wish I could have done something to help her."

"I know, love, it must have been awful, but the fact that you were there must have been a great comfort to her," she said, stroking his hair.

"I'm afraid she might die. She looked so frail." He buried his head in his hands.

"Well, she *is* eighty-two and she's had a good innings. Maybe she'll pull through this. People often do."

"I hope so, though I don't want her to spend the rest of her life an invalid."

"Don't worry. God is good," she said taking his hand. "Let's go to bed."

He fell instantly asleep and she hadn't a chance to tell him about their weekend. Somehow it seemed very unimportant in the face of his mother's illness.

Yves awoke with a start to find that it was already dark. Looking at his watch, he saw that it was nine o'clock. Jazz stirred beside him, reaching out for him. What the hell, I'm late anyway, he thought, reaching down for her and stroking her gently. She woke to the delicious sensation and, rolling over on top of him, guided him into her once more.

When it was over, he kissed her deeply. "I'm sorry, *chérie*, I want to stay with you but I have to go."

She clung to him wishing he could stay the night but understanding that he had to leave. She saw him out and they kissed until the moment that he pulled away, afraid that he would want to take her again.

"Till tomorrow, *ma petite*," he murmured, and then he was gone.

Jazz opened the window wide and watched him until he walked away around the corner, turning to wave at her. She sighed. She knew with a certainty that he was the man for her despite what all her friends said. She knew that he wouldn't break her heart.

She poured a glass of wine and sat on her balcony, thinking of Yves. She watched the night cruises, their lights twinkling, as they sailed up and down the Seine. She could hear the music wafting upwards and spied some couples sitting at candlelit tables, having dinner and dancing. It was impossibly romantic. How she wished that she and Yves could do romantic, normal things like that, but of course they couldn't. It had been a wonderful, wonderful evening but it was heartbreaking every time they parted.

Yves was very apprehensive as he made his way home. He really had got carried away and lost all sense of time. Now he had to face the music and Sophie. She was sitting quietly in the dark, waiting for him.

"Sorry, I lost sight of the time," he said, kissing her lightly.

She looked up at him solemnly and he saw the fear in her eyes.

"You weren't at work, were you?" she asked.

"No," he said honestly. There was no point lying to her. Sophie was too clever for that.

"You were with a woman." It was a statement, not a question.

"Yes," he sighed, looking at her guiltily. "I'm sorry."

"Who is she? Do you love her?" she asked, needing to know the truth.

"Of course not – I love *you*," he said, sitting down beside her and putting his arm around her.

It was obvious that he didn't want to tell her the identity of the woman in question, so she didn't persist. But she was consumed with curiosity to know who it was. He was late home practically every night now and when he did come home he was distracted, his mind obviously elsewhere. She figured that he might as well not have come home at all.

She was also beginning to get angry. They had an agreement, one that she'd always adhered to, that if there was any fear of involvement with a third party, they would immediately end the relationship. Now, it seemed, Yves was breaking his part of the bargain. She'd always known that he was a serial womaniser which was why she'd agreed to have an open marriage. She'd been sure that his love for her and for Pierre was strong enough to cope with other women. Now she was frightened that this was not the case.

She knew there was nothing she could do other than wait it out. He was obviously in the first flush of lust – she refused to call it love – so to confront him now would be foolish. She knew his attention span with women was very short and he very quickly tired of his paramours so she could just hope and pray that this one wouldn't last long. Meanwhile she'd just get on with her life.

After she'd gone to bed, Yves sat with a brandy thinking that he'd really have to tread carefully. He loved Sophie and didn't want to hurt her. Tonight had been stupid. He was also concerned about the fact that Jazz had said that she loved him. He hadn't meant for that to happen. He'd thought that they could have a mutually advantageous sexual relationship but he was beginning to think that Jazz wanted more than that. Maybe it was time to cool it.

37

Marilyn was feeling guilty about Taylor and went to visit her in the hospital on Monday. She was shocked when she saw the state her friend was in. Her lips were all swollen and her face and arms were black and blue. Taylor wasn't too happy to see her as she reckoned that if Marilyn had got her the cocaine she wanted from Louis in the first place, she wouldn't have been forced to go on the streets of Montmartre looking for it. She told Marilyn as much.

"You can make it up to me by getting me some now," she said sulkily.

"Honey, I promised Brandon I wouldn't bring you anythin'. I don't wanna upset him." Marilyn took her hand but Taylor winced and pulled it away. "Well, you can leave right now, if that's how you feel!" she screamed at her.

Marilyn gathered up her things and exited in a hurry as the nurse came running in.

"Gawd," she told Louis later, "she's freaked out. What a mess! Poor Brandon, my heart goes out to him."

Louis looked at her, his eyes hooded. He knew she'd always had the hots for Brandon. Now that Taylor was out of the picture, he'd no doubt she would fancy her chances with him. Louis had no illusions where Marilyn was concerned.

On Tuesday, on the way to the airport, Taylor rang Marilyn to apologise.

"Don't worry about it, honey. I understan' that you've been through a lot," her friend assured her. Taylor was relieved. Marilyn promised to keep in touch.

By nightfall, Taylor was safely deposited in the most elite rehab clinic New York had to offer. It had been a nightmare few days.

Bob had suggested to Brandon that he take her pills away from her and dole them out to her, as little as possible at a time.

"No point in her goin' cold turkey until we get her into the clinic, buddy," he'd advised. "But you'll have to control what she takes until she gets here. It won't be easy, Brandon ole boy, I'm warnin' ya!"

He wasn't kidding. Taylor was querulous and bad-tempered and pestered him hourly for more Vicodin. It made him realise just how addicted she'd become. In a way, the mugging had been a blessing in disguise. Now, under Bob's care, she should be able to recover. It was with a sigh of relief that he left her there.

Bob had said that she should have no contact with the outside world, which meant no visitors or even phone calls, for six weeks. That meant Brandon could return to Paris immediately. There was no point in staying in New York.

He had wanted to go to California to tell the twins what had happened but Taylor had pleaded with him not to say anything to them.

"When I'm cured, I'll tell them," she stated, "not before."

He agreed to say nothing.

Wednesday night he flew back to Paris and slept like a baby the whole way. He arrived in the office Thursday morning refreshed and invigorated. Jazz was delighted to see that he was back to his old self. She'd found it a strain to keep everything going without him although it had taken her mind off Yves a little.

38

It was Friday and Brandon and Jazz were having lunch in the Excelsior café.

"It will be strange being alone in Paris for the weekend," Brandon remarked. "I guess I'll work tomorrow and catch up."

"Join the club. I'm fine during the week when I'm working but I hate weekends. Everywhere you go you see nothing but couples. It makes me feel a bit freaky, if you know what I mean."

Brandon thought she sounded wistful. "Well, you would have no shortage of suitors to spend them with, if you were interested."

"Unfortunately, I'm not," she replied, as she finished the last of her toasted cheese and ham sandwich. "So I guess I'm destined to spend them alone."

Then she was struck by a brilliant idea. "If you've no other plans for Sunday, Brandon, I'm thinking of visiting the Louvre and I'd be delighted to have some company." She looked at him hopefully.

"Are you sure?" he asked. "I *am* rather at a loose end."

"Of course. I would be very lonely on my own there."

"Well then, let's be lonely together." His smile lit up his face.

God, he's handsome, Jazz thought. That Taylor is a fool. The weekend was suddenly looking up.

Kieran had arrived home so late every night that week that he never got to see the girls at all and by the weekend they'd forgotten all about Corey so there was no need for Ashling to mention him. Her mother and her sister Fiona were coming for a visit and the girls were in a state of excitement by Friday afternoon when it was time to go to the airport to meet Nana and Auntie Fee. Ashling was dying to show her mother and sister the city that she'd come to love. Kieran, unfortunately, wouldn't be around as he had to go to Ireland again to visit his mother, who still hadn't rallied.

Ashling and the girls travelled to Charles de Gaulle airport with Kieran as his flight time coincided with the incoming flight of her mother and sister. After seeing Kieran off they went to the arrivals hall to wait for them. Ashling saw Fiona first, waving and jumping up and down as she came out the doors. Running towards Ashling, she hugged her and swept the little girls up in her arms. Ashling's mother followed more sedately, beaming as she hugged her daughter and little granddaughters.

"You look fantastic, love," she said, standing back to look at Ashling. "You've lost weight."

"Thanks, Mum. It's just so great to see you. I've missed you."

"You look fab, sis," Fiona cried. "Wow, you're gone all chic! I love your hair. It suits you. I just can't wait to see Paris!" Her voice was high with excitement.

Ashling laughed at her enthusiasm. "I've a whole programme planned for you," she told them as she led them to a taxi.

Orna and Ciara talked nineteen to the dozen all the way home, telling their nana all about their new school and their new life. Ashling couldn't get a word in edgeways.

"I can't believe we're in Paris," Fiona sighed as she stepped out of the taxi on to the Paris pavement. She almost felt like doing the whole papal thing and kissing the ground!

Ashling showed them round the house and when they'd unpacked and given the girls the presents they'd brought and Ashling the sausages and Lyons tea, she opened a bottle of champagne.

"Welcome to Paris!" she toasted them.

"*Bienvenue à Paris!*" Orna said as she clinked her glass of Sprite to theirs.

Ciara naturally parroted her sister, causing them all to laugh.

"My God, you're speaking French," Fiona cried, astounded by her little nieces.

"And with such a great accent," their nana added.

Ashling beamed proudly at her daughters. They should have been in bed by now and she didn't know how she'd ever get them to sleep tonight, they were so high, but it wasn't every day that her mother and sister came to visit.

She'd prepared a coq-au-vin earlier followed by a chocolate mousse and was delighted by their praise and to see they'd cleaned their plates.

When the girls were finally settled – after Fiona had read them three stories – the three women sat chatting and Ashling opened a bottle of Lynch-Bages 1985.

"This is a divine wine," Fiona exclaimed, licking her lips.

"Yes, it is very special," Ashling told her. "The Minister of Finance gave Kieran three bottles of it for his birthday. Kieran isn't that into wine but I've started a wine course at the Cordon Bleu school. It's fabulous and I hope to know my Bordeaux from my Burgundy by the end of it," she laughed.

"Oh God, you're *sooo* lucky," Fiona said. "I'd give anything to be living here. It's such a romantic city."

"It is beautiful," Ashling agreed with her. "I absolutely love every minute of it."

"I'm green with envy," Fiona sighed dramatically. Then she had a brilliant idea. "Maybe I could take a year out and come over and stay with you," she announced, looking at her mother hopefully.

"God, Fee, that would be fantastic! I'd love to have you here," Ashling replied excitedly. Having Fiona around would be great, both for her and the girls. Kieran would agree to it, she was sure. After all, when was he ever there to notice?

"You'll do no such thing, young lady," their mother said stiffly. "You'll finish your degree and if you want to come to Paris then, Ashling will still be here."

"Oh Mum," Fiona moaned, "pleeese! It would be a brilliant opportunity for me." She turned to her mother, looking at her with pleading eyes, hoping to change her mind.

"Love, it's only another six months. If you give up now it will be very hard to get back into it next year. Am I not right, Ashling?" She turned to her older daughter for support.

"Yeah, Fee, Mum's right. Six months will fly and once you've done your finals you can come over and we'll have a fabulous summer."

Fiona knew when she was beaten. "Okay," she said sulkily.

39

Ashling had planned a full day for her mother and sister. Firstly they were taking the tourist bus around all the famous sites then they were going up the Eiffel Tower. She was pleased to be so au fait with the city and couldn't resist showing off her French a little. She took them to a lovely bistro overlooking the Seine for lunch where her baby-sitter, Nicole, met them and took a tired Orna and Ciara home for the afternoon. Then she took her mother and Fiona shopping on Boulevard Haussmann which they thoroughly enjoyed.

She had invited Felicity, Max, Jazz and Hugh to dinner that evening to meet her family. She would like to have invited Sophie and Yves but with Jazz coming, it was out of the question. It had made things rather difficult for everyone.

They all had a great night and everyone got on famously. Her mother was very taken with Felicity and they spent the evening exchanging recipes and talking about cooking. Fiona thought Jazz was cool but it was Hugh who really took her fancy. They got on like a house on fire and spent the evening discussing the latest bands and TV shows.

"I adore Paris. You're *sooo* lucky to be living here. I'm definitely coming over to live with Ashling when I finish my exams in May," she told him, her eyes shining.

"That will be fantastic," he replied. "I'll introduce you to all my gang. They're great *craic*. You'll love them."

She laughed at his use of the Irish expression. He thought she looked so very pretty with her golden curls dancing and her emerald-green eyes sparkling. She was such fun. All his friends would adore her.

"Hey, maybe you'd like to meet them tomorrow. We're going down the Seine in a boat for lunch at my friend's bar. I'd really love you to come."

"That'd be brilliant. I'll have to check with Ashling but I'm sure she won't mind."

"I've got an even better idea. I'm meeting up with them after I leave here and we're going on to a club. Why don't you come and I'll show you a bit of Paris nightlife?" He flashed his boyish sunny smile.

She would have followed him to hell and back if he'd asked her.

"Cool," she said, thrilled with the idea. "But what about Jazz?"

"Nah, she wouldn't come. She won't mind. There's no romance between us, we're just good friends."

"Okay so," she grinned at him, happy to hear that.

Fiona went into the kitchen to find her sister there with Jazz. They were dishing up dessert.

"Ash, is it okay if I go out with Hugh to a club after dinner? He wants me to meet his friends." Fiona was practically jumping for joy. "And tomorrow he wants me to go on a boat down the Seine to his friend's bar for lunch. You don't mind, do you?"

"Of course not," Ashling replied, laughing at her sister's enthusiasm.

"Is that alright with you, Jazz? Maybe you'd like to come too." Fiona looked at her earnestly.

"No way! I'm much too old for clubbing. You go, girl, you'll have a great time," Jazz grinned at her.

"Thanks, and thanks, sis," Fiona said, giving Ashling a kiss and blowing one to Jazz before she bounced out to give Hugh the good news.

"They're great together," Jazz remarked. "I'd really like Hugh to meet someone special. He's a fantastic guy and he deserves it. Maybe Fiona is that someone."

"Wouldn't that be something?" Ashling agreed. "I really like him too."

Jazz stayed on after the others had gone and sat chatting with Ashling's mother while Ashling went to check on the girls.

"I hope you don't mind that Fiona went off with Hugh," Ashling's mother, Nora, said to Jazz. She was a little concerned as they had arrived together.

"Not at all," Jazz assured her. "Hugh and I are just friends. I find weekends very lonely and he kindly lets me tag along with his friends. They're all much younger than me." She smiled ruefully.

"Don't you have anyone special?" Nora asked gently.

"Indeed I do," Jazz told her, "but unfortunately, he's married to someone else." She didn't know what made her reveal this to a practical stranger and a woman old enough to be her mother at that, but somehow Nora had that same trait as Ashling which made you want to confide in her.

"Oh, you poor dear," Nora said with sympathy. "Do you love him?"

Ashling had returned to the room in time to hear this and Jazz's heartfelt reply.

"Desperately. I can't bear a moment I'm away from him."

"Does he love you?" Nora asked.

"I don't know if he loves me," said Jazz, sounding like a forlorn little girl.

"Do you have any future together?" Nora wanted to know.

"I don't know if he'd leave his wife for me. They have a son, you see." She looked so downcast that Ashling's heart went out to her.

"Oh, dear," said Nora. "That does rather complicate things."

Ashling poured them all some more wine and sat down beside Jazz, taking her hand. Jazz smiled wanly at her.

"It's so awful when there are children involved," Nora said. "I hate to sound negative, my dear, but these things rarely work out and I'm afraid you're the one who will get hurt in the end. I know," she added, sadly, "I was in that position once and my heart was broken."

Ashling looked at her mother, shocked to hear this. It was the first she'd ever heard of it.

"But you and Dad –"

"Oh, yes. Hearts heal, you know. I met your father two years after that and have been happy with him ever since." She smiled at the two girls. "Best thing I ever did. It would never have worked out with the other man. I realised afterwards it was just passion and I'd have felt guilty forever after if he'd left his family for me."

Ashling looked at her with shock. She'd never considered her mother as the passionate type. She was so down to earth. Well, well!

Jazz looked at her wretchedly. She knew Nora was right. She couldn't think past the passion that enveloped her when she was with Yves. It was like a drug. But she also knew that passion cools and as for Sophie and her little son, well, she couldn't even dare to go there.

She left them with a heavy heart, missing Yves more than anything and feeling more miserable than ever.

Fiona had never enjoyed herself so much. She had a brilliant time with Hugh's friends and they went clubbing till two in the morning. They were so friendly and welcoming and such free spirits. Hugh had been very attentive to her and she fancied him like mad. She suspected he felt the same way about her.

On Sunday, after Fiona left with Hugh, Ashling took her mother to the local market where Nora exclaimed at all the wonderful fruit and vegetables on offer. Everything was so fresh and much cheaper than in Dublin. She bought some lovely scarves with scenes of Paris on them for her sisters and snow-globes for the girls with the Eiffel Tower and the Arc de Triomphe inside. Orna and Ciara were fascinated by them and shook them non-stop all through lunch in Les Deux Magots.

Remy was delighted to see Ashling with her family and made a big fuss over her mother and the girls.

"My God, you're like a local here," Nora said, pleased with all the attention.

"Well, I do come here three days a week."

"Why so often?" Nora asked.

"Well, I come here to write," Ashling told her mother. "I've started writing a novel and it's going really well." She blushed as her mother beamed at her, delighted with this news. "Please don't say a word to anybody. I haven't told Kieran yet."

"Why not?" Nora was puzzled.

"To be honest, I hardly see him and when I do he's exhausted and is just not interested in my life." Ashling couldn't keep the resentment out of her voice.

"Is he still working as much as ever?"

"Even more, if anything. He rarely sees the girls, especially now that he goes to see his mother every weekend."

"That's a shame. He really needs to get his priorities sorted." Her mother couldn't help but criticise him. "Before he knows it the girls will be grown up."

"I know but I can't get that through to him. He says he's doing it for us but, honestly, if he's not careful there will be no 'us'," Ashling said bitterly.

Nora was very worried and wished Kieran would realise just what he had.

After lunch they walked into the Luxembourg Gardens where the girls played in the playground as the two women chatted. Before they left, Ashling brought her mother to see the bridge players in the park. To her surprise, Corey was seated playing with them.

The two girls ran up to him and he hugged them warmly.

"Who's that?" Ashling's mother asked her.

"He's a writer that I meet often in the café where we had lunch," she replied, blushing as she spoke.

"Oh?" Nora raised her eyebrows.

He came over to them and kissed Ashling on both cheeks.

"Corey, I'd like you to meet my mother, Nora."

"Another beautiful Irish colleen," he said, his dazzling smile creasing his face.

He took Nora's hand and brought it to his lips. "*Enchanté, Madame.*"

223

Ashling could see that her mother was utterly charmed by him.

"What do you say that we take Grandma to have some ice cream?" he asked the girls.

"Yes, please, Corey," they squealed, dancing around him.

"I'd love that," Nora smiled at him. "Just what I need right now."

Ashling knew when she was beaten. "Go on then. You're a terror," she laughed at him.

They walked to the Île de la Cité and this time they went into a café to order the delicious Berthillon ice cream.

They had a great time and Corey kept them amused with his storytelling and jokes.

"Your daughter is a talented writer, you know, Nora," he remarked, smiling at Ashling who blushed again.

Nora had never seen her daughter blush so much. She was sure there was nothing going on between them but it was obvious that Corey was enchanted by Ashling. She wondered if Ashling was aware of this. Probably not. She figured that Kieran would want to get his act together, and fast, if he wanted to hold on to his wife. Nora sighed. Life was so complicated. She would definitely *not* like to be young again.

When Brandon met Jazz on Sunday morning he barely recognised her. She was wearing cropped denims with a simple white T-shirt and flat ballet pumps. He thought she looked about twenty, with her hair in a pony-tail and her face glowing and make-up free. She was nothing like the suave businesswoman, nor the glamorous party-goer that he knew. He liked her like this – natural-looking and fresh.

"Sensible girl," he said pointing to her flat shoes.

"I'm not so stupid as to wear heels to a museum," she replied, wondering if he'd expected that from her. "How's Taylor? Have you spoken to her?"

"No, Bob says that she is to be totally cut off from the outside world. No visitors – no phone calls."

"That seems a bit harsh."

"I thought so too, but he assures me it's the best way. I have to take his word for it that they know what they're doing."

"I suppose," she replied, but she didn't sound convinced. "God, it must be awful for her."

He sighed. "No doubt, but she did bring it on herself. And she absolutely has to be weaned off all that stuff or she'll kill herself." He sounded sad.

"Well, let's get this culture trip on the road," she smiled, trying to lighten the mood.

The hours flew by as they walked from room to room, admiring all the marvellous paintings they'd only ever read about. Away from the work environment they were relaxed and happy in each other's company and got on amazingly well.

There was something to be said for being with a woman when there was no sexual relationship between them, thought Brandon. She was great company and he was thoroughly enjoying himself. He could see that she was equally relaxed with him. He noticed the envious glances of other men as he squired her around the Louvre. If only they knew, he chuckled to himself. To his amazement she was amazingly well informed about art.

"You're full of surprises," he said as they took a break for coffee.

"You don't know the half of it," she laughed back at him, teasingly.

"I'll bet," he said, throwing back his head and roaring with laughter.

Exhausted, they called it a day at four thirty and went to a local café where Brandon ordered a bottle of red wine and some cheese. He had enjoyed his day with her so much that he didn't want it to end.

"Are you busy this evening?" he asked her. "If not, I'd really like to take you out to dinner, to show my thanks."

"I've got a better idea. I love to cook and I brought some *choucroute* back from home with me. Why don't you let me cook you a real Bavarian meal?"

"It's a deal! I love *choucroute*. I've had it before in Alsace."

"Well, you've tasted nothing like the one we have in Bavaria. It's the best," she said proudly.

"What's the difference?" he asked.

"Ours has cabbage marinaded for weeks in Riesling wine, as well as smoked bacon, ham hock, bratwurst sausage, smoked sausage, potatoes and –"

"Stop it, you're killing me! I can't wait," Brandon cried, almost able to taste it. "I take it's a date then," she said coquettishly, before she started laughing.

Fiona reckoned she'd just had the best day of her life. Hugh had collected her at midday and they had sailed down the Seine to meet up with his friends again, for lunch. It was so romantic. What a life! She couldn't wait until she would be finished studying and living in this fabulous city.

It had been a wonderful day. They sailed home that evening, Hugh standing with his arms around her waist as they admired the Paris skyline. She was blissfully happy and dreaded having to return to Dublin the following day.

He nuzzled her neck and it seemed the most natural thing in the world to turn around and kiss him. She was in heaven.

"Will you come back again soon?" he whispered huskily.

"If you'd like me too," she replied breathlessly.

"Of course, I would. I really like you . . . a lot." He kissed her again.

Fiona thought she'd died and gone to heaven. She'd had a few romances in the past but nothing like this. She was a virgin, unlike most of her friends, and she'd always wanted the first time to be with someone special. From the way she was feeling about him, she guessed Hugh was that someone. She'd never believed in love at first sight but now within twenty-fours of meeting him, she knew she was falling in love. She hated having to leave him but, as he said goodnight, he promised that he'd keep in touch.

Brandon arrived at the address Jazz had given him and looked around the cosy apartment as she put the Alsace Riesling wine he'd brought in the fridge.

"Thank you. It's the perfect wine for my *choucroute*. You *are* a connoisseur," she grinned at him.

"Not really. The guy in the wine shop told me what to buy," he admitted sheepishly.

"You are too honest," she said, liking his modesty.

She opened a bottle of champagne and he noted that she had changed for the evening. She was now wearing a short white floaty dress with white sandals and her hair, which fell in dark curls on her shoulders, had a white camellia pinned in it. He thought she looked like a nymph or an ethereal fairy. They took their glasses out to the terrace and he was enchanted by the view of the Seine from there.

"What a wonderful apartment you have here. I'd love to live in an old place like this – and the view – it's spectacular," he said, waving his arm around. He found it mesmerising and could just imagine himself sitting out here every evening with a whisky. It would certainly de-stress the most stressed-out businessman in the world.

"Did Sophie find this for you?" he asked.

"Yes. I told her exactly what I wanted, and where, and she came up with this perfect place."

"How did you know what you wanted?" he asked her, curious as to how she could have known.

"Well, I spent a year in Paris when I was twenty-one and I have fond memories of the Île Saint-Louis," she told him, blushing.

Fascinated, he took a guess. "Memories of a lover?"

"Yes."

"Tell me more," he said, leaning back in his chair and looking at her quizzically.

"It's a long story." She was blushing furiously now.

"I'm not going anywhere. I've got all the time in the world." He was teasing her now and dying to hear all about it. He wouldn't let her off the hook and before she knew it she was telling him all about her affair with Yves, fifteen years previously.

He listened in silence, shocked at what she was telling him.

"Are you sure he doesn't remember you?" he asked, finding it hard to believe.

"Quite sure," she replied, her eyes filling with tears. Embarrassed, she went to get more champagne.

What a cad, Brandon thought, cold fury building inside him. Yves was despicable and now here he was playing with her feelings once again.

"Do you think it's wise getting involved with him again?" he asked gently as she poured more champagne.

"Of course not," she replied, her eyes sad. "But I can't help it. He's like an addiction and I can't pull myself away."

Brandon wanted to clobber Yves there and then. How dare he trifle with her affections like that! He felt like telling him exactly what he thought of him.

"Promise me you won't breathe a word of this to anyone," she begged him, worried that he might approach Yves. "Please, Brandon? I'll never forgive you if you say anything. I told you in confidence, as my friend." Her eyes were pleading. "Promise me?"

"Okay," he said, against his will. As she went to serve up dinner, he ruminated on what a bastard Yves was. To think he doesn't even know that he was with her before, he thought bitterly. Just how many women has he had? I wouldn't even hazard a guess.

He had no doubt that it would all come to a messy end and that it would be Jazz who would be hurt.

The meal was wonderful and the wine was perfect with it.

"This is delicious," he said, his mouth full of bacon and sauerkraut. "The best I've ever tasted. Real comfort food – just what the doctor ordered."

"Have you heard how Taylor is?" Jazz asked him as she speared a piece of sausage.

"Yes, my friend Bob who's looking after her keeps me informed. She's not too happy there, seemingly," he grimaced.

"Things are not good between you, are they?" she asked gently.

Brandon rarely discussed his marriage with anyone – he felt it was disloyal to Taylor – but now, after Jazz's revelations, he felt they were good enough friends to share his problems with her.

"They're worse than not good," he confided. "I thought that the year in Paris might help us but things have actually got worse since we arrived here. She changed utterly. She started drinking a lot and I suspect the drugs she was taking have affected her personality too."

"It must have made life very difficult for you," Jazz sympathised.

"Hell, actually," he admitted, with a wry smile. "I had planned to seek a divorce when we got back to the States and then all this happened."

"What about Chantal?" she asked him diffidently, afraid he might tell her it was none of her business.

"She's a sweet girl and we have a mutually pleasing relationship. She doesn't want any romantic involvement and neither do I. Taylor decided twenty-two years ago, when the twins were born, that she wanted to have nothing more to do with sex so, of course, she accepts that I have a woman from time to time. I've never got involved with any of them but, suddenly, it's not enough." He looked downcast.

Jazz reached across the table and patted his hand. "I'm so sorry," she said, sympathetically. She was shocked at his revelations.

"It's not just sex I need any more. What I miss is a loving relationship, someone to share things with. That's why I'd decided to look for a divorce from Taylor. Now I don't know what's going to happen. We'll have to see how things go." He smiled sadly. "So, that's my secret. Now you must promise not to tell anyone either."

"I promise," she said, crossing her heart.

He crossed his heart too and smiled at the childish gesture.

"We're a right pair," he said, refilling her glass. "You, in love with a married man and me trapped in a loveless marriage. You'd think we'd have enough sense at our age to have it sorted."

"That's life," she said, raising her glass to him.

40

Ashling had loved having her mother and Fiona to stay over the weekend and wished they could have stayed longer. As she left them at the departure gate at the airport, she hugged them both.

"You'll have to come again soon," she said. "It was brilliant having you here."

"We will, love, we will," her mother replied, hugging her again. "You mind yourself now."

Fiona was busy texting Hugh again. She'd done nothing else since she'd got up this morning. "Hugh says he's going to come to Ireland to see me," she cried, her eyes shining.

"Oh my God, what have we started here?" Ashling laughed.

Nora threw her eyes to heaven. She could see that she'd be forking out for flights to Paris for her romantic daughter in the future. Still, she was delighted to see Fiona so happy and this guy Hugh seemed like a very decent fellow.

As soon as Ashling entered the gym, Hugh bounded over to her.

"Did Fee get off okay? Was she lonely going?" he wanted to know.

"Yes and yes," she replied, laughing. She was pleased to see that he was as smitten as Fiona was. Thank God it wasn't one-sided. She'd hate her baby sister to get hurt.

"She's brilliant. I really like her. I'm planning to go to Dublin to see her in two weeks' time."

"That's great. She'll give you a good time there. She has loads of friends."

"I can imagine. Everyone must love her," he said, his eyes dreamy.

Lordy me, he has it bad too, Ashling thought as he bounded away to answer the phone. Just as she was leaving the gym she saw him texting, a big grin on his face. She wondered if it was her sister who was on the receiving end.

It was. Hugh came over to her, his face split in a smile.

"They've landed safely in Dublin," he reported.

"I guess your texting bills are going to be quite high for the next few weeks," she laughed.

"I hope so," he replied, beaming at her.

Corey was seated at his usual table when she entered the café and she joined him for a quick coffee.

"What a lovely woman your mother is," he remarked, as Remy appeared with two coffees.

"She was equally charmed by you," Ashling laughed, remembering how coquettish her mother had become in his presence.

"What a beautiful family!" he sighed. "And I wasn't joking when I told her you were a talented writer. I've just heard back from my agent and he likes the six chapters of your novel that I sent him."

"Oh my God!" Ashling's hand flew to her mouth. "You're not serious? I can't believe it!" Her face was flushed with pleasure. "I didn't know you were going to send it to him."

"Well, when I realised how good you were, I thought I'd suss it out. My agent suggests that as it's based in Europe, it would be best to go with a publisher in the UK. As you know, Philippa Gregory's novels have been hugely successful there and yours are in the same genre. He's willing to approach them, on your behalf, as he has great contacts there. He's convinced it's a winner, so you go, girl, and get the rest of that novel finished, pronto!" He laughed at her incredulity.

"Oh I will, I will!" She jumped up, overcome with delight. She couldn't believe it.

Blowing him a kiss, she went to her own table where she got down to work with a light heart. *Me, a published author! I can't believe it,* she said to herself, over and over.

Yves had passed a miserable weekend. Sophie was angry with him and he didn't blame her. He'd have to cool it with Jazz. She was getting too involved and that was the last thing he needed. No, great as the sex was, he'd have to finish it. He really did love Sophie and couldn't imagine his life without her and Pierre. He just found it so hard to resist chasing women. He loved the excitement of it. He loved the sex and Sophie understood his need but it had to stop at the sex. No romantic involvement – they'd both agreed on that.

On Monday morning he went into Jazz's office, as he did every morning, but he avoided looking at her directly.

"How is Taylor?" he asked Brandon.

"She's doing fine," Brandon replied. "Happy to be back in the States." That wasn't strictly a lie. She was glad to be out of France although she wasn't exactly happy with *where* she was in the States.

"Give her my regards," Yves said before starting to discuss the agenda for the week ahead.

He left the office without saying a word to Jazz. She was worried. Had something happened? Normally he couldn't take his eyes off her and dallied on the least excuse. Today it was different. He didn't text to ask her to meet for lunch. When he hadn't contacted her by four o'clock she swallowed her pride and texted him, 'Are we meeting tonight?' He replied, 'Sorry, not tonight.' In a moment of weakness, he added, 'Tomorrow night? Your place?' Relieved, she texted back, 'Can't wait! xx'

Yves knew that this was probably a mistake but the thought of Jazz's voluptuous body was irresistible. Just then his phone rang.

"Hi, lover boy, remember me?" He recognised the American drawl but couldn't visualise the owner. He hesitated for a second – then it came to him.

"Marilyn! How could I not remember you? You've been on mind since last week," he lied.

"Well, how about my being on your body instead," she purred, her voice husky and incredibly sexy.

Maybe this was what he needed to give him the courage to finish with Jazz. "Anytime," he smiled to himself.

"Tonight?"

"My pleasure," he replied, his voice low and smooth.

"Mine too, I hope," she pealed with laughter.

She had the sexiest laugh he'd ever heard. He gave her the address of the Hôtel Lutèce and they arranged to meet there at six thirty. He then rang the concierge, Guy, and asked him to put two glasses and a bottle of champagne on ice in the room for him.

Guy laughed. Another new conquest for Monsieur Yves! He had to be the randiest man in Paris. He wished he knew from where he got his stamina. Guy did as he was asked, knowing that Monsieur Yves would reward him with a generous tip, as he always did.

When Yves rang Sophie to say he'd be late, she decided she'd had enough. She had to find out who her rival was. Kissing Pierre goodnight, she told him to be a good boy for Cosette before setting out for the Île Saint-Louis. She had known about the Hôtel de Lutèce since Yves had first brought her there many years previously. She also knew, from his bank statements, that he rented the room on a yearly basis. She guessed that this was where he brought his lovers but it had never bothered her till now.

Parking her car, she put on the long blonde wig and sunglasses and made her way to the little café directly opposite the hotel. Taking a seat where she had a clear view of the hotel door she didn't have long to wait. Within twenty minutes, Yves swaggered along. He entered the hotel looking neither left nor right as he took the stairs two at a time.

Filled with apprehension, sipping slowly at her glass of wine, she saw the taxi draw up and the blonde alight. From a distance it could have been Marilyn Monroe. Then it dawned on her. It was Marilyn – Taylor's friend. I might have guessed! Sophie grimaced. She remembered how Marilyn had been flirting outrageously with Yves at Taylor's party and how he'd obviously enjoyed it. So that's the mystery woman! In a way, she felt relieved. Marilyn was sex-on-legs and there was no way Yves would have wanted her for anything other than sex. She was happy that the mystery was cleared up once and for all, yet somehow she felt deflated. The fact that Yves would rather spend his evenings with this bimbo rather than with her and Pierre left her feeling demeaned. What did it say about their marriage?

Making her way back to her car, she wondered if it was her fault that he felt this need for other women. She had hoped that once he became a father he would slow down. Even though he was now past fifty, he showed no signs of that – except with her. Their love-making had declined lately and become much more infrequent. Perhaps Marilyn was exhausting him so much that he had no energy left for her when he got home.

She sighed as she got into her car and pulled off the wig and sunglasses. She couldn't go on like this. Things would have to change!

Jazz and Yves had arranged to meet in her apartment the following night. He was apprehensive about the meeting and she sensed from the minute he walked in the door that something was wrong. They made love straight away and as they were lying together afterwards, he smoking a Gauloise as he always did after their love-making, she asked him if everything was okay.

"*Chérie,* I am sorry, but we will have to cut back on our meetings because my wife is not happy that I am out every night with you," he told her.

Jazz felt like she'd been punched in the stomach.

"Does Sophie know about me?" she whispered, panic in her voice.

"No. She does know that I have a mistress but she has no idea who it is," he assured her.

She flinched at the word 'mistress'. It sounded seedy somehow. She didn't want to be his mistress – she wanted to be his love.

"So you understand that I cannot meet you so much now," he continued, unaware of her feelings.

She felt let down and cheap. She'd hoped that he'd discover that he truly loved her and somehow find a solution. Now it appeared that he was more concerned with appeasing Sophie than pleasing her. Unfairly, she knew, she felt jealous of Sophie. And how would she survive not seeing him every night? She couldn't bear to think of it.

"And how often can you meet me?" she asked in a whisper, afraid of the answer.

"Maybe two nights a week," he replied, cupping her face in his hands. "You understand, *ma petite*, I want to be with you all the time, but it's not possible."

She wanted to believe him and when he started caressing between her thighs once more she put all these thoughts from her mind as she succumbed to his touch. After they'd made love once more, he said he would have to go and left abruptly, leaving her feeling empty and dejected.

Mistress, she said to herself, hating the word. I'm just his mistress!

On Wednesday Sophie rang Ashling. "Pierre has me pestered to let him go to your house to play with the girls. Do you mind?"

"Of course not," Ashling laughed. "They'll be delighted. Is Friday okay? I'll pick him up from school and you can collect him later."

"That would be great. I'll pick him up around six."

It was a very happy little boy who greeted Ashling on Friday afternoon. The three children got on extremely well together and Ashling wondered where they got their energy from.

"Pierre's my boyfriend," Orna announced over lunch, as the little boy sat beaming at her.

"He's my boyfwend too," Ciara lisped.

"No, he can't be yours too," Orna informed her. "Can he, Mummy?"

Before Ashling could think of a way out of this dilemma, Pierre saved the day. He had it all worked out.

"I'll be your boyfriend on Monday, Wednesday and Friday," he told Orna, "and on Tuesday and Thursday I'll be Ciara's. Is that all right?"

Ashling laughed at the ingenuity of it.

Orna looked perplexed until she realised that she would have him more days than Ciara. She seemed happy enough with that.

"Today's Friday, so it's my turn," she exclaimed, with a pleased smile.

Sophie arrived at six, as agreed, but the children were in the middle of a game and Pierre begged to be allowed to stay a little longer.

"Oh, do let him stay another hour. They've no school tomorrow and Kieran is gone to Ireland to visit his mother again. I could do with some adult company," Ashling admitted, pulling a face.

"Why not? There's no one waiting for me either," Sophie said, sitting down as Ashling poured two glasses of wine for them.

"Is Yves working?" she asked the pretty French woman.

"Not exactly," she grimaced. "To tell you the truth he has a new mistress and he's seeing her every night."

Ashling almost dropped her glass in shock. She didn't know what to say. "I *am* sorry," was all she could manage. Her voice sounded like a squeak even to her own ears.

"Well, I've never minded him having a mistress but I was getting worried as this time he had begun meeting her every night. I was concerned that perhaps he was getting involved but when I discovered who she is, I realised that my fears were unfounded." She smiled over the rim of her glass.

Ashling felt the blood drain from her face. "Why is that?" she couldn't help but ask.

"Well, it's Taylor's friend, Marilyn."

Nothing could have prepared Ashling for this piece of news.

"Marilyn?" she squeaked. Felicity had told her all about the sex-siren. "How do you know?"

"I know Yves holds his little trysts in the Hôtel de Lutèce and I spied on him last Monday night. I know it's not a nice thing to do but I had to find out who he was seeing, as he wouldn't tell me."

Ashling realised with horror that this was the same hotel that he'd been taking Jazz to. Not only that but Jazz had arrived on

Ashling's doorstep last Monday, very dejected because Yves had been unable to meet her. God, what a mess! It looked like Yves was two-timing Jazz as well as his wife. She felt equally sorry for both women.

"What can I say?" she said feebly.

"I'm sorry for unburdening myself like this," Sophie apologised, "but somehow you are so kind, you invite confidences."

Ashling had heard this so many times before that she now wished to God that she wasn't so bloody kind! What should she do now?

She refilled their glasses, relieved that Sophie had not noticed her shock.

"I guess it will burn itself out, like it always does, but I think maybe it's time to call a halt to all his philandering."

"I don't know how you do it," Ashling said truthfully. "If Kieran went with another woman, I'd kill him." From the tone of her voice, Sophie knew she meant it.

"Yes, well, it's the way it is," Sophie replied, not sounding too happy about it.

They discussed Taylor and Kieran's mother's illness until it was time for Sophie and Pierre to leave. Ashling closed the door with relief. And to think I wanted some adult company, she thought, having got more than she'd bargained for with Sophie. I'll settle for children from now on!

Brandon was very concerned about Jazz. They went out for a drink on Friday night and she told him that Yves was pulling back on their relationship. She'd only met up with him twice that week and she was very depressed about it. Brandon wished to God that Yves would finish it completely and let Jazz move on with her life but, knowing the bastard, he guessed that he'd hang in there as long as it suited him.

He also wasn't happy with the reports he was getting from Bob. Taylor had been three weeks in the clinic now and had seemingly made friends with another patient there – a young man who was a serious drug user. He came from a very wealthy family but according to Bob he was an utter waster. Bob was afraid that this friendship would not be very helpful to Taylor's recovery. He had spoken to Taylor who had told him to fuck off and mind his own business. She'd make friends with whoever she chose, she'd informed him. There was nothing that Brandon could do except wait and hope. He had made up his mind. He would wait for Taylor to recover and be well again and then he would seek a divorce. He couldn't kick her while she was down, so for the moment, he'd have to stick by her.

Marilyn had been calling regularly asking for news of Taylor. He appreciated that she was concerned and had come to realise that he was wrong to blame her for Taylor's predicament. Nobody had forced his wife to take drugs. She had chosen to do so.

At the same time that Jazz was pouring her heart out to Brandon and Sophie was doing the same to Ashling, Yves was enjoying Marilyn's favours once more. She was a tonic! She was funny and witty and, best of all, she wanted him solely for sex. She'd told him that Louis had asked her to marry him.

"But, if I say yes, that doesn't mean that we can't still see each other from time to time," she'd winked at him.

She was fun in bed. The sex wasn't as good as with Jazz but she was a nice antidote to Jazz's intensity. He reckoned he had the best of both worlds. If he could keep this going it would be ideal. Jazz a couple of nights a week, Marilyn another one or two, and the weekends would be spent with Sophie, whom he really loved. Yes, life was *absolument parfait* – just perfect, he smiled smugly to himself.

Brandon took Jazz and Ashling out for a meal on Saturday night and Jazz's mood had lightened somewhat. Thank God she had Ashling for a friend, he thought. That girl was a rock of sense. He wished that Taylor could have made friends with the lovely Irish girl when she'd been here. She might not be where she was now if she'd had someone like Ashling in her corner.

Ashling really didn't know what she should do about Sophie's revelations. Should she tell Jazz, or not? She wished Kieran was here to discuss it with her but he wasn't flying back from Ireland till Monday morning and was then going straight to work from the airport.

41

On Monday morning after her gym session, Ashling went as usual to Les Deux Magots. She lost herself in her book and, over lunch with Corey, she told him about her dilemma, not mentioning any names of course.

"So," she finished up, "I honestly don't know what I should do."

"If it was you, in your friend's position, would you want to know your lover was cheating on you?" he asked.

"Yes. Definitely," Ashling replied.

"You have your answer, then. You should tell her," he said quietly.

"Thank you, Corey. I will," she replied, relieved that she'd made a decision.

The women had started getting together once a week and tonight it was Ashling's turn to have them at her place.

Jazz knew that if Yves asked to meet her, she would be tempted to cancel Ashling's and go to him. She texted him to ask him if he wanted to see her.

'Sorry, chérie, can't see you tonight. Have to stay home. Tomorrow night, your place?'

Well, no decision to be made there then, she thought bitterly.

"I nearly didn't make it tonight," Sophie remarked, as they ate supper. "Monday is Cosette's night off and Nicole was busy. I was worried I wouldn't get a baby-sitter but luckily, Nicole's friend stepped in at the last minute."

"Is Yves not baby-sitting for you?" Jazz asked, curious.

"Good heavens, no. Yves couldn't stay in midweek to save his life. He goes out every night. I wouldn't dare interfere with that." She laughed but it sounded hollow.

Felicity thought how awful it was that she only saw Yves at weekends. If Max was out every night, Felicity would kill him.

"We have an open marriage," Sophie explained. "We're both free to have other partners as long as we don't become involved."

Felicity gasped. She stared open-mouthed at Sophie.

"Oh Lord," she said, sounding distressed, "I could never manage that."

"I'm afraid I wouldn't be able to cope with that either," Ashling agreed. "Is it not . . . difficult?" She'd been about to say impossible. Jazz said nothing.

"Well, it seems to work for us," Sophie mumbled, aware of their disapproval.

'For him maybe,' Ashling wanted to say, 'but not for you.' She kept mum.

"He does spend all weekend at home with Pierre and me, though, so I can't complain," Sophie added. Although she was smiling Ashling could see the bleakness in her eyes.

She also saw the puzzled frown on Jazz's face. Please, please, don't say anything, Ashling prayed silently. She was terrified that Jazz might let the cat out of the bag. Luckily, she didn't but Ashling could see that she was pondering what Sophie had said.

Jazz was very quiet for the rest of the night and when the others had left she turned to Ashling, who knew what was coming.

"Ash, did you hear what Sophie said about Yves being out every night? He told me that he had to be home tonight and that he had to spend more time at home during the week but, according to Sophie, that's not true. Why would he lie to me?"

Ashling took a deep breath. "Jazz, I've been debating all weekend whether I should tell you this or not, but I was talking to Sophie on Friday and she told me that Yves is having an affair."

"She knows about me?" Jazz was shocked.

"No, she says he's having an affair with Marilyn, Taylor's friend."

"Marilyn?" Jazz repeated, shaking her head in disbelief. "Why does Sophie think that?"

Ashling wished that she could have done something to spare her friend the truth but she knew she had to be honest with her. Taking Jazz by the hand she told her, "Because she spied on him last Monday – the night you came around to me – and she saw him with Marilyn, at that hotel you told me about. I'm so sorry, sweetheart." She stroked Jazz's hand in an effort to comfort her.

Jazz looked at her, stunned. "He's probably with her tonight, isn't he?" she whispered. This thought devastated her. "Oh God, I've been such a fool," she cried.

"You weren't to know," Ashling consoled her. "He *is* very persuasive."

"No, I was a fool. I *am* a fool to have believed him," she said, her voice low.

"What else did Sophie say?" She looked at Ashling, her face stricken.

"Well, she seems to accept that he always has to have a mistress but that he truly loves her." Ashling hated having to say these words.

"*Mistress*, that's what he said I was, his mistress," Jazz said bitterly, "but at least I thought that I was the only one. But he's just been using me, hasn't he?" she turned to Ashling, tears in her eyes. "I never meant anything to him. I was just another notch on his bedpost."

"Honey, I know it's hard to believe right now," she told her gently, "but even if he did love you, he wouldn't have treated you any differently than he's treating Sophie. He's a serial womaniser and there will always be mistresses."

"I so much regret that I was one of them. Poor Sophie! How does she bear it?" Jazz looked at Ashling with a tear-stained face. "I feel so guilty about her. She was so sweet to me tonight."

"Yes, well, thank God she never discovered that you were one of his conquests," Ashling said grimly.

Jazz looked devastated as she got ready to leave.

"Are you okay? Would you like to stay here tonight?" Ashling asked.

"No, no, I'll be fine, honestly. I need to think about this." She looked in shock and Ashling wished she could do something to help.

"Well, if you need me, I'm at the other end of the phone."

"Thanks, Ash. I'll call you tomorrow." She gave a grim smile. "I feel so betrayed."

"I know, honey. Try and get some sleep if you can," she said, hugging her devastated friend. Bloody men, she thought, not for the first time.

When Jazz got home she made herself a hot chocolate and, taking the duvet off her bed, wrapped it around her and went out to sit on the terrace. Sipping the hot chocolate, she thought about what Ash had just told her. To think that Yves had been cheating on her with Marilyn, the silly bimbo that Brandon and she had laughed about. Had he no taste whatsoever? He'd been with her last Monday night and probably again tonight when he could have been with me, she thought. She started to get angry, firstly with him for his lying and then with herself for being such a bloody fool. No fool like an old fool, she laughed harshly. Well, at least she'd found out before she'd made a complete ass of herself.

"Monsieur Yves, I've wasted enough of my life on you! *Adieu!* Good riddance!" she said aloud to the night sky.

She didn't get much sleep that night. She tossed and turned until daybreak, when she finally fell into a restless sleep. She would never meet him again. Nor would she let him know why. It would be small comfort for the dreadful betrayal she was feeling.

Brandon noticed that Jazz was very subdued on Tuesday morning but he had enough problems of his own to worry about. His daughter, Mia, had rung very late last night and asked to speak to Taylor. He was running out of excuses to give her for her mother's absence. He knew Mia was suspicious that all was not well if

Taylor was still out at one in the morning. Although there was no love lost between mother and daughter, Mia was a dutiful girl. Her twin, Mike, on the other hand, believed whatever you told him.

Bob had also rung last night and left a message to call back. When Brandon called him, it was to be told that Bob was getting more and more concerned about Taylor's friendship with Dylan, the other patient at the clinic with whom she'd become friendly.

"I can't prove anything, but I suspect he's getting drugs from somewhere. You know how money talks," he said grimly. "Problem is, I think he may be sharing them with Taylor which means that her treatment here will be worthless."

"Oh God, what can we do?" Brandon asked him.

"Nothing except keep an eye on her. She's being very uncooperative." Bob sounded pissed off.

"Well, I appreciate all you're doing, Bob. Thanks."

"No problem, buddy. Anything for an old friend."

Brandon felt that he should probably go home straight away but things were very hectic at work and anyway he would be going back to the States shortly for Christmas. Bob was being brilliant but, at the end of the day, Taylor was *his* problem. And he'd have to tell the kids then. He hated lying to them.

Thank God for Chantal. He'd spent last evening with her and, loath to leave her loving arms and uncomplicated mind, had stayed much longer than usual. He longed to tell her his problems but was afraid that she might let it slip to one of her friends in the office and then it would be all over the building within minutes. No, he'd restrict his confidences to Jazz whom he knew he could trust. She was acting very strangely today, he noticed.

Jazz kept her head down and spoke very little all day. She was still reeling from the disclosure of last night and when Yves came into the office it was all she could do not to hurl her computer at him. However, she kept her cool and greeted him civilly but kept on working, avoiding his eyes.

Ashling had rung earlier and Jazz had assured her that she was fine.

"Would you like to come around here this evening? Kieran is coming home early but you're welcome to come and have supper with us."

Jazz knew that Ash had hardly seen Kieran in five days so she figured they'd need some time alone.

"Sorry, Ash, but I'm planning an early night."

"Well, if you change your mind, just drop in."

"Thanks, Ash. You're a pal." Jazz thought what a great friend Ashling was turning out to be.

She had arranged to meet Yves that evening but planned not to be there when he turned up.

"Brandon, can you meet me after work and we'll go for something to eat?" she asked.

He had intended working late but something in her tone of voice alerted him that all was not well.

"Are you not meeting anyone?" he asked her, nodding in the direction of Yves's office.

"No. That's what I want to talk to you about."

Brandon wondered what the hell was going on. He'd noticed her coolness to Yves that morning. Well, he'd find out soon enough.

Ashling could see that Kieran was exhausted. He had come home early, as promised, and they had a lovely family meal together. The girls were talking nineteen to the dozen, giving him all their news and he winked at Ashling who couldn't get a word in edgeways. After he'd put the girls to bed she opened a bottle of red wine and they sat cosily on the sofa, ready to catch up on each other's news.

There was no change in his mother's condition and she could go on like this for months, they said.

"I feel like I'm chasing my tail all the time," he said, "and I'm just exhausted. I feel like it will never end."

"It will, sweetheart. It's a shame that this happened to your mother while we're here. But you can't change anything."

"I know. I did wonder if I should pack in this job and go back to Dublin to be near her . . ."

"Oh no!" Ashling cried.

"No, babe, don't worry. I wouldn't do that to you. I know how much you and the girls love it here, but I miss spending time with you."

"Honey, if you could get home earlier every night, then we could have many more evenings like this," she suggested, gently. "You work too hard."

"I know. You're right. I will definitely make a huge effort to leave the office by six at the latest," he said, slipping his arm around her. "Now tell me, what have you been doing with yourself?"

"Well . . . I've started writing a novel and a writer in the café has shown the first six chapters to his agent and guess what?" she cried, her eyes shining. "He thinks it's good and wants to see more!"

"My God, when did all this happen?" Kieran asked, stunned.

"Well, I didn't want to tell you until I knew I could write but Corey – that's the writer guy – he thought my stuff was good and *voilà*!" She raised her hands.

Kieran didn't like the sound of this one bit. It must have taken her a couple of weeks at least to write six chapters and yet she'd never mentioned it.

"Why didn't you tell me before now, Ash?"

"Darling, you're never here and when you are you're always so tired. I never really got a chance."

He sat looking into his glass quietly as she got up to pour some more wine. Was it really like that? Being honest, he had to admit that it was. God, he was a fool! He'd seen so many colleagues losing their wives and families because they were so caught up in business that they'd let things slip away. Well, he wouldn't be one of them. He loved Ashling more than anything in the world. Without her nothing had any meaning. Yet, they were drifting apart – thanks to him. Things would have to change. *He'd* have to change, if he didn't want his marriage to be one of those casualties.

"I've decided that I'm not going to see my mother this weekend," he said. "And I'm taking you out for a romantic dinner on Friday night."

Ashling clapped her hands. "Fantastic! There's this cute little restaurant that my friend on the wine course told me about. I'd love to go there."

"Okay, you make the reservation," he smiled at her.

Finishing their wine they went up to bed where he made sweet, gentle love to her. Just before he fell asleep he found himself wondering what this guy Corey was like. He'd have to find out.

Yves arrived at Jazz's apartment to find that she wasn't there. Perhaps she was in the shower getting ready for him, he thought smugly. She was always so fresh and clean and delicious-smelling. He couldn't wait to be inhaling her gorgeous musky scent. He went for a stroll around the block, smiling as he passed the Hôtel de Lutèce. Marilyn had been in great form the night before. She had him almost exhausted. Ten minutes later he was back at Jazz's ringing her doorbell again. Still no reply. Maybe she couldn't hear the bell. He called her mobile phone and got her voicemail.

"Hi, *cherie*, I'm here outside your apartment but you're not answering. Can you let me in please?" He waited a few minutes. Still no reply. He rang again and left another voicemail. "Jazz, where are you? For God's sake answer the door." He was getting more irritated by the minute.

Jazz was, at that moment, sitting in a restaurant in Les Halles with Brandon. She listened to the voicemails and smiled. She ignored them. Brandon wondered what the hell was going on. She still hadn't mentioned anything about Yves.

Five minutes later she received a text. "Excuse me a moment while I answer this," she said to Brandon.

'Sorry, can't make it tonight. Jazz' she texted back.

"Now, would you mind telling me what all that was about?" Brandon asked her when she had finished texting and had turned her phone off.

"Sweet revenge," she replied, giving him a little smile.

"On who? Come on, don't keep me in suspense."

"You'll be pleased to hear it's on Yves."

She then told him about Yves's betrayal and what she'd found out the night before.

"The bastard!" Brandon cried, banging his fist on the table. "And with Marilyn, of all people. What a cad!"

"I agree, but it was as much my fault for having anything to do with him," she said sheepishly.

"The main thing is that you found out now. Better now than later. I always knew that it would come to a bad end." He shook his head.

"I know, I know. Everyone warned me about him but I wouldn't listen. Anyway, let's forget about him now and enjoy our evening."

"Are you sure you're okay?" he asked, concern in his voice.

"I'm fine, truly. I'm over him. I have that much respect for myself," she smiled tremulously at him.

"Good girl! Now let's order."

"Thanks for being here and listening," she replied as she turned her attention to the menu.

Yves read the text from Jazz with disbelief. What was going on? She was always ready and hot for him when he arrived. This was unbelievable! He texted her again and again but she didn't reply. Where was she? How could she do this to him! He'd been aroused and looking forward to some great sex and now this! Furious with her, he left and went into the nearest bar. He rang Marilyn but her mobile phone was turned off. She'd warned him never to ring her at home. Louis wouldn't take too kindly to it.

Frustrated, he rang Chantal.

"Hi, baby, I was wondering if you're free tonight?" he asked his young secretary.

"Sorry, Yves, I can't. I'm seeing someone else at the moment so it's out of the question," she replied.

"*Merde*!" he cried, hanging up.

Thoroughly annoyed now, he spotted the girl sitting alone at the bar. She smiled at him. He raised his glass to her and she sashayed over to him. He bought her a drink and within twenty minutes she was leaving for Hôtel de Lutèce with him. They undressed and he was delighted to find that she certainly knew how to get a man aroused. As he was about to enter her, she put up her hand.

"Let's get business out of the way first, shall we?" she whispered.

"Business?"

"Yes. I charge one hundred euro. Five hundred if you want me to stay all night."

Yves looked at her disbelievingly. He'd teamed up with a hooker!

"And if I decide I don't want to continue?" he asked. She was stroking him sensually all the while and he still had a hard-on.

"I'm afraid you'll still owe me the hundred euro. But you don't want to stop, do you?" she smiled, stroking him faster.

"Noooo," he moaned. "Okay," he agreed, reaching for his wallet and taking out a hundred euro. There was no way he wanted her to stay the night!

It was over in less than an hour but he reckoned he'd got his money's worth. Disgusted with himself and raging against all women – Jazz in particular – he took a shower, then went out to the nearest bar and drank himself into oblivion.

When Jazz turned on her phone again there were fifteen texts from Yves and a couple of drunken voicemails. Great, she thought, feeling some satisfaction.

The following morning he looked like hell when he came into their office. Hungover as he was, he could feel the frosty atmosphere that greeted him. Jazz left, giving him a curt nod and Brandon was extremely cool with him. What did I do wrong? he asked himself. He couldn't figure it out. Everything had been going so swimmingly. Mid-morning he received a text from Jazz saying that she didn't want to have anything more to do with him. He was flabbergasted. Had Sophie found out and said something to her? He quaked at the thought.

Jazz had to call on every reserve of strength she possessed to get over Yves. Yes, she missed his lovemaking but what was that worth if there was no love in it? She'd thought that she was in love with him but realised now that she'd been in lust with him. She could not have loved anyone as despicable as he had turned out to be. More importantly, she now respected herself again. She'd felt so horrible and guilty, especially where Sophie was concerned, but now that guilt was lifting and it felt good. She would mark the whole thing down to experience and never make the same stupid mistake again.

Yves pestered her all week with texts and voicemails but she refused to discuss it with him. She kept her phone off most of the time. Finally, he'd nabbed her as she was leaving the office on Friday. She gave him no excuse and refused to discuss it.

"Just accept it. It's over," had been her parting shot as she walked away. The look of incredulity on his face had given her great satisfaction.

She couldn't believe her stupidity in getting involved with him again. She felt such an idiot and, when she saw cute little Pierre at Orna's birthday party the following Sunday, she was truly grateful that she'd seen sense.

Ashling was delighted to see that Jazz was back to her old self, playing with the children and keeping them entertained. Orna had invited four little friends from school and three from the park, so Ashling had quite a handful to cope with. She'd shooed Kieran off to golf with Max that morning and he'd promised they'd be back in time for the birthday cake. He seemed to be making a big effort and, true to his word, had come home early almost every night. Last night they'd had the most wonderful romantic evening out and had made love afterwards. Twice in one week! Things were looking up! She smiled at the memory.

Just as they were about to have tea, Fiona rang to wish Orna a happy birthday. She was bubbling with excitement as she told her sister that Hugh was coming over to Ireland to see her the following weekend. She was obviously crazy about him.

Thankfully, Yves hadn't put in an appearance. Well, it *was* a kiddie's birthday party but you never knew what could happen. She guessed that he wouldn't take Jazz's put-down lightly. Doubtless his male ego had been bruised.

After the tea, when the other children had all gone home, Orna, Ciara and Pierre snuggled up on Ashling's bed to watch *Toy Story 3*. Max and Kieran were playing a golf game on the computer – as if playing eighteen holes of golf that day had not been enough!

"Men! They're worse than children," Ashling exclaimed, and the other three women agreed wholeheartedly.

With the men and the children thus occupied, the women sat chatting over a bottle of wine. They all agreed that the move to Paris had gone swimmingly. Except for poor Taylor, of course!

Poor Taylor, as they called her, was up to her old tricks. Dylan, her new BFF, had her completely in thrall. He was younger than she, handsome and from a filthy-rich family who bankrolled him but wanted to have nothing to do with him. Best of all, he understood her need for the drugs as it mirrored his own. With his unlimited access to funds he had no problem getting people to supply him with them. He very generously shared his stash with Taylor. She'd decided that he was her soul mate.

She knew Bob was watching her and doubtless reporting her every move to Brandon so she had to be very very careful. The only place she could snort or swallow was in the ladies' room. She even half-expected him to follow her in there!

"I'm sick of this place," she confided to Dylan one night after Bob had been on her case all day. "My husband's spy will hardly let me go to the john!"

"Okay so, let's split," he said, nonchalantly.

"We can't just walk out."

"Who says we can't? It's rehab – not a prison. We're here of our own free will. They can't detain us."

And just like that, she gathered up her belongings and walked out with him. They got a taxi to his place in Greenwich Village and, in the early hours of the morning, topped up with umpteen vodkas and cocaine, they fell into bed together. He wasn't demanding as a lover, not at all like Brandon, and in five minutes it was over. She felt happier than she'd ever been and fell asleep with his arms wrapped around her. They were a team.

Brandon was wakened out of a deep sleep by the ringing of the telephone.

"Hello," he mumbled, switching on the light to see what time it was. The clock read 5.30 a.m. That meant 11.30 p.m. in New York.

"Hi, buddy," said Bob. "Bad news, I'm afraid. Taylor walked out of here tonight with that waster I told you about. I tried talking to her but I could do nothing to stop her if she wanted to go."

"Christ!"

"I can't help her any more, pal, and neither can you. I guess it's her choice to live like this."

"Oh God! Thanks, Bob, I appreciate all you've done. I guess you're probably right. Do you know where she might be?"

"Probably crashed out in his pad. He has a place in the Village, I believe. I can check it out for you."

"Hey, Bob. Thanks again. I owe you big-time. Maybe you can tell me what I can do to help her."

"Buddy, I hate to have to tell you this, but I think Taylor is past help. She doesn't want to give up the drugs. Until *she* wants to do it herself nobody can make her."

Brandon let out a long sigh. "Let me know where she is anyway. I can't get away from here until Friday, I'm afraid."

"I don't think it will make any difference when you come, to be honest with you."

Brandon thanked him again and hung up. This was the end! He wouldn't take any more crap from Taylor. She obviously didn't want to get well. Either she cleaned up her act pronto or he was out of there! Even Bob had given up on her. Angrily he got out of bed. There was no way he could get back to sleep after this bombshell. Going on-line, he found a flight leaving on Friday evening. He booked himself on it. How he missed Concorde!

He showered, made himself breakfast and was at his desk by seven thirty.

Jazz knew from his hunched shoulders that something was wrong.

She took off her jacket and pulled a chair up to his desk.

"What is it?" she asked, looking into his troubled eyes.

"It's Taylor. She's left rehab and is shacked up with some waster who has been supplying her with drugs. He's a serious drug user, seemingly."

Jazz wanted to reach out and comfort him but at that moment Yves came into the office so she went back to her own desk, nodding curtly at him.

As soon as he had left, she made two coffees and set one in front of Brandon.

"You look like you could do with this," she said, her voice full of sympathy as she sat by his desk once more. "What are you going to do?"

"I'm flying to New York on Friday to try and find out what's going on. My friend Bob thinks there's no hope of saving her," he said bleakly.

"Oh God, I'm so sorry." Jazz could find no words of comfort for him. What can one say in this situation, she wondered?

"I shouldn't be away for too long," he said.

"Take as long as you need. I'll keep things running here for you," she assured him.

"God what a mess," he said glumly, as he finished his coffee and reopened his computer. Jazz had to agree with him.

Lying in Chantal's arms that Thursday night, Brandon felt grateful for her calm and gentleness. He told her that he would be away for a couple of days and might not be able to see her the following week.

"You want talk about it? I know you very worried," she said gently.

"Thanks, but I can't talk about it at the moment – maybe someday." He smiled at her, grateful for her concern. She was such a sweetie.

Sophie had been taking stock of her life. Remembering how the other girls had reacted to her 'open marriage' confession, she was now seriously questioning if they weren't right. She suspected the affair with Marilyn was over as Yves was home most nights now. He seemed depressed and she often caught him just staring into space. When she asked him to sit down and discuss the problem, he'd stormed out.

"*Merde,* woman! Leave me alone!"

She felt near to tears at that. She wondered whether perhaps she'd been mistaken about Marilyn and whether he was in fact in love with her and that she'd been the one to finish the affair. She had no way of finding out. He certainly wouldn't discuss it with her. He did keep assuring her that he loved her but he never wanted to make love. She wanted very much to believe him. Whatever it was, something was seriously bothering him.

42

Taylor didn't know what day of the week it was. Life was one big merry-go-round of drugs and parties. She loved it. Dylan was fantastic. He had loads of friends who came and went at all hours of the day and night. She felt like a teenager again, except she'd never done anything this wild back then. She was finally getting to live the hippie lifestyle and it was fun.

She was high as a kite when Dylan answered the knock on the door. She got the shock of her life when he came back into the room with Brandon and Bob in tow.

"Oh my God, what are you doing here?" she cried, her face as white as a sheet.

Brandon took in the dishevelled clothes and hair and the messy apartment and wondered how she had come to this.

"I'm here to take you home," he said, his voice quiet and steely.

Dylan stood by, in awe of this elegant man who oozed authority. He reminded him of his own father and he felt nervous in his presence.

"I'm not going anywhere," she said. "This is my home now."

"Do you mind if I have a private word with my wife," Brandon asked Dylan.

"C-course not," Dylan stuttered nervously. He shrugged his shoulders and looked at her helplessly. He left the room with Bob as Brandon looked at her with pity and disgust.

"Taylor, what has happened to you?" he cried. He tried to take her hand but she yanked it away. "Taylor, please let me get help for you."

"I don't want help – I'm happy here," she said sulkily.

"Taylor, I came all the way from Paris to try and help you but if you don't want my help then there's nothing more I can do."

"There is one thing you can do for me," she replied. "I want a divorce."

He thought he was hearing things. *She* wanted a divorce! He felt like laughing.

"Yes," she said, brazen now. "Dylan and I want to get married."

Now he did laugh. "Are you serious?" he asked incredulously.

"Very. Will you see to it?"

"With pleasure, *madame*," he said. Turning on his heels, he walked out.

"It's no good, Bob, there's nothing we can do any more to save her," he said sadly as they walked back to Bob's car. "Can you believe it? She wants a divorce so she can marry that guy! What did I do wrong?"

"I've seen what drugs can do to people, Brandon. Don't blame yourself. It's her choice." He patted his old friend on the back. "What next?"

"I'll consult my lawyer tomorrow morning and set it in motion and then I'll fly straight to California and explain things to the kids." He let out a long sigh. "That won't be easy."

And it wasn't easy. They were delighted to see him but not so happy when they found out the reason for his visit. Mia burst into tears and Mike looked shaken. He hated having to hurt them but he owed them the truth.

"Can we go and see her?" Mike wanted to know.

"I wouldn't advise it, but it's up to you," he replied, frowning. "Bob will take you to her, if you want, but I must warn you, she's not the mother you knew. You'll be horrified at how she is and the conditions she's chosen to live in." He stressed the word 'chosen'.

He also promised that they would spend Christmas together, at his expense.

"How does Barbados sound?" he asked. "First class all the way of course," he added, lightening the mood for the first time since he'd arrived.

He enjoyed spending time with them and hearing all their news, before catching his flight back to New York. The night before he left LA he had dinner with them and their partners. He really liked Mia's boyfriend, Doug, and it was obvious that they were very much in love. Mike's girlfriend, Star, was an actress and very beautiful. They had a great night and he was happy that his children were in good relationships.

He didn't try to see Taylor again. What was the point? His lawyer assured him that the divorce could be finalised very quickly. He knew that she'd probably have a list of demands but at this stage he would have given her anything just to be free of her.

On Tuesday morning he was back in his office in Paris.

"How did things go for you in New York?" Jazz asked him.

"Not good. I'll tell you this evening. Are you free for dinner?"

"Why not come around to my place and I'll fix us something," she offered.

"Lovely," he replied, his voice tired and emotional. "What a bloody awful weekend!"

Jazz handed him a whisky almost as soon as he came through the door and he gulped it down quickly.

"I needed that," he said with a wry smile.

"You've had a hectic weekend alright," she smiled back at him.

"Understatement, my dear," he said stretching out on her sofa.

He then recounted all that had happened in New York and Jazz's eyes got rounder and rounder as he went on.

"*She* wants a divorce?" she said with a harsh laugh, when he'd finished.

"I know. That was my reaction too. Anyway, it's with my

lawyers and under way now. She's filing in Nevada where things are very speedy so I should be a free man within weeks." The whisky was doing its work and he was beginning to feel some warmth in his body again.

They were both subdued as they ate supper and he left shortly afterwards, exhausted and jet-lagged, to make his way back to the big lonely apartment.

43

The next few weeks flew by in a flurry of Christmas preparation. Every time Ashling visited the gym Hugh spent the time extolling Fiona's virtues. He'd been to visit her in Dublin and it was obvious they were madly in love.

"I had the best weekend of my life," he enthused. "Fee is the sweetest girl I've ever met. As you know, she's coming here when she finishes her degree and then we'll decide where we'll go. Maybe I'll go spend a year in Dublin before we head to California. Anyway, we have plenty of time to decide." He flashed a brilliant smile at her.

Ashling noticed the 'we, we, we' littering his conversation. Thank God he was as mad about her sister as she was about him. Fee was constantly on the phone to her and all she could talk about was Hugh. This was serious indeed. Ashling was delighted for them, as was Jazz.

"I knew he'd find someone special, and I'm glad it's your sister," she told Ashling.

Ashling was busy putting the finishing touches to her novel and was quite pleased with how it had turned out. She couldn't believe how easy it had been in the end. The characters had written their own story. Corey was as encouraging as ever and his agent was waiting to receive the finished manuscript. He had convinced her that she had real talent. He was also busy editing his latest book so they had put their museum outings on hold for the moment.

On the 5th of December, the Eve of St Nicholas, when Santa Claus comes to the children of France, they all gathered for a girls' night at Ashling's. Jazz and Felicity arrived laden down with presents to leave by the chimney for Orna, Ciara and Pierre. As a special treat, Pierre was allowed to stay the night.

The little fellow had taken a huge shine to Jazz and sat on her knee playing with her hair. He was so like his father that it was heartbreaking but thank goodness he had Sophie's sweet nature. Jazz hoped he wouldn't turn out to be a love-rat like his father.

The four women had been meeting once a week for a girls' night and had become firm friends. Jazz had to try and bury her guilt over her affair with Yves but it was getting easier as she and Sophie became close. She prayed that Sophie would never learn of her indiscretion although the better she got to know her, the more she began to think that Sophie might understand.

When the children were in bed the four women gathered around chatting over a bottle of wine.

"Any word on Taylor?" They all looked at Jazz, knowing that she and Brandon were close.

She told them what had happened. Now that their divorce was going through and Taylor would not be back in Paris again, Brandon saw no reason to keep it a secret any longer and had given Jazz permission to the tell the others about it.

"My God, so much has happened to all of us since September. I can't believe it!" Ashling remarked.

"I wonder if the next nine months will be as exciting," Jazz smiled at her and gave her a little secret wink. Felicity and Sophie knew nothing about Ashling's book as she didn't want to tempt fate by saying anything about it until it was a done deal.

"It's wonderful having such good friends," Felicity said, thinking that these friends were much more genuine than any she had back in London. But then of course, she had changed so much that she was a different person now.

She had the others in stitches telling them of her conversations with Georgina.

"God, I can't imagine calling my mother 'Nora'," Ashling laughed.

"My mother would kill me if I called her anything other than Mami," Jazz told them.

They had a lovely evening and arranged to meet in Jazz's apartment the following week for their last girls' night before the Christmas break.

Felicity's mother had come to realise that her daughter had finally developed some backbone and wouldn't be bullied any more. She had phoned Felicity to say that she expected her for Christmas, as usual.

"Sorry, Mother, but we are staying in Paris for Christmas. The girls are coming over and you and father are more than welcome to come here too."

She steadfastly refused to call her mother Georgina any longer and her mother had finally accepted it. After much wheedling and bullying, Georgina realised that Felicity was standing her ground. Reluctantly she agreed to come to Paris.

Her father rang that night when Georgina had gone to her Women's Institute meeting. "Good girl! How did you manage it? I've been dying to come and visit it you. Jolly great stuff!" he said admiringly.

Next she received a call from Penny. "Congrats, sis! At last you've cut the umbilical chord. Georgina is mighty miffed."

"Tough shit!" Felicity replied, shocking her sister into silence. She'd never, ever used language like that before. "Father is delighted and I know we'll all have a jolly good time."

"Well, I'm just thrilled. I've always hated having to spend Christmas in that draughty, cold house. Jeremy is delighted too that we can stay home here for once."

"Great! Everyone's happy then!"

"Except perhaps Georgina!"

"She'll get over it."

Penny laughed with glee. "Whoa, Mother's finally met her match!"

Brandon asked Mimi to get Taylor's things together for shipment back to New York. He would send them to their apartment there until he heard what she wanted to do with them. He was amazed at the amount of clothes that she had amassed since coming to Paris. Mimi filled box after box and, when it was done, he shipped the lot off. Bob would organise collection at the New York end. He held on to her jewellery, putting it in the safe. He reckoned that she would hardly have any call for it in this new life she was living.

He had decided he would let the apartment go and move to a bijou place such as the one Jazz had. Sophie was already busy looking for one for him. He sadly would have to let Mimi go. She wasn't too bothered as she was bored rattling around the big apartment all day with nothing to do. Sophie found another position for her, starting in January, and Brandon paid her up until then but told her that she could have the intervening weeks off. She was more than happy with that.

He and Jazz were having dinner together three or four times a week now. He loved eating at her place as she was a great cook and in return he took her out to restaurants. He hated eating in restaurants alone and so did she so the arrangement suited both of them. Both Ashling and Felicity invited them around at weekends so, in fact, Brandon hardly missed Taylor at all. He certainly didn't miss the rows – that was for sure. His life was now peaceful.

He was looking forward to the Christmas break and spending time with the kids. He'd booked them into the Sandy Lane Hotel in Barbados for the week and it would be a badly needed break for him too.

Jazz was going back to Munich for Christmas and hoped to get in some skiing while there. She realised that she was actually weary and was looking forward to the break. All the emotional ups-and-downs with Yves had taken their toll and the work-load had been relentless these past few weeks. It was time to recharge the batteries.

She'd gone all-out for her girls' night and they'd all got pretty drunk on the exotic cocktails she'd served. It had been a hilarious night and they'd exchanged gifts with each other. They'd been in high spirits and all were looking forward to the Christmas break.

Sophie told them that she was spending Christmas with her sister in the French Alps. They hoped to get in some skiing too.

Ashling was getting organised to go back to Ireland for Christmas the following weekend. She had never been so busy and there were parties and lunches coming out her ears. Firstly, there was a party in the Irish Embassy that they'd been invited to, then her wine course party and lastly Kieran's office party. Corey had also invited her out for a special Christmas lunch.

Everything was happening so fast that she barely had time to catch her breath.

Orna and Ciara were also madly excited about the Christmas party that they were having at school on the last day of term. Ashling took them to Tartine et Chocolat, the beautiful children's boutique, and bought them the most adorable matching outfits she'd ever seen. They would also wear them on Christmas Day back in Ireland.

Ashling and Jazz went shopping on Saturday and met up at Galeries Lafayette. To her surprise Jazz took her to the Herve Leger boutique and insisted that she try on some of his dresses.

"I told you you'd be wearing one of these dresses by Christmas and I was right," Jazz said, pushing her into the changing room with at least six dresses over her arm.

"Oh God, I'll never fit into these," Ashling cried.

"Of course you will. Just shut up and try them on!" Jazz was being very forceful indeed.

Ashling did as she was told. To her amazement they not only fitted her but they looked fantastic too. As she came out of the dressing room with her favourite – a midnight-blue one – Jazz let out a wolf-whistle. "Wow, amazing! You look sensational. You're going to wow them all at the office party."

Ashling could hardly believe it was herself looking back at her from the mirror. She looked slim and glamorous and . . . actually sexy! It was unbelievable.

"Oh, my God, it's gorgeous," she said, turning this way and that.

"You're gorgeous," Jazz said, hugging her. "This is my Christmas present to you."

"Oh no, I couldn't possibly . . ."

"Bullshit! I insist." Jazz would hear no argument and went up to the cash desk to pay for the dress as Ashling got changed.

"Thank you so much, Jazz. I'd never have had the confidence to buy this myself." She felt like crying.

"Nonsense! You've lost so much weight, you deserve it. And you've been a wonderful friend to me through all my drama." Jazz's voice was filled with emotion. "Now let's get you a pair of shoes to match," she said, ushering Ashling to the shoe department.

"God, you're real bossy when you want to be," Ashling laughed.

"You should see me in the office! I'm being a pussycat now."

They both roared laughing.

"God help the men. You're a right ball-breaker," Ashling cried as the saleswoman came towards them.

The office party was held in a restaurant close to Jazz's apartment on the Île Saint-Louis. It wasn't the kind of Christmas party that Ashling was used to back in Dublin where everyone got mouldy drunk and all kinds of shenanigans took place, leaving red faces all around the following morning. This party was a more civilised affair and although everyone enjoyed the fantastic food and wonderful wine it was all rather genteel.

She wore her new Herve Leger dress and she felt like a million dollars in it. The compliments she received echoed Kieran's comments that she looked more beautiful than he'd ever seen her. He said he couldn't wait to show all their old friends in Ireland this chic new woman his wife had become.

Jazz had been dreading being in such close social contact with Yves but Brandon and Ashling made sure that they were kept apart, seating her at one end of the table with them, and Yves at the other end with Felicity and Max in between. She noticed that Yves was very quiet and almost morose and there seemed to be some tension between him and Sophie. Jazz took care not to drink too much so that she wouldn't get emotional and, when the meal was over, invited Brandon, Ashling and Kieran back to her place where the party turned out to be rather more fun.

The following day was the final day of work before they broke up for holidays. Mid-morning, they decided to finish up as no one was in much of a mood for working. They went to l'Excelsior to share a last Christmas drink and left at midday amid shouts of 'Happy Christmas!' and 'Have a good holiday!'

Kieran rang Ashling and she told him that she was writing in Les Deux Magots. He decided to surprise her and take her out for lunch. His taxi pulled up outside the café just in time to see Ashling leave it with a very handsome silver-haired man. She was laughing up at him and, as they crossed the street, the older man took her hand to guide her. Passers-by smiled at the happy, good-looking couple. Kieran sat transfixed. This couldn't be happening! Who was this man? Where were they going? Kieran felt as though his whole world was falling apart. He asked the taxi driver to drive him home where he sat slumped in the chair waiting for Ashling to arrive.

The phone rang and he listened as the answering machine picked up. It was Ashling's mother.

"Hello, love. Just checking that you're all set for tomorrow. Fee will pick you up at the airport. By the way, I just finished Corey's latest book. Tell him I loved it. What a charming man he is too! Can't wait to see you tomorrow. Bye, love."

Corey! The writer fellow Ashling had mentioned. Was he the man he'd seen holding Ashling's hand earlier? How come her mother knew him? Kieran was sick to his stomach. Was it possible that his wife was having an affair behind his back? He never asked her what she did with her days. He knew she'd been writing a book but that surely didn't take up the whole day, every day? He didn't believe that Ashling would do this to him. They'd always been honest and truthful with each other. Still, he couldn't forget the way she'd looked up at the other man, her face alive and laughing, or the way he had so casually taken her hand. Oh God, what will I do if she loves him? He felt anguished.

"Kieran! What are you doing home so early?" Ashling cried, when she came in later with the girls in tow. Her eyes were sparkling and it was obvious that she'd had a few drinks.

"We finished early," he replied, not looking at her as he helped Orna off with her coat.

"We had a great time at school today, Daddy," Orna told him.

Ashling busied herself with Ciara, who was also relaying all that had happened at their Christmas party.

"That's great, love," she said, getting out some juice for them. "Have you eaten, Kieran?"

"I'm not hungry."

"No, me neither," she replied.

He waited for her to say something more but she didn't, busying herself with the girls. She then went upstairs to pack for their trip to Ireland the following day.

As the evening went on he waited for her to say something about this Corey guy but she never mentioned him. She listened to her mother's voicemail and still she never said a word.

"When did your mother meet this Corey guy?" he asked her nonchalantly.

"We met him in the park on the Sunday Mum was here," she replied, equally casual.

"*Corey, Corey!*" Ciara chanted.

"Daddy, he knows where to buy the bestest ice cream in Paris," Orna informed him.

"Yeah, Corey gave us yummy ice cream and his beard is tickly," Ciara giggled.

"When did my daughters meet this Corey guy?" Kieran asked Ashling, glaring at her.

"As I said – when we went to the park," she replied without meeting his eyes.

"Two times," Orna stated matter of factly.

"Corey is a nice man. Mammy likes him too. Don't you, Mammy?"

Ashling blushed. "Yes, he is a nice man. Now come on, girls, and let's get your toys ready to take with us," she said, ushering them upstairs.

Kieran sat with his head in his hands. Now he was sure there was something going on. Why had she never introduced *him* to this Corey? He felt scared and didn't know how to handle it. What did one do in this situation?

His thoughts were interrupted by a phone call from his sister in Dublin. His mother was failing fast. Her doctors reckoned that it was only a matter of days. He hoped that she'd last till he got there the following day.

He was quiet and subdued all evening and Ashling supposed it was because of his mother. She just hoped it was nothing to do with Corey.

44

Kieran's mother did live just long enough for him to say goodbye. She died peacefully, two hours after he arrived at the hospital in Dublin, with all her family around her. She'd had a good life and they all agreed that it was a merciful release as she would have hated being an invalid for the rest of her days. Still, Kieran missed her and felt unutterably sad.

He was very grateful to his colleagues in Paris who all rang him to sympathise with him. Ashling was a great support throughout the next few days and he pushed his fears to the back of his mind as they celebrated a quieter Christmas than usual.

Brandon spent a lovely relaxing week at the Sandy Lane Hotel in Barbados with his twins. For the first time he saw them as adults and he liked the people they'd become. They had matured a lot in the past year and he had no fears for them in the future.

They'd gone to visit Taylor the previous weekend and had been shocked by what they'd found. They'd hoped to convince her to come with them to Barbados but after two minutes in her company realised that what Brandon had told them was true. She was too far gone to be saved. She wasn't too happy to see them and after half an hour told them to leave. They reckoned that they were interfering with her drug-taking. Mia cried all the way to the airport and Mike tried to comfort her in vain. They now understood Brandon's devastation at how low she'd fallen. They knew how unhappy he'd been with their mother and that he'd stayed in the marriage for their sake. They both hoped that he would meet some nice woman who would make him happy. Judging by the attention he was receiving from the wealthy women in the resort, they knew that he would have no problem attracting a new partner. They grinned at each other as they saw Brandon smiling at a text he received on Christmas Day. It was from Jazz and he rang her back to wish her a Happy Christmas.

The three of them had a fabulous holiday together swimming, sailing and snorkelling and getting to know each other better. Although none of them would have voiced it, they all secretly thought that the presence of Taylor, with all her demands, would have made for a much more stressful holiday for all around.

Jazz was glad to be back with her family in Munich where they had a white Christmas. She enjoyed catching up with all her old friends and felt her heart was finally healing after all the heartbreak inflicted by Yves. The fact that she wasn't seeing him every day probably helped. On Stephen's Day she was going skiing with a group of her old university friends and she was looking forward to catching up with all they'd been doing while she was away.

That Christmas was the year Felicity came into her own. She organised the festivities with such flair that even her mother was unable to find any fault whatsoever. The apartment was beautifully decorated and the food she produced worthy of any Michelin-starred restaurant. Max beamed with pride and the girls were thrilled with this new relaxed mother who didn't keep after them all the time about untidy rooms or unsuitable clothes.

Felicity's father, Nigel, was delighted with this change in his beloved daughter. He looked on in amazement as she deftly put Georgina in her place, time and time again. To his surprise his wife accepted it and became quite mellow. Maybe this is how *he* should have treated her all these years. If Felicity could manage it, surely he could too. It gave him hope.

Felicity was in her element, doing what she did best which was taking care of her family. It gave her great satisfaction to see the look on her mother's face when she told her that she planned on going into the catering business. "Well, well," was Georgina's only response.

Her parents left on the 29th of December and Georgina reluctantly agreed with her husband that it was indeed the best Christmas they'd ever had.

"We'll come to you in Holland Park next Christmas," her mother announced haughtily.

"Well, we'll see," Felicity replied. "It all depends on what other plans we may have. We may not stay in England for it at all."

Pippa and Alex had to smother a giggle at their grandmother's outraged face. However, Georgina simply pressed her lips tight together and said nothing before kissing them all goodbye.

The two girls had met up with Nicole and her friends again and were out partying every night. Alex had kept in touch with one of the boys, Jean Michel, and it looked like young love was in the air. Two of her friends and two of Pippa's were coming to visit the following day, from London, and Felicity had agreed that they could throw a New Year's Eve party and also invite their new French friends.

She and Max opened a bottle of champagne at midnight on New Year's Eve after wishing the youngsters a Happy New Year. They took it up to bed where they watched the Hogmanay parties on television as they toasted each other. They were both looking forward to an even more exciting year to come.

Sophie did not have as good a Christmas as the others, thanks, in part, to Yves's moodiness. Even her sister, Vianne, noticed that he was not his usual self and worried that there was something serious bothering him. Sophie could throw no light on the matter as he wouldn't discuss it with her. She hoped it wasn't because he was missing Marilyn. Although he assured her that he loved her, their lovemaking was practically non-existent.

They returned to Paris on New Year's Day and Sophie was relieved when he returned to work the day after.

45

Kieran was not in good form as they arrived back in Paris. Because of his mother's death, followed by the funeral and Christmas, he'd had no chance to sit down and have a talk with Ashling. He knew it would have to happen soon. He couldn't go on like an ostrich any longer, burying his head in the sand. They would have to have it out.

Hugh had been over to Ireland for Christmas and Fiona had returned to Paris with him and would stay until college started back. They were madly in love and making plans to live together once she had finished her degree. Ashling was delighted for her sister and was happy that she'd see her every day while Hugh was working. She asked Fiona to baby-sit the day after they arrived back in Paris so that she could go to Les Deux Magots and see Corey.

He greeted her with delight and gave her the news she'd been hoping to hear.

"I can't believe it, I just can't believe it," she cried, hugging him. "Are you serious? My book is going to be published?" She had to sit down as she was shaking. "Oh my God, I can't believe it!"

Corey laughed at her reaction. He'd never had any doubt but that she'd be published. She was a talented writer and he was delighted that he'd been able to help her.

Brandon and Jazz were both looking tanned and relaxed as they started back to work on January 2nd. Brandon had gone back to New York from Barbados to talk with his lawyer. To his amazement Taylor wanted very little from him. He'd been expecting a long list of demands. This proved to him, more than ever, that she'd lost the plot. Bob had told him that Taylor and Dylan were still hard at it partying and doing more and more drugs every day. Dylan's family wanted him to go in to rehab again but he was refusing. Probably because he now had a partner in crime!

Brandon would wait until he returned from Paris to decide what he would do with the apartment on New York's Upper East Side. It was too big and ornate for him. He would prefer something simpler. Sophie, true to her word, had found a lovely little place for him on the Île Saint-Louis, very similar to Jazz's and just two houses down from hers. It was perfect for him and he moved in on New Year's Day, the day he'd come back from the States. Now he and Jazz were neighbours.

Jazz checked her diary the day she got back from Munich. Shocked, she discovered that she was two weeks late with her period. This was very unusual as she was normally as regular as clockwork. Probably all the stress, she thought, collapsing into bed. When it still hadn't arrived a week later and she found herself feeling sick three mornings in a row, the penny dropped.

"I couldn't possibly be pregnant, could I?" she asked her reflection in the mirror. She remembered the one night that she'd had unprotected sex with Yves. It was the first night that he'd come to her apartment. Neither of them had had a condom but they'd gone ahead anyway. Surely that one occasion couldn't have made her pregnant, could it? Of course it could, she realised, thinking that she was acting like a naïve young teenager who thought it couldn't happen to them.

She put her hands on her stomach. Could there be a little person in there? She felt confused. One part of her was enchanted to think that she might be carrying a baby inside her and the other part was horrified to think that Yves would be the father. She really did not want any permanent tie with him but, still, she knew he'd have a right to know if she was carrying his child. God, what a mess! She'd have to think this through carefully.

Kieran came home to find Fiona there as Hugh had to work that night. No chance of a serious talk then!

"Put on your glad rags," Ashling told him. "You and I are going out to dinner. Fee is baby-sitting for us."

He couldn't mask his surprise. "What's the occasion?"

"Do I need an occasion to take my husband out to dinner?"

Mystified, he did as she asked and was just ready when the taxi she'd ordered arrived.

"Where are we going?" he asked, wondering what this was all about.

He was shocked when she ordered the taxi to stop at La Tour d'Argent, the most famous and expensive restaurant in Paris. He paled.

"We can't afford this," he hissed.

"Don't worry, we're not paying," she laughed. "Trust me," she replied, her eyes shining as she led him into the building.

Nothing could have surprised him more than to see the silver-haired Corey sitting there, a bottle of Roederer Cristal on ice.

"What the hell!" Kieran exclaimed.

"Kieran, I'd like you to meet my friend, Corey Danz. He has some exciting news for us," Ashling said, grinning from ear to ear.

"I'm happy to meet you, at last," Corey said, pumping his hand. "Ashling has told me so much about you."

He was obviously American and, Kieran had to admit, very charming. Corey beckoned the waiter to open the champagne.

As the waiter poured Corey beamed at them both and Ashling was glowing so much that Kieran thought she might combust at any moment.

"What's this exciting news?" he asked, looking from one to the other.

"Your wife is a very talented writer and the exciting news is that one of the top UK publishers has agreed to publish her novel."

Kieran was gobsmacked. He didn't know what to say. "Are you serious?" he asked, finding it hard to take in.

"Absolutely." Corey smiled broadly, handing them both a glass of champagne.

"To a bright future!" he toasted Ashling.

She clinked her glass to his and then turned to Kieran and kissed him on the lips.

"When did all this happen?" Kieran asked, taken aback.

"Well, Corey's agent in New York has contacts with the UK company – they've published just about anybody who's anybody really – well, he read it and thought it was good enough, so he sent it off to them the day before we left for Ireland. Corey took me out to lunch that day to celebrate. I didn't want to say anything to you in case nothing came of it. I was afraid I'd jinx it. But now it's really happened!" Her eyes were sparkling with happiness. She took his hand and squeezed it. "What do you think of that? Corey has been a fantastic help and support. I couldn't have done it without him." She smiled at her friend.

"Of course you would," Corey replied. "Talent will out. And now I'd like to invite you both to dinner to celebrate the occasion."

Relief flooded through Kieran. So that's what she was doing with Corey the day he'd seen them together. They weren't having an affair. He'd been helping her with her book. Kieran felt a fool for having doubted her. When they stood up to go to dinner, she kissed him again and held his hand as they were shown to their table. She was bubbling with happiness and he thought she'd never looked more beautiful. He was so lucky!

It was the best table in the house and they had a magnificent view across the Seine to Notre Dame Cathedral. The maitre d' came and greeted Corey like an old friend and it was obvious that he was a valued customer. Kieran couldn't believe it when he discovered that Corey was in fact the famous writer Dan Corey. He was a big fan of the author and had read all his books. The dinner was a huge success and Corey recommended that they try the duck which was a speciality of the house. It was the most divine duck that they'd ever tasted.

"You'll have to come and have lunch with us some Sunday,"

Kieran said as they parted. He had been utterly charmed by Corey and had found him to be fascinating company.

"I can't think of anything I'd like better. You're a very lucky man, Kieran, to have such a beautiful family."

As they rode home in the taxi Ashling was on cloud nine.

"I'm really glad you two got on so well," she said. "Corey has been such a great help to me with my writing."

Kieran looked at her sheepishly. "I have a confession to make. I actually thought that you and he were having an affair."

"You're not serious? How could you think that?"

"Well, the day we broke up for the Christmas holidays I came to Les Deux Magots to surprise you and take you out to lunch and I saw you walking out of there hand in hand with Corey and I put two and two together and – "

"You came up with five," she said reproachfully.

"Well, you looked awfully happy together and – oh, Ash, I was terrified of losing you." He looked at her and she saw the pain in his eyes. "Then I discovered that your mother and the girls had met him and that you'd never even mentioned him to me – and well you know –"

"You didn't really think that, did you?" She looked at him, her eyes wide.

"Yes, I did."

"Surely you know I'd never be unfaithful to you." She leant in close to him. "You're the only man for me." She took his face in her hands. "You silly clown! How could you ever have thought that? You know I love you more than anything." She kissed him then, to show him how much she meant it.

"Oh, Ash. I went through hell. Then with Mam dying and everything I just couldn't face bringing it up –"

She took him in her arms then and the taxi driver, who hadn't understood a word they'd said, smiled as they kissed again.

"You poor darling! To think you had that on your mind all that time." She had tears in her eyes as she thought what he must have gone through.

"Well, it's taught me one thing." He smiled at her. You're the most important thing in my life. More than my work, or golf or even rugby," he added.

"Wow! That really means a lot," she said. "More than rugby! I feel honoured."

They laughed together then, knowing everything was okay again, and when they got home they went straight to bed where they made wonderful love.

Looking at her afterwards as she lay back on the pillow smiling sleepily at him, he knew how lucky he was. He'd learnt his lesson. He'd never take her for granted again. From now on Ashling would be his top priority. Without her nothing would have any meaning.

As they curled up and prepared to go to sleep, he nuzzled her neck.

"Just think, I'm in bed with a soon-to-be-famous author," he murmured.

She sighed with happiness as she drifted off to sleep.

46

Jazz tried to put it out of her mind during the following week but all she could think of was the fact that she might be pregnant. Eventually, when her period still hadn't come, she bought a pregnancy test. She waited another three days before she had the courage to use it. She hardly slept a wink the night before, wondering what she would do if the test was positive.

At six the following morning, she went into the bathroom and taking a deep breath took out the kit. She could barely breathe as she waited the required time before reading the result. She looked at the strip. There was no mistaking it. Pregnant, it said.

In a trance she made a coffee and curled up on the sofa. I'm pregnant, she thought, something that she'd often thought about but never actually dreamed would happen for her. Rubbing her tummy, she tried to imagine the new little life that was starting in there.

She felt desperately confused. The thought of killing this baby was abhorrent to her but what other choice did she have? If it was anyone other than Yves who was the father she would have bravely faced off all criticism, but what about Sophie and Pierre? Could she do this to them? She was sure that it would rock Sophie's world if she were to have Yves's child. There was no way she could hide it from them either. God, what a mess! The only person that didn't deserve consideration in all this was Yves. He'd taken his pleasure without a thought of the consequences. Now, it was her problem. She hadn't prayed in ages but now she found herself calling on her favourite saints to guide her and help her to do the right thing. She hoped they were listening.

Sophie was at the end of her tether. She knew there was something bothering Yves and was beginning to suspect that it was more than just Marilyn but she had no idea what it could be. She found out a few weeks later when two plainclothes gendarmes called to the door one Sunday evening. They were flashing their badges at her. Fraud squad, they said. They were looking for Yves and asked to come in. When Yves saw them, he paled.

"Monsieur Durbuis? We have a warrant for your arrest on charges of embezzlement and fraud."

Sophie thought she was going to faint. "There must be some mistake," she cried, the colour leaving her face.

"There's no mistake, madame," the older man said.

She looked to Yves for confirmation that it wasn't true but he was hanging his head, not able to look at her.

"Yves, tell me it's not true," she begged him.

"I'm sorry, Sophie," he said softly. "I didn't mean for this to happen."

Without so much as a word or a kiss, he left with the two gendarmes. She sank to the floor, unable to comprehend what was happening. Cosette, seeing the two gendarmes, had spirited Pierre off to the playroom. On hearing the door close she came quickly downstairs. Picking Sophie up gently, she led her to a chair and then handed her a brandy which she made her sip.

"Thank you, Cosette," Sophie said, her eyes brimming with tears.

"I'm sure there's some mistake, madame," Cosette said quietly.

"No, I don't think so, Cosette. Yves didn't deny it."

She finished her brandy and then rang her father who came straight over along with her mother and brother.

"I'll find out what's going on," her father, who was a lawyer, reassured her. "Leave it to me."

She felt shattered and empty and was happy to let them take over.

Nothing could have prepared Brandon for the bombshell that Sophie dropped when she rang on Monday morning. Yves was in jail, accused of fraud and embezzlement from his bank.

"My God, that's terrible news. How are you holding up?"

"Oh, Brandon, it's been hell. Yves refuses to see me. He says he's too ashamed to face me. I don't know what's happened. I thought it must have been some dreadful mistake but his lawyer says he's pleading guilty. I feel like I'm living a nightmare. If only he'd talk to me. His hearing is tomorrow." Her voice was so anguished that it broke Brandon's heart.

"What about Pierre?"

"I'm trying to keep things as normal as possible for him. My family are with me and they've been fantastic. I just rang Ashling and she's taking Pierre from school today and keeping him till after the hearing tomorrow."

She told him the time and place of the hearing and he assured her that he'd be there. Her voice was pitiful as she thanked him.

"Well, I can't believe it! What was he thinking of?" Brandon exclaimed as he put down the phone, looking at Jazz in astonishment.

Jazz wondered what was so terrible. "What is it?"

He told her and she was as shocked as he had been.

"How's Sophie?"

"Devastated, as you can imagine. The poor girl doesn't know what way to turn."

"The poor thing," Jazz said with feeling. "She doesn't deserve this. Did she say what happened?"

"She has no idea what went on. Yves refuses to see her or talk to her. All she knows is that he's pleading guilty. The hearing is at ten o'clock tomorrow. I said I'd be there to give them some support."

"I'll come too and I know Ashling and Kieran would want to be there also."

"That's good. They need all the support we can give them. It's at times like these that you find out who your true friends are," he said bitterly.

He went into Max and Kieran's office to find they were as shocked as he was. Ashling had contacted Kieran with the awful news. They both agreed that they should all show a united front in support of Sophie and Yves the following day.

"Poor girl," Kieran said. "I know Ashling wants to come too."

Brandon knew that within minutes the news would be all over the building. He called into Yves's office to find Chantal in floods of tears. The news was already on the grapevine.

"Isn't it awful?" she whispered, her face streaked with tears. "Poor Yves . . . and his poor wife and little boy," she said through her tears.

He could think of nothing to say to comfort her.

They were all there the following day. Even Felicity had taken a day off from her cookery course. They hugged Sophie and shook hands with her parents as they filed into the seats behind them. They were shocked to see how haggard Yves looked when he was brought into the court.

He had aged ten years since they'd last seen him. He looked dishevelled and unshaven and gone was the swagger that they were used to. They all felt sorry for him although they were also angry with him. To Jazz he seemed like a stranger, not the man she had made love to and who was the father of her unborn child. Ashling was holding her hand but she needn't have. Jazz felt nothing for him but contempt.

It was over quickly. The prosecution stated that he had borrowed bank funds to invest in the stock market and, instead of making a fortune, as he had hoped, he had lost it all. He had acted from greed, as had so many others in the banking world before him. This was nothing new to the four bankers present. They'd all come across this before.

Yves was sentenced to one year in prison and Sophie let out a cry and called his name when she heard it. He looked up at her then, for the first time, and the look in his eyes was heartbreaking. It was full of remorse and regret and love. His shoulders were slumped and he gave her one more look as he was led from the court. Sophie's father and brother had their arms around her, supporting her, as the others pressed forward to sympathise with her.

Brandon hugged her. "He'll be out in six months, I'm sure," he whispered to her.

"You think so?" she asked, hope in her eyes.

"Yes, they never have to serve the full sentence."

She thanked them all for being there as they hugged her and then she was led away by her father and brother who had to practically carry her. They tried to shield her from the cameras that were flashing like mad outside the courthouse.

It was a very subdued gathering that adjourned to a local café for lunch.

"You know it could have happened to any of us," Kieran remarked.

"I have a couple of friends who did the same thing and got away with it," Max admitted. "They're filthy rich now," he grimaced.

"Sure, the temptation is always there," Jazz agreed.

"But there *are* risks, we all know that," Brandon replied. "Yves decided to take those risks."

"Well, he's paying for it now," Ashling said sadly.

They all nodded their heads in agreement.

Brandon and Kieran were called into the French Finance Minister's office the following day. There were two other officers present. Monsieur Fournier, the Minister, informed them that they had decided not to replace Yves. Brandon heard the sympathy in the Minister's voice when he spoke Yves's name.

He asked them if they felt that together they could take over the project and run it alone. Kieran thought about it for ten seconds and then replied that, due to family commitments, he didn't think that he could take on any more responsibilities. Brandon looked at him sympathetically. He knew that Ashling had been unhappy with the hours that Kieran had been putting in. Since Christmas, she'd told him happily, Kieran had cut back and was spending more time with his family. Brandon was pleased to hear that.

"I have no problem taking over," he said, to the relief of all the others. Kieran, in particular, looked relieved and winked his gratitude to him. Why not, Brandon thought, I have damn all else to do with my time. Why not work?

On Thursday, Brandon visited Chantal to find that she was still very upset about Yves's imprisonment.

"I sorry, but tonight is last night with you," she murmured, crying softly. Apparently, now that Yves was gone, she no longer had a job. She had asked for a transfer to Caen, which they'd happily agreed to.

"My 'usband and me 'ave decide to 'ave baby, so I cannot see you no more," she said sadly, still crying softly.

He held her gently as she wept, sorry that it was over between them but knowing that it was inevitable. They made love one more time before they parted forever. Now he really was alone.

47

Ashling and Sophie had become even closer since Yves went into prison. She had Pierre around often to play with the girls and he and Sophie joined them regularly on their weekend jaunts. Sophie was now visiting Yves weekly and confided to Ashling that he had become a changed man. He regretted deeply the pain he had caused her and vowed to make it up to her when he came out. "Maybe this is the best thing that could have happened," she said to Ashling. "We'll start again afresh and no more 'open marriage' for me."

Jazz had also showered Sophie with kindness since the episode and called regularly to visit her, always bringing some toy or goody for Pierre, whom she had come to adore. *Tante Jazz,* he called her. She was delighted that he considered her his aunt. She hoped and prayed that Sophie would never learn of her liaison with Yves.

Jazz worried constantly about the decisions that she would have to make pretty soon. Should she resign from the project once she could hide her pregnancy no longer and go back to Munich? Could she lie to Yves and say the baby wasn't his? She knew this would be a dreadful thing to do but she suspected Yves might prefer to believe this rather than wreck the fresh start to his marriage that he had promised Sophie.

It was a mess! The only sure thing she knew was that she was going to keep this baby.

Now that she and Brandon were neighbours, they met up often in the evenings and she cooked dinner for him regularly. They had become close friends and on Valentine's Night he invited her out for a special meal. To his delight his divorce had come through that day and he was now a free man.

He ordered champagne in the restaurant to celebrate. To his surprise Jazz took just a small glass, which she barely sipped, and then refused to have any wine. He said nothing but as he was having a brandy in her apartment later that night and she was having only a diet coke, he said, "I notice you're not drinking alcohol any more. Is there something you want to tell me?"

She looked away from him.

"Come here!" he said, patting the sofa.

She came and sat down beside him and he put his arm around her.

"You can tell me," he said gently. "I'm your friend and your secret will be safe with me."

He saw the tears welling up in her beautiful brown eyes.

"I'm pregnant," she whispered.

"Yves?"

"Yes," she murmured, as a tear slid slowly down her face.

He brushed it away. "What are you going to do?"

"I haven't decided yet but I know I could never get rid of it. It's a little person already," she added as she unconsciously laid her hands on her tummy.

Brandon sighed. "Does Yves know?"

Her head shot up and she gave him a look of panic. "No, and I don't want him to know."

"Well, it's your decision but I think you'll have to tell him eventually." He sighed. "Anyway, whatever you decide, I'll be here for you."

"Thank you," she whispered. She laid her head on his shoulder, grateful for his presence and his support.

It didn't take Ashling long either to suss out the fact that Jazz was pregnant. She had drunk no alcohol at their girls' night and Ashling noticed that she had gained a little weight around the midriff. No doubt about it! She knew it could only be Yves's baby. God, what a mess! She wondered what Jazz was going to do about it but she didn't like to say anything until Jazz confided in her.

She didn't have long to wonder. Jazz rang and asked her to call around the following night. Over coffee she broke the news.

"I'm pregnant," she whispered, her voice emotional.

"I thought as much," Ashling replied, giving her a hug. "How do you feel about it?"

"I don't know. I'm so confused. One minute I'm up in the air and the next minute I'm down in the dumps."

"I take it it's Yves's baby?"

"Of course."

"That makes it a bit complicated, I suppose," Ashling said gently.

"I know I couldn't have an abortion, so I'll have it but whether I leave Paris and return home early – or stay on here, that's my dilemma." She looked wretchedly at her friend.

"Well, you have a little time to decide," Ashling said, wishing that she could do something to help.

"Brandon has been a rock. I don't know what I would have done without him."

Ashling was aware that Brandon and Jazz had become very close and she was happy that Jazz could rely on his support. She herself had become very fond of him and had come to see what a good, kind person he was. She often invited him around to dinner with Jazz. He seemed much more relaxed now that his divorce had come through and Taylor was off the scene.

Ashling received her contract from the publishers in late February and as she had no agent and neither she nor Kieran had any legal knowledge, she took Corey's advice and joined The Society of Authors in London. They looked over the contract for her and advised her on some minor changes. She was very excited about the whole thing and everyone was delighted for her.

She was still going to Les Deux Magots three times a week and had started writing a children's book, something she'd always wanted to do. God knows, she'd read enough stories to the girls in the past few years to know exactly what was required. Her little daughters were the inspiration for it and the story was of two little girls who travelled around the world with their parents. She hoped to show the magic of exotic places, as seen through the eyes of children, to all those children who never did get to travel. She hoped to have it finished by May when she would have to do the editing on her first book, but meanwhile she felt a need to write every day. She loved it.

Corey was a regular visitor for lunch and dinner at her home. Kieran and he had become good friends and often had long, deep conversations together as Ashling prepared a meal for them all. The girls absolutely adored him and he never arrived without his arms full of presents for them. She often included Sophie and Pierre in these invitations and was delighted that Sophie and Corey seemed to get on so well together. Sophie was doing well, considering the situation she was in, and was 'standing by her man', much to her credit.

Brandon, Max and Kieran had all offered to go and visit him in prison but she informed them that, for the moment, Yves did not want to see them. He also forbade her to bring Pierre to visit. Although he was pining for his son, he did not want the little boy to know his father was in prison. He insisted that Sophie tell their son that he had gone away on a business trip.

The four women still met regularly for girls' nights out and if Sophie and Felicity noticed that Jazz wasn't drinking, they never passed a comment.

Jazz felt the first cramps in the morning. They got steadily worse as the day wore on and by lunchtime she told Brandon that she would have to go home. She looked wretched and he was very concerned about her. He offered to take her home but she assured him that she could manage so he called her a taxi and saw her into it.

When she got home she made a coffee and then curled up in bed with a hot-water-bottle held to her stomach. She dozed off and woke to feel the wetness between her legs. With a sinking heart she suspected what was happening. Dragging herself to the bathroom she was shocked at the amount of blood she seemed to be losing. She realised that she'd have to call for help. She rang Ashling but only got her voicemail. Scared and frightened, she then called Brandon who insisted that she call for an ambulance immediately.

"Please ring me when you find out where they're taking you and I'll come straight away." He knew she was frightened and she had nobody else to support her.

The ambulance came very quickly and within five minutes she was on her way to the hospital. She rang Brandon, as she'd promised, and was grateful that he would be by her side.

The pain was pretty dreadful but they could not give her anything for it. The nurse who was in the ambulance with her tried to reassure her but Jazz sensed that she was just doing her job.

The next hour passed in a blur as the hospital staff buzzed around her. Jazz tried to think positive thoughts and prayed like she'd never prayed before but it was to no avail. Eventually, a very nice doctor came to her and told her that, as she'd suspected, she'd lost the baby. She was devastated and felt a great sense of loss. They did a D&C on her then and, a little woozy from the local anaesthetic, she came out of the theatre to see Brandon waiting for her, a concerned look on his face. He stayed by her bedside, holding her hand and wiping her face, until they told her she could go home. The doctors and nurses obviously thought that he was the father. He didn't disillusion them.

He put her to bed and brought her a hot chocolate, insisting that he would stay the night in the guest room. She was grateful for that as she didn't want to be alone. She cried herself to sleep and woke the following morning with a feeling of dread in her stomach. She wanted to go to work but Brandon insisted that she stay home. He rang Ashling and explained what had happened and she came straight to Jazz's apartment after dropping the girls to school. She was shocked at how pale and drawn Jazz looked.

"I really wanted this baby," Jazz told her, her eyes filling with tears. "Now, I'll probably never have a child." The tears started to flow. "Sorry," she sniffled, as Ashling handed her a tissue.

"Cry as much as you want," Ashling said gently, cradling Jazz in her arms. "It's important to grieve for this baby. And of course you can still have a child. You're still young."

"I'll be thirty-six in two months' time," she sobbed, blowing her nose. "And I don't even have a prospective father in sight."

Ashling held her and let her cry on. She made lunch for them both and was pleased to see that Jazz ate it and looked much better than she had that morning. She made her lie down for a rest before she left to go to collect the girls from school, happy that Jazz was on the mend, physically at least. How long it would take her heart to mend – that was another story.

48

Brandon was surprised by how concerned Marilyn was about Taylor. She rang often and in early March rang to say she was going to the States and would like Taylor's address. He rang Bob in New York to see if he knew whether Taylor was still at the same place.

"She sure is. Dylan's family have been in touch with me. They want him to go back into rehab but he's refused. They've cut off his allowance but he's still refusing. I guess Taylor is supporting him at the moment."

Brandon sighed. As part of their divorce settlement, he had given her one million dollars and an apartment which he owned in Soho and which was rented out. The rent, along with the very generous alimony he was paying her, would keep her in style but it wouldn't go far if it was supporting two drug habits. Luckily, their apartment on the Upper East Side had been a gift from his father and was still in his father's name, so she had no claim on that. The bulk of his family's great wealth was tied up in trusts so that was also safe for his children. Now the news that she was supporting Dylan made Brandon appreciate his father's astuteness with his finances. At least she couldn't waste the twins' legacy.

He met Marilyn for a drink before she left and he gave her Taylor's address. She was in fact returning to New York to have some work done on her face and body. Louis had very generously agreed to foot the bill for it all and she had booked into a clinic for liposuction, botox, a bottom tuck and an eyelid lift. She was quite frankly relieved to be getting a break away from him as he was proving to be overly possessive. Just as well Yves was in prison because she would have had no chance of meeting with him, not with Louis's beady eyes on her every movement.

Her heart skipped a beat when she saw Brandon sitting in the bar. He was more gorgeous than ever. She would have left Louis in a flash if she could have had a chance with him but unfortunately he didn't seem to have any interest in her. However, perhaps when she'd had all this work done that would change. She enjoyed his company and he was being very pleasant to her. He seemed much more relaxed since his divorce. She promised to meet up with him when she got back and bring him news of Taylor. Who knows, he might even see her in another light then. Wouldn't that be something!

Life for Taylor had taken a downturn. The first couple of months had been one long party but now the gloss was wearing thin and she was getting tired of the endless stream of 'friends' who passed through Dylan's apartment, day and night. She had come to realise that they were more like scroungers and hangers-on, the type of sycophants who often surrounded wealthy people, pretending to be their friends.

Catching sight of herself in the mirror one morning, in one of her more lucid moments, she wondered how she had come to this. Her skin was grey and dull, her eyes dead and her once beautifully coiffed hair now lank and lustreless. She would never dream of visiting her old hair or beauty salons, terrified of running into some of her old friends, so she mostly stayed in, living her life in a drugged haze.

Lately however, she wasn't getting the same buzz as before. It took more and more of the drugs mixed with ever more alcohol to make her feel good. Dylan assured her that what she really needed was heroin. It was *the* best feeling in the world, he insisted. She wasn't so sure. She'd seen TV programmes about heroin addicts and it had scared her to death. She had been shocked to find that he was injecting himself daily. She hated needles although she'd succumbed to botox, but that had been administered by a professional not something she'd had to do herself. So she resisted all his attempts to introduce her to the lethal drug.

Then there was the problem of money. Previously, he'd always agreed to go into rehab to keep the money flowing from his family but now with access to Taylor's money he could tell them to go to hell, which he did. They responded by cutting off his allowance. He'd taken her debit card from her and hadn't given it back. When she'd asked him for it, it had made him very angry and he'd even slapped her around a couple of times. Heroin made him very violent. Taylor was beginning to wonder if she'd made a dreadful mistake.

Since her divorce had come through he'd made no mention of marriage. Now she wasn't sure that marrying him was such a good idea. This was where she was at when she opened the door one morning to find Marilyn on her doorstep.

"Marilyn," she cried, delighted to see her old friend. "It's wonderful to see you!" She hugged her tightly.

Marilyn couldn't keep the shock from her face. "Oh my Gawd, honey, what's happened to you?" she cried, before she could stop herself.

She took in the slovenly hair and make-up free face, the dirty clothes and the messy apartment and was appalled. Taylor, who had always been so impeccable, living in this pigsty. It was incredible! Then she was introduced to Dylan and with disbelief she wondered how anyone in their right mind could have traded in the gorgeous Brandon for this weedy little man. He was small and skinny with long lank dirty blond hair framing his stubbly face. He had a ring in his nose and if you tried, you couldn't imagine anyone more different than the tall clean-cut Brandon. Was Taylor out of her mind?

Dylan took her hand limply and it was all she could do not to flinch away from his touch. He made her skin crawl and she unconsciously snatched her hand back. He looked her up and down slowly, taking in the expensive clothes and jewellery. He also saw the voluptuous curves and big breasts and made her squirm as he leered at her. He made her feel dirty and she wanted to rush home and shower after being in his presence. How could Taylor stand it here?

She couldn't even bring herself to sit down on the dirty, rubbish-strewn sofa and insisted that Taylor put on her coat and come out for breakfast with her. Taylor obediently did as she was told, ignoring Dylan's disapproving glare.

Once they were seated in the restaurant, Marilyn couldn't hold back. Taylor sat quietly as Marilyn berated her and asked her if she was out of her mind.

"I know, but it's not as bad as it looks," Taylor mumbled.

Marilyn insisted on taking her friend to her own hair and beauty salon and was shocked to find that Taylor had no money and no debit or credit cards. She was appalled to be told that Dylan held all control of her finances. It took Marilyn until seven o'clock that evening to persuade Taylor that she had to get out of this mess.

"You're comin' to stay with me, sweetie," Marilyn informed her.

"He'll kill me," Taylor whispered, her fear showing in her eyes.

"Not with me around, honey," Marilyn assured her. "If he lays one finger on you, I'm callin' the police." She looked fearsome and Taylor didn't doubt her for a minute.

She needn't have worried. Dylan, like all bullies, was completely cowed when faced with a stronger character than himself. He meekly handed over Taylor's debit and credit cards to Marilyn and stood silently by as they packed up her things. He was obviously under the influence of some drug.

"Taylor, babe," he slurred as she was leaving, but Marilyn swept her out imperiously, not giving her a chance to say anything.

She felt a strange sense of relief and looked to Marilyn as her saviour.

When they got back to Marilyn's apartment she gave Taylor a sleeping pill and hot chocolate and tucked her up for the night. Taylor slept till noon the next day and then soaked in the tub for an hour, feeling refreshed and half-normal for the first time in months.

For the next three days Marilyn looked after her like a baby and by the fourth day had convinced Taylor to go back into rehab again. She chose another clinic, way up in the Hamptons, just in case Dylan should decide to revisit the one they'd met in. Taylor was humbly grateful to Marilyn, convinced that she'd saved her life, and entered the clinic determined to get her life back on track. They were both tearful as they parted, Marilyn on her way to check in for her plastic surgery. She promised to visit Taylor the following week, when she was released.

49

Jazz had been having a hard time since her miscarriage. She had been very down in herself and had found herself crying at the drop of a hat. If it hadn't been for her job and the support she got from Ashling and Brandon, she feared she would have gone under.

Ashling had finally persuaded her to go and see a doctor who explained that her feelings were perfectly normal and that most women felt that way after a miscarriage. Seemingly, it was her hormones that were in upheaval so the doctor gave her some medication to correct this. She also gave her the name of a counsellor who could help her with the grieving process she was experiencing. Soon Jazz felt much better but she recognised that the sense of loss would always be with her.

Brandon was surprised when Marilyn called him to tell him that Taylor had re-entered rehab voluntarily. Marilyn was turning out to be a better friend than he'd ever have imagined. Maybe he'd misjudged the old girl, after all. What perfect timing! Mia and Mike were arriving the following day for a five-day visit and he looked forward to giving them the good news about their mother.

It was with a light heart that he met them at Charles de Gaulle Airport and they were overjoyed to hear that their mother had re-entered rehab and was trying to get her life back on track. It set up a happy note for their holiday. Jazz had very kindly offered him her spare guest room so that they wouldn't have to go into a hotel and in the end it was decided that the kids would stay in his place and he would sleep in Jazz's.

"April in Paris," Mia sighed as they drove down the Champs-Élysées. "Could anything be more romantic?"

The kids went to bed for a couple of hours while Brandon went into the office. He wanted to wrap up as he was taking the following day, Friday, and the next Monday and Tuesday off, to show them around. He was so looking forward to spending the time with his kids. He was taking them to his favourite local restaurant, Au Sergent Recruteur, for dinner and had invited Jazz along to meet them.

It was a lively trio that converged there that evening and, as they waited for Jazz to join them, Brandon ordered a bottle of Bollinger as an aperitif.

The waiter was pouring the champagne when Mike let out a low whistle.

"Wow! What a babe!" he murmured, looking towards the door.

"She's beautiful," Mia agreed, following his gaze.

Brandon turned around to investigate the object of their admiration, only to find out that it was Jazz who was making her way towards them, stopping to kiss the patron and two waiters along the way. She was wearing a short, fitted, black-wool dress with a black-leather bomber jacket. The skirt ended mid-thigh and her high suede boots came to just over her knee. She wore her hair up and she looked sensational.

She kissed Brandon on both cheeks and then kissed both Mia and Mike. Mike was enthralled with her and Mia looked enviously at her figure. She noted, with typical female intuition, the glow in her father's eyes as he took Jazz's jacket. Ha-ha, she thought, there's more to this than meets the eye!

They had a wonderful evening and Brandon announced it was the best night he'd had in years.

They walked the five hundred metres to his apartment and he saw the twins comfortably settled. He then made his way to Jazz's apartment where she had a cognac waiting for him. He stretched out on the sofa and sighed happily as he sipped it.

"They're great kids," Jazz remarked, delighted to see him so relaxed. "You must be very proud of them."

"I sure am. They are wonderful, aren't they?" he said, bashfully.

"They take after you, much more so than Taylor," she said.

It was true. They were both blond and blue-eyed and had Brandon's sweet nature. Thank God for that, Jazz thought uncharitably.

Mike, meanwhile, was extolling Jazz's attributes to his sister.

"Do you think I might stand a chance with her?" he asked his twin.

"Not a hope in hell," she replied, in her forthright manner. "Not with Dad around as competition."

"You don't think . . . ?"

"She's crazy about him. Can't you tell?" she stated, with all the arrogance of a twenty-two-year-old expert in love.

"Well, blow me down!" Mike let out a low whistle, feeling a little jealous. "Dad's a lucky dude! She's a wow."

"But so nice too," his sister replied. "I'm delighted for Dad. He deserves some happiness."

"You're right," Mike agreed generously. Both of them were thinking of the awful life he'd shared with their mother. They hoped that she would also be able to move on with her life.

Brandon was incredibly proud of the adults his children had become and he enjoyed their company enormously. He was also delighted to see how well Jazz was getting on with them. Mike was obviously smitten and forever trying to attract her attention which made Brandon smile.

Mia was charmed by her and admired Jazz's style, pumping her for information about her clothes and shoes. Jazz promised to take her shopping on Monday.

"That's if my boss will give me the day off," she said, looking hopefully at Brandon.

"As if I could stop you," he laughed, throwing his eyes to heaven.

Brandon had wanted to have a party to introduce the twins to his colleagues and their families but obviously his bijou apartment was much too small. He asked Felicity and Ashling if they knew of anywhere he could hold it, as there would be quite a crowd.

"Why not let me host it for you here?" Felicity had said, when he'd been there for dinner the previous week. "I'm off for the Easter break and we've plenty of space here. I'd love to do it. It'll be good practice for me."

"I couldn't impose on you like that," he'd replied.

"Nonsense, man, she loves to entertain. She's a born hostess," Max had said proudly, beaming at his wife.

"Well, only on condition that I pay for all the food and drink," Brandon had insisted. "Otherwise it's no deal."

"Done!" Felicity had smiled at him. "I'll make you proud."

They all gathered in Felicity's at noon on the Sunday and the twins were very impressed with her apartment.

"Gosh, we've nothing this nice in LA," Mia had told her. "Everything's so modern there. I like this," she'd said, looking around the room appreciatively.

Pippa and Alex had arrived for the Easter holiday and Mike and Alex seemed to hit it off extremely well. Max raised his eyebrows at Brandon as the young couple sat close together on the sofa, joking and laughing.

Ashling was there with Kieran and the girls and she and Mia found themselves discussing wine for the afternoon. Jazz was enveloped with hugs and kisses by Orna, Ciara and Pierre, who were all fighting for her attention. Mia noticed how wonderful she was with the children.

"Does Jazz have any children?" she asked Ashling tentatively.

"No, unfortunately. She'd make a great mother."

"Maybe Dad and she will have one. I'd love a little sister," Mia remarked nonchalantly.

"What?" Ashling asked, thinking she'd misheard.

"Dad and Jazz. They're an item, aren't they?"

"Well, they're very close but they're just friends," Ashling replied, looking at the young girl in surprise.

"No way! They're crazy about each other," Mia stated matter of factly. "Look at the way they smile at each other and they even finish each other's sentences."

Ashling felt rocked out of her usual equilibrium. She looked across to Brandon and Jazz who were laughing over something the children had said. With a shock she realised that Mia was right. They were like two parts of a whole but she knew that they were not aware of it.

"Well, well," she murmured, turning back to the smiling Mia.

"Trust me, I know true love when I see it," said Mia.

The afternoon went with a bang and Felicity had done her usual wonderful miracle with the food. Even Sophie was happy and laughing. Yves was doing fine and had said he would like Kieran to visit him in the prison. Sophie felt it was a good sign that her husband was ready to see someone else. She'd been very worried at his isolation of himself. Kieran was surprised that it was he Yves wanted to see and not Brandon or Max. He promised Sophie that he would go to visit Yves on Tuesday.

Jazz did as she'd promised and took Mia shopping on Monday. Brandon had given her his credit card and told her to buy something very special with it. Jazz could think of nothing more special than a Herve Leger dress and when Mia saw how flattering and glamorous it was on, she immediately bought two.

"Dad won't mind," she said, mischievously.

Jazz laughed. The young girl obviously had her father wrapped around her little finger.

They met up with Ashling and Felicity and her girls for lunch and had a lovely time.

That evening Mia declared to her father that it had been a brilliant day.

"Jazz is so cool," she said, looking at Brandon slyly. "I really love her."

"She is pretty special," he agreed. "She's become my best friend since your mother left."

"I think she's a little in love with you," Mia said casually, looking for his reaction.

"Oh, I don't think she'd be interested in an old fogey like me." He smiled at the very idea.

"You never know," Mia said mysteriously. "She'd make a cool stepmom."

Brandon laughed. "So that's what this is all about?"

"Why not?" Mike joined in. "All my friends would be madly jealous of me."

Brandon threw back his head and roared laughing at the transparency of his children. They were priceless!

He felt his spirit had been renewed by the time the twins left for California. It had been a wonderful five days and he reckoned that he had caught up on some of the time he'd missed with them when they'd been little. They promised to come again in summer and this time Doug and Star would come too.

"We'll maybe take a trip and see a little more of France," Brandon suggested.

"And Jazz could come too," Mia said, all innocence, as they said goodbye.

"Maybe," he replied, thinking it was just as well she was going or she'd have had him married off by summer.

50

Jazz felt sad after the twins had left. She'd felt like part of a family with them and she genuinely liked Mia and Mike. She had to admit that she'd also liked having Brandon stay in her apartment and it somehow felt empty after he'd left. He was such a fantastic father and she thought, for the hundredth time, how foolish Taylor had been to let him go. The good news was that Taylor seemed to be getting her life back together again.

Jazz felt melancholy all week and couldn't shake off that feeling. She wondered if it was the youthfulness of the twins that was making her feel her age. Her birthday was less than a month away and she was not looking forward to it. If she was honest, she was in denial about it. Thirty-six! She didn't want to go there.

She was going back to Munich the following weekend, which was Easter, but even that prospect couldn't lift her gloom. Two of her friends had just got engaged and were having parties. Another had asked her to be godmother to her new baby. Jazz somehow had the feeling that she was missing the boat.

Kieran went to visit Yves on Tuesday and was shocked at how much he had changed. Besides the fact that he looked years older, his whole demeanour was different. Looking around the cold bare walls of the visiting area, Kieran shivered. He guessed it must be no picnic being locked up in a dismal place like this. He couldn't begin to imagine how he would cope, away from Ashling and the girls, with his freedom curtailed.

"How are you?" he asked Yves gently, feeling desperately sorry for him.

"I'm fine, all things considered," Yves smiled wanly. "I've had plenty of time to think about my life and to realise what a dickhead I've been." He spoke quietly and kept twisting his hands as he did so. "I feel I've let everyone down and I've brought dishonour to the project. Please apologise to everyone for me."

"Look, we all know how easy it would be for any one of us to have done the same thing," Kieran assured him. "We all have colleagues who made a lot of money on schemes like you tried. And the project is on track. It hasn't been affected by your actions."

Yves looked relieved at that but then a shadow crossed his face again. "The worst of it is what I did to Sophie and Pierre."

He put his head in his hands and Kieran could see that he was crying. He reached out and rubbed Yves's arm.

"Listen, Yves, Sophie loves you and that's the main thing. You'll have a chance to make it up to her, and Pierre, when you get out of here."

"I hope so. She's wonderful to be sticking by me. I wouldn't have blamed her for leaving me." Yves's eyes were distraught as he looked up at Kieran.

"She would never consider doing that. She loves you and you'll get the chance to start again when you get out. Any idea when that'll be?"

"By August, my attorney says."

"You won't feel it," Kieran assured him gently.

He left, giving Yves a hug, and promising to take care of Sophie.

"I really appreciate what Ashling and Jazz are doing for her. Can you please tell them that?" Yves said, as they parted.

Kieran said he would.

51

Kieran and Ashling left for Dublin to spend Easter with their families. They'd invited Corey to visit for a few days and he was very much looking forward to it. Felicity and Max were taking the girls to the south of France for a week and Sophie was taking Pierre to visit her sister, Vianne, in Grenoble, in the French Alps. With Jazz gone to Munich for the weekend, Brandon felt very alone. He thought often of Jazz and wondered what she was doing. She had texted him a few times and he gathered that she was not enjoying herself too much either. 'Miss you', she'd signed off her last message and he wondered if this was true. He had a spring in his step on Tuesday morning and was looking forward to seeing her again.

Her face lit up when she saw him walk into the office.

"Hi," she grinned, "good to see you again. How was your weekend?"

"Lonely. How was *your* weekend?"

"So so. All my friends seem to have partners now. To be honest I felt a bit like a spare thumb!" She laughed hollowly.

They quickly resumed their easy, friendly relationship, spending most evenings together.

Marilyn called from New York to say that Taylor was doing well in rehab and was trying really hard to conquer her addictions.

Brandon was grateful to his ex-wife's friend and invited her out to dinner when she got back to Paris. She promptly accepted. Little did he know that she was hoping that her newly lifted bum, boobs and eyes would make him see her in a new light.

The following Saturday was Jazz's birthday and on Friday night, as Brandon was leaving after dinner in her apartment, she said to him, "Dinner tomorrow night, as usual?"

"Sorry, no can do. I'm taking Marilyn to dinner. Remember her? Taylor's old friend."

Jazz was frozen to the spot, shocked with this piece of information. Remember Taylor's old friend? How could she ever forget her! Did he not remember that it was with Marilyn that Yves had cheated on her? Was Brandon to be Marilyn's latest conquest?

She said nothing but when he'd gone, she sat hugging herself tight, feeling a strange sense of betrayal.

The four women met for lunch on Saturday. Felicity had some good news for them. She'd made the decision to go into business with Becky when she got back to London and was very excited about it. They all congratulated her and she insisted on ordering champagne to celebrate. Jazz noticed that Ashling took only one sip and left the rest.

"Are you feeling okay?" she asked her.

"Fine, just a little hungover from last night and we're going to a party in the Irish Embassy tonight. I don't want to arrive there drunk," she laughed.

Jazz had been about to ask her to go out to dinner that evening but that was obviously not on now. The others were all otherwise engaged too. Felicity and Max were going out with Becky and her husband to celebrate their new venture and Sophie was having her family to dinner. Even old reliable Hugh was unavailable as he had gone to Ireland to visit Fiona. She didn't want to think of what Brandon would be doing.

Ashling noticed that Jazz was not her usual bubbly self.

"Are you okay? You seem very quiet today." Ashling was concerned about Jazz. She was still at times very down since her miscarriage.

"I'm fine," Jazz replied, but Ashling wasn't convinced.

"Will you come around with Brandon for lunch tomorrow?" she asked. "Corey is coming too."

"Well, I can't answer for Brandon but I'd love to come," Jazz replied, just a little too sharply.

Ashling hoped that they hadn't had a falling out. She sighed. Relationships were so complicated!

"I have something to tell you," Ashling said to her when Sophie and Felicity had left. "It's not because I've a hangover that I'm not drinking – it's because I'm pregnant!"

Jazz was surprised. "Congratulations!" she said, hugging Ashling. "I didn't know you wanted another baby."

"Well, I think three is a nice number and it would be nice if it was a little boy. Kieran would love to have a son."

"That would be great," Jazz agreed. "I was wondering why you turned down the champagne. It's not at all like you."

"Yeah, thank God my wine course is finished. I couldn't bear not to swallow all the gorgeous wine they served us," Ashling laughed.

Jazz was delighted for her friend but more anxious than ever about her own prospects of ever becoming a mother. Feeling very down, she decided that if no one else would, then she'd treat herself to a birthday dinner. Firstly, she went on a shopping spree in Galeries Lafayette and, laden down with bags, then visited the famous Parisian delicatessen, Fauchon. She treated herself to some foie gras and a jar of pheasant with truffles and Armagnac. She also bought a bottle of Sauternes to go with the foie gras and a bottle of Lynch-Bages, the lovely red wine she'd enjoyed so much in Ashling's house. I'll have my own party, she thought, feeling very sorry for herself.

Brandon had offered to pick Marilyn up at her apartment but she quickly shot that down.

"Good heavens, not a chance, daahling," she laughed, her voice low and husky. "Louis would go crazy with jealousy if he thought you and I were sharing a cosy dinner together."

Brandon was a little worried by this remark. Was she expecting a cosy romantic evening? If so, she was in for a shock. He was taking her out to hear how Taylor was progressing and to thank her for taking care of his ex-wife. That was as far as it went. He arranged to meet her in Willi's, a bar and restaurant that he'd heard was nice and casual.

Marilyn was fashionably late and he knew, when he saw the glossy mink coat she was wearing, that she was expecting the Ritz or the George V for dinner. Underneath it she was wearing a very low-cut tight red dress which left nothing to the imagination. She had obviously burnt her bras years ago and all the men at the bar were ogling her breasts, much to Brandon's embarrassment. She looked different – years younger – and he realised that she'd obviously had some work done on her face and body while she was back in the States. Well, he wouldn't hold that against her.

She greeted him in a warm embrace, kissing him full on the lips which made him feel very uncomfortable. She never flinched when he told her that he had reserved a table in Willi's despite the fact that she was dressed for the Moulin Rouge or Maxim's.

He told her he was very happy to hear that Taylor was doing well in rehab. He was very appreciative of Marilyn's efforts to get her there and for getting her away from the dreadful Dylan. She, of course, embellished her part in the whole thing, hoping that Brandon would see what a wonderful person she was.

"Now, enough about Taylor, let's talk about you and me," she began.

He squirmed in his seat. He felt her leg rubbing against his and pulled away. The next hour was pretty torturous as he tried to evade her advances. She kept leaning towards him, giving him an eyeful of her newly enhanced breasts. She constantly ran her tongue over her luscious red lips which were certainly much more swollen than he remembered. She even resorted to dipping her finger in her cream dessert and licking it suggestively while looking at him from under her newly lifted eyelids. She made him feel ill. She was all fake, down to the tan which was more deep orange than anything the sun could have produced.

He couldn't help but compare her with Jazz who was the essence of natural beauty. He desperately wanted to leave this manufactured woman and go to Jazz. Marilyn reached for his hand once more and suddenly he'd had enough.

"Sorry, Marilyn, I have to go," he mumbled, pushing back his chair so hard that it fell.

She looked up at him in surprise. "Brandon, honey, don't go yet. I was kinda hopin' that we'd go dancin' after this."

Even her voice now irritated him beyond all reason. "Sorry, Marilyn," he said, turning on his heel, aware that he was being rude but not caring. He'd had enough.

He paid the bill and practically ran from the restaurant, afraid that Marilyn might actually come after him. Luckily, he found a taxi before she had the chance. Ten minutes later he was ringing Jazz's doorbell.

Jazz had spent her thirty-sixth birthday wallowing in self-pity. What had she achieved in all those years? Nothing, precisely nothing – at least nothing that was important. Yes, she had a good job but that didn't keep her warm at night. Nor did it love her or help her come to terms with being alone for the rest of her life.

She was a little drunk when she heard the doorbell ring. What the hell, she thought, what bloody idiot forgot their key tonight? She pressed the intercom.

"Hi, Jazz, it's me. Can I come up?"

"Brandon?" she asked, surprised. Wasn't he supposed to be with Marilyn tonight?

"Yes, Jazz. Can you buzz me up?"

She did as he asked and he could see straight away that she'd been drinking and obviously crying. He looked around the candlelit room, thinking that maybe she had company.

"What's the matter?" he asked her gently. "Are you alone?"

The tears started again. "Yes, I'm alone – all alone. And, it's my birthday and no one wants to be with me . . . I'm a failure really," she said between sobs.

He put his finger on her lips. "Hush, hush, don't say that. You're not a failure and you're not alone. I'm here now. Why didn't you tell me it was your birthday?"

"Well, you were going out with Marilyn . . ."

"I would have cancelled her if I'd known it was your birthday."

"You would?"

He led her to the sofa. "Of course I would. I only took her out to thank her for taking care of Taylor but I would have cancelled it if I'd known it was your birthday."

She stopped crying and looked at him with wide eyes. "I thought you were interested in her."

He roared laughing and she smiled tremulously.

"You can't be serious!" he said.

Now she started to laugh with him.

"I couldn't wait to get away from her!" he said. "She irritates me beyond belief."

Jazz gave a sigh of relief. She'd been riveted by jealousy at the thought of him with Marilyn.

"And what are you doing sitting here alone, drinking?" he asked, smiling indulgently.

"I know," she replied sheepishly. "I was feeling sorry for myself."

"Come here, silly," he said, pulling her to him.

She leaned into him, loving the feel of his arms around her.

"You know, I miss you terribly when I'm not with you," he said. "I couldn't wait to get back to you tonight. Doesn't that mean something?" He stroked her face gently.

"I feel the same way. I was terribly jealous tonight thinking of you with her," she whispered. In fact, it had shocked her to find out just how jealous she'd felt.

Brandon found it hard to believe that Jazz could feel jealous of anyone, least of all the trashy Marilyn.

"You have no one to be jealous of," he told her, taking her face in his hands. Before he knew it he was kissing her and to his amazement, she was kissing him back. She tasted delicious, sweet and fresh and her mouth was so soft. He didn't want to stop.

Jazz couldn't believe what was happening. This was what she'd been waiting for all her life. Yves and Hans both now paled into insignificance beside Brandon. The feelings she had for him went so much deeper. He was her best friend and the kindest person she'd ever known. She felt like they were part of a whole. When he took her hand and led her into the bedroom, it seemed the most natural thing in the world to do. He was such a gentle considerate lover that after they were spent she found herself crying.

"What is it, my darling?" he asked, kissing her tears away.

"I'm so happy," she smiled up at him.

"Me too. I love you very much," he murmured.

"I love you too," she whispered. "And thank you for making this the best birthday ever."

"I know someone who will be delighted with this news," he grinned.

"Who?"

"Mia. She practically tried to throw me into your arms when she was here. She says you'll make a cool stepmom."

"Thank you, Mia," Jazz said, smiling.

He stayed the night with her and every night after that, although he held on to his own apartment.

Marilyn couldn't believe it. Things had been going so well. When Brandon had asked her out to dinner she'd thought that she'd finally got her chance with him. She figured that when he saw how great she was looking since her latest surgery, he'd fall hard for her. And there was no doubt that he'd noticed how well she was looking. He hadn't missed the envious looks he'd been getting from all the other guys in the bar. She had been a bit disappointed when he'd told her that they were eating there in the restaurant at Willi's. She'd expected that he'd take her to the Ritz or the George V at the very least.

Then just when she'd felt that she was getting somewhere with him, he'd upped and left. No apology, no future invitation, nothing! She couldn't understand it. Maybe it was all too much for him. She'd call him in a few days and invite him out to dinner and this time it would be the Ritz or George V. This time she'd make sure he'd end up in her bed.

Ashling was pleased when Brandon rang on Sunday morning to say he could make it to lunch. Jazz and he arrived together and appeared to have made up as they were smiling and joking together. As always, the girls leaped on Jazz and monopolised her while Corey and Brandon got into a conversation about American politics. Kieran was doing the cooking and served up a delicious pasta meal. They had a lovely afternoon and Jazz and Brandon left about five o'clock.

"Those two are very much in love," Corey remarked, as he sat sipping a brandy in Ashling's living room after they'd gone.

"What?" she exclaimed.

"Oh, definitely. Did you not see the way they were looking at each other?"

"I did think they were much more touchy-feely than usual today," Kieran agreed.

Ashling couldn't believe it. "Gosh, I hope you're right," she said, grinning broadly at the two men. "They're both fabulous people. I'll be delighted if they got it together."

"I think they already have, my dear," Corey smiled at her.

Kieran nodded his agreement, grinning broadly.

"Well, I never!" Was she the only one who hadn't twigged?

She couldn't wait to ask Jazz about it. She didn't have to wait long. Jazz rang later that night to thank her for lunch and share the news that she and Brandon were now a couple. Ashling could hear the happiness in her voice and was delighted for both her and Brandon. They deserved some happiness. She'd always known that there was a Mr Right waiting out there somewhere for Jazz. She just hadn't expected it to be Brandon.

"So Mia was right after all," Ashling said to Kieran as they were curled up in bed that night.

"*Out of the mouths of babes,*" he replied sleepily as he drifted off to sleep.

The following Saturday Brandon went out shopping and was all smiles when he returned to Jazz's apartment. He got out the ice-bucket and opened the bottle of Cristal he'd put in the fridge earlier.

"I have a little present for you," he said, taking a long slim package from his inside jacket pocket.

Jazz was agog with curiosity and excitement as he toasted her.

"A belated happy birthday, my darling," he said, handing her the box.

When she unwrapped it she saw the Cartier insignia on the box and caught her breath. She opened it slowly to discover a stunning pair of the gypsy earrings that she wore so often – but these were not plain gold, they were made of sparkling diamonds. She was so touched that she started to cry.

"Hey, don't you like them?" he teased.

"They're the most beautiful earrings I've ever seen," she said, through her tears. "Thank you so much, darling," she murmured, kissing him deeply.

"Put them on," he told her, happy that she liked them.

She went to the mirror and did as he asked. He came up behind her and lifted her hair gently off her neck as she turned her head this way and that, watching how the light caught the beautiful stones.

He kissed her neck and murmured huskily. "I think I could appreciate them more if I wasn't being distracted by your clothes."

"You think so?" she asked, watching him steadily in the full-length mirror. Slowly she undid the buttons of her dress and let it fall to the floor. She could feel his excitement as she undid her bra and let it fall also. She saw his eyes slide over her body as he watched her in the mirror and then she was naked except for the beautiful diamond earrings. Within seconds he had ripped off his clothes and started caressing her body while still looking at her in the mirror. It was the most erotic moment either of them had ever experienced. The champagne forgotten, they made love right there and then, she still wearing the earrings. It was the best sex either of them had ever had, bar none.

52

Two weeks later Fiona arrived in Paris, having finished her final physiotherapy exams. She knew that she'd done very well and was over the moon at having finished her studies, at least for the moment. She and Hugh planned to move to Ireland in October where she had enrolled in a Sports Therapy course. Hugh had already secured a job in a Fitness Centre there and, when she qualified the following May, they would move to California. He would open his own Fitness Centre and Fiona would open a Sports Therapy practice in conjunction with his business. They had it all worked out.

Ashling was delighted to have Fiona's help, especially as she had to edit her book. The publisher had assigned her an editor who had marked all the changes that she needed to make to her manuscript and she baulked at the sheer number of them when she first saw it.

"I felt exactly the same when I got my first manuscript back from my editor," Corey assured her "Trust me! They know what they're doing. You'll learn a lot and next time round you'll have much less editing to do."

"I hope you're right," she grimaced, a little overwhelmed by the daunting task. Luckily, Fiona was around a lot. She was staying with Hugh but came to Ashling's whenever he was working. Orna and Ciara were delighted to have their favourite auntie baby-sitting them and it left Ashling free to work on her editing.

Fiona now joined in the girls' nights out and the occasional Saturday lunches as did Alex, Felicity's oldest daughter, who had come to stay for the summer, now that college had finished. Alex, who had studied French for years at school, was now taking lessons from Nicole. She and Felicity would natter away in French, much to Max's amazement. Alex was currently madly in love with Nicole's friend, Jean Michel, and Felicity guessed that he was behind this sudden desire to become fluent in the language.

Felicity and Becky were making plans for the catering company they were going to open when they got back to London. It was all incredibly exciting. They spent two weekends in London checking out premises and it was looking very promising.

Marilyn rang Brandon several times but he declined all her advances and invitations to dinner or drinks. She couldn't figure out what his problem was and was piqued by his behaviour. She informed him that Taylor was still doing well in rehab and had agreed to stay there until she felt strong enough to face the world again.

Now that Brandon was so happy, he hoped that Taylor would find happiness too.

Jazz felt like she was living a dream and was incredibly happy loving him and being loved in return. She didn't think of the future. She was happy living in the blissful present and was falling more and more in love with Brandon with each passing day.

Kieran went regularly to visit Yves in prison and finally he agreed to see Max and Brandon. He spent the whole time apologising to them and they felt desperately sorry for him. It looked like he would be freed in August which was good news. Sophie was very hopeful that they could start over again. They all agreed that he was a changed man but Jazz resolutely refused to visit him and Brandon was secretly pleased about that.

He'd rung Mia with the news that he and Jazz were now a couple.

"About time, Dad," was her succinct reply. "When are you getting married? Can I be bridesmaid?"

"Whoa, whoa there! Who said anything about marriage?" he cried.

"Why not? You love each other, don't you? God Dad, you don't want some other guy coming along and stealing her from under your nose, do you? You're not getting any younger, you know!"

Brandon thought about what she'd said. The thought of losing Jazz, now that he'd found her, was unimaginable. Maybe Mia was right. Mike was equally anxious to have Jazz as his new stepmom.

"Gosh, Dad, I can't wait to see my friends' faces when they see how gorgeous she is."

Well, no problem there then. His kids certainly approved.

The following Saturday night he told Jazz to dress up as he was taking her somewhere special. She decided to wear her silver Herve Leger dress and spent the afternoon at the beauty salon, wondering where he was taking her.

He arrived at her apartment wearing a tuxedo and she thought he'd never looked more handsome.

"I suggest you wear a warm coat as it may be a little chilly," he said.

Mystified, she did as he asked and felt like a princess as she stepped into the limousine he'd ordered. She looked surprised as they pulled up at the Eiffel Tower. She hoped he didn't expect her to climb the steps in her four-inch Brian Atwood heels. Luckily he didn't! They took the private elevator up to the second level where they entered Le Jules Verne, the famous Michelin-starred restaurant.

Jazz had read about this restaurant and was immensely impressed with the décor and not least the fact that Brandon had managed to get a reservation there. The maître d' showed them to their table which was situated in a bay window with the whole of Paris spread out below them. Jazz was blown away by the view. The lights of the city twinkled like a million jewels. It was breathtaking.

"I read that you have to reserve here weeks, if not months, in advance. *And* we have the best table in the house," she remarked. "How did you manage it?"

"To be honest, I asked Monsieur Fournier to make the reservation for me," he told her sheepishly.

"The Finance Minister? You clever boy," she grinned at him.

"Anything for my lady." He gave a little bow.

The food was out of this world and everything was served under a silver dome which the waiters whisked away with flair, revealing a work of art on the plate. The flavour of the food was like nothing Jazz had ever tasted and the accompanying wines were simply divine.

To finish, they'd ordered a trio of chocolate desserts and they came under the usual silver dome. The waiter whisked hers away with a flourish and there sitting in the centre of her plate, surrounded by the chocolate was a tiny velvet box in which sat the biggest diamond ring she'd ever seen. She looked up at Brandon, bewildered, to see him smiling.

"Will you marry me, Jazz?" he asked softly.

She was dumbstruck. She was so in love with him and now he wanted to marry her.

She looked back at the ring again and tears welled up in her eyes.

"I love you so much, Jazz. Please say yes," he said, taking the ring from its box.

"Oh, yes, yes," she cried the tears spilling down her cheeks.

He slipped the ring onto her finger. It was exquisite and fitted her perfectly. He leaned across the table and kissed her.

"I love you too and I promise I'll make you happy."

She was glowing and the waiters and the other diners nearby smiled at the lovers as they realised what was happening.

He took out a pristine white handkerchief and wiped her tears away.

"You'll have to stop crying every time I give you a present or you'll be shedding many, many tears in the future," he said, smiling at her.

"I'll try, honestly I will," she smiled back at him.

He thought she had never looked more beautiful.

She kept turning her hand this way and that, admiring the beautiful ring. She thought she must be the happiest woman in Paris tonight.

As they left the restaurant, the staff congratulated them and gave Jazz a little bag of their famous Madeleine biscuits.

"So you will remember your evening here," the maître d' said.

"Believe me, I'll never forget it. Thank you." She gave him a smile as dazzling as the new ring on her finger.

Brandon led her to the banks of the Seine where they boarded a boat for a cruise back down the river. They toasted each other with champagne, she warm and cosy, wrapped in Brandon's arms and his love.

When they got home they decided to ring Mia and Mike to give them the good news. Jazz could hear Mia squealing with delight.

"Can I be bridesmaid?" she cried.

"Of course, I wouldn't have anyone else," she said, laughing at her future step-daughter's excitement.

Mike was equally delighted. "When are you getting married?" he asked.

"As soon as possible," Brandon replied, surprising Jazz.

"Why not?" he said, after he'd come off the phone. "I'd like to get married here in France, wouldn't you?"

"That would be nice but it doesn't give us much time," she replied.

"We'll manage. I want you as my wife, as soon as possible." He pulled her to him, marvelling again at how lucky he was to have this fabulous woman in love with him.

The following morning, she had to look at her ring again to make sure she hadn't been dreaming. It was real. The first thing she did was to phone her mother in Munich.

"Mami, I have some good news," she said, happy to be giving her mother the news she'd been hoping for so long.

She was overjoyed that her daughter would have someone to look after her as she grew old and from what Jasmin was saying her future son-in-law was pretty special. And maybe now she would finally have the grandchild she'd always longed for.

"She's crying," Jazz whispered to Brandon as she let her mother pull herself together.

"What a family!" he teased. "I know who you take after now. I suppose if I'm joining this family, I'd better get used to all these tears."

Jazz promised to take Brandon down to Munich the following weekend. They decided to get married in September as they would all be finished the project and would be taking holidays before returning to their home countries. They both wanted a small intimate wedding with just close family and friends present. Jazz was on cloud nine.

They spent the next hour phoning all their friends to give them the good news.

Ashling was thrilled for them and promised to help Jazz with the preparations for the wedding. She insisted that they come around for celebratory champagne that evening. When Jazz and Brandon got there they found that Ashling had gathered the troops and there were banners and balloons plastering the walls. Felicity, Max and Alex were there along with Sophie, Pierre, Corey and of course Fiona and Hugh. They all descended on the pair, hugging and clapping them on the back as they congratulated them.

Orna, Ciara and Pierre were dancing around and clapping their hands. Jazz was close to tears – tears of happiness – at the love that surrounded her. Brandon saw this and clasped her hand as she accepted their good wishes. All the girls oohed and aahed over her ring and insisted on trying it on, making a wish while turning it round three times. Even Orna and Ciara got in on the act.

Ashling had somehow managed to turn it into a great impromptu party with nibbles and canapés and some fabulous cakes that Felicity had contributed.

Jazz was very touched. She knew she was very lucky to have such great friends and to think that nine months ago she'd never even met any of them!

53

Brandon went to visit Yves the following Wednesday and Yves congratulated him on his engagement to Jazz. He was much more upbeat now as he'd been told that he would definitely be freed in August.

"What will you do when you get out?" Brandon asked him.

"I haven't decided yet. My priority will be to try to make it up to Sophie and Pierre for what I've done."

"Everyone deserves a second chance," Brandon told him. "I think you've paid for your mistakes."

"Thanks for that, Brandon, and I really hope that you and Jazz will be very happy. She's a wonderful woman."

"I know that. I'm a lucky man." Brandon did not let on that he knew of her relationship with Yves. What was the point? It was over now, that's all that mattered.

Brandon couldn't stop thinking about Yves since his visit to the prison. It looked like he really had changed, as Sophie had said. Things would be very difficult for them when he got out because he would now be unemployed. There was no way the bank would take him back. Brandon had an idea.

At his Friday meeting with Monsieur Fournier, the Finance Minister, he presented him with a bottle of wine in thanks for making the reservation at the Eiffel Tower.

"We had a wonderful night, thank you," he said. "It was very special. I actually asked Jazz to marry me there." He couldn't stop smiling.

"I take it she said yes?"

"Oh yes, she did."

"Well, my heartiest congratulations. She's a lovely young woman."

"Yes, I feel very lucky," Brandon told him.

He then broached the subject of Yves. As he'd suspected, the Minister was sympathetic to Yves's predicament.

"So hard on the family and Sophie is such a sweet girl."

"I was wondering if there was any way you could find a position for him here or anywhere," Brandon asked. "Not in charge of money, of course," he added hastily.

"Mmm, leave it with me. I would like to help him. I'll see what I can do."

Brandon was relieved. He knew that Monsieur Fournier was a fair and generous man and was pleased that he'd brought it to his attention.

Jazz and Brandon flew to Munich the following weekend to meet Jazz's family and friends. He couldn't get used to everyone calling her Jasmin. He thought that the name Jazz actually suited her better. Mami, as she insisted he call her, received him with open arms. Here was the son she'd never had. She was much younger than he'd expected and quite a beauty. It was obvious from whom Jazz had inherited her looks.

Her mother threw a big engagement party for them and he got to meet all of the neighbours and cousins and Jazz's school and university friends. All of her friends agreed that Brandon was very cute. They all met up again in the enormous English Beer Garden on Sunday afternoon and he looked on in amazement at the way they lowered the huge litre pots of beer without batting an eyelid. They had great fun and he loved their jolly banter. They were different to any other Germans that he'd met before. As they left that night to catch their flight back to Paris, he was exhausted but happy that the visit had been such a success.

With a sigh of relief Ashling finally typed the last word of her edited manuscript. It had been a tough job but she was happy with the end result. She had learnt so much while editing and realised now just how naïve she'd been when she'd blithely decided to write a novel. Now it was done and dusted and she felt much more confident about starting her second one. She'd finished her children's book and had sent it off to the publisher also. Her morning sickness had disappeared and she was blooming. She knew that she had to watch her weight with this baby. Hugh was almost like a personal trainer making sure that she didn't strain herself in the gym. He needn't have worried. She would never take any risks and was only doing gentle exercises.

She was really looking forward to this baby and staying home to care for him – for some reason she felt it was a boy – and she could continue her writing as well. It was all working out beautifully.

Felicity finished her cordon bleu course in June and was ecstatic to gain the top place of all the students. Her prize was a course in Advanced Studies in Taste at the University of Rheims in Champagne. It was a two-week course of workshops and tasting, with one week spent in Rheims and the other week in the Cordon Bleu School itself. She was overwhelmed to have won it and planned to do it in July. Pippa had come from England to join the family at Felicity's graduation and Max and the girls were extremely proud of their mother. When she stood on the stage and thanked everyone involved, *in French*, Alex and Pippa thought that Max would burst with pride.

Felicity and Becky left for London on Monday, to finalise plans for their business and they were all shocked when Felicity said that she would drive so that she could drop Pippa off at school for her last week before the summer holidays.

They finally found premises that had a perfect location and a very reasonable rent and signed up for it on the spot. They planned to be up and running by October and now had to start choosing what food they would prepare and sell. Max was going to help with the financial side of things and keep the books, which was great. Becky's husband would take care of the marketing. It was all working out very satisfactorily.

When she rang her mother to arrange to visit, there was no prevaricating from Georgina.

"Of course, darling. Come down any day you wish. I'll make sure I'm free."

Her father, hearing his wife saying this, couldn't resist a little smile and Felicity also felt a sense of satisfaction that her mother now respected her. When she visited and told her parents of her success and the new business she was starting, Georgina could hardly believe it.

She said to Nigel, when Felicity had left, "I honestly never thought she had it in her."

He smiled smugly. "Oh, I always knew she had."

Jazz and Brandon kept to their plan of tying the knot as early as possible in September, before everyone returned to their countries. Monsieur Fournier had called in to their office to congratulate Jazz, bearing a big bouquet of flowers. On hearing that they were planning to get married in Paris, he suggested that she call his daughter, Élise, who had got married recently and could advise her where to go. Jazz rang Élise and she recommended Sabine, the wedding planner that she had used.

"She was fantastic. Everything was just perfect. I had a fairytale wedding." She sighed with happiness, thinking about it.

Jazz contacted Sabine and they arranged to meet. Sabine's resumé was impressive and they could see she was very professional. She showed them photos of Monsieur Fournier's daughter's wedding.

"That's a beautiful château," Jazz exclaimed admiring the gardens and the setting.

"Where is it?" Brandon asked.

"It's only an hour from Paris. It's magnificent and very exclusive but horrendously expensive, I'm afraid."

"I want no expense spared – I want to give Jazz the most wonderful wedding that she could ever have imagined." Brandon said, taking his fiancée's hand and bringing it to his lips. She blushed with pleasure as Sabine smiled happily at them. She loved it when her clients were as much in love as these two appeared to be.

"I'll check out the château immediately," she said. "Have you any thoughts on a dress, Jazz?"

"Not really. I haven't thought about it. I have seen some beautiful Monique Lhuillier wedding dresses in magazines though."

"Perfect, she's exactly who I would have recommended. You can see her bridal collection on Rue d'Échelle. I'll call and make an appointment for you, if you wish."

This wedding was going to be just perfect, Sabine could feel it.

She rang Jazz that evening to say that the château was, unbelievably, available for the weekend of the 2nd September. They agreed to book it provisionally and arranged to go and see it the following Sunday.

Jazz took Ashling with her the following Saturday morning to check out the Monique Lhuillier collection and they were both mesmerised by the beautiful bridal dresses on show. The saleslady was very helpful and showed them all the various styles available. Jazz knew exactly what she wanted and, the moment she saw it, she knew she'd found the dress of her dreams. It was exquisite and Ashling caught her breath when she saw how sensational Jazz looked in it. She was like a beautiful princess and when the salesgirl added the tiara and long veil, Ashling felt tears come to her eyes. Jazz stood looking in the mirror hardly able to believe that she could look so beautiful. She bought the dress on the spot.

While there, they had a look at bridesmaid's dresses for Mia and Jazz was ecstatic when she spotted a pale-green, silk, strapless bridesmaid dress she thought would be perfect for Mia. The saleslady told her that Mia could visit the Monique Lhuillier Salon in Los Angeles and try it on. She offered to email the details of the dress to them. Jazz fervently hoped that Mia would like it.

Then, to Ashling's surprise, Jazz said, "Let's look at dresses for Orna and Ciara now."

"What?"

"Didn't I mention that I would like them to be my flower-girls and Pierre my page-boy?"

Ashling clapped her hands. "Oh, they'll just adore that. They'll be so excited!"

They spotted two adorable little dresses that they both loved and a cute page-boy outfit for Pierre and arranged to return with the children the following Saturday.

On Sunday Brandon and Jazz visited the château with Sabine and were entranced with it. They booked it on the spot. They would stay in the Bridal Suite, which was magnificent, the night of the wedding. A fleet of limousines would take their guests to and from the château. It was idyllic, just perfect! All the arrangements would be left in the extremely capable hands of the efficient Sabine. She would source the caterers, flowers, invitations, photographer, music etc. All Jazz and Brandon had to do was choose which one they preferred. The fact that money was no object made it all very easy for Sabine.

Pippa was ready and waiting for Felicity when she picked her up from school on Thursday for the start of her summer holidays. She was practically dancing with excitement.

"Two whole months in Paris! Imagine!" she cried, throwing herself at Felicity as the porters lifted her cases into the boot of the car.

They drove back to the house in Holland Park and would pick Becky up the following day before driving back to Paris. Pippa was very impressed with the way her mother handled the right-hand-drive car on the French roads and the way she was able to speak French to the staff in the restaurant where they stopped for lunch.

She had enrolled Pippa and Alex on an intensive French course for the following two weeks, which Felicity thought would benefit them greatly. She herself would spend the following week in Rheims, on the tasting course she'd won. Then after the next week in the Cordon Bleu School, she would have six weeks to relax and enjoy a well-earned break before they returned back home. She realised that she would be very sad to be leaving Paris. It had been a wonderful experience and she felt she had grown a lot as a person.

It was just as well, Jazz thought, that they had Sabine there to organise their wedding as things had become very hectic at work now that the end of the project was in sight. Their Asian counterparts would be coming to Paris for a week in August, to finalise their findings together and it looked like the whole project had been a tremendous success. At their meeting the following Friday, Monsieur Fournier told Brandon as much. He was very pleased at what they had achieved, he said, as was the President. Brandon couldn't help but feel proud of his team.

"I've two pieces of good news for you," the Minister said. "Firstly, the President would like to invite all of you to the Élysée Palace to thank you personally and secondly, I have managed to find a position for your colleague, Yves, on my staff."

Brandon wanted to whoop with joy. Everything seemed to be coming up roses. "Thank you so much, Minister. My team will be thrilled and I know that Yves and Sophie will be very grateful for your offer. May I tell them?"

"Yes, of course. The President's office will be in touch with you soon about a possible date."

"Thank you, Minister. I very much appreciate all your help."

"I'm happy to be able to help. How are the wedding plans coming along?"

"Wonderfully well. Sabine is taking care of everything and we're having it in the same château as your daughter's wedding."

"You'll have a superb day." Monsieur Fournier smiled at the memory. "It's idyllic there."

Jazz, Ashling and Sophie, flanked by three very excited children, converged on the bridal shop the following Saturday morning. The girls loved the ballet-length white tulle dresses and twirled around and around like ballerinas. Pierre looked darling in his pageboy outfit. Mia had called during the week and judging by the squeals of excitement over the phone, Jazz gathered that she loved the pale green dress too. Jazz ordered it for her. The Los Angeles bridal salon had sent Mia's measurements already to the Paris store. Orna and Ciara would have sashes of the same green on their white dresses and little coronets of green and white flowers in their hair. Everything was falling into place.

The next few weeks sped by so fast that Jazz could hardly believe it. She was in contact with Sabine almost daily. She and Brandon went to Antwerp, in Belgium, to choose their wedding rings and Jazz also found the most exquisite satin bridal shoes there. They were studded with seed pearls and had white ribbons around the ankles. Everything was now in place. Brandon was keeping their honeymoon a secret. No amount of probing could get him to reveal what he'd planned. He wanted it to be a surprise.

The invitations went out in the middle of July. They had kept it to thirty guests plus the three children. Alex and Pippa were delighted to be invited and Monsieur Fournier replied immediately to say that he and his wife would be honoured to attend.

Jazz got a surprise phone call from Hans.

"I believe congratulations are in order," he said, sounding surprisingly cheerful.

She still felt a little guilty about him. "How did you hear that?" she asked.

"My fiancée is from Munich and she met some of your friends who told her," he replied.

"Well, congratulations to you too," Jazz said, relieved that he'd met someone.

"I've got a transfer to Munich so I'll be leaving your apartment next month. Are you coming back to Frankfurt after your marriage?"

"No. I'm moving to New York. I've applied to the bank for a transfer there and they've agreed to it."

"That's good news. And, Jazz . . ." he hesitated, "I hope you'll be really happy."

"Thanks, Hans. You too," she replied softly, glad that there was no bad feeling between them and hopeful that they'd both found true love.

54

Taylor was feeling like her old self again, at last! She felt that the stint in rehab had been a lifesaver and she realised now what stupid mistakes she'd made. Initially she'd been uncooperative but, when she read in the newspaper that Dylan had been found dead from an overdose of heroin, it had brought her to her senses.

This new clinic was nothing like that dreadful place Brandon had sent her to earlier, where the awful Bob had stalked her day and night. The staff here were very understanding and helpful, but adamant that if she reverted to taking drugs she would have to leave instantly. She'd been savvy enough to know this wasn't an idle threat and so long as they allowed her to have a drink when she wanted, she could handle it. After all, nobody could expect her to give up drink *and* drugs, all at the same time!

The last couple of weeks there had been very pleasant, almost like a stay in a health farm, and she'd finally felt ready to face the world again. Her first stop, obviously, would have to be her plastic surgery clinic. She'd been shocked to see how ravaged she'd become but, of course, since she'd missed her six-weekly botox and filler treatments, what else would you expect? She urgently needed to redress this so she left the rehab clinic and took a cab straight to that of her plastic surgeon. He agreed with her that she was a mess and suggested a full face-lift, bum-lift, breast enhancement and liposuction on her thighs and arms. She gratefully put herself in his hands and now here she was, two weeks later, almost a new woman.

She called her hair stylist and got him to come to the clinic where he'd been shocked by the state of her hair. She warned him that if he ever mentioned it to anyone, she'd ruin him forever. He was scared enough of her reputation to agree. The frosted highlights that she'd always been so fussy about were now a mousy-brown and her hair was long and straggly. He suggested a complete change and keeping some of the length, he restyled it and coloured it a lovely champagne blonde. She was delighted with the result. He knew that, much as he wanted to spread the gossip, he daren't. If he kept his mouth shut, Taylor would be a huge asset to his business. So, difficult as it was, he kept his mouth shut!

The day before she was due to leave the clinic, her beautician visited and spent several hours waxing, eyebrow-threading, eyelash-tinting and giving her a manicure and pedicure. She oohed and aahed over Taylor's smooth skin and wonderful new full lips, "Just like Angelina Jolie's," she remarked. High praise indeed! Taylor had smiled smugly to herself. Now she was ready to face the world, New York society and Brandon.

She left the clinic and arrived at the apartment on Park Avenue, to find her keys wouldn't open the door. She couldn't understand it. She called Brandon in Paris.

"Brandon, darling, it's Taylor, how are you?"

She heard his sharp intake of breath. "Taylor, how are you?"

"Fine, dear, just fine. I'm out of the clinic and happy to say that I'm completely cured."

"Where are you?"

She could hear a slight panic in his voice.

"That's the thing, dear. I'm outside our apartment in Park Avenue but my keys don't work."

"It's not *our* apartment any more, Taylor. You got the Village apartment in our divorce settlement. This apartment still belongs to my father and he's had the locks changed."

"I don't believe it!" she cried, outraged. "What about my clothes and things? I need to have them. And where am I supposed to stay? You know I have tenants in my place."

"I'll contact Dad and have him meet you so you can collect your belongings. As for where you'll stay, that's up to you, Taylor. There are plenty of nice apartments for rent in New York. You're not my problem any more. We're divorced, remember? And you were the one who asked for it." He couldn't resist that last dig.

She couldn't believe he was treating her like this. Yes, she'd made mistakes but she hadn't been herself – she'd been ill. Now she was better and she'd expected him to say it had all been a misunderstanding and they could go back to their old way of life once again.

"Oh, Brandon darling, don't be so horrid. I didn't mean any of it," she said, her voice simpering. "I'm sure we can sort things out."

"I'll get Dad to give you a call to make an arrangement to collect your things. Now I have to go," he said, hanging up on her.

She was astounded. What had got into him? This wasn't like the Brandon she knew. He sounded so cold. She'd have to think this out carefully.

Brandon's father met her at the apartment two days later.

"Hello, Taylor," he greeted her coldly as he let her into the apartment. She knew he'd never liked her. He'd never thought that she was good enough for his precious son.

"Hello, Chase."

"Kindly, take your clothes and personal belongings and nothing else," he instructed her, without preamble.

Brandon had warned him not to let her take any of the paintings or other valuables from the apartment. Chase stood guard over her to make sure she didn't touch anything that was not hers. Pompous ass, she thought, glaring at him as she packed her shoes and bags into boxes. The removal-van driver had already gone down with several boxes of her clothes. It took more than two hours to clear out her bedroom and when it was done she sighed and looked around the apartment, thinking how beautiful it was. She wouldn't let all this slip away without a fight. There was nothing else for it – she would have to go to Paris and woo him back.

55

Life was unbelievably hectic and Jazz thanked God every day for Sabine. The wedding plans were now in place and everything finalised which was just as well as the financial group were working twelve-hour days to have everything ready for the big global meeting. The group from Beijing arrived and it gave them all a tremendous sense of satisfaction to know that the project had been a superb success. On the night before they were due to return to China, both groups went to the Élysée Palace for a reception hosted by the President and First Lady of France.

The wives had been invited too and Ashling and Felicity were wild with excitement. The President thanked the group for their contribution to this very major global development and he finished his speech by saying, "I would also like to congratulate Brandon and Jazz on their upcoming nuptials and wish them a long and happy life together."

Everyone raised their glasses to the blushing, smiling couple and wished them good luck. Jazz thought that she'd never been happier.

The following night, exhausted from their intense week of work and socialising, they decided to have a quiet night in. Jazz was preparing *choucroute* in the kitchen, when Brandon's phone rang. It was Marilyn.

"Brandon, honey, I must see you immediately. It's about Taylor. Can you meet me in Willi's?"

"No, Marilyn, honestly, it's not my problem . . ."

"Please Brandon, it's urgent," she cut in on him. "Please?"

"Okay, I'll be there in ten minutes. But I can only stay for a short while."

If this was another ploy to get him to take her out to dinner, it wouldn't work. Jazz looked at him enquiringly as he came into the kitchen.

"That was Marilyn. It's about Taylor. I said I couldn't meet her but she says it's urgent," he explained, hoping she'd understand.

"You won't be long, will you?"

"I promise I'll be back within the hour. This better *be* urgent," he said as he reached for his coat. He kissed Jazz tenderly before leaving. "I love you, you know that – more than life itself," he murmured, before he pulled away. "I won't be long, promise. Love you."

Then he was gone.

Fifteen minutes later, he arrived at a crowded Willi's. He spotted Marilyn sitting at a table and saw that she was with another blonde. It looked like her sister. He did a double take when he realised that the 'sister' was in fact Taylor, a Taylor that he barely recognised.

"My God, what are you doing here?" he exclaimed, shocked.

"Aren't you pleased to see me, darling?" she asked, wrapping her arms around him as she kissed him.

He was so shocked he could hardly move. Coming to his senses, he roughly pushed her away.

"What's the meaning of this? You tricked me, Marilyn!" He glared at her menacingly.

"Don't blame Marilyn. It's my fault. I wanted to surprise you."

"You certainly did that!"

Marilyn could see how angry he was and decided to make herself scarce. She should never have agreed to do it. God, he was handsome when he was angry, she sighed, as she left.

"Champagne?" Taylor asked, lifting a bottle sitting in a stand beside the table.

"No, thank you. What is this all about, Taylor?" He sat down opposite her.

"I came to Paris to apologise," she said demurely, looking up from under her lashes at him. "I was such a ninny. I'm sorry," she purred, leaning in closer to him.

He looked at her with disgust. He noticed that she'd had a lot of work done on her face – and those lips! Looking further down he saw that she'd finally had the boob job she'd always wanted. No wonder he'd thought she was Marilyn's sister. They were like two peas in a pod. Two manufactured peas. All fake!

"What exactly do you hope to achieve?" he queried, his eyes half-closed.

"I think we should try and make a go of our marriage once again," she said, her voice low and husky.

"Are you out of your mind?" He couldn't quite believe what she'd just said. "We have no marriage. We're divorced. And frankly, that was the smartest thing I've ever done."

She recoiled from the vehemence in his voice. "Please, baby," she simpered. "I made a mistake. I'm a changed person. I'm sorry. Forgive me and let us get back together again."

How did I ever stay married to her for so long, he asked himself, filled now with disgust and disdain for her.

"Actually, I am getting married again to a wonderful woman whom I love very much."

Taylor's eyes widened with shock although because of all the botox the rest of her face stayed immobile. "You're what? When? To whom?" she shrieked, making the other customers around them stare.

"I'm getting married next week. To Jazz."

"You bastard!" she yelled, throwing her glass of champagne at him.

At this, all the customers in the bar stopped talking and watched with interest.

With as much dignity as he could muster, he stood up and said quietly to her, "Goodbye, Taylor, I never want to see you again. You haven't changed. I'm a lucky man to be rid of you." With that he turned on his heel and left.

The manager of the bar had become aware of the fracas and approached Taylor. "*S'il vous plaît, Madame* –" he began.

"Oh, fuck off!" she shrieked, grabbing her bag and coat and chasing out after Brandon. He was just getting into a taxi as she exploded from the bar waving her bag at him and shouting.

"Quickly, l'Île Saint-Louis," Brandon instructed the driver, looking back at Taylor who was frantically waving her fist at him.

"Lovers' quarrel?" the driver grinned at him in the mirror.

"Not exactly," Brandon replied, sighing.

That was the end of it.

Jazz was surprised to see him back so soon. Shocked, she saw that he was all wet.

"What happened?" she asked, intrigued.

Briefly he told her. She couldn't believe her ears.

"Poor baby," she said gently. "Let me take you into the shower and wash you."

"That nearly makes it all worth while," he grinned, as she started to undress him. She led him into the bathroom, letting her silk kimono slip from her naked body as she did so.

"What about the *choucroute*?" he asked.

"That'll keep," she said, smiling sexily at him. "This is more important."

Once again he thought he was the luckiest man in the world.

The following night Jazz was having her hen-night and Brandon his stag-night. Yves had been let out of prison the previous Tuesday and had spent the past few days relaxing with Sophie and Pierre. He was very grateful to Brandon for securing the new job for him and rang to thank him. Brandon insisted that he join them for his stag party. Yves was very reluctant to do so but, as Sophie was going to Jazz's hen party, she persuaded him to go.

The girls went to a lovely little bistro on the Place du Tertre in Montmartre while the boys went to the Irish pub, Kitty O'Shea's.

"Typical," Ashling pronounced. "No doubt Kieran's idea."

At about eleven Brandon rang Jazz and said he missed her so much and wondered if the girls would consider joining the guys in

Kitty's. They happily obliged and the hen and stag parties merged. They had a brilliant time together and everyone was happy to see Yves free again. Even Jazz hugged him warmly. She felt it was time to let bygones be bygones now that she was so very happy with Brandon. This time next week they would be husband and wife.

Sophie clung on to Yves's arm as if her life depended on it. He seemed very happy to have her do so and was very amorous towards her. They seemed to have found each other again. Everyone was happy for them.

Taylor arrived back at Marilyn's apartment, still furious at the bombshell Brandon had dropped. Marilyn was equally flabbergasted at the news. Bloody hell, she thought, why didn't I try harder with him? If I could have gotten him into my bed, he'd have been mine by now. She felt no sympathy for Taylor, who'd had him and thrown him away.

She listened to Taylor ranting and raving as she knocked back martini after martini. At one stage she even asked Marilyn whether she had any Vicodin or coke. Marilyn knew better than to give her any. Louis had warned her that under no circumstances was she to give Taylor any drugs. He didn't want that problem under his roof.

"Hey, honey, give over, give it a break," Marilyn said. She was fed up with Taylor's rantings. "Just accept it. It's not gonna happen with him any more. Brandon is finito. Look, why don't I give Christophe a call. He has the hots for you. He's always askin' for you."

"He is?" Taylor was surprised. She remembered Louis's friend who, Marilyn had told her, was filthy rich. Well, why not? If Brandon could get married again so quickly, then so could she. "Yeah, sure, give Christophe a call."

56

The project wound up the following Wednesday and they all felt a little sad as they cleared out their offices but at least they had the wedding to look forward to. It was all systems go now for Jazz and Brandon. They were at the airport early Thursday morning to meet the guests who were arriving from the States. Mia and Mike were staying in Brandon's apartment with their partners Doug and Star. Sabine had block-booked rooms in the Ritz for the others and for Jazz's friends and family, who arrived that afternoon from Germany.

Jazz and Brandon had dinner with them all that night in their favourite local restaurant, Au Sergent Recruteur, quite close to their apartments on the Île Saint-Louis. It was wonderful to be surrounded by those they loved and Brandon's kids got on great with Jazz's friends. Brandon's father, Chase, and Jazz's mother agreed it was a very happy occasion for both of them, seeing as how their two children were so obviously in love.

Sabine had arranged for a fleet of limousines for Friday, to take the visitors on a tour of Paris and that evening all of the guests met in the Ritz for a pre-wedding dinner.

"Congratulations!" Mia said as she hugged Ashling. "Dad told me you were expecting another baby. When is it due?" she asked, patting Ashling's tummy gently.

"Six more weeks. Not long now," Ashling replied, smiling at the young girl's enthusiasm.

"That's fantastic and how are the girls? I'm dying to see them again."

"They're so excited about tomorrow that I doubt they'll get a wink of sleep tonight. It's going to be a wonderful wedding," she sighed. "Do you like your dress?"

"I lovvve it – and the girls' dresses too. I'm dying to see Jazz's dress. She's keeping it a secret till tomorrow. I can't wait!"

They had a wonderful evening and it was almost midnight when Jazz and Brandon said goodnight.

The morning of the wedding dawned bright and sunny. Jazz and Brandon shared a last shower and breakfast together before they became man and wife.

Mia and Mike arrived at the apartment just as they finished and all four of them went to the Hôtel de Ville, where the official ceremony – a necessity in France – was to take place. Brandon's father and Jazz's mother were there waiting for them. Thirty minutes later, they were officially married but what they all considered the real wedding would take place that afternoon in the château.

The girls then went to the hair salon where the stylists made a big fuss of Jazz. Odette opened a bottle of champagne and they all toasted the bride who was overwhelmed by all this kindness.

Her mother and Mia helped Jazz get dressed in her wedding gown and when Mami saw how radiant her daughter was, she couldn't help but shed a tear.

"Please, Mami, don't make me cry. I'll ruin my make-up," Jazz said, as she hugged her mother.

"You look so beautiful," Mia whispered, hugging her tight as they made their way down to the waiting limousine.

It was a glorious warm sunny day, with not a cloud in the sky and the château looked spectacular as they drove up the drive. Sabine had done a wonderful job and the whole setting was magnificent, with beautiful flowers everywhere.

Ashling and Sophie were waiting at the entrance and the children looked adorable. The ceremony was to be held at four in the gardens, where Brandon was waiting with the guests.

As the music started, he looked around and caught his first glimpse of his gorgeous bride. Her beauty took his breath away and his heart overflowed with love for her. She had eyes only for him as she made her way up the red carpet. Orna and Ciara were strewing rose petals before her and Pierre carried the rings on a cushion. They made a very pretty picture. Mia walked behind Jazz, smiling broadly at everyone. As Brandon reached for Jazz's hand there were very few dry eyes in the audience. Their happiness was there for all to see.

After the ceremony, which went without a hitch, there was a champagne reception in the beautiful gardens. Everyone hugged and kissed them as they congratulated them and Brandon never let go of Jazz's hand for even a moment.

The dinner was held outdoors on the terrace and it was absolute perfection. Jazz had never felt such happiness as she looked around the table at her guests. As the sun set, candles were lit and it was magical. A quartet played at the other end of the terrace and under the moonlight, Jazz and Brandon had their first dance.

The party went on until the wee small hours when the happy guests were ferried back to Paris by a fleet of limousines. Everyone agreed that it was the best wedding they'd ever attended. Jazz and Brandon stayed in the château that night, in a candlelit, four-poster boudoir, strewn with rose petals. It was as romantic and enchanting as any lovers could ever have wished for.

The following evening they all met for dinner again, this time at El Mamounia, the famous Moroccan restaurant where they ate outdoors again, on the candlelit veranda. After the wonderful meal, Jazz and Brandon said goodbye to everyone as they were flying out on their honeymoon the following morning. Jazz still had no idea where they were going but had been told to pack bikinis and beach clothes, so presumed it was somewhere hot.

The first surprise was that Brandon had hired a private jet to take them there, so it wasn't until they landed in Nice that she realised the French Riviera was their destination. A chauffeured limousine met them and they were whisked down to the port where they boarded a private yacht that was theirs for three whole weeks.

"I could get used to this style of living," Jazz told him as they lay in each other's arms that night.

"I certainly hope so," he replied, nuzzling her ear, "because I intend to treat you like this for the rest of our lives, Mrs Hartford."

"I like the sound of that," she grinned, snuggling down in his arms.

Ashling had felt a terrible wrench when saying goodbye to Jazz. They'd become so close over the past year but now they had to go their separate ways. She had spent the week before the wedding packing up and now it was time to say goodbye to Paris. It had been such a wonderful year and so much had happened to them all. They were all going home changed women. If it wasn't for the fact that her baby was almost here, she would have been totally miserable leaving.

Corey took them to the airport and he hugged them with the promise that he would come to Dublin for her book launch on the 1st of December. That was another exciting thing that would be happening for her. Fiona and Hugh would be living in Ireland by that time so they would be there for the launch too.

Sophie had also promised to come and said she would bring Pierre with her. They had already agreed that the children should visit each other every year to keep up their languages and their friendship. It was more difficult for Sophie as she was the one staying and they were all leaving. However, she and Yves were experiencing what was almost a second honeymoon and he had indeed changed, as he'd promised he would.

Felicity was leaving Paris with a heavy heart too but she had her exciting new catering business to get stuck into and of course she'd see more of her daughters too, which was a good thing. She had improved her relationship with her mother, who could no longer intimidate her. She planned on keeping up her French as they would more than likely holiday in France every year from now on. Max was even talking of perhaps buying an apartment in the south of France for their retirement. How wonderful would that be!

Taylor had accepted the inevitable, i.e. Brandon was gone forever. She'd heard from Mia about the wonderful wedding he and Jazz had had. Bitch! she'd thought, with envy. She was living with Christophe now but he was getting a bit tiresome about her drinking. It was almost enough to make her go back on drugs! She regularly saw Marilyn who was still with Louis but as usual always on the lookout for someone even wealthier. *Plus ça change!*

57

Three Months Later

Ashling was in a tizzy as she got the girls dressed for her book launch. She was quivering with excitement and as nervous as hell. When she had finished brushing their hair she lifted baby Corey from his pram to feed him. He was the sweetest natured baby in the world and Orla and Ciara were crazy about him. He was, however, a hungry baby and as she was breastfeeding him, he kept her fairly busy.

She had called him after her great friend Corey who, as always, had been extremely supportive. He had come to Dublin the previous week and every TV show, radio programme and newspaper had been clamouring for interviews from him. It wasn't every day that a world-famous author came to town. He mentioned Ashling's book in every interview and as a result she'd been invited on a few shows herself and was getting lots of free publicity. He was such a pet!

He was very moved that she had called her little son after him and was looking forward to the christening the following day when he would be the baby's godfather. But first there was the book launch to enjoy.

Ashling had been terrified that no one would turn up but she needn't have worried. There was hardly breathing space in the hotel room she'd booked and every journalist in Dublin was there, as well as some from further afield. It was a huge success and once Ashling saw that, she relaxed and started to enjoy herself.

She was thrilled that all her friends from Paris had come as they'd promised and she was looking forward to catching up with their news later at dinner.

Jazz was looking sensational and still sported the tan that she'd got on her wonderful honeymoon. She was loving New York and it was obvious that she and Brandon were still madly in love. She had sent Ashling the biggest bouquet she'd ever seen, on the birth of Corey, and was thrilled that she was going to be his godmother. She'd also sent a complete layette of Ralph Lauren baby clothes and had set up a bank account for him in which she and Brandon had lodged a substantial sum. Ashling knew that she'd chosen great god-parents for her son.

Felicity and Max came over from London and Sophie and Pierre came from Paris. Yves, unfortunately, could not get off work.

They'd booked into the Unicorn that night for dinner and it was a happy group who caught up on all their news. Ashling presented all of them with a signed copy of her book. She'd thought long and hard about what to say on each one and everyone was delighted to have it.

"Imagine, I know two famous authors now," Felicity exclaimed. "Corey *and* Ashling. None of my friend's know even one!"

"Hang on, I'm not famous yet," Ashling laughed.

"You will be, you will be," Corey said calmly. "Mark my words." All the women loved him.

After the Irish coffees were served, Jazz said she had some news to share. They all looked at her expectantly and Ashling, looking at Brandon's beaming face, guessed what was coming.

"Brandon and I are expecting a baby . . . in May," she said shyly, smiling around the table.

Ashling jumped up to hug her and Felicity and Sophie followed suit.

"Congratulations! How wonderful!" they all exclaimed.

"I know, I have to pinch myself every now and then to make sure I'm not dreaming." She was radiant with joy.

Max, Kieran and Corey were busy clapping Brandon on the back before they came to kiss Jazz and offer her their congratulations.

"I'm so happy for you," Ashling whispered to Jazz as she sat down.

"Thanks, we're both over the moon about it."

Baby Corey was as good as gold the next afternoon as he slept in Jazz's arms. He never even cried when they poured the water on his head. Pierre was fascinated with him and jealous that he didn't have a baby brother too.

"Maman, can't we have a baby too?" he asked Sophie as they left the church.

"Yes, maybe. Papa and I would like that too," she replied, causing the other women to look at her enquiringly.

"Actually, I've just discovered I'm pregnant," she confided in the other women, when Pierre was out of earshot. "I didn't like to say anything last night so as not to spoil Jazz's good news. And of course it's much too soon to tell Pierre yet. But Yves and I are both thrilled," she said, glowing with pride.

"Fantastic!" Jazz hugged her and the others did likewise.

"So I hope that means that you'll all come to Paris next September for a re-union and the christening." She looked from one to the other hopefully.

"But of course we'll come. Who could resist an invitation to Paris, the wonderful city of love?" Jazz said raising her glass.

"To Paris, the most beautiful city in the world!" Ashling toasted.

"To Paris, the city where true friends are made!" Felicity added, as they all clinked glasses and smiled happily at each other.

"To Paris and a year like no other!" Sophie said.

"Hear, hear! To Paris and a year like no other!" the four women chorused, smiling at each other as they raised their glasses once more.

THE END.

If you enjoyed
A Year Like No Other by Pauline Lawless
why not try
If the Shoes Fit also published by Poolbeg?
Here's a sneak preview of Chapter One

if the shoes fit

Pauline Lawless

1

Amber was sitting on the balcony of her penthouse apartment in Malahide, watching the little boats bobbing about in the beautiful marina below. Her face, a golden tan and make-up free, was turned to catch the rays of the morning sun and her bare feet were curled up under her. She was wearing a comfy Juicy Couture velour leisure suit and her long blonde curls were caught up haphazardly in a ponytail. She sipped a vodka and orange as she reached for a glossy magazine and started leafing idly through it. It was then that she spotted the advertisement.

"I don't believe it!" she exclaimed as she read it. "I don't bloody believe it!" She smiled to herself as she realised that she sounded just like Victor Meldrew, that crazy character from the TV sit-com *One Foot in the Grave*. She read down through the ad again.

CALLING ALL SHOE ADDICTS!

Are shoes your passion? Are you enthusiastic and ambitious? Would you like to work for yourself? Not be tied to specific hours? Do you get on well with people? If you answered "yes" to all of the above, you may be the person we're looking for.

IF THE SHOES FIT
(buy them in every colour!)

We are launching in Ireland soon and we require part-time area sales managers to introduce our fabulous range of designer shoes to Irish women. No age limit. No experience required. No initial cash outlay.

Applications with CV to:
If the Shoes Fit, 54, Lower Mount St., Dublin 2.

"Buy them in every colour" was Amber's motto. How often had she bought the same shoe in two or three different colours! "Am I a shoe addict? Are they my passion? Are they *what*?" she exclaimed aloud. "Just come and see for yourself!"

She wasn't joking. Amber was the proud owner of the most fantastic shoe-room in Dublin, if not Ireland. Not a closet or a couple of racks, like most women, but a customised room, especially for her shoes – and their matching bags, of course. All her girl-friends were madly envious of her collection of some two hundred pairs (give or take a few) and she did sometimes feel a bit guilty about it. But what the hell, she thought, Imelda Marcos had 1250 pairs! Everyone had a passion and shoes just happened to be hers. And she rarely paid full price for them. Most of them she'd bought in sales in New York, Paris, Rome and Madrid for a fraction of the original cost.

It had always been that way. She'd always been a sucker for shoes.

This love affair had begun when, as a three-year-old, she'd fallen in love with a tiny pair of red patent shoes. Her mother had chosen a pair of sensible brown leather Clarks but Amber wouldn't even try them on and had thrown herself on the shop floor, refusing to get up until she could have the red patent ones. Embarrassed by this tantrum and shocked at her little girl's determination, her mother had given in and had left the shop with her golden-haired, angelic-looking daughter clutching her shoes and smiling in triumph. Amber could still remember every detail of them. They had narrow ankle-straps with the cutest bows on the front and they were so shiny that she could see her own face reflected in them. How she'd loved them! She'd felt like a princess every time she'd worn them.

She read the ad a third time, hardly daring to believe it. It sounds too good to be true, she thought. She got scissors and cut the page out of the magazine, then poured herself another vodka and orange. This called for a celebration! Yes, she knew it was still not quite midday and she'd already had her mid-morning drink, but this job was just perfect for her and as the song said: *"It's five o'clock somewhere."* She'd always thought that was strange – saying five o'clock – as six o'clock was the boozing hour in Ireland. Mind you, we make up for that extra hour real quick, she admitted to herself with a wry smile.

She hadn't always been a drinker. When she'd first met Dermot, her ex-husband, she'd never touched the stuff but it used to infuriate him when she'd ask for a Diet Coke at the fancy corporate dinners and receptions they attended regularly.

"For God's sake, just try and drink a glass of wine. It won't kill you!" he'd say in exasperation.

So, to please him, she'd tried, although she'd hated the taste of it. Eventually of course, she'd grown to like it and now she couldn't get through the day without it. She knew she drank too much but she didn't know how she would have survived the past twelve months, since her divorce, otherwise. Twelve months of heartache – her *annus horribilis*, as she called it – during which her self-esteem and confidence had sunk to an all-time low.

Reading the ad, she had her first glimmer of hope. Be positive, she told herself. I adore shoes, I'm enthusiastic, good with people and I'm willing to work hard. I'll do anything to get back to the old me – to get back living again.

So, with a sense of purpose, she pushed away her vodka and went to the computer to print out her CV and application. She went straight to the post-box and sent it on its way, before she could change her mind.

Susie, her best friend, rang that afternoon. "I've something really interesting to show you," she said, excitement in her voice. "I'll pop in on my way home."

She arrived beaming and brandishing a copy of *It Magazine*.

"This is just perfect for you. Look!" She shoved the page with the ad for If the Shoes Fit at Amber. "You adore shoes, you're great with people and it's only part-time. It's made for you!"

"Oh, I don't know . . ." Amber shook her head.

"What do you mean you don't know?" Susie banged the table, exasperation showing in her face. Then she saw that Amber was smiling.

"Actually, I've applied for it already – this afternoon!" Amber replied smugly.

"You've what?" Susie couldn't believe her ears. For months now she'd been trying to get Amber interested in getting back to work, with no success. Susie had been very worried. She was aware that Amber was drinking too much and wasn't making any effort to move on with her life. Thank God, at last she'd found something to interest her.

"I'm so happy," said Susie, giving her dearest friend a hug. "The minute I read it I knew it was made for you. You're an expert on shoes, as we all know!"

"I have to agree with you there," Amber replied. "Have you time for a quick cafè latte?"

Susie looked at her watch. "Yes, if it's real quick. I have to collect Rachel and Joshua from the crèche in ten minutes."

They chatted enthusiastically about the ad as Susie gulped down the coffee – then she flew out the door, blowing a kiss at her friend as she did so.

Amber appreciated Susie's concern. She knew she was worried about her drinking and it touched her. There was nobody else who gave a damn. She owed it to her friend to make an effort. Feeling bad about her behaviour and grateful for Susie's loyalty, she decided then and there to put a stop to it. This new opportunity had given her something to aim for. She made a decision. That's it – no more drinking on my own any more! This is my chance to get my life together again and I won't blow it. With determination, she took the bottle of vodka and poured it down the sink. It felt good!

Niamh was waiting in the doctor's surgery in Clondalkin with her little son, Ian, when she spotted the advertisement. She couldn't call herself a shoe addict exactly, mainly because she couldn't afford to buy shoes for herself very often, but she did adore them and if she had the money she had no doubt but that she would indulge herself. As a teenager, while her other friends were spending their money on cigarettes and drink, piercings, tattoos and the Lord knows what else, Niamh had spent every penny of her precious pocket money on shoes. Now twenty-three years old with three children (four, counting her husband) and a mountain of debts, there was very little chance of her buying a pair of glamorous shoes anytime soon. Intrigued, but not thinking it could have anything to do with her, she read down through the ad. She did have a passion for shoes – those she saw on other women – and yes, she was ambitious and enthusiastic and did get on very well with people. She read on. Was it possible? No age limit, no experience needed and most importantly, no money outlay. That would have been a problem. She began to feel a tremor of excitement. Was God possibly taking pity on her and bringing this opportunity her way? She desperately needed to get a job to help pay off all her debts and now that the twins had started school . . .

It says part-time, she thought, and it looks like you can choose what hours you work – this would be perfect for me.

There was no way she could afford to pay a child-minder for three kids.

She felt buoyant with hope. She despised people who tore pages out of magazines that didn't belong to them – but she had no choice. She could never afford to buy the glossy magazine herself and she desperately needed this ad.

After the doctor had assured her that Ian was merely suffering from a cold, she rushed home to make out her application. Her hopes took a bit of a bashing when she realised that her CV was pitiful. She couldn't very well say: "Mother of three at nineteen and excellent at the job." She guessed that wasn't quite what they were looking for. However, she had achieved a very good Leaving Certificate and would have gone on to University to study law if fate hadn't intervened. Fate in the form of charming, sexy, handsome Gavin Byrne who had seduced a very naïve seventeen-year-old Niamh, which resulted in her getting pregnant. She didn't want to go there.

Wrapping Ian up well, she collected the twins, Lily and Rose, from school. They looked so cute and tiny in their uniforms and as they hugged her, her heart swelled with love for them. Yes, she had it tough, but not for anything would she give up one minute spent with her three precious babies.

She posted her application and then they took the five-minute bus ride to her mother's house. Normally they walked but today, what with Ian's cold and her exciting news, she decided to splash out and take the bus.

"Come in, my darlings, and give Nana a big hug!" Her mother, as always, was delighted to see her grandchildren and wrapped her ample arms about them.

"How is your cold, pet? And what did you do at school today, girls? I've baked some lovely fairy cakes for you and I'll make some of your favourite hot chocolate."

When the three kids had babbled their news and were seated at the kitchen table happily munching, her mother turned her attention to Niamh.

"You seem in high spirits today, love. What is it? Has Gavin got a job?"

"No such luck, Mam. But maybe I have," and with eyes glowing she handed her mother the advert.

Eileen raised her eyebrows as she read it. "No experience needed, no money outlay and you can work whatever hours you choose. This seems perfect, love. You should apply for it."

"I already have, Mam," Niamh replied.

"That's great, love. You know, you'll never get out of your mother-in-law's house if you don't do something about it yourself. You certainly can't rely on Gavin to help!"

"Ah Mam, give him a break," Niamh sighed. They'd been down this road many times before. "I don't want to breathe a word of it to him just yet, in case I don't get it."

It killed Eileen to see her bright, smart daughter tied to a waster like Gavin. She often thought that Niamh would have been better off as a single mother – as least she'd have had her own house by now and not be stuck living with that dragon of a mother-in-law. Eileen sighed. What a mistake we made! she thought. We should never have agreed to the marriage. Her dad never wanted it – I should have listened to him. Thank God he's not alive to see how hard it is for his little girl now. It would break his heart. She sighed again.

Niamh hated having to leave her mother's warm, homely kitchen and face back to the drab, cold house they shared with Gavin's mother, Bridget. The cottage was tiny – certainly not big enough to accommodate three adults and three children. Bridget had kept the biggest bedroom for herself and Niamh and Gavin had to make do with the box-room and a bed that wasn't quite a double one. The kids had no space to play with their toys and it was impossible to keep them from messing things up. On top of that, she had a job trying to keep them quiet while her mother in law watched the endless procession of daytime chat and game shows on television.

Her mother was right – she had to get out of there – and it would be up to her to achieve it. Thank God for Mam, she thought. What would I do without her?

Niamh had left the advert with her mother just in case Bridget should find it. She knew all hell would break loose if she did. Bridget did not approve of working mothers and Gavin sided with her on this. In fact, he sided with his mother's views on practically everything.

Niamh's older sister, Val, dropped in to her mother's later that evening.

"Great news," Eileen announced, as she cooked up a big fry for her daughter. "Niamh applied for a job today. It sounds great."

"What kind of job?" Val asked, already munching on her mother's brown bread.

"It's a part-time job, selling designer shoes. She saw an ad in a magazine. It's there in the drawer." Eileen nodded towards the dresser.

"Let's have a look at it," Val said, full of curiosity.

Eileen dished up the bacon, egg and sausages and when she'd poured them both a cup of tea, she found the ad and handed it to her daughter.

"Mmm . . . interesting," Val remarked as she read it.

When she'd finished eating and her mother had left the room to answer the phone, Val slipped the magazine page into her pocket.

If you enjoyed this chapter from
If the Shoes Fit by Pauline Lawless
why not order the full book online
@ www.poolbeg.com

POOLBEG WISHES TO
THANK YOU

for buying a Poolbeg book.

If you enjoyed this why not
visit our website:

www.poolbeg.com

and get another book delivered straight to
your home or to a friend's home!

All books despatched within 24 hours.

POOLBEG

WHY NOT JOIN OUR MAILING LIST
@ www.poolbeg.com and get some
fantastic offers on Poolbeg books

Also by Poolbeg.com

Because We're Worth It

Pauline Lawless

When Kate's husband lands a high-profile contract in London and her youngest son heads off to boarding school, she suddenly feels that she's surplus to requirements. To boost her self-esteem, overweight Kate joins Slimforever'. Will it help her find herself again?

Jenny longs for a baby but time is running out. If she lost weight, would it help her to conceive? She joins 'Slimforever' in a last ditch attempt to beat her biological clock. Is it the answer to her prayers?

Their friend Lauren, a beautiful ex-model, decides she could lose a few pounds too. Lauren appears to have it all – elegant Georgian home, barrister husband, two lovely children and a successful business as an interior decorator. But is it all as it seems?

Meanwhile sexy, voluptuous Diana craves excitement and detests being buried in the backwoods of Ballyfern.
She'll stop at nothing to get what she wants – even if it's another woman's husband.

Four women – different goals – can they all be winners?

ISBN 978-1-84223-373-3

Also by Poolbeg.com

if the Shoes fit

Pauline Lawless

'*Calling All Shoe Addicts*', said the advertisement that triggered a response in four very different women, each at a difficult time of her life.

Niamh, at 23, the mother of a five-year-old and twin girls aged four, is desperate to have a home of her own. She longs to escape the house of her vicious mother-in-law but her charming, irresponsible husband and the mountain of debts they have makes this seem ever more unlikely.

Amber, former air stewardess whose husband Dermot left her for a younger woman, has lost all her confidence and is drowning her sorrows with alcohol.

Tessa, beautiful former model, paid the price for living life in the fast lane when she almost died from a heart attack. Her reliable friend, George, persuaded her to come and live with him in Ireland. She now realises that she's made a dreadful mistake.

Rosie, recently widowed, can't come to terms with the loss of the man she loved so much. Life without him doesn't seem worth living.

All of them, needing a way out, find it with the Italian designer shoe company, '*If The Shoes Fit*'. This leads them to a new career, great friendships and a life-changing experience.

ISBN 978-184223-388-7